F.S. Hamilton was born in Cumbria, the son of a village schoolmaster. Following a scientific career, he trained originally as a biologist, later specialising in environmental toxicology and with a wide range of employment. This included a term with UNIDO where he gained an international reputation.

Now living in Cambridgeshire, he is an active member of the Church of England, with an interest in theology – particularly of the Celtic Church and early Christian heresies. Besides being a story, his first book, *The Queen Behind the Veil*, represents an allegorical challenge relevant to the present time.

Published work

The Queen Behind The Veil
(Vanguard Press 2009)
978 1 84386 573 5

The Queens of Cornwall

F.S. Hamilton

The Queens of Cornwall

Or

The Brocelliande Myrmidons

Vanguard Press

VANGUARD PAPERBACK

© Copyright 2014
F.S. Hamilton

The right of F.S. Hamilton to be identified as author of
this work has been asserted by him in accordance with the
Copyright, Designs and Patents Act 1988.

A CIP catalogue record for this title is
available from the British Library.

ISBN: 978-1-84386-808-8

*Vanguard Press is an imprint of
Pegasus Elliot MacKenzie Publishers Ltd.*
www.pegasuspublishers.com

First Published in 2014

**Vanguard Press
Sheraton House Castle Park
Cambridge England**

Printed & Bound in Great Britain

This book is dedicated to Saint Catherine of Siena.

The Last Battle

Epilogue

CHAPTER I
The Fiddler and the Queen

It was all because of that confounded accident.

Jennifer Parsloe took a deep breath and tried once again to force the incident from her thoughts. She had to finish her concerto, and within five days, but whenever she tried to rally her concentration the accident came back to her mind. It had been horrible. On the promenade. The little Citroen had swerved to avoid a child, and a big Range Rover moving far too fast had hit it, broadside on, on the driver's side. He had been killed almost at once, and the Rover driver had gone through the windscreen. No safety belt, and she had seen it all from twenty feet away. People screaming, and police and questions; and she could not finish her concerto. The music had all been there in her mind, waiting to be written down. Also it was good. She knew it was, and her first real opportunity. But what was she to do? In time her ideas might come together, but time she had not got. Maybe it would help to talk to a friend. Perhaps if she talked it out with someone her thoughts would come under control. But with whom? Then an idea formed, and Jennifer turned away from the sea front of the Cornish town, and walked uphill in the autumn sunshine. Old Laura Trepennick might do. People said she was batty, but she was all right and had a deal of insight. Jennifer had always known her, as had half the town. She had always been old; in school days the girls were terrified of her, although for no good reason so far as Jenny could remember.

Soon she was ringing the bell of the big Victorian house high up on the hill. Laura would think it strange, but the old lady must be lonely and might welcome an unexpected call. At the second ring, the door was opened and a maid asked her business, Laura herself appeared, and Jenny was ushered in.

The grey eyes of the enigmatic old lady fixed Jenny with a penetrating stare, but the tale was heard out kindly enough.

"So. You can't get it out of your mind my dear, and you've no time and a consuming panic. Why come to me? People say that I'm fey, but I'm no psychiatrist. What can I do?"

"I don't know," Jenny lamely replied. "I felt that if I told you about it perhaps ..."

But Laura interrupted her, with advice as strange as it was unexpected.

"Why not go up to the wood, and see if something happens. It often does for someone in your condition, only don't blame me if you dislike the consequences. Whatever you do, don't be afraid. The place is more benevolent than evil, but there is no way of saying which way things will jump, if you take my meaning."

"Saint Catherine's Wood?" said Jenny. "You really believe the tales about it? Noises at midnight, and mysterious lights and all that?"

"No. By and large I don't," replied Laura. "But the place is powerful enough in its own fashion. Try it – but on your own head mind you. Come, I'll set you on your way."

Jenny noticed that Laura had clearly foreknown that the advice would be accepted, and soon the young lady and the old one were walking together. Laura was over eighty, but remarkably nimble. They took a by-road over the hill, down into the next valley, past St. Catherine's Church, along a path up the farther hill and so towards the wood. Here they parted.

"Goodbye and good luck my dear," said Laura, as Jenny ascended a stile.

Soon she was across the sheep pasture, and at the wall surrounding the wood. There was no easy means of ingress, although it looked harmless enough in the afternoon sunshine. Not much of a place really, about fifty trees on the crest of a hill. People said that originally St. Catherine's Church had been built there and later replaced by the one down in the village. Certainly there were some traces of old walls, and a larger stone plinth which was supposed to be the focus of the genius loci, or whatever the word was.

Jenny climbed the dry-stone wall and entered the wood. She felt little sense of fear, but a curious notion of heightened awareness. Probably it was no more than a reaction from a subconscious belief that something would happen. But she was being ridiculous. 'Belief' was far too strong a word. Of course there would be nothing unusual. She had only come to avoid offending old Laura. The whole thing was clearly a waste of time, but having come she might as well explore the place. Walking through the trees, Jenny reached the wall on the further side. Beneath her in the hollow was Trevanions' Farm and the nearby St. Catherine's Well. Who was this St. Catherine anyway? Jenny had little religious knowledge, only a vague belief, but she thought of the Communion of Saints, or whatever they called it, and people who had been here before to worship in a long-abandoned church. Perhaps they were coffin dust beneath her feet. Jenny returned to the old stone plinth, sat down with her back to it, and thought of the Communion.

There was a little air moving higher up in the trees, with the sound resembling a gentle surf breaking against the promenade. The promenade, with people, and cars and the accident. Jenny closed her eyes. A rest would do her good, half an hour or so in the quiet. The sound was very like waves; my God but it was waves, surf against the promenade. She was dreaming of course. She had to be, because the accident was happening all over again. It was horrible, but this time there was something different. Another person was present; a tall young woman was standing by her side.

The newcomer was highly elegant, almost six feet tall, and wearing a loose fitting jacket and skirt in dark coloured silk. Pricey by the look of it. She wore her hair well up, emphasising her height, and retained behind by a silver comb. The face was calm and serene, with large brown eyes and a strong chin. She had an air of authority.

"Hello Jenny," said the stranger. "You're Mary Parsloe's girl aren't you? The brilliant young violinist. What a horrid accident, but we can't do anything physically. Come and walk with me for a while. I am a musician too. The piano and the harpsichord are my instruments; it would be good to talk to you."

The two women turned away from the promenade and strolled down a side street. Jenny felt a trifle faint, and experienced a strange rushing sensation; her companion took her arm in sympathetic support. But Jenny soon realised that she was not walking through the well loved town of her birth. This place was totally different. There was a medieval feeling; people were dressed rather differently, and treated her companion with great deference. A woman curtsied, and was rewarded with a smile and an inclination of the head. This was no nightmare, but Jenny felt nonplussed; that confounded wood and the meddlesome Laura. Then she felt her companion's eyes upon her.

"Have no fear," said the tall lady. "You are more than safe with me."

Jenny felt her anxiety fall away, but curiosity remained.

"Where have you brought me?" she asked.

"To the City of Ys, as was known in a different form to your Celtic ancestors, but don't worry about it. We are going to a concert."

Dusk was falling as they entered a large square with an enormous church on the farther side, where a Galilee Porch provided access. A teenage girl was seated at a table. She stood up immediately, and coloured slightly.

"We can't charge *you* Donna," she said. "May I show you to seats?"

"Nonsense my dear," came the reply. "I shall pay the same as everyone else. My coming is unexpected, and we need no ceremony."

An affectionate smile counteracted the slight reproof; Donna placed what looked like a sovereign upon the table, and moved on to a descending staircase, Jenny walking behind. But the girl came running after, and put a coin in Jenny's hand.

"The Donna forgot her change," she said, as they reached the foot of the stairs.

Jenny looked at a large silver piece, and saw with a start that the portrait was that of her companion. The likeness was excellent and allowed no ambiguity. Jenny felt a little embarrassed, but Donna was surrounded by a knot of people – a clergyman, a woman in military uniform, and two or three more.

"Please, please, no fuss," Donna was saying, "I have brought an unexpected guest, and we are late. Two extra chairs at the back will do nicely."

Soon they were seated in what was clearly the crypt of an ancient church, but surprisingly well-lit and lofty. The orchestra was small, about twenty instruments all played by young women. They looked like senior girls from a ladies' academy.

The concert began with some elaborate chamber music, and then the main event of the evening. With a sort of foreknowledge, Jenny heard a violin concerto being announced. As the music developed, it became clear that it was 'her' concerto. Essentially what she had composed, but wonderfully improved. It was superb, subtle and powerful, and with a further fullness which was difficult to describe. The leader rose to play a solo passage, and the notes of the violin rose in a rainbow of limpid sound, filling the old vault with an effortless cascade of notes. Jenny was a professional, but she had never heard the like of this! It was more than virtuosity; truly magnificent music played with a skill beyond belief. Then she realised that they were giving her back her music. The wood was genuinely enchanted; it had to be.

"Donna, Donna, it is too beautiful," she murmured, with tears filling her eyes.

"Donna is a title, not my name. You may call me Catharine – with two 'A's," was added with a conspirator's smile.

Jenny lost her sense of time, but all too soon the performance was complete. Refreshments followed, served with a heady effervescent wine. Catharine pressed her to drink, but shielded Jenny from the attentions of the audience – clearly the Donna had enormous personal command. And the wine seemed to magnify Jennifer's sense of awareness; the music was engraved upon her mind. But presently Catharine slipped an arm about her waist.

"Time to take you home my dear," she said, kissing her gently on the forehead.

Again, a sudden rushing sensation and a feeling of faintness.

Catharine's lips had felt slightly moist, but with a sense of dismay Jennifer realised that her forehead was wet from a raindrop, and there was wind in her face. She was no longer in the heavenly Ys with the compassionate and wonderful queen – she was in St. Catherine's Wood; and it was dark and midnight, with bats and beetles, and raining on her. O dear, O dear; she scrambled over the wall, and with stockings laddered and hair awry she fled towards the stile. But the taste of wine was still in her mouth, and the music as vivid in her mind as the stars in the storm-tossed sky. She paused for a moment outside Laura's massive house – a light was burning, and she thought that a curtain moved. Jenny 'knew' that the old lady was awake and sentient, but she turned and walked on as briskly as she could. An hour later she was home, both wet through and wildly elated. But there was no time for sleep. Her hand flew over the manuscript blanks, note after note, with a speed and confidence never achieved before. She finished at three the following afternoon, then collapsing into an exhausted sleep.

It was shortly after the concerto's first performance that Jennifer was sitting with a friend in a Kensington café, reading revues and drinking coffee; her music had received adulatory praise from the major papers to the point of embarrassment.

'Magnificent first major work by Britain's leading young composer.'

'Remarkable music, fresh and original with great depth and sincerity.'

And much else besides.

"Darling," said Jenny's friend Elaine, "how absolutely super. I feel more than jealous – we all knew you were good, but glory be, I'd never heard the like of it! Although the third movement reminded me of Sir Peregrine Barry. You always admired him, I know."

Sir Peregrine Barry, but this was praise indeed. Probably the greatest living modern composer and exponent of stringed instruments!

"It was dreadful wasn't it," Elaine chattered on, "and such a stupid way that it happened. You haven't heard of the accident!? Gracious, but you must have been busy. It happened in your home town. He was driving that crazy little deux chevaux Citroen of his, and a Land Rover ran into him; he died at once – it was in all the papers – Jenny, whatever is wrong?"

But Jenny was too pale and shaken to reply immediately. The familiar café seemed to turn about her as she sought to rationalise the coincidence. Then to cover her confusion she thought to pay for their coffee – a £1 piece from her purse, and a 50 pence from her pocket. But the waitress rejected the coin.

"Sorry madam, but that's foreign; you've mistaken it for a fifty."

Jenny stared at the large silver coin, there in the palm of her hand. Serene, calm, and confident, Catharine's profile gazed on, through time and through eternity.

CHAPTER II
Samuel Mordecai

Jennifer soon abandoned any attempt to rationalise her experience in St. Catherine's Wood. The sequence of events which had filled her mind while she was apparently asleep had been unlike any usual dream. It was too rational, albeit in a bizarre sort of way, and she could recall the whole experience in complete detail. Also, there was that extraordinary piece of money. How had she come by it? Conceivably someone had come upon her as she slept and placed the coin in her pocket. This notion frightened her when she first considered it; the thought of some weird-minded person stealing up to her in that psychically active wood, when highly vulnerable to malice or harm. Alternatively, she had passed into some form of somnambulistic trance, wandered off to God knows where and found the coin for herself. But both ideas seemed so unlikely that she dismissed them with little hesitation. Moreover, the coin itself was exceedingly strange. The obverse bore Catharine's portrait in right hand profile, but the wording was in foreign letters which Jennifer recognised as Greek:

ΚΑΘΑΡΗΝ ΙΙ ΒΑΣΙΛΛΙΑ
translating to CATHARINE II QUEEN

The reverse showed the elevation of a medieval castle, with the legend (in English) 'Kingdom of Lyonesse, Ynys

Afalon, and the Auroras. Six Crowns'. Even more curious was a continuous circle of letters, engraved around the edge of the disc:

NIΨONANOMHMATAMHMONANOΨIN

This was also probably in Greek, but made no sense to Jennifer. The coin was struck in silver, very little worn, and almost one and a half inches in diameter. Who on earth would possess such money? But Jenny had little time to continue thinking about the coin and her dream (if dream it were), because of a career which now developed with meteoric speed.

The violin concerto was recorded and sold well, engagements followed, both to play and conduct; incidental music was commissioned for a television series, and pupils came flocking. So she was busy, and found herself a moderately wealthy woman. Jennifer was vivacious and humorous, beautiful in the Celtic fashion, and with many people about her, including numerous young men. About five and a half feet tall, she was dark haired with an oval face, and being also full breasted and well formed round the hips males came like bees to a honey pot, but she had little time for them, preferring her work and the company of other women. Therefore time flew past, and it was not until twenty months or so after the concerto's first performance that she returned to Cornwall for a few weeks' much needed rest.

Her mother provided the usual unquestioning affection, but Jenny felt restless, thinking once more of St. Catherine's Wood and the mysterious queen. She was now convinced that something supernatural had occurred, but probably not of an evil nature. She also wanted to offer some sort of thanks to Catharine, and indeed felt drawn to associate with the Donna, whoever or whatever she might be. A visit to Laura proved somewhat negative. The old lady was kindly and welcoming, but evasive about the properties of St. Catherine's Wood, and Jenny refrained from showing her the six crowns piece. In fact it had been shown to no one. The money was not her property, and although she had not truly stolen the coin, she felt an intuitive reserve about it, rational or otherwise. And so it was with mixed feelings that she set out for a return visit to St. Catherine's Wood.

The Saturday afternoon was exhaustingly hot as she parked her car beside the village church. Time seemed suspended in the heat, and no one was stirring as she paused to inspect the notice board beside the churchyard gate. 'Saint Katherine of Sienna' was painted across the top in the usual formal manner of the Church of England; one half beneath announced the times of services, and that the rector was the Revd. Samuel Mordecai, M.A., D.D. – surprisingly well educated for this part of Cornwall. The second half bore two handwritten notices: a jumble sale in aid of the Girl Guides, and a flower festival.

The June heat felt even more inanimating as she turned away and toiled slowly upward towards her destination. Flowers drooped in full bloom beside the path, the newly shorn sheep sought such shade as they could, and even the birds seemed enervated by the warmth. Nevertheless, Jenny felt her perceptions heighten as she climbed the dry-stone wall and entered the comparative cool of the wood. She composed her mind, endeavouring to speak within her thoughts as though Catharine could hear her. She offered profound thanks to her mentor, and then asked if she could do something of service, some gesture in return for Catharine's generous aid. But nothing happened. No inward response, no mystical experience, no sense of silent presence. Jenny felt rejected, and a vague feeling grew that Catharine might grant a royal favour, but desired nothing in return. So she leaned against the stone plinth, and thought:

"Perhaps I could do something on behalf of the Communion of Saints, even here and now? Some contribution of practical use. I would like to help the cause if I can."

Presently she became peaceful, ceased to struggle, and allowed the sultry calm of the afternoon to invade her mind. Time passed, until on consulting her watch Jenny found that she had been in the wood for over two hours. She returned to the village, finding the walk pleasant in the lessening heat.

The scene looked no different from before, but a third handwritten notice had appeared on the notice board. It was on rectory notepaper, and in a flowing copperplate hand.

"MOST URGENT," it was headed, in large capitals, "Due to the sudden illness of Mr Appleton, an emergency organist is immediately required. Will any parishioner knowing of a suitable person kindly inform me at once.
God bless you all,
Samuel Mordecai".

"I would like to help the cause if I can." Jennifer's thoughts returned to her, and it felt as if an icy cold finger were moving very slowly down through the perspiration on her spine. She had asked to be given something of practical use to do, and Catharine had answered. By choice Jenny was a violinist, but like many professional musicians she could play a keyboard instrument passingly well. "Something of practical use;" but where was Samuel Mordecai?

She opened the gate, walked along the path between the gravestones and entered the church. There was gentle activity within. The building had been extensively decorated with floral arrangements, and three or four women were moving to and fro with cans of water. They ignored her. Jenny moved onward to a door on the further side of the font – it looked like the priest's vestry, and knocked gently.

"Enter," said a man's voice, and she went in.

"Mr Mordecai?"

He rose as she spoke, from a seat at the vestry table.

"At your service ma'am; what may I do for you?"

"Please, it is about your notice," said Jenny, a trifle nervously. "May I play the organ for you?"

"Good God almighty!" he exclaimed, and sat down again on his chair. "You're Jennifer Parsloe, aren't you – the finest musician in England!"

It was not surprising that he recognised her. Jenny was a local celebrity and her picture had been in the papers. She scarcely knew how to reply, but the rector continued:

"Excuse my reaction my dear. Oh ye of little faith." (Does he mean me? thought Jennifer.) "Everything has gone wrong in this parish for the last twelve months, and here we are beginning the village festival week, with choral evensong tomorrow and the important concert on Friday. And Appleton has been working like a badger for weeks past. He's in intensive care with a heart attack – I was over to see him this morning. But what to do? Organists like him don't grow on trees round here. So half an hour ago, I sat down in this very chair, and I said out loud 'Catherine, this church has been dedicated to you for centuries past, and now you'll have to help. I need a good organist, and I need one now,' and something said 'Put a notice on the board, and you'll be sent one!' And so I did, and ten minutes later a famous professional musician walks in through the door!"

"You've got your Catherines mixed up," replied Jenny. "You need one with two 'A's, and also I'm not an organist,

25

although I can play one. Frankly I've never played for a congregation before."

She began to get a sense of déjà vue, but this was combined with a mixture of joyfulness and an unexpected anxiety. She desperately wanted to help. Catharine had brought her to great professional success, and it was the least that she could do. Moreover, Mordecai was clearly convinced that she had arrived in answer to his appeal, and who was she to argue? But Samuel's next remark was somewhat bathetic.

"Would you like a cup of tea?" he said, "The kettle is over there – put it on while I find tomorrow's music."

Clearly, Jennifer was now admitted to the parish staff, albeit with scant ceremony. The tea making equipment could not have been more typical of a vestry – a stove enamel electric kettle of 1950's vintage, an aluminium teapot, and an assortment of eight cups and saucers. There was a half empty bottle of milk standing in cold water in the vestry sink. Mordecai was back by the time the kettle boiled.

"Tomorrow we are having a processional entry, aetherial responses, and an anthem by Orlando Gibbons, all good stuff; the lead soprano's in church now watering the flowers. Let's drink our tea and then we'll have a look at the organ."

He was easy to talk to. One of those rare people with the ability to generate enthusiasm in others. They spread the sheet music on the vestry table. The anthem was straightforward, but the canticles were in a complex polyphonic chant, ambitious for a country church. And she was expected to play this tomorrow, besides coping with the choir. Clearly, to Mordecai, Jennifer Parsloe could do anything musical.

"Time to see the organ," invited Samuel, and forth they went into the nave.

Behind the temporary splendour of the floral festival, the building was a trifle dilapidated. Obviously it was large for the modern village, and upkeep was a problem. But the organ was different. Mordecai unlocked the shutters, and turned on the blower and lights for her. Glory be, it was a five manual Willis! Jennifer started to play the first tune which came into her head. It was Blake's 'Jerusalem'. Gently at first, as she came to terms with the enormous power of the instrument, and then the lead soprano started to sing, and so did old Mordecai, in a fine clear tenor.

"Bravo my dear," he cried, and then in a manner characteristic of the man, he insisted that Jennifer and the lead soprano (introduced as Caroline Owens) should join him and Mrs Mordecai for tea.

It was a most entertaining meal. Mary Mordecai was younger than her husband, and engaged Caroline Owens in a continuous repartee, most of it humorous nonsense. Samuel contributed intermittently, and then started to tell Jenny something of the history of the church.

The existing building dated from the late sixteenth century and had been built by one of Elizabeth's merchant adventurers, perhaps in penitence for his activities on the Spanish Main. It was a pity that the ancient church on the hill had not survived; certainly it was Saxon, and might well have been built on an even earlier Celtic Christian site. There was much continuity in Cornwall, and some local families had been associated with the church for centuries. These included the Trepennicks, of whom Laura was the last surviving example. Indeed she was a remote descendant of the man who had built the present church. Also, the original foundation of the church was so ancient that there were legends which appeared to date from Arthurian times. Chief among these was that known as 'Merlin's Myster' or 'The Curse of Cornwall'. According to this, St. Catherine's Church guarded an evil mystery, preserving an object of forgotten identity which in the hands of knowledgeable but wicked men could be used for the most dreadful and diabolical of purposes, avarice being the least of these. The old church on the hill was a woodland chapel where the Holy Grail had appeared, and had therefore been selected by Arthur as the site of safe repository for the curse. Samuel doubted if there was much truth in any of this, but there was one strange and undoubted fact. The present St. Catherine's Church was built over a crypt which had been sealed up many years before.

"So you think St. Catherine's is built on top of the Curse of Cornwall?" said Caroline with a smile.

"No, of course not," replied Mordecai. "It's romantic nonsense, but I'd like to know why the crypt was sealed. The old doorway is in the tower. You can see where the masons blocked it off."

"Couldn't you satisfy your curiosity," said Jenny, "and have the doorway reopened?"

"I have thought of that, but feel an intense and irrational disinclination. There is one other odd fact. A piece of metal has been let into the masonry closing the doorway. It is made of lead, in the form of a long strip, like a barrier across the entrance, and it has incomprehensible writing cast into it.

I have made a rubbing of it; I shall show you if you will excuse me while I fetch it from my study."

The strip of paper was about three feet long. As she looked at it, for the second time that afternoon Jenny felt a cold finger move down her spine:

NIΨONANOMHMATAMHMONANOΨIN
read the legend before her frightened eyes.

CHAPTER III
Hermione De Lamarac

A month later Mordecai sat in his church and contemplated some problems. Things seemed to be going wrong again. The architect's report had arrived barely an hour before and was dismal reading. Then there was the Penvithick family. A long-standing problem; the husband had disappeared, the wife was ailing and a four-year-old son seemed to be verily possessed by the devil. Also Mordecai had an irrational but deep seated disquiet concerning recent visitors to the church. Firstly there had been Arthur Marazion. He seemed to be an honest young man with a legitimate historical interest, but those two other types were a different matter. Weird questions, and offering to put up some money for restoration in return for permission to excavate around the building. What did they really want? 'Menenius' was the name they had given at the village inn. Cousins, according to the landlord. Was there a connection between them and Arthur Marazion? Mordecai thought not; but it was odd. They seemed evil, and he trusted his impressions.

Still it was not all bad. Jennifer was a cheerful young maid in a difficult time. Mordecai realised that he needed some sort of help, but irrationally enough, he did not know what it was. To whom could he talk? No one, because he scarcely knew what he wanted to say.

He leaned back in the pew and closed his eyes. Let it go for a bit, and perhaps his mind would clarify of its own accord. But then he realised that someone else was in the church; a strange young woman was standing at the end of his pew. In itself this was not remarkable since tourists often paid a visit, but the lady's garb was unusual – she was fully vested in a manner resembling a priest in the Church of England! Unfortunately Mordecai was opposed to the ordination of women. Also her appearance was against etiquette, if not canon law. This was his parish, and there were things which one didn't do!

He was disarmed instantly.

"Good morning," she said, with a smile like the roses of heaven. "I'm called 'Hermione de Lamarac', and would like to see your church. You must be Samuel Mordecai. It's a great pleasure."

She was a superb young woman, and a brusque reply was out of the question. Copious dark chestnut hair framed a sensitive face. Clearly Celtic – large dark eyes and a smooth complexion – with her embroidered robes and serene expression she could have been a Rossetti painting come to vibrant life. Tall for a Celt; Mordecai had momentary visions of Arthurian Romance with stately ladies in courtly chivalry. Nonsense of course. Probably it was a world of great barbarity. Then a further thought struck him. At the end of the legend, Guinever had entered a convent and risen to be mother superior; such ladies were ordained in those days. And here was a female priest of Celtic appearance, appeared out of the blue. It was as if time had gone into reverse, or had remained inanimate for a millennium and a half. Odd things happened in Cornwall. But how to respond?

"Permit me to show you round," he said.

"I would rather sit and talk for a bit," she replied, and sat down uninvited beside him.

Mordecai felt a rush of both emotion and interest. Who was she, and why had she come?

He found that he already desired her company. She was a total stranger, but nevertheless he wished to talk to her. But he did not understand his own reaction, and so felt somewhat confused.

"A cup of tea perhaps?" he suggested, as usual for him. "We keep a kettle in the vestry."

She accepted readily, and soon they were tête-à-tête in the homely room. Mordecai realised that he had lost all resentment at her unexpected visit, and apparently pointless priestly garb. Ceasing to wonder at her background, he found that he was talking to her with ease and inner relief. Far from dismissing his worries, she took them seriously indeed.

"You believe that there is some evil factor threatening your church, but are unable to define it?" she asked. "You may be right, do not dismiss old legends too easily. My friends and I also think that the abandoned church on the hill was of Celtic origin, and may well be mentioned in the Morte d'Arthur, although in a garbled way. It was one of the chapels where the Sangreal appeared, and this endowed it with exceptional power. What happened later I don't know, but we think that the chapel may have been used as a place of safe keeping for some article of potential evil, to make it less accessible to the powers of darkness. Centuries have now passed, and the energy implanted by the Grail has lessened with the passage of time. I fancy that your Menenius visitors are attempting something which would have been too dangerous for their ilk in earlier years. If you like, I shall arrange help for you. Be careful, because as pastor of the church you may be an early target. It is difficult to say what form their devilry may take;

perhaps it will be a purely psychic assault, but a combination of this with physical methods is more likely. I would like you to have a bodyguard. A good friend of mine is a formidable army officer – a lady called 'Ystelle Zabuloe', or 'Canti' to use her maiden name. You will be safe enough if she is in charge."

At first Samuel was a trifle abashed. Surely Hermione was over-reacting and making too much of the position. It was difficult to believe the legend of Merlin's Myster and all that. Was she pulling his leg? No, he felt ashamed of the thought. Clearly she was totally honest. Also he had a growing presentiment that her visit was not by chance and she possessed information beyond what he was telling her. Moreover, she seemed to have some sort of authority. She was young and beautiful, and very well spoken, but also had a maturity far beyond her apparent years.

And so they toured the church. She found it beautiful and interesting, and Mordecai told her of the financial problems associated with so large a building in a small parish. To his surprise, he now found her naive. For a clergywoman she knew little of parish finance, but seemed to have a simple trust in divine providence taking care of such things. Yet he continued to find her highly intuitive, indeed almost embarrassingly so. She expressed interest in several of the memorials which ornamented the church, haphazardly enough. The oldest was to Sir Christopher Trepennick, very elaborate, and with a deal of bad Latin.

"So he wasn't really an evil man," she remarked. "He certainly seems to have taken care of his tenantry. Perhaps by his lights he was justified in slaying Spaniards. Long live Good Queen Bess and all that."

Some of the local names fascinated her. Paul Pendrea, and Ahab Choone, eighteenth century gentlemen, Captain William Trevayne with a cameo of a Victorian battleship, and Brigadier

Jonothan Nanjulien V.C., departed in 1932, 'Not dead, but gone before' the letters read. Their survey of the building ended in the tower, with an inspection of the leaden strip across the built-up doorway. She looked at it quizzically, and suddenly the realisation burst upon Mordecai that the inscription formed a palindrome – the message (if it were a message) was the same whether you read the letters forwards or backwards. Strange that he had never noticed the point before. Even stranger was the impression that he had 'caught' the information from his companion – Hermione's mind had in some way informed his own. It was a little disturbing; who was this remarkable woman? He said nothing, but soon his impression of intuitive transfer was confirmed. Thus he felt obliged to offer hospitality to a visiting priest, but Mrs Mordecai was from home and he had only a pound or two in his pocket. But the thought had barely entered his mind before Hermione said:

"Can I persuade you to join me for lunch? I'm staying in the village inn, and the food isn't too bad. Please come – the hotel bill is on my superiors!"

Clearly, she could see into his mind. It was disturbing, but still he liked her. The empathy of it was fascinating. He realised that she was drawing his spirit towards her, into an aureole of both power and compassion.

In fact the inn was an hotel of some little size, and Samuel waited in the foyer, thinking about the Menenius cousins, and what Hermione had been saying. Soon she reappeared, wearing a flame coloured dress in some thin silky material, her only ornament an elaborately enamelled Celtic Cross on a fine gold chain about her neck. They were shown to a table in a window recess, and while his companion consulted the menu, Mordecai caught sight of his Menenius adversaries in the adjacent bar.

Clearly, they could see him, but not Hermione who was sitting within the recess. He was about to speak, but again the gentle smile, this time almost naughty. Had she anticipated the situation? His notion was rapidly confirmed.

"Why not ask them to join us?" she said, although she could not have seen the pair. "It might be funny."

"Perhaps, but it might spoil a pleasant occasion. The less I see of that pair the better."

"Don't worry. They won't accept. Or at least they will, and then change their minds when they meet me. Try it. You will be amused by the experiment."

So Mordecai strolled through to the bar as nonchalantly as he could, noticing that the atmosphere seemed to change as he did so. Perhaps it was merely because the bar was in the old dark part of the Cornish inn, whereas the restaurant was of new construction, with large windows and ample head room. But he knew the bar well enough, and had never previously experienced the alien force which now seemed to be oppressing him. The Meneniuses were heavy fleshy men of middle height, and with the dark complexion typical of South Europeans. Spanish or Italian perhaps, with a touch of eastern blood. They seemed surprised when Samuel approached them; the interview in the church had not gone well.

"Would you like some lunch," he said. "I'm eating in the restaurant with a friend. Bring your drinks with you."

The cousins exchanged glances, and hesitated for a second or two.

"It is indeed courteous of you," replied one in an oily voice, "and we shall be delighted to accept the felicity. Rumour has it that there is a sad difficulty with the church architecture – the roof is in disrepair they say. Perhaps our financial proposals may now be reviewed in a more favourable light …"

Mordecai interrupted his monologue.

"Please come along," he said.

The pair seemed surprised that he had a lady companion, but to Samuel's disappointment showed little immediate interest.

"This is the Reverend Hermione de Lamarac," he said, "paying a visit to the parish."

Clearly the Meneniuses were a trifle puzzled. And then Samuel noticed something in Hermione's behaviour which appeared positively arch, although in fact this was not entirely the case. Her dress was low cut, and she had slipped the Celtic Cross within her bosom, so that only the top of the ornament was visible. But this part of the cross was enamelled in an iridescent green, which, gleaming bright as an emerald with reflected light, inevitably drew the eye to the creamy white valley between her firm young breasts.

"Pray sit down," she said with her gentle smile, "and order anything you choose. My principals are paying."

The pair seemed edgy, but duly seated themselves. Samuel realised that Hermione was playing a mischievous game. He had no idea what the rules were, but it was enjoyable for all that.

And then it happened. Hermione leaned forward to pass the menu to her guests. More of both the cross and her bosom became thus visible, but then the fine gold chain supporting the ornament became undone (apparently of its own accord) and the cross slipped down out of sight.

"O dear," she said, "I'm losing my favourite pendant," and standing up, she vibrated her body with a sinuous undulation, so that the cross slipped down inside her dress, and appeared on the floor at her feet. The action was sensuous indeed, but now Samuel realised that although she was entirely virginal, she was using this tactic to raise her opponents' tension, leading their minds to herself, and also into a focus of perilous attention. It was thus that they entered a psychological pitfall.

She bent forward, picked up the cross, and placed it on the table. The cousins' eyes had been upon her as she leaned forward, but they now turned to the Celtic Cross, and with electrifying effect. There was a pause, lasting perhaps three seconds, and then they rose simultaneously.

"Please excuse us," said one. "I now remember that we have an appointment, we must go at once."

And so they fled, like a pair of fat rabbits.

"God bless my soul!" said Mordecai. "May I see that cross?"

"Certainly. It is a Saint Catherine's Cross, although none of the six Saint Catherines was Celtic."

She passed him the ornament, and he looked at it closely. It was very beautiful, intricately made, and wrought in an interlocking arrangement of colour and filigree that gave an impression of depth beyond what was physically possible. Samuel well knew that all great art was alike in that it contained something indefinable. This cross had it in high degree.

There was a Greek inscription.

"Cleave the wood and I am there," he translated.

It was a quotation from Saint Thomas' Gospel, and borderline heretical.

"You remember your Greek," she said, but he was not sure that he had truly translated it, perhaps this magical priestess had passed the information into his mind. He was about to ask why their enemies had reacted so strongly, but she sidestepped.

"That is an interesting piece of Greek in your church tower," she said.

"You know what it means?"

"Yes indeed, but we mustn't talk shop in the mess. The braised salmon looks a fair choice, perhaps with some Liebfraumilch."

CHAPTER IV
Langarrow

The moon was high in the Cornish sky as Laura Trepennick walked slowly homewards. Her Newfoundland was in front, snuffling after imaginary rabbits when the stranger spoke to her. It was startling, although he appeared, understandably enough from a lane which joined her own. She was glad of the dog; big and powerful he would be there in an instant if she called. But the stranger was civil and clearly harmless.

"Pardon me ma'am, but can you direct me to Langarrow? I must have missed my way, and am hopelessly lost."

He seemed a pleasant young man, dressed for walking, so far as she could see in the moonlight. A large haversack suggested that he was on holiday. It had happened before; walkers often became confused in the Cornish lanes.

Langarrow? The name seemed familiar, and Laura stretched her mind. She felt sorry for the young man. It was nearly ten o'clock and there was a spatter of rain in the wind.

"Langarrow?" replied Laura, struggling to bring an old memory into her mind. "The name is familiar."

"Yes," he said, "I met two fellows in a pub at lunch time and they told me of it. Apparently it's a village of ancient interest. I'm writing a project on Celtic history."

He continued by giving a detailed account of his instructions for finding the site. Laura was puzzled. What he said seemed geographically accurate, but there was no village where he claimed there to be. Still, he was a nice youngster, and she decided to help him.

"Young man, I think you had better come home with me. My house is just along the lane, and I'll ask my chauffeur to drive you over. It's getting late."

He demurred; too much trouble he said, but Laura overruled him easily enough, and soon they approached her imposing residence.

But there was a car already there. Laura recognised it as belonging to Jennifer Parsloe, the recently appointed choir mistress at her parish church. She had called on Laura before following choir practice, but what was strange was the note under the wiper blade, clearly visible in the light from the porch. 'Laura' was written on it in large letters, but the light was not bright enough to reveal the contents. Laura was puzzled, but being involved with her newfound friend, she slipped the note into her pocket and they entered the house, finding Jennifer by the drawing room fire.

"Laura," she began, but was then confused by the unexpected presence of the stranger.

There was a difficulty in introducing an unknown person, but the young man assisted her.

"Arthur Marazion at your service ladies. I was born in London, but my family is of Cornish extraction. We still feel that we have roots here."

Laura now saw that he was younger than she had thought. Her heart went out to him. He might have been the son she had never had. They exchanged pleasantries for a minute or two, until Laura sensed that Jenny had some news to impart.

"Dear me Laura," said Jennnifer. "The rector has the Church architect's report; received it this morning, and the roof's got both dry rot and death watch beetles. Poor old Mr

Mordecai. He tries so hard but can't win. God alone knows where the money will come from."

For a cynical moment Laura wondered whether this was a subtle appeal for funds. She was a woman of considerable wealth, and with no one to leave it to. But the thought was soon rejected. The Revd. Samuel Mordecai was too direct for such tactics – if the rector wanted a subscription he would ask her for it himself.

So Laura found the situation a little awkward. Clearly Jenny had come to talk to her; equally she felt obliged to her new friend. She decided to combine their respective needs.

"Jenny my dear," she said. "Could you do me a favour in the form of some transport? We can talk while you drive, if I may so presume upon you."

She outlined Arthur's difficulty and her offer of help, and out they went towards Jennifer's car.

Events were now beginning to seem strange to Laura, and indeed the sensation grew as she paused to read the note, remembering as they crossed the hall.

"Dear Laura," it began, *"You do not know me, but soon we shall meet. If you go to Langarrow, and are asked for money, tell Jennifer to pay in Catharine's coin. And remember, there are Myrmidons in Brocelliande."*

The note was signed *"Hermione de Lamarac"*, and the pen had almost gone through the paper in underlining the advice to Jennifer. Laura returned the note to her pocket. The message was both intriguing and a little frightening. It would be best to take the dog. Like a fair sized bear, he packed into the rear seat beside her, lying with his muzzle on her lap.

And so they set out. With the ladies' help, Arthur recovered his bearings, and the car rolled on along his described route. They were heading for a low-lying locality near to the coast, but both of the ladies knew full well that there was no village there.

Let us prove it to him directly, thought Laura; then Jenny could drive them home and she would give him a bed for the night.

It was raining harder now, with clouds scudding across the moon, and as the car moved on towards the coast some large dark birds became active, calling and swooping around despite the gathering wind. Also the dog became restive, whimpering and fidgeting about. Laura soothed him, scratching his ears and talking to him. Usually he was a contented animal – perhaps the change in routine was upsetting him.

Then the road became rough, with the car bumping and jolting over the ruts. Jennifer commented on it. The Cornish roads were well maintained as a rule. Also they were conscious of a tension in the car, with the young people talking in rapid and nervous sentences, mainly of a trivial nature. Laura in particular was aware of something uncanny, as if they were moving into a situation of an almost dream-like quality. And then they found it. Indeed it was almost as if the village found them. The car jolted round a bend in a deep-set lane, climbed a slight incline, and there it was, and surprisingly large. The full moon appeared from among the clouds, showing them a long badly paved street with perhaps a hundred buildings. Cottages, two or three shuttered shops, and in the background the squat tower of a small church. The only brightly lit structure was the inn, half way down the street and in front of the church.

"I don't fancy driving the car down there," said Jennifer. "I'll park here and we can walk with Arthur as far as the pub. Frankly, I don't like the look of the place."

There were lights in some of the cottages, but no one was about, until they came to the inn. A sign swinging in the wind was illuminated by an oil lamp. 'The Langarrow Arms' it read, above some sort of heraldic device, obscure in the lamplight. They all felt an unspoken reluctance to enter, but having come so far it seemed stupid to turn back. Arthur pushed open the door, and they went in.

It was large inside and full of men, wearing what could have been seventeenth century country dress. Most looked like farm labourers, but a few had a nautical air about them. The place fell silent, and all eyes were upon them. It was frightening, but their tension lessened as two men in modern dress came forward and greeted Arthur.

"Marazion, my dear fellow," said one. "So you have arrived at last, and on the day of the local carnival – very interesting to a history student. But we had thought that you would be alone. Who are the ladies?"

Arthur explained what had occurred; refreshments were offered, and they moved forward into the room. There was no valid reason for fear. The strange dress was now explained, presumably they had chanced upon a drinking session following some sort of village fete. But the place stank. Not only of beer, but of decay and unwashed bodies. The dog stood between Laura and Jennifer, tail between his legs, but wide eyed and alert.

A group of men gathered around, talking in a rough manner, and including phrases which Laura recognised as ancient Cornish, half way between Breton and Welsh. The trio stood close together near a table which seemed to serve as a bar, while their hosts, introduced as Charles and Percival, ordered drinks. Cider for the women, spirits for themselves and Arthur. A room would be arranged later for Arthur, and then the ladies could return home. But the other occupants thought otherwise. The newcomers clearly had money, and should not be allowed to depart without observing the local customs. Was it not usual for strangers to pay for drinks? And was not Jennifer a comely lass? Should she not be obliging to a few of the lads in some other way? She felt a hand moving over her buttocks, but thought best to keep still and ignore it; no sense in making a scene. Charles and Percival appeared to be in difficulties. They seemed to have some sort of vague authority, but clearly had not expected anyone to accompany Arthur. Also the local men were drunk and hard to control. Jennifer felt the hand moving again, and pressing forward into her cleft. She wriggled uncomfortably, but the hand interpreted this as encouragement, and the fingers pressed deeper. Laura spoke to the dog; there was a snarling snap, and the hand was withdrawn with an obscure curse. A round of drinks was again demanded, and then Laura remembered that extraordinary note.

"Tell Jennifer to pay in Catharine's coin", it had read. What it meant she had no idea, but it seemed wise to speak to Jennifer.

"Offer to buy some drinks, but pay with Catharine's money," she said speaking softly in her ear. By now Jenny was terrified, indeed so much so that she did not recognise that Laura had no obvious means of knowing the existence of the large silver piece. She took it from her pocket, and placed it on the bar table.

Startled, the barman looked at it hard indeed.

"She's paid with an Ys silver noble," he called excitedly. "Where come they from?" (His voice was rising.) "We want no coin from cats of murdering hell!"

"Be thou from Brocelliande?" demanded a man at Arthur's side. "It's Brocelliande money for sure."

Then Laura entered the fray.

"Brocelliande, where the Myrmidons come from," she called, as loud and clear as possible in the fug and noise of the room.

There was panic.

"The Myrmidons are coming," screamed the man. "The Brocelliande Myrmidons, run lads, run. Remember the last time. These bitches are Catharine's helots, sent on in advance, run for your lives!"

"Stop, stop, stop, don't be bloody fools," shouted Charles at the top of his voice. "These are harmless local women, no need to fear."

To no avail.

"The coin," shouted the barman. "Castle of Ys on it. A six crowns bit with the Greek round the edge. How came she by that master? Answer me that?"

Clearly Charles could not, and the panic continued. Several men had already left the inn, and others were following.

"What of the gold?" called one tall fellow, seemingly some sort of rough leader.

"Let's bury it fast," said another man, "and come back for it later when the troopers have gone."

The whole scene seemed so extraordinary that all three of the adventurers had a feeling of witnessing something not truly real, but it was all happening right enough.

"By the church tower," said the tall man. "They'll think it's a fresh grave should they see it."

The inn was now almost empty, but two men emerged from a side room, struggling with a leather sack. It might have held a stone of potatoes, but was much heavier.

And then the place was empty. Except for Charles and Percival, and the three companions. Percival looked at the women with a glance so malevolent that they were glad of the indifferent light.

"So you have defeated us," he snarled, "but we'll be even with you soon. The saints won't help you for ever, and you won't like it."

Then he and Charles went out into the night. And thus the inn was deserted; spilled ale, broken mugs and overturned furniture testified to the vigour of the rout.

"Let's get out of here," said Arthur. "I feel awful for getting you into this."

Only too keen to follow his suggestion, they slipped outside, Jennifer first reclaiming her silver coin from the table. The street was deserted, but the moonlight showed two or three men digging frantically beside the church tower. Of Charles and Percival, there was no sign.

And so they returned to the car, Nathan the dog walking quietly in front. Conversation was muted on the way home. Events had been so extraordinary that they found it difficult to form rational thoughts. But this was not the end of it.

Laura insisted that both Jennifer and Arthur remain with her overnight, and following a generous ration of brandy they retired about two a.m. However, they were up in time for breakfast, and towards the end of the meal, Laura telephoned Mordecai, he offering to come over. Meanwhile they continued to talk.

"Brocelliande," said Arthur, "is or at least was, the French equivalent of Lyonesse. I believe in the legend of Lyonesse, because a French account describes the loss of a similar tract of land off the coast of Brittany, and it must have happened simultaneously. Two such similar stories would not arise by chance – there has to be a basis of fact behind them. Ys was the capital city of Brocelliande, and Sir Lancelot du Lac of

Arthurian fame was its ruler. The coin is a mystery. It doesn't look old to me. And why there would be Myrmidons in Lancelot's army is beyond reason. Myrmidons were Greek heavy infantry in the time of Achilles, and in their day the most formidable soldiers on earth. Surprisingly enough, a fair proportion of them were women."

Then Mordecai arrived, as they were finishing some more coffee. He was bursting with both curiosity and interest, but to the ladies' surprise was already acquainted with Arthur, whom he had met a few days before.

"Langarrow," said Mordecai, "was a place of great evil which traditionally came to a sticky end in the sixteenth century, and is the basis of another legend associated with Saint Catherine's. Murder, the medieval equivalent of white slaving, the distribution of illicit liquor, devil worship, and every imaginable vice were attributed to its residents. Even Agravain the parson was involved. The place existed all right, but legend has it that it was destroyed by the wrath of God. Most likely it was engulfed by the sea – gone down to join Lyonesse – but the tale has it that there was an invasion by an army of vengeful female harpies who butchered all the men, and then burned it to the ground. The story also says that they were sent by Saint Catherine, but which Saint Catherine remains obscure. A variant is that the Catherine was a queen."

"Female Myrmidons?" enquired Laura.

"Why not?" replied Mordecai with a gentle laugh. "But let us go forth in the morning sunshine and visit your village. I have a fancy to see the place."

Jennifer said nothing.

And so they set out to Langarrow for the second time, the previous evening's events seeming unreal in the daylight. During the journey, Arthur explained that he was a post-

46

graduate history student, working on the thesis for his doctorate, and had visited the rector a few days before to discuss the history of Saint Catherine's Church. There was much material there he said, albeit a trifle mysterious.

The car ran smoothly on along well-metalled roads; the rain had blown away and the morning pleasant as they arrived at their destination. Everyone save Mordecai was dumbfounded, for all about the area was nothing but a few low lying fields and dry-stone walls. Had it all really happened? The trio knew that it had, and Mordecai had too much insight to deny the supernatural.

"I say," said Arthur, "that derelict pile of stones could have been where the church stood, a little way back from the village street; assuming this lane we are in follows the original route. Let's go over and have a look."

Sure enough, the pile could have been a church tower. An arched doorway was more or less intact, with paving beneath it, and by scratching away grass and sheep droppings, they found an inscribed slab with the lettering disfigured with age.

"The name looks something like 'Menenius'," said Jennifer. "Are you sure you didn't murder one last night Arthur? Or perhaps they got left behind after our adventure?"

They all laughed, but meanwhile Laura's mind had been working with the mixture of logic and fey intuition for which she was well known.

"We must dig," she said. "They buried the gold about here."

Mordecai borrowed a pick and spade from a nearby farm and obtained leave to excavate. Half an hour later they found it, about eight hundred gold coins, some rings and other jewellery, a quantity of silver, and also a few rotten shards which might have been the remains of a leather sack.

"There's your new church roof," said Jennifer.

CHAPTER V
The Islands of the Dawn

It was an excited party which accepted Laura's invitation to lunch. Clearly, their new valuables were treasure trove, but nevertheless it seemed likely that a goodly sum would be available for repairs. Thus they talked obsessively, and Samuel (tacitly assumed to be some sort of chairman) had difficulty in maintaining rationality. There was a growing conviction that there was an underlying link between events, and after a while Samuel restored order by asking each member to speak in turn. So for the first time, Jennifer described her visits to St. Catherine's Wood, and explaining the origin of her Ys silver noble, she passed the coin round for examination. This led to her first meeting with Samuel, and the Greek palindrome, inscribed both on the coin and across the doorway to the church crypt.

Then Arthur took over the running. He had already spoken on Brocelliande and the mysterious City of Ys, and he now suggested that there had been some sort of time reversal, although in Jennifer's visit to Ys a geographical relocation must also have taken place. It was weird, but on the whole the company agreed with him. Conversely, Jennifer mentioned that her dream-like experience had begun with Catharine, wearing modern dress and also apparently at ease in modern Cornwall. She also insisted, surprised by her own vehemence, that Catharine was wise, kind, and good to the point of saintliness.

However, Arthur's contribution was not yet complete. His historical research had included a visit to the diocesan archives, and information had been unearthed. The parish was now in the Diocese of Truro, but this was a modern foundation; when built the existing church had come under Exeter. But the ruined St. Catherine's on the hill was so old that it predated the parochial system, and therefore had originated under the auspices of a long-forgotten religious house. (Known to Guinever, wondered Samuel?)

So Arthur had first visited the Truro authorities. They were co-operative, advising him that the records relating to Cornish Churches had been transferred from Exeter to Truro following the founding of the new diocese in 1876. As for the ancient St. Catherine's, its origins went back at least to the old diocese of Crediton, and therefore before 931. But to the archivist's embarrassment it proved impossible to find any documents relating to either church! So Arthur went to Exeter. Here the response was somewhat different, and he sensed that the archivist was being defensive. Initially, irritating advice was given to return to Truro, but on persistence a reluctant permission was given to search. Since Marazion was a legitimate historian under the aegis of a major university it seemed inexplicable, but the archivist became increasingly obstructive. The man was clearly well over seventy; Arthur wondered if he were unbalanced. Usually such professionals welcomed a student as a temporary colleague in their work.

Then Arthur found a locked box, covered in dust and labelled 'St. Catherine's', but the archivist had no key to it. Or so he said. However, when the man's back was turned, Arthur turned the simple lock with a key from his desk at home, and examined the contents. Most of the papers were comparatively modern, but the box also contained some in Dog-Latin, and most interesting of all, drawings which appeared to be the sixteenth century architect's plans for the church. There was much detail on the upper parts of the building, and also a sketch of what might be the crypt. Here there was a deal of fine writing, mainly in bad Latin and well nigh illegible. He could make neither head nor tail of it. But the lay-out was totally different from any crypt which he had seen before. Thus there was a single central room, with other smaller rooms opening from it, in some cases with doors communicating one with another. Also, and most mysterious of all, a stairway was indicated descending to a lower level. Then the archivist returned, and clearly surprised and angry at Arthur having opened the box, he asked his visitor to depart. The day was Friday, and the hour was late; Arthur fled.

This account tantalised the company, but as Marazion explained, St. Catherine's was one church among many, and the present building was not particularly old. His interest was in the Celtic Church, and therefore until the recent events, the present St. Catherine's had not been of special concern to him.

They talked on for a while. Who was Hermione de Lamarac? Why and when had she placed a note on Jennifer's car instead of making herself known to Laura? Clearly, she was aware of the Menenius duo, but where did they fit in? Presumably they wanted to get into the crypt, but why? So Arthur offered to return to Exeter, taking Samuel with him. The archivist could hardly be awkward then. Damn it all, it was Mordecai's church. So they agreed, but things turned out differently.

Next day was the Sabbath, and Samuel was occupied by his usual duties. Monday dawned wet and cold, and he felt depressed, possibly a reaction from his recent excitement. Tuesday found him in a mood of great tension, edgy and unable to settle to anything. He wandered round the church, looking at this and that with confused thoughts flitting about with no rationality. And then Hermione came into his mind with irresistible force. An awareness of warmth and kindliness came upon him, but combined with a notion of sustenance and a warning of perils unseen. She was there, vivid in his thoughts, and he wanted her as a sick child may want its mother. But how could he find her? She had left neither address nor telephone number. His thoughts raced on – of the ancient church on the hill, of Celtic Christianity, of Guinever, of old forgotten things which he believed were in some way caught up behind Hermione's visit. Perhaps if he went up to the old church there would be some sort of message. Yes indeed, he knew it – intuitively, but yes indeed. Probably a note, left there for reasons beyond his present understanding. He threw on his coat, and her encouragement waxing ever stronger in his mind, hurried up the hill.

The wood remained moist and humid from the previous day's rains, redolent of wet foliage and damp earth, and with small noises in the boskage. But there was no sign of any physical communication from the Reverend Hermione. He leaned against the plinth and meditated. Jennifer had described the wind in the trees as sounding like surf. Apt enough; ceaseless waves flowing free, for ever. He looked down at a tiny patch of lichen growing upon the stone, seeing it with a clarity and detail which he had heard described as resulting from psychedelic drugs, but which could also be caused by a personal concentration of unusually great intensity. It was a trifle disturbing; he closed his eyes, while continuing to think of Hermione, and her promised support. Then he had a falling sensation, but the feeling of the maritime continued; indeed the very odour of the sea was upon him. So he opened his eyes, still looking down, and incredibly enough, a rippling surf was breaking gently a short distance from his feet. A great emotional surge sprang up within him. Joy and warmth, and an unreasoning happiness. What had happened? He did not know, but it was ecstatic. Impossible, dreamlike, but ecstatic.

He looked up, and then around him. Nearby was a patch of sea holly; bright blue flowers and a tiny blue butterfly of exactly the same shade, gathering nectar. Burnet roses were growing a little further up the beach. Sand dunes, and coarse grass, and a moderate breeze. He absorbed the scene in minute detail, seeing nuances of form and colour which he had never realised before. The foreshore curved round into a sizeable bay, and looking across it he saw waves breaking against a rocky headland, spray flying high, all with a surreal clarity. A village occupied part of the headland; a small harbour with some fishing boats, and houses rising above it. Higher still, indeed on the summit of the headland was a church. Large for the village, and oddly sited he thought.

To the left, a promontory thrust out into the bay, and rising above it he could see the top hamper of a large ship. Something about it suggested a gunboat and it was presumably a sizeable vessel, for the promontory was well over fifty feet in height. Otherwise of human life there was no sign. No one was visible in the village and the beach and promontory were equally deserted.

The atmosphere was quiet; not physically silent, he could hear the wind, the sea, and the calling of sea birds, but still with an implication of great peace. He stood motionless for several minutes, wondering. Where was he? What had happened? Hermione and Laura and supernatural forces, and their extraordinary wood! He looked around again.

Three women and a man were walking towards him along the beach. The tallest lady he recognised, both from Jennifer's description and the portrait on the silver noble. Undoubtedly she was Catharine of Ys. The man was tall, well made and soberly dressed, in contrast to the Athene on his arm who was diamond bright in an elaborate uniform; much gold braid, and a becoming peaked cap. There was something in her bearing that gave an impression of vitality and superb physique. Samuel assumed that this was Ystelle Zabuloe – Hermione's 'formidable army officer'. The fourth member of the party was Hermione herself, now wearing well cut tweed.

Samuel's sense of the surreal continued. He was living more than intensively – his accustomed limits of human reality had gained a perspective which he could neither describe nor understand. Every step that the party took seemed an eternity, and the wind in Hermione's hair stirred her chestnut locks into an ecstasy of form and colour. Then she raised her arm to wave to him, and the spell was altered, not broken but made different. This place and these people were of his own kind, but in some sort of superior condition. He knew both from intuition and Arthur's analysis that he was in a latter-day Lyonesse, and that here he was accepted, even as Catharine had accepted Jennifer. Ys and Lyonesse and the Celtic Church.

The party hurried on towards him, Catharine speaking first as they gathered round.

"Samuel, Samuel, my dear Samuel. How wonderful that you have come to us; it is good that your faith was strong."

She extended her hand, and in a burst of uncontrollable emotion, Samuel found that he was bowing before her, her hand clasped in both of his own. But raising him up, she caught him into her arms, and he felt as if he had found a home for which he had been searching for the whole of his life. She held him close for a second or two, then released him, and holding him at arm's length with her hands upon his shoulders, looked at him, smiling gently. And he loved her. Not in any erotic sense, but because he knew in that instant the person who she was.

"Samuel, dear Samuel," she repeated. "You are in danger, but do not fear unduly because now we are with you. Stephen Zabuloe" (she blandly assumed that he knew who people were) "has been watching over your parish for some time past, indeed it was he who recommended Hermione as my ambassador. You will also need some material support, but now is not the time for a conference."

Poor Samuel was at a loss for words, but Zabuloe came to his aid.

"It is good to see you Mordecai," he said. "Men are in short supply here, as you will shortly come to understand. We would ask you to stay for a few days to go into the position, and sort out a plan of action; there is much to talk about."

Samuel was hopelessly out of his depth. Moreover, he could not disappear inexplicably from the village, and Mrs Mordecai was coming home that evening. But how could he refuse?

"You are very kind," he replied, "but I have duties to do, and my wife will panic if I am not at home. Can we make some arrangement for these things?"

"To be sure," said Zabuloe. "Laura Trepennick will meet Mary at the railway station, shepherd her into the Rolls, and persuade her to stay with her for a few days. The tale will be that you have been called away suddenly on a matter to do with the treasure trove, which is true enough as it happens, if not in the way that your wife will think."

"But how will Laura know?" persisted Stephen, although he saw that the question was obvious.

It was Hermione who replied.

54

"Laura Trepennick responds to intuitions which she does not understand, but has learned to trust. She will do as I ask. Have no fear; your wife will be cared for."

"Courage Samuel." It was the Athene who spoke. "Hermione wants me to help you. If anyone menaces Mary Mordecai they will have me to reckon with."

Heavens, but she looked strong. And she meant what she said. A warm open face, not beautiful, but with what the Americans called 'that other'. Tawny blonde hair curled in to her collar; broad shouldered and upright she could have felled an ox. But there was nothing masculine about her. All woman, and lots of it. Samuel almost felt jealous. Then the Athene continued:

"It so happens that Donna Catharine has for long honoured me as Killiarch of her personal guard, and I know that she will lend troopers as necessary. A killiarch is a colonel. Soon you will meet an admiral; our launch is coming."

Sure enough, a sleek boat was racing across the bay, its noiseless propulsion had failed to draw Samuel's attention. He also noticed that a small wooden jetty was near at hand, and a floating pontoon, presumably to accommodate the tides. They walked towards the jetty, arriving simultaneously with the launch.

A woman wearing a flamboyant light blue uniform stepped onto the platform, and Samuel gazed upon her. Hermione was a beautiful woman, Catharine handsome in the classical Grecian mode, and Ystelle had her own vigorous attraction. But this woman! Moreover, Catharine read his thoughts:

"Was this the face that launched a thousand ships," she said softly, "and burned the topless towers of Ilium? She is

Admiral Lucilla Mantzini. You can see the masts of her flagship on the other side of Goose Rock. Lovely, isn't she?"

The lady was indeed exquisite. Her face was perfect, framed by auburn hair and with a tricorne hat bearing an elaborate silver brooch. And yet she was no china doll. He sensed there was a great deal of steel about her, and the ability to command. She bowed slightly to Catharine.

"Greetings Donna. At your service."

Catharine embraced her.

"It is good to see you Lucilla. Things are stirring again on earth, as we shall presently explain. This is Samuel Mordecai. He is in the front rank against our enemy. Hermione has persuaded him to visit us, that we can lend him some aid."

"Your ally sir," she said, looking him full in the face.

It was disturbing. He felt that she could see into his mind – her eyes were deeper than the depth of waters stilled at even. Who were these extraordinary women? Their characters were clearly manifold, although paradoxically enough it was equally clear that there was a common factor in their natures. Catharine, according to Jennifer was a saint, and Hermione had something of the same spiritual character, but the other two were like the wrath of God. But what to reply to Lucilla?

"I am out of my depth ma'am. Perhaps you will help me to understand."

Once more, Stephen came to his aid.

"Don't worry Samuel. Shortly all will be made clear. If I may make a start, here the leading ladies are called 'Donna'. Ma'am is short for madam, which can mean more things than one!"

They all laughed, very gently, and Samuel felt better.

"Come along children," said Catharine, and thus they boarded the launch.

Swift and silent the boat slid away towards the village on the further side of the bay, Zabuloe continuing his partial explanation.

"Events developed in a bit of a rush," he said, "or I'd have handled things differently. By coincidence, Ystelle, Hermione and I are here as Catharine's holiday guests – she is taking a few days in a villa which she has nearby. Today's jaunt has nothing to do with your problems, but Catharine wants to help you personally, and as it happened she could not cancel today's arrangements. Here the Church and State are close together, and she is to preach in the church which you see on top of the hill. The village is associated with Lucilla's battleship, which explains why she is here. You will see the ship in a minute when we are a little further across the bay."

Samuel's mood was now altering swiftly; his feeling of peace and relaxation was being replaced by a growing excitement. Things were happening. He was part of it all, and seemingly an important part, caught up within a tide of events not of his own making and at present beyond his understanding. Perhaps the sight of the warship contributed to his changed condition, although as yet he had small impression of the vessel save for its enormous size. The bows rose from the water like a great metal wedge.

'ΑΓΙΟΣ ΘΟΜΑΣ ΑΠΟΣΤΟΛΟΣ', he read, gilt letters against a fawn ground.

"Saint Thomas the Apostle," he translated, but why O why in Greek?

The launch sped on. Soon they entered the diminutive harbour, and by now a further curiosity was being forced upon him. Apart from Stephen Zabuloe all of his newfound friends were women, and young women at that. Alert young ladies in their early or mid-twenties. Perhaps the vigour of their ages was vitalising him. Certainly he felt strong; he was absorbing the experience with the detail and clarity which he recalled from his own long-gone youth.

Their path led them into a village street, a steep cobbled ascent between white-painted houses. It was immaculately kept, indeed almost too perfect to be real. Tubs of flowers in sheltered corners, a small shop with everyday goods in the window, all seemed more normal than normal, and Samuel found himself envying both the village and the pattern of life which it seemed to represent.

And so they went on towards the church, his professional interest expanding. He knew full well that communication was important in all liturgy, and he looked forward curiously because his new friends were showing him a different dimension in the art. At least Hermione had the ability to transfer information by unusual psychic pathways. Many people (dare he say 'ordinary beings'?) could be aware of a fellow person's moods or needs by intuitive means which might be less than rational. But Hermione's ability went far beyond this.

As Zabuloe had said, it was Catharine who preached. She spoke in English, although the canticles had been sung in the original Greek. Her words seemed childishly simple – until a person reflected upon their content, when a current of almost paranormal intensity developed within the mind of the listener. She held the attention of Samuel and the entire congregation with an effortless command. Much of it was heretical. He felt vague stirrings of half forgotten knowledge, a little recalled from his student days, but more arising from a growing awareness of ancient churches and schools of theology buried long since from earthly minds. He thought of the Cathars of eleventh century France, of priests chanting in Syriac, of Pelagius, and the second century Valentinus and his Gospel of

Truth, of Saint Catherine's Cross and its inscribed quotation from the Gospel of Saint Thomas. He knew that in the early days theology had not settled down; diverse schools of thought had existed concurrently. And Catharine held a Gnostic theology; it was heretical but her mind had entered his, and she took him by storm. What she said did not contradict his orthodox belief, but rather confirmed and extended it into a higher Christianity which he had not known to exist. Her faith was more developed and parallel to Anglicanism, but not opposed to it. And it was dangerous, old and powerful and dangerous; too powerful for ordinary men. Marazion would have been fascinated. Was there a connection here with Arthur's apparently fortuitous involvement with the company? Mordecai suspected so. And what were the powers formerly exercised by the Celtic priests, and now apparently by Hermione and Catharine? The great Pelagius was said to have been a converted Druid, and that this was a salient factor in his dispute with Saint Augustine. Who and what were Merlin and Morgan le Fey: what was the significance of Guinever?

What indeed lay behind the recent events? There was some common factor involved, indeed there had to be.

Then the service ended.

"Come into the vestry," said Catharine.

The room was large, but contained several half dressed women, so Samuel gazed out of the window, looking down to where Lucilla's dreadnought was riding to her anchors close offshore. The setting sun illuminated the ship in a shadow-casting light which contributed to the drama of the scene. The vessel was truly enormous. Brightly painted with no attempt at camouflage, the gunboat had colours that could have come from a medieval ship-of-the-line. But the overall form was that of a super dreadnought; there were four quadruple turrets furnished with tremendous guns, and a conning tower a hundred feet in height. Yet these women were profoundly Christian people. He looked again at the guns, and thought of the wrath of God until Catharine was by his side.

"We could have our meeting on the ship," she said, "but I would be honoured to entertain you in my country house for a day or two. Also the triennial visit here is a bit of a party for the ship's company, so we can join in their festivity this evening, and Lucilla will take us back to the mainland through the night. The Saint Thomas is a Trisagion Battleship, and enormously fast."

"My kingdom," said Catharine, as she sat beside Samuel during dinner in the ship's wardroom, "is one of the many mansions of low heaven. It is our duty to contend against the powers of darkness.

"This activity takes diverse forms, in fact this great ship is an example of one of them – no don't worry, we shan't send her to Cornwall! But," she continued, "I would like to send Ystelle, as she has already mentioned, to take care of you for a few weeks. She will need some little force, so if you agree, a few picked troopers from my personal guard. Also, for reasons historical but almost beyond earthly belief, a few of our Brocelliande Myrmidons. The land of Lyonesse as you now experience it, is in a sense parallel to that of King Arthur, but exists in a different aeon. We have many islands, and the largest, Lyonesse proper, is divided into three provinces. These are Brocelliande, Ysbathaden, and Westland. In former earthly times, Brocelliande extended from Brittany far out into the Atlantic, and was part of Sir Lancelot du Lac's French domain. Ys was its capital city, but the land was engulfed by the sea at the same time as Lyonesse. Brocelliande is the eastern part of Lyonesse, but my country house is in the Westland, at the other end of the island. It is called 'Plas Llyntawn'. Maybe you will like it. Most people do."

Catharine was not disappointed. Next day dawned fine and bright, but by the time they arrived at Llyntawn, several magnificent thunderheads had appeared, and the house was illuminated by a great shaft of sunlight streaming down between them. Catharine was clearly at pains to welcome Samuel, for she stopped the car at the west gate, to stroll for the last half mile or so along a gravel walk to the house. They were accompanied by Ystelle, and the trio paused for a moment to look at Catharine's favourite abode. It was indeed a royal residence. A right-angled terrace faced south and west, and was supported on a colonnade of arches with a Palladian balustrade. This formed an elegant platform for the house itself, which rose beyond it with an airy grace. Samuel was reminded of Lutyens, but the house had an air of dream-like presence never achieved by the great architect. And so for a long half minute he stood enthralled, finding it impossible to analyse the nature of the Queen's residence, because attempts to identify individual architectural features were self defeating. The structure had to be seen as a whole.

The gravelled walk extended before them, bordered by occasional urns overflowing with pendulous flowers of assorted colour and form. He was almost reluctant to move onward lest the spell break, but with a lady on either side of him and the gravel crunching beneath his feet, the walk commenced. And then the rain began. At first a few large drops as the harbinger of a deluge, with the house three hundred yards away.

"O my word," cried Catharine. "It is hurry that we must!"

And hurry they did. Samuel was a slightly built elderly man of indifferent physique, but without exchanging a word, the two women caught him up on their linked arms, and ran like a pair of chamois towards the house. He felt a little unmanned at first, although he readily recognised that the lithe young ladies were far stronger than he. And he became acutely aware of them as women; Catharine's hair was rustling across his face, he could feel their breasts nudging against him as they ran, and he also noticed that they were both wearing scent, although of different perfumes. It was a sensation of exotic and intimate luxury, heightened by the growing downpour and an initial crash of thunder. In fact they covered the distance in a little over a minute, and ignoring the stone staircase to the terrace, Catharine sprinted under one of the arches and on through an open door into a low-ceilinged room which was furnished as an adjunct to the garden. Here they collapsed in a heap upon a wickerwork sofa, the women laughing hilariously. Samuel found himself caught up within their mood. He had arrived at Llyntawn!

Catharine's study is a beautiful room. In plan elliptical, it has walls decorated in a continuous rural scene, with a window at one end, glazed partly in stained glass and opening onto an arcade. The whole is contrived so that the vista appears to form an extension of the room, and combines with a domed ceiling rising upward in a decreasing shade of celestial blue to terminate in an oval lunette. It happened that as Samuel entered, sunlight was creating a chiaroscuro of light and shade which confirmed the elegance and architectural proportion of the room. Wonderful indeed.

"And did those feet in ancient time walk upon England's mountains green?" said Catharine to the small party when they were seated around her central table. Samuel's mind reverted to Jennifer playing the hymn at their first meeting, and Caroline Owens' superb soprano singing Catharine's quotation. But what had Blake's 'Jerusalem' to do with this meeting, called to explain the queen's concern for his Cornish parish?

"The answer," continued Catharine, in reply to her own question, "is probably not, but William Blake's sentiments are indeed apposite. I believe that Joseph of Arimathea did in fact visit England, but Hermione is a greater authority on this than I am, therefore I shall ask her to take up the story with some help from Stephen."

"Thank you Donna," said Hermione. "At the risk of seeming vainglorious I shall borrow one of my own books from your shelves."

She left the table, and Samuel realised that the rural scene was painted onto sliding panels which concealed bookcases; Hermione selected a slim volume, and passed it to him. It was entitled 'The Acts of Pontius Pilate', and in letters small in their humility 'Translated and with commentary by H.J. de Lamarac, Dean of St. Mary All Souls, and Mistress Emeritus of Theology, University of Ys'.

Well, well, well, thought Samuel. He had heard of the book, also called 'The Gospel of Nicodemus'. It contained the legend of Joseph of Arimathea, but never having examined a copy, he was little familiar with it. The work dated from the fourth century, many years after Pilate's time.

"The book as it is known on earth," continued Hermione, "is less complete than the version from which that translation was prepared, and it was also somewhat edited for political reasons. I believe that the original is accurate in certain unpleasant details concerning the death of our saviour, and in the subsequent history of Joseph of Arimathea. He had possession of the extraordinary chalice known as the Sangreal, and also of the spear belonging to the Roman soldier Longinus, one of the three soldiers recorded as present at the death of Our Lord. We know where the Sangreal is, indeed it is now safely in our possession – but don't let us go into all that. Both objects are imbued with enormous spiritual resources." She paused as if ordering her mind. "I don't know for sure where the Spear of Longinus is," she went on. "There are contradictory accounts of its history. William of Malmesbury claimed that Charlemagne used it in conflict with the Saracens, although I don't believe it myself. Other vague mentions crop up here and there, but Mallory's account in the Morte d'Arthur is based on fact, although subject to histrionic exaggeration. What Mallory does not record is precisely what happened after Sir Balin fought with King Pellam, despite some vague allusions later on in the book. He claimed that Sir Balin's dolorous stroke caused the devastation of three counties; a statement which in itself is romantic nonsense, but it conveys a notion of magnitude and the human reaction felt at the time. But what became of the spear?"

In a flash of dreadful intuition, Samuel realised that he knew the answer, but Stephen Zabuloe took up the tale:

"Like you Samuel, I hail from Cornwall, as did King Arthur a few years back. The definitions of 'King' and 'Kingdom' were different then from those understood today. Most kings were little more than petty chieftains ruling over whatever they could control. One of Arthur's achievements was to make a realm by drawing together the allegiances of such people. I have studied both the earthly records, and fuller documents available here, and it is clear that while Arthur was a profoundly Christian man; he retained an earlier credulity which made it easier for him to accept factors that would probably be rejected by a modern believer. Sir Balin and King Pellam were out of their depth, and to prevent further mischief, Arthur decided to place the spear in safe keeping. And safe in two senses, firstly physically safe to prevent anyone from stealing it, and secondly psychically so to guard against intervention by the forces of an antichrist, which could have drawn energy from its undoubted reserves. Let us consider what sort of place he would choose."

Stephen caught Samuel's eye, before continuing:

"Physical security would not be particularly difficult for him – several castles were available which were well-nigh impregnable in pre-gunpowder days. But what of the diabolical influences, ghostly entities which were nearer the surface then than now? If the spear were locked up in Lonazep or Sir Lancelot's Joyous Guard, who would guard the guardians? Better to rely on his army of heavily armed knights to repel material enemies, and place the spear in a place of spiritual power and the custody of Christian men."

"Or women," contributed Ystelle, "Guinever comes into the story."

"What we believe to be the story," her husband replied.

"Now children," said Catharine. "This is meant to be a serious meeting! What will Samuel think?"

"Yes Donna," said Stephen. "We shall come to Guinever in a few moments. I believe that Arthur selected a Cornish chapel for the custody of the Spear of Longinus, a chapel where the Sangreal had previously appeared, and he also caused a crypt to be built specially for the purpose. Perhaps the spear was continuously watched over by a relay of religious dedicated to the purpose, or perhaps Arthur relied upon the influence imparted by the Holy Grail to ward off what they feared. Perhaps some forgotten ritual or even sacrament was applied to ensure its safe keeping. All very mysterious, but sacrament means mystery, musterion, in the Greek. It is also probable, as Ystelle may well remind us, that following the death of Arthur – or his departure to Avalon – Mallory gives an account which is not fully clear – custody was continued by nuns from the order where Guinever became Mother Superior, and hence one of the first women in England to be ordained priest. And, as Samuel has by now guessed, the Arthurian chapel was the original Saint Catherine's, up there on top of the hill, and within his parish. No wonder the wood has some extraordinary powers!"

In fact Samuel was not surprised by Stephen's description, because he had realised where the tale was leading. And he felt a sense of comfort; the gage was down, the challenge out, and these people were his powerful friends. Moreover, he was not alone. He felt the excitement of team membership in a common cause, and some sort of zany sense was being made of recent events. It was as if Arthurian times were reawakening, with old ideals coming back to life. As an orthodox Christian, Samuel did not believe in metempsychosis, but he felt as if something very like it were going on. Old influences, if not characters were being born again. Odd that Marazion was named 'Arthur'. Furthermore, 'Marazion' was an exceedingly ancient Cornish name, and it was he who had found the plan of the crypt. A Guinever would appear next! But then he felt Catharine's large brown eyes full upon him, and a thought sprang (or was entered) into his mind. Guinever, he recalled, was a name that had disappeared in the seventeenth century, but by transliteration – 'Jennifer' – was the modern use. But why the involvement with the present Saint Catherine's? The queen answered his unspoken question.

"I fancy that Laura Trepennick's ancestors moved the spear, or Merlin's Myster, or whatever they called it, from the old church to the newly built one, but without understanding the significance of what they were about. Also, they built a crypt like that under the original church, and sealed it."

She opened her handbag, and smiling gently passed him a coin.

"A present from Catharine," she said; however this was no silver noble, but a great piece of gold.

"A sophia, Samuel. The currency unit in Lyonesse, but don't admire my portrait, read the rim."

He had small need to, for he knew already what would be there, but he did as she asked.

"ΝΙΨΟΝΑΝΟΜΗΜΑΤΑΜΗΜΟΝΑΝΟΨΙΝ," he read aloud, stumbling a little over the Greek.

"Apart from the altar, what is the holiest place in a church?" she asked.

"Why – the font," he replied.

"Exactly, and the wording on the coin, which incidentally is the earliest known example of a palindrome, means: 'Wash my transgressions, not only my face'. It was formerly used as an inscription on fonts, engraved around the basin. I fancy that Guinever attempted to block the power of the spear by baptising it, or by some such ceremony, to wash away its supposed sin. Clearly, this did not work, as I could have told her it wouldn't, but then I wasn't around at the time."

"Thank you Donna," said Samuel. "You are embarrassingly kind."

CHAPTER VI
Jonothan Nanjulien

"Come," said Hermione a little while later. "We must return to Cornwall. Ystelle will follow and Stephen will maintain a rapport. Stand close to me, and don't fear."

It was with mixed feelings that old Mordecai felt the delightful young woman take him into her arms. Again, a sensation of falling, a rushing movement in a direction which he did not understand, and he was looking out over the dry-stone wall of St. Catherine's Wood, down to where an immaculate Rolls-Royce was standing near to Trevanions' Farm.

"How kind of Laura to send the car," said Hermione. "We can collect Mrs Mordecai from Trepennick Chase before taking you home."

And it was good to be home, although if Hermione had not been there Mordecai might have had difficulty in believing that he had ever been away. But there she was, and the calendar had moved on. He was surprised at the ease with which a rapport developed among the women, even as Hermione explained the situation. Both Laura and Mary accepted her words readily enough, asking little more than questions of clarification.

"We are much on our own in this," Hermione concluded, "and cannot involve the earthly authorities. They would not believe what we say, and also Catharine is against it. She says that supernatural forces are behind the earthly events, and we must fight in similar terms. On the whole I agree with her."

"It seems to me," said Laura, "that we have three issues. Firstly we must defend Saint Catherine's from physical assault. This includes ourselves as well as the building. Secondly we must arrange protection from satanic forces, and thirdly decide what to do with whatever it is that the enemy is after. We still don't know for sure that it is the Spear of Longinus. There is nothing in the Trepennick family records about it."

"I agree, but an immediate attack is unlikely," said Samuel. "Hermione has frightened off the Meneniuses, and they will need some time to think."

But events proved him wrong.

They agreed to form themselves into a Christian fellowship, although as Hermione remarked, this appeared to have formed of itself. So they were seven all told: Samuel and Mary Mordecai, Laura, Hermione, Arthur Marazion, Jennifer Parsloe, and at Laura's request, Caroline Owens. Not many thought Samuel, and Laura and he were old people. He suggested that they meet next evening in the vestry to make more definite plans – he had a feeling of suspense – what course would be taken by events? Trouble was forecast, but how to prepare for it?

The first event was the great storm, remembered for decades after. Much timber came down, although, curiously none in St. Catherine's Wood, and this together with torrential rain effectively isolated the village. The telephone lines followed the trees, and the road to the local town was under water. So it was a wet and excited company which met next evening.

Hermione appeared surprised at the suddenness and severity of the storm, but said little. Unexpected news was that the Meneniuses had returned to the village, and there was a lot of disjointed talking. All of the women apart from Hermione were in favour of opening the crypt, but were clearly unaware of the canon law on such matters. Arthur was against, wanting to conduct further research before doing so.

Hermione continued to say little, but Samuel sensed that she was tense, unusually so for a woman of her numinous faith and personality. Maybe it was the weather. The church was like a ship in a gale, wind wailing round the corners, rain splattering against the windows, and the churchyard trees waving and blowing like the roaring forties. Samuel felt that Hermione's mind was working overtime. She seemed to be thinking of Sir Christopher Trepennick, navigating his man o'war through the storms of the Spanish Main. Of Captain William Trevayne, triple expansion engines, and half speed ahead though it blew like the devil himself. But there was something else in Hermione's mind. A vague suspicion about the origin of the storm, the consequent isolation of the village, and the presence of the Meneniuses. Some sort of diabolical influence. She was about to speak, but was frighteningly forestalled.

For at that moment the vestry door opened, and four men entered, one carrying a sawn-off shotgun. There was a moment's pause, and then:

"If you lot had any sense, you'd have stayed at home on a night like this. We're locking you in. Too much fuss to shoot you. Come morning, someone may come looking for you, otherwise you can starve to death for all I care. Don't try to break out or you'll get shot. No meddling, no questions, nothing stupid, and none of you'll get hurt. As for you," he continued, glaring evilly at Mordecai, "you've got some gold belonging to our lot, and we'll want it back."

And without waiting for a reply, they filed outside.

Samuel had left the vestry key in the outside of the lock; he did not carry it with him, because the key was secreted nearby for mutual convenience – the churchwardens, choirmistress, and such people. It had all happened so quickly that the company was more dumbfounded than frightened. It was Marazion who spoke first.

"I had a quick look through the vestry door," he said. "There are some more of them over in the tower, and they've got a thing like a jack hammer for taking roads up. And I think I saw that Agravain character – the ancient archivist from Exeter, he was there along with the Menenius pair. There must be eight or ten of them altogether, counting those that came in here."

"Could someone get out of here," said Caroline, "and get help?"

It seemed a hopeless suggestion, the vestry window was impractical for the purpose, and there was no other exit apart from the door, but Samuel spoke:

"I have a second key – kept on my key ring," he said, "and I don't think that they left the first key in the outside of the lock. But I wouldn't fancy going out there."

He was finding it difficult to concentrate. Apparently illogical thoughts were surging through his mind, of Catharine and her people, particularly of Stephen and the formidable Ystelle. He noticed that Jennifer and Laura were standing close to Hermione, as if forming a group within the company. Physically they were in a weak position. He himself was too old to be much use. Marazion was a well made young man and Caroline Owens an exceptionally powerful woman, but they could not take on the opposition, and the other lot had a gun, possibly more than one. Then they heard the rattle of the jack hammer – presumably one of the electrical variety, a compressor could hardly have been brought up to the church. In a matter of minutes the enemy would be into the crypt!

There was some disjointed conversation, then to Samuel's surprise Jennifer took the lead.

"I have a plan," she said. "The fuse box is here in the vestry, I have a small torch in my handbag, and the door has a large bolt on the inside. So, we unlock the door but don't open it, then switch off the electricity at the fuse box. Two of us, say Arthur and I, slip out of the door the instant the lights go out. I'll leave the torch with you. The other lot will be confused by the sudden dark, and most likely we'll get away with it. You shut the door behind us. Re-lock it and bolt it, but don't leave the key in the lock so that if they come back and try to open it, they won't know that you've got another key. Refuse to let them in. They don't know about the second key, so they won't suspect that the door has been opened. Pretend that the storm has caused the power failure, and that you won't open the door for fear of violence. Jam the table against it to help the bolt, and try to keep them talking. They won't suspect that Arthur and I are loose in the church. While they are flapping we'll be escaping."

"The difficulty," said Caroline, "will be in getting out of the church. They are close to the tower door and are sure to have torches with them. Also the chancel door is a pig to open because it's hardly ever used, and it's me that's going, not Jennifer. I was born and brought up in this parish, and it's my fight more than hers."

But Hermione interrupted her:

"There are several memorials in this church, and to valiant men. The evil ones are using supernatural forces against us. Have no doubt of it, and therefore we shall reply in like kind. I agree with Jennifer's plan for getting out of the vestry, but I am going outside with her and Laura. The rest of you stay in here, but think very hard of some old parishioners, hardy men who stood up for their church in the past. I shall write their names down. Read them by the light of the torch."

The intermittent rattle of the jack hammer continued, and using a sheet of Samuel's notepaper, she wrote as swiftly as possible:

'Jonothan Nanjulien, William Trevayne, Ahab Choone, Paul Pendrea, Christopher Trepennick'.

"I wrote paragraphs on all of these when we produced a Parish History," said Mary Mordecai, "but this is no time to be playing psychological games."

"Hermione isn't playing games," said Laura. "I remember Brigadier Nanjulien well. He was a friend of my father, and I wish he were here now. Hermione means to raise what some people call ghosts. I'm going to help her."

This produced a momentary pause, no one contradicting. All present were aware of the tension and urgency of the moment – the storm howling about the building, the noises from within the tower, and an underlying sense of the paranormal combined to raise their sensibilities to the sticking point. Truth to tell, it was only Hermione who understood what was happening. Laura's intuitive mind was following her mentor's lead, but without rationalising what was involved.

"Now," said Arthur.

He was standing with his ear to the door panels, trying to time their opening stratagem with both the clatter of the jack hammer, and an unusually noisy movement of the storm. Samuel threw the switch, and with his heart in his mouth, Arthur opened the door. Praise be, there was no answering shotgun blast. It took the women perhaps four seconds to slip out, and two more for him to close the door, re-lock it and remove the key. As rehearsed, Mary shot the bolt, and Caroline had the vestry table in place within the instant. All seemed to be going well, but it was Hermione's party which was taking the bulk of the risk. Arthur had his ear to the door again, but could hear nothing new. How would the enemy react?

In fact they were at first nonplussed. The Meneniuses had assumed that they would find the church unoccupied, and having made no advance planning for the contrary, they were taken doubly off guard.

Hermione led onward into the Lady Chapel, added to the main building centuries before by the Choone family. Indeed it contained their memorials and mortal remains, including those of Paul Pendrea, married to Ahab's youngest daughter. And still the tempest raged without, its violence invading all within the church, as Hermione strained her ears to catch sound of their enemies. She realised that the other side were as tense and extended as the Christians, even though she was now convinced that the storm had been raised by their necromantic resources. It sounded as if huge malevolent birds were involved in the clangour, screaming and calling all around the church, but Hermione's training told her that this was not the case. No birds were present, indeed it was doubtful if birds could have flown in such a gale. It was evil entities which were gathered about the church. Thank God that it was a consecrated building, and they thus lacked the power to enter. But gusts of air were forced inward under the doors and round ill-fitting windows, rain dripped from leaks in the roof, and a few dead leaves rustled here and there across the floor, adding to a feeling of abnormal energy, and indeed a fighting struggle on the part of the building itself.

She could now see the light of torches within the tower, and between the gusts voices could be heard expostulating loudly:

"I tell you the power went off the minute the hammer touched that bit of lead with the writing on it. I'm for getting out of here ..." Then a renewed rush of wind erased the rest of the words.

The Lady Chapel was removed from the tower, and it was evident that the miscreants suspected nothing; Hermione was in little immediate danger.

"Stand close by me," she said to her companions, "and think hard. Concentrate your belief on the Communion of Saints."

And then she was chanting, very softly, and in Greek. Her contralto voice rode along in that mighty tongue with practised ease; the diphthongs, complex vowels and resonant consonants of an ancient liturgy seemed to fill the chapel with a mystical energy opposing that which raged without.

Meanwhile, Samuel and the remainder of the company waited in the vestry. Their nerves were on edge, but more for Hermione than themselves. There was nothing to be heard apart from the fury of the storm. Samuel directed the torch onto Hermione's list of bygone parishioners, and they repeated the names aloud.

"Jonothan Nanjulien, William Trevayne, Ahab Choone ..."

And then a key was thrust into the outside of the lock, the wards were turned, and a thunderous hammering beat upon the panels when the door failed to open. There was a coarse expletive, but the voice sounded frightened as well as angry.

"Open up you lot. Or we'll have the door down." A series of obscene threats followed.

Samuel was about to make the agreed reply, but was forestalled. A stentorian voice reverberated through the vestry.

"Brigadier Nanjulien here. I've got a loaded Webley in my hand, and if you force that door you're dead men. Queen Catharine is onto you fellers. I'm here on her orders, and I'll take no nonsense."

And at that moment a gunshot sounded from within the church. The noise seemed odd, a dullish flat boom, unlike a rifle or shotgun.

Uncharacteristically, Samuel was paralysed by indecision. But not Caroline.

"Hermione wants the lights on," she said. "Don't ask me how I know, but she does."

"Put 'em on then," said the strange voice. "Electric it'll be by now I suppose."

The illumination showed Nanjulien to be a massive man, wearing a uniform reminiscent of the First World War. A large black moustache, and eyes as bright as diamonds. He seemed to accept the situation phlegmatically, and apart from the dated uniform, looked little different from a modern senior officer.

"Where is Laura?" he demanded. "Charming girl. Great to see her again. Credit to her family."

At that moment, Marazion took it upon himself to open the door. Apart from the sanctuary lamp, the only lights burning in the church were those in the tower, and a single bulb at the end of the nave. It was difficult to recognise what was happening. The men had scattered away from the vestry door, and a dreadfully lacerated corpse lay outside the tower arch. Nearby, a squat figure wearing medieval dress was reloading an enormous fowling piece. The dead man was he who had threatened the company with the sawn-off shotgun. Samuel walked over to the switches at the end of the nave, and turned on more lights. The scene was somewhat macabre, with smoke from the fowling piece drifting over the pews. Jennifer had taken possession of the shotgun, and was menacing a group of five or six men, whom she had herded into a group near the tower. But where were the Meneniuses? The question was answered in a scuffle which emerged from beneath the pews at the far side of the church, where a large white dog

76

(subsequently identified as a Basset Hound) flushed them out, locking its teeth into Percival's ankle in the process.

"Aah, bytheid y lluan brathu," exclaimed a heavily built man, carrying a firearm as large as that recently discharged.

"He's speaking ancient Cornish by God," said Nanjulien. "It means 'Go on dog, bite the louse.' I'd better take charge or they'll commit a bloody massacre. Those weapons are punt guns, meant for wild fowling from boats."

Charles Menenius fled into the Lady Chapel, but emerged a moment later with a cut on his cheek, and pursued by an elaborately dressed gentleman who was armed with a rapier.

"That must be Sir Christopher Trepennick," exclaimed Mary. "Hermione has certainly started something!"

And then Hermione and Laura appeared from the Lady Chapel, escorted protectively by a man wearing Victorian naval uniform, and identified by Nanjulien as Captain William Trevayne.

"He was a grown man when I was a lad," he said. "Damned good old family as well."

It seemed to Samuel that the situation was beyond control, but Nanjulien took immediate action. Dammit he was the senior officer! Therefore he assumed command. Any alternative action never occurred to him.

He walked over to the man who had fired the enormous hand gun, and grasping his hand, addressed him warmly.

"Quite a firing piece you've got there."

"Aaah," came the reply.

"My name is Nanjulien, Jonothan Nanjulien," continued the brigadier.

"Aaah Zurr. Ahab Choone. At the Queen's duty. I'm for shooting the lot of them."

"Let us show some charity," said Nanjulien, "and round them up. Before that lady kills someone with the shotgun."

Two or three members of the Menenius faction were still at large in the church, but the Basset Hound proved effective. Surprisingly, none of them had left the building, maybe because they themselves feared the diabolical forces which raged without. Alternatively, the presence of the stalwart gunman discouraged them from re-entering the tower, where was the principal doorway. Nanjulien bowed very slightly to Hermione.

"Please carry on Brigadier," she said.

"Now listen to me you lot," he began, addressing the miscreants. "You had better take yourselves off from here, and don't come back. Some of you are pawns in a game you don't understand, but by Heaven, and I speak no blasphemy, if you continue to use supernatural force against this place, the Queen of Lyonesse will do likewise against you. And you won't like it. As for you," he continued to the Meneniuses, "I'm minded to let the Choones shoot you out of hand."

But at that moment the diabolical gang broke away and ran for the tower door in a terrified rout. No one fired at them, although the hound made pursuit until Pendrea called him off.

"Let them go," said Nanjulien. "They won't be back in a hurry. As for the corpse, we had better bury him. At least there's a graveyard handy. Perhaps he should have a Christian ceremony. The Padre will know, but we ought to get on with it." He paused to inspect the body.

"Hell of a mess. The whole charge went into his chest, and at short range by the look of it. All by the light of the sanctuary lamp as well."

"Ah Zurr, he were threatening about him with that horse pistol that he had. I reckoned I'd shoot him first, before he shot one of us Zurr."

"And quite right too," said Nanjulien.

Samuel was eyeing the medieval gun with apprehension. It was about five feet long, and an inch or so in calibre. The tension of the moment was now beginning to wear off, and he felt physically sick at the sight of the corpse. Not so the valiant Caroline.

"I'll clean the mess up," she said. "A bit of blood doesn't worry me."

Samuel recalled that she had been a theatre sister before she married and took up district nursing. Thank God she was there. But why was she there? Answer, because Laura had insisted. And why had Laura insisted? A good question. Samuel had thought that their band of friends was a fortuitous association, but now he wondered. Laura appeared to have had a fey and possibly unrecognised relationship with Catharine's people for some time past, and it was Laura who had brought all of the earthly members into fellowship. It was she who had sent Jennifer to Saint Catherine's Wood all those months before. And so they stood for a few moments in a small incongruous group.

Later Samuel felt surprised that they had all accepted the situation so readily, contradicting as it did the rationality of every-day experience. Five men from a different order of existence had been peremptorily summoned to return to a parish church with which they had been associated many years before, and defend it against forces which the company could hardly begin to understand. Also, how had Hermione achieved this? Much later, Hermione explained a good deal of the background to what had happened, but at the time Samuel could only recognise that Queen Catharine's arm was long and her powers mysterious.

A further factor was that all of the men had memorials in the church, and their earthly remains were there interred, either within the building itself or nearby. Did these new allies know anything of the early history of the church? But Samuel's thought had been forestalled by Arthur Marazion.

"You must be Sir Christopher Trepennick," said Arthur, addressing the tall esquire with the rapier. "My name is Marazion, Arthur Marazion; an old Cornish family, if not so august as yours."

"You are well named sir," replied Trepennick. (The courteous use of the plural 'you' did not escape Marazion's trained mind.) "I am pleased to return and be of service. Catharine of Lyonesse is a most gracious sovereign lady. In truth a Gloriana, albeit of a different aeon."

"You are yourself gracious sir," responded Marazion, in what he judged to be appropriate language. "Perhaps it was your generous self who built Saint Catherine's? You will know of the Mystery beneath our feet?"

"No, no dear sir; it was my father who raised this church. The Mystery was moved at dead of night, with a strange liturgy sung by an ancient priest, Nacien by name. I know not the language, but it was not the Latin. There was fear at the time. Great fear, with talk of an assault upon the old Saint Catherine's like that which we have repelled tonight. And we had a fellowship then, a small brotherhood of older men, who handed on a secret from father to son. It was judged that with the new Saint Catherine's all would at last be laid to rest and the trust discharged. God's wounds, but they were intolerant times! The brotherhood also feared a charge from the civil authority. Idolatry, or even worse; so there was the devil on one hand and the witch prickers on the other."

"Tell me about the old church," said Arthur. "The one on the hill."

"I was christened in it," replied Sir Christopher, "and can remember it from boyhood. It was small but beautiful, with a sense of ghostly presence. There were stained glass windows that were ancient then. Some people wanted to take the windows out and bring them here to grace the new church, but the brotherhood would not have the old building defaced. For a time we continued to maintain it, although it was but seldom used. There was a service held there, every third year, but not from any prayer book known to me, and for a time this was continued. All I can remember of it is that we were given grapes to eat. There was a crypt under the ancient church, but it was always locked, except that some of the brotherhood went down into it, after the service was complete."

"But what of Merlin's Myster?" persisted Arthur.

"Whatever it was, I believe that it is now beneath the present church," replied Trepennick. "But mark thee I was not the eldest son until my brother died, and was never told the whole secret. One thing more I can tell you. It was said by the stannary workers that the crypt of the ancient church led down into the tin mines. Some of them were of immemorial age. The captain of the Rose Jane claimed from Roman times. The truth of it all I cannot tell. The Choones may know something, but they were then unlettered men."

And then Hermione interrupted.

"This is a fascinating conversation, but we must dispose of the corpse. Let us bury him."

"Put 'en on the midden ma'am," contributed Pendrea. "No need for Christian burial. He be for the Amente I'm thinking."

"Have charity," said Hermione. "He was more ignorant than evil. You were born into the Church Militant and followed its teaching. That man probably wasn't, and no one informed him."

"Aaah ma'am, but some men are just plain bad. I may be rough, but I'm not bad."

It was Captain Trevayne who came to Hermione's support.

"Has the church got a mattock and spade available?" he asked Samuel. "I'm sure that Ahab and Paul can dig like badgers, and I'll lend a hand myself."

Samuel's thoughts were now moving on to the legal position. He had a very dead man on his hands, obviously murdered, and in his church.

"There is a recent interment in the churchyard," he said. "It should be easy to re-open the grave and put this fellow in on top of the coffin."

"There are some old choir surplices in the back of the cupboard," suggested Mary, "and we can bundle him up in some."

Digging tools were produced from the churchyard shed, and Choone and Pendrea set to work with a will. The earth came up easily. It was a recent grave – one of two interments conducted by Samuel a few days before. Meanwhile, Caroline set about clearing the mess in the church. Nanjulien and Trevayne gave help; they had treated injured men before, and were not unduly distressed.

Soon the new corpse was in the grave and the earth being replaced. The scene was indeed macabre; torchlight and the waning storm. Thank God the rain had abated. Hermione, Laura, Arthur and Samuel were clustered round. They said the Nunc Dimitis and some of the Common Prayer funeral service. Hermione added a Grecian prayer: it seemed to be some sort of absolution for the dead.

The remainder of their people had returned to the church, removing signs of the night's activity. The jack hammer lay abandoned in the tower. The damage to the masonry was superficial but impossible to conceal. Best to leave the hammer where it was, 'find' it next day, and blame the damage on some weird black magic practitioners. Their task completed, they turned off the main lights, and withdrew to the vestry.

"I'll put the kettle on," said Mary, but events were not yet over.

Pendrea was replacing the turfs, when a figure appeared out of the darkness, and illuminated them with a powerful torch.

"And what's going on here then?" asked a voice.

It was the local policeman. Laura assumed command, and replied with great mental dexterity:

"Ah, good evening Mr Nanskillien. A wild night to be out. We have had a most embarrassing occurrence – an interment in the wrong grave, and we are quietly sorting matters out, at night and in a tactful way. Strictly, there should be a dispensation, obtained from the diocese, but it seemed best to proceed informally – more discreet as you will understand. If you hadn't happened to come along in the course of your duties, no one would have been any the wiser."

The constable seemed undecided. Laura, as he well knew, was the chairman of the parish council, and he also noted that the rector was present. Even so, it was a strange business. Had the relatives of the deceased been informed? And what of the strangers? Two looked like grave diggers, but who was the young man?

"Who might you be sir?" he said, addressing Arthur.

"Arthur Marazion, Officer. Please accept my card. May I add that this is a matter of ecclesiastical law, and with respect is of small concern to the civil authority."

The constable inspected Arthur's card by the light of his torch.

"University of Cambridge, I see sir," he said, and was about to continue when his torch caught the epitaph on the tombstone. The lowest line read:

"And of Isabella Marazion, dearly beloved wife of the above, who departed this life on the 14th January 1968, aged 84 years."

"Ah, quite so sir; I understand entirely," continued the constable. "I'll be on my way and keep my mouth shut. No need to make a report. Like you say sir, ecclesiastical law is not my job."

Samuel's mind was working furiously. He had forgotten that it was the Marazion family plot. Indeed the name was now extinct in the village; the recent funeral had been of Isabella's married daughter. The coincidence was astounding. But was it entirely by chance?

"One last thing Rector," said the constable. "I was taking a walk round the village, mainly to see if anyone was in distress from the storm, and I met Bill Trelawney. He said that a group of men came running out of the lychgate as if the devil himself were after them, climbed into two cars and a van, and drove off. Queer do. You saw nothing of it I suppose?"

"I've seen no one in the churchyard," replied Samuel, truthfully enough, "and it's a wild night for anyone to be out without reason. What was Bill Trelawney doing?"

"Better not to ask sir, begging your pardon, you being a Minister of Religion and all that."

"Now that's enough, Nanskillien," commanded Laura. "Good night to you."

"Good night ma'am," said the policeman, and to the relief of all, off he went into the night.

So they returned to the vestry. Hands were shaken all round, and many thanks expressed, where after their visitors disappeared as mysteriously as they had arrived. And then, suddenly, all of the company felt tired, as if the strain had snapped and undone their nervous energy.

"We must all be very careful," warned Hermione, "because we have not seen the last of it. Scotched the snake perhaps, but we haven't killed it."

She wanted the company to keep together, and ask Laura for hospitality, but Mary and Samuel demurred, insisting on returning to the rectory. So it was about two thirty in the morning when the meeting finally broke up.

But the Mordecais had scarcely reached their habitation, before there was a sharp knocking at the door. Who could desire entrance at such a time, apart from the Menenius faction? With his heart in his mouth Samuel approached the door. Outside he could see a group of figures. Should he telephone Laura or Nanskillien? He was very tired. What was the use? They should have taken Hermione's advice and kept together. A second knock, but gentler. He opened the door.

"Hello Samuel," said Ystelle Zabuloe. "Sorry if we startled you."

CHAPTER VII
Chthonic Forces

"We came as quickly as we could," Ystelle continued. "These ladies are light infantry from my own Killiad – Catharine's personal guard, usually called 'The Queen's Girdle'. You can all feel safe now."

Donna Canti (so addressed by her troopers) had marched her force from Saint Catherine's Wood, but despite the ravages of the dying storm they seemed but little extended. Also, each carried a carbine rifle and a sizeable kit bag.

"I don't know exactly what happened to you tonight," said Ystelle, "but I fancy that it was nasty. Tomorrow you must tell me all about it."

"Will Laura be safe?" Mary enquired anxiously. "And Caroline? The Menenius' gang were horrible."

"No need to worry. It's true that the enemy would like to attack them; more so than you, because they are petrified of Hermione and want her out of the way. So I've sent Laura some support. A lady called Louise Long-Clark. She is a Lieutenant Colonel, Demiarch in our terms, and her troops are Myrmidons, from the Brocelliande Killiad. They will have arrived by now. But we all need some rest. Anywhere in the dry will do. The girls have their sleeping bags."

Then Ystelle answered a question that Mary would have been too well mannered to ask.

"Do not be alarmed Mrs Mordecai. We are all fully domesticated and you will suffer no embarrassment. As for forage, don't feel concerned. Catharine sends you a gift, with the humble request that you ask for more whenever necessary."

She produced a small bag, of yellow silk, and gave it to Mary. It contained one hundred Elizabeth the Second sovereigns, freshly minted in bright gold.

"Struck especially, as soon as Samuel left Lyonesse. Forgeries of course, but all true metal, so don't worry about it. We shall change a few for sterling in the morning."

But the morning brought a meeting, in Laura's library. It began as a social muster, but assumed a more formal dimension, Hermione becoming leader. She spoke with great lucidity.

"It is now abundantly clear that the creatures who attacked the church last night were directed from what Samuel would call 'the other side'. A truly diabolical influence is behind what is happening, and as we thought, the Meneniuses and their riff-raff are working for satanic masters. Thank God there is now little immediate risk because of last night's victory. Also, we have Ystelle and Louise to constrain their evil ways." She paused for a moment for her words to gain effect.

"Let us therefore take the offensive. It seems to me that the enemy has been seeking information on Saint Catherine's Church and parish for some time past. Agravain, the archivist from Exeter is a suspicious character. Interesting that he bears the same name as the rector of the long-gone church at Langarrrow. But I have a feeling that the enemy must have an observer nearer the scene. I would expect this person to be an unwitting catspaw, and it may be that the Amentans are observing Saint Catherine's through the eyes of a parishioner recruited for the purpose. It could be almost anyone, but a child or person of low intelligence would be the probable victim. Someone naive, whose unformed mind would serve purely as a vehicle. Also, distress of an emotional nature increases vulnerability. A broken family, or someone suffering from mental illness perhaps."

Samuel began to pass a series of parishioners through his mind, but Hermione continued:

"Ystelle will tell you that a good rule in warfare is to know your enemy, and a factor which Satanists overlook is that their diabolical practices can be inverted against them. Hoist with their own petard or whatever. Therefore I would hope to identify whichever demon is behind the Menenius gang, and confront him through the mind of his possession. Ystelle can, if she will pardon the analogy, deal with the monkeys; I shall attack the organ grinder."

Samuel looked around the meeting. Catharine had certainly kept her promise about sending support. The newcomers included Ystelle's Sergeant Major, referred to as a 'Sarissa' in their military terms. At well over six feet tall she towered above both Mary and himself. They were now sitting three together in one of the window seats, and she had put her arm round Mary in a protective gesture when the Meneniuses were mentioned. The Sarissa had been introduced as Rosalind du Lac, but she told Mary that the troopers called her 'Boadicea'. Like many of the Lionelles, she looked like a Celt, dark eyes and black hair, but much larger made. She was quiet in manner, but with a dry and occasionally devastating sense of humour. She obeyed her officers implicitly, but Samuel sensed that she could lead well enough herself if the occasion required it.

Louise Long-Clark was as fair as du Lac was dark. She had a strongly extroverted personality, with a winning smile, and was easy to talk to. Almost as tall as the Sarissa, she had a willowy grace that would have done credit to an antelope. She had assumed the role of secretary, sitting at the library table and writing notes in a bold flowing hand.

Others present included a surgeon to the Queen's Girdle – Michelle de Ligny – and the same killiad's chaplain – Pearl Esyllt – usually called 'Margeritos' because of her tendency to pray in Greek. There was also a second Sarissa, to the Brocelliande Myrmidons, with the elaborate name of Georgina Burton-Coggles. She was as different from her mistress in appearance as chalk from cheese. Of middle height she looked as if she could have felled an ox. The women had all discarded their uniforms and were wearing tweedy clothes, apart from Louise in a grey silk dress. Looking back on the scene some months later, what surprised Samuel was how easy it all seemed, although in fact he was caught up in events of a strongly supernatural nature.

But the immediate conversation soon turned to the paranormal, in an attempt to deduce which of his parishioners might have been unfortunate enough to come under diabolical influence. Samuel thought hard. Domestic distress, erotic displacement, emotional strain, ill-health, a rebellious child if she were right, he had to consider the welfare of the persons concerned as well as the wider issues before them. Thirdly, if he judged wrongly he could both impede their cause and make a fool of himself.

Once again, it was Laura who gave a lead, and again by intuition rather than logic.

"Try the Penvithicks," she said. "The husband disappeared two years ago, the teenaged daughter will end on the streets if something isn't done, the son is a limb of Satan, and the mother desperate. It's rumoured that she's ill with cancer and won't do anything about it."

"With Samuel's permission I shall call on the Penvithicks," said Hermione, "and perhaps with Michelle.

Lyonesse' medical knowledge is of a high order. Particularly if it is a woman's cancer."

And Samuel knew that they were right. The mother was an occasional churchgoer with his and Mary's sympathy. Best to clear an approach for Hermione. She knew more about these things than he did.

Nevertheless, Hermione felt some trepidation a few days later as she rang the bell on Polly Penvithick's door. She recalled Samuel's introduction to the lady, and also a story which had arisen spontaneously in the village to the effect that the visitors were from an American religious society. The tale was useful, and had been permitted to run unchecked. Hermione pushed the bell for the second time, whereon the door was opened by the daughter; predictably hostile.

"What do you want?" she said.

"Would you like to go to America?"

It was interesting to watch the panorama of diverse emotions which paraded sequentially across the teenager's face. From the sulky hostility, came first a struggle to comprehend and rationalise, then a coming to terms with the idea, followed by a desire 'to go one better on mother', and lastly hesitation as she realised the consequences of leaving home, both to herself and her ailing parent. Despite her wilful rebelliousness, the child truly loved her mother.

"Who'll take care of Mum?"

"Perhaps I might, although it would be good if you helped me with it."

By now the daughter's personality was an open book before de Lamarac's priestcraft, and the psychological moment achieved, she transposed a strong sense of compassionate warmth directly into the girl's mind. As de Lamarac had calculated, she burst into tears.

"You had better come in," she sobbed. "I can't go off and leave Mum alone with the boy. It wouldn't be right."

The mother was a wan creature. A lined face and hopeless expression betrayed her emotional exhaustion. Hermione's heart went out to the pair of them. Of the boy there was no sign, but the girl continued tearfully:

"This is Miss de Lamarac Mum. Mr Mordecai's new lady curate, and I'm sorry I've been bad to you. Something seems to get into me sometimes. But I'll be different now Miss de Lamarac is here."

The girl was frowsily dressed, with bad make-up and tatty hair. Hermione put her arm round her, holding her in close, but saying nothing.

"I'll make some tea," said Polly, "please sit down."

Clearly, the mother had not heard the conversation on the doorstep and was puzzled by her daughter's sudden penitence. And it was the daughter who made the tea. Polly seemed somewhat bemused, but was favourably impressed. And thus Hermione maintained her advantage.

"Your daughter is a spirited girl, Mrs Penvithick, with an outlook not uncommon in young ladies of her age. I don't want to intrude, but I like being with young people. I can do a lot for her if she'll let me."

Polly Penvithick was intelligent, if little educated, but she continued nonplussed by the unexpected visitor.

"It is good of you ma'am," she replied, perhaps a little diffidently. "It's true I'm having a bad time, and you've certainly made an impression on Trudie. This is the first time she has made me some tea for months past. Everything is on top of me, but I don't see how you can do much to help."

"Most of us need help one way or another," said Hermione. "You're run down, and I'd like you to see a lady doctor. She's a friend of mine, and easy to talk to."

So all was developing well, until the four-year-old boy appeared. He was called Simon, and at first he stood silent, close to his mother but not touching her. He fixed Hermione with a wide-eyed stare; then:

"Who's she?" he demanded, but before his mother could reply, he ran over to de Lamarac and started pummelling her with his tiny fists. Then he started shouting in his shrill little voice, kicking and screaming like a terrified animal. But Hermione had anticipated something of the sort, and she broke the rules.

The child's mind was partially clear to her, and recognising that he was responding helplessly to an alien compulsion, she pressed her own trained and powerful psyche directly into his. This procedure was in a sense an interference with free will, but arguing that the infant had been similarly influenced by a diabolical agency, she felt justified. The boy froze. Wordlessly, Hermione gathered him into her arms, and so soothed him, whispering gently, and pressing his little head close against her breasts. He snuggled close to her immediately. The mother gasped.

"How did you do that?" she asked. "Simon is uncontrollable at times and I can do nothing with him, but you stopped him just like that."

"We'll talk later," said Hermione, continuing to murmur softly to the child, before returning him to his mother.

"Maybe it would be helpful to us both," she continued, "if you could accept me as a paying guest. I am staying at the hotel, but it isn't very convenient, and I would prefer to stay with another woman if you could find room for me."

By now Hermione's faculties had penetrated Polly's mind. It was against the spiritual rules to eavesdrop in this way, but de Lamarac was playing for high stakes. She could see that Polly desperately wanted her companionship, but was ashamed of the run down state of her house. To Polly, Hermione was an upper class woman: an educated lady. So the priestess proceeded carefully.

"Polly my dear, I am weary of the hotel. It would be wonderful to be in an ordinary house with another ordinary woman. I could help a bit with the cooking and so forth. The person inside this cassock is not unlike you. And I'd like to be with the boy. He responds well to me."

And so Hermione achieved agreement. Polly would be 'pleased to welcome her'. Trudie was moved to Trepennick Chase, where Laura persuaded her to wear some newly purchased clothes, and sent her as a day pupil to a secretarial college. She continued to see much of her mother, but was now relaxed; Hermione 'was there with mum'.

Meanwhile, de Lamarac continued to study the family. Polly was indeed a sick woman, but she agreed to talk to de Ligny (the Lyonelle's surgeon), and seemed relieved once the contact was made. Canti was worried about Hermione's physical safety; renewed violence was possible from the Menenius clan. She also wished to bring matters to a head. Catharine's instructions were clear: to protect the earthly Christians, to defeat the diabolical forces, and thirdly to recover the Spear of Longinus, and (assuming their deductions were correct) prevent it from falling into evil hands. Hermione seemed little concerned by Ystelle's fears, possibly because she was deeply absorbed in protecting Simon, for whom she soon developed an affection beyond the line of duty.

"The boy is subject to some form of visitation," she said to Ystelle. "During the day he keeps near to me almost all the time. I can sense some sort of presence. At first it seemed to be within him, but I believe that I have pushed it back a little – it now seems more upon him. He stays near because he then feels safe, and the oppressor is becoming angry, probably because he thinks that he is losing his hold on the child. I see the boy into bed, but he cries with fear if I leave him. At least he did until I started tying my priest's girdle round his cot. This forms a spiritual barrier, and he sleeps secure."

(The girdle referred to was the vestment worn by many episcopal clergy, and signifying mission. In Lyonesse it is a long linen cord, worn three times round the waist, and with tasselled ends reaching almost to the floor.)

"Soon Michelle is taking Polly into hospital," continued Hermione. "Then I intend to take the initiative and would ask your support. From what Simon has told me I fancy that the demon is none other than Archaroch. We have crossed swords with him before, as you well know."

"I shall ask Polly's permission to move in with you while she is away," said Ystelle. "This will also relieve my anxiety about your physical safety. You need a bodyguard."

De Lamarac had mixed feelings – Ystelle carried a Lyonesse army automatic pistol; flagrantly illegal in England. Moreover, the company had killed one man already, albeit in extraordinary circumstances. They had narrowly got away with it, but Hermione did not want any more dead bodies. Great affection for the Killiarch did not exclude an understanding of her temerarious nature.

Nevertheless, she agreed with Ystelle's desire to bring the enemy to conclusions. This made a complete victory more probable than would a result from drawn out guerrilla combat.

Simon claimed that the 'nasty man' came in the night, to ask him questions and give him orders; mainly to find things out on the nature and disposition of Samuel's people. The child was too young to give a fully objective account, but it seemed improbable that Archaroch yet realised that the company included a contingent of Lyonelles, let alone some Brocelliande Myrmidons. This caused a difficulty, because the ladies feared that if the enemy discovered this, they might back off, only to resume their assault at some indeterminate time in the future. Taking on the Revd. Samuel Mordecai and the local Church of England was one thing; Catharine of Lyonesse and the Church Celestial was another matter.

"Supposing we managed to capture this creature from the other side," said Hermione. "We would cause them great confusion, particularly if it is Archaroch. They must regard the campaign as important if he is personally involved in the front line."

"True," replied Ystelle, "but how do you propose to bell this particular pussy cat?"

"I have a plan," came the reply. "My idea is to watch over Simon as he sleeps, so using him as bait, but sheltering him from harm. Then we confront Archaroch when he appears. Hoist with his own petard, I think Shakespeare said."

Rather than sit beside Simon's cot, where the sight of the two women might have discouraged the demon from materialising, they removed their shoes and took the child into bed between them, where Ystelle could also boost the mite's confidence by holding him in her arms. He was so small – her thoughts went out to her own child, safe at home in Ys with her father and nursemaid. And so she snuggled him in, as a cold controlled anger welled up within her. There was small danger of physical violence, although the Menenius faction was still at large. She had her army automatic beneath her pillow, fully loaded, but with the safety catch on.

Hermione occupied the same bed, so sheltering Simon between Ystelle and herself. She had set a low light burning on a bed-side table, and beside some equipment covered by an embroidered veil. And so they waited. Simon alone felt relaxed, secure between the two women whom he had come to love and trust. Time passed, so very slowly. Would the necromancer come? Or would he sense the presence of the boy's guardians and fail to make his usual visit? Hermione thought not. She believed that her previous protection of the child by tying her priest's girdle round him while he slept would provoke the necromancer rather than warn or frighten him.

Midnight came and went. Simon was now in an innocent slumber, but presently he became restive in Ystelle's arms, murmuring and twitching in his sleep, with his little body intermittently shivering. And then he was awake, with the women becoming aware of a presence developing within the bedroom. As yet nothing could be seen by them, but Hermione believed that the child was more aware. As agreed, Ystelle kept him close in her arms; he was now fully awake, and she spoke softly in his ear.

"We are going to show this beast who frightens you that he can't get you any more. Don't be afraid, because you are safe with us. Be a good boy, and do what we say."

Simon snuggled closer to her. She knew that he felt secure in their custody, as indeed he was. De Lamarac was an experienced priest of the Celestial Church – let the demon beware!

In fact de Lamarac believed that the appearing necromancer would be seen at first by the child, but unless checked would grow in substance until he became a physical presence, visible to all. Her objective was thus firstly to observe through Simon, but to do this without either exposing the tiny boy to harm, or alerting the apparition to their presence. As planned, Ystelle made the next move.

"Simon," she said, "we want you to sit up and tell us what you can see, but to keep you safe, stay very close indeed to Hermione. She will lean over you, so that her hair forms a curtain over your face. Look out through it – you will be able to see the nasty man, but he won't be able to see you."

Ystelle sensed that the mite was starting to enjoy what was happening, indeed vengeance was in his soul. She had feared that he might give way to frightened tears, but he had a Cornish sturdiness remarkable for so small a boy. She eased him upwards, but keeping her hands close about him, lest his determination fail. Hermione's copious chestnut tresses formed a protective curtain between him and the evil one. He looked out confidently towards the apparition even then growing at the end of the room.

"He's there now Auntie Ystelle," he said. "I can see his face coming clear, all yellow and horrible, and he's got his funny coat on, like before."

Hermione was tense, but not displeased. Now her task was to time things carefully lest Archaroch withdraw too soon.

"I can see his eyes now," continued Simon. "All sort of green and yellow, and he's got his fancy hat on. But I'm not frightened of him. He's not able to get into me like he could before."

It was a surprisingly succinct statement for so small a child; Hermione feared that the necromancer might scent a rat. But now she could see the apparition herself, one more minute and she would act. Ah yes! It was he, longish black hair, and a red and gold headdress.

Now! Ystelle drew Simon into her arms, and Hermione moved her hand sideways, raised the embroidered cloth close by, and rested her fingers on the silver cup beneath. And then she was speaking softly, and in ancient Greek! Ystelle recognised the words – the prayer of consecration from the

97

classical liturgy of Lyonesse. Simon's part in the drama was now almost over. He had been the bait, but it was the predator who was now entering the snare. She drew the child down into the blankets, covering his head with her hands.

Hermione stepped onto the floor, took up the chalice, and stepped calmly forwards, saying:

"To de en toi Poteirioi toutoi timion alma tou Christou. Metabolon toi Pneumati sou toi hagio.[1]"

It was the moment of epiclesis – the chalice no longer held a simple mixture of water and wine, but the substance of the risen God.

She continued to walk forward, and the necromancer suddenly became aware of her presence. The light was indifferent, and it was difficult to read his face, but his expression seemed to be one of surprise rather than alarm. Yet the tall man retreated before the woman, his expression hardening as he recognised the presence of an adversary – but without realising it, he moved backward into a horseshoe shaped area marked on the floor by a long silken scarf, and found to his consternation that this was something which he was unable to cross. Hermione advanced to within two feet of him, holding the chalice like a shield before her. The expression on Archaroch's face became one of enormous fear. The scarf was in fact one of Hermione's stoles, indeed the same vestment which had lain on the high altar of the cathedral church of Saint Mary All Souls, when Catharine of Lyonesse had made her priest all those years before. Archaroch could no more step across the silken strand than an ordinary man could

---

1 And what is in this cup the precious blood of thy Christ, changing them by thy Holy Spirit.

walk through a brick wall. Neither dared he move forward; he was terrified of the contents of her chalice. Hermione extended one delicate little foot, very slowly and deliberately, and moved one end of the stole so that it formed a complete circle.

"So, Archaroch," quoth she.

There was a lengthy silence, the necromancer's face twitching in impotent fury. He was trapped, and he knew it.

"Release me," he snarled, "or my colleagues will soon destroy you."

"Threats will avail you nothing," replied Hermione. "Were I to throw the contents of this chalice into your face they would burn you like molten lead, but have no fear, the sacrilege would be too great. In a while I may release you. Before then you will open your mind to my scrutiny, and also withdraw what remaining hold you have upon the little innocent even now asleep in my colleague's arms."

True enough, Simon was fast asleep. Ystelle took him back to his cot, and soon returned, after donning the jacket of her Killiarch's tunic, which she had previously removed.

Meanwhile, the exchange continued. Archaroch, badly humiliated, hurled out an extraordinary stream of vainglorious malice. Hermione replied calmly, reminding him that her Queen was Catharine of Lyonesse, whom he defied at his peril.

"You will get nothing out of me," was his rejoinder, "except a retribution which will enslave your body and soul for countless ages to come. You milksop of a female priest, who are you to…?"

And then he paused. Hermione was removing her Saint Catherine's Cross from around her neck, to hold the jewel before him, suspended on its fine gold chain. Archaroch had heard of these crosses. Bestowed as a personal gift by the Queen of Lyonesse, they were seldom awarded, and reputedly had mystical powers. He was aware of such factors. Indeed, they were part of the stock in trade of his evil profession, albeit in a converse manner. Could he learn from this, to his advantage? Despite himself, Archaroch's curiosity was aroused – a victory for Hermione, although he did not know it.

She began to move the cross, swinging it slightly from side to side. Archaroch's eyes followed the movement, left to right, right to left. Ystelle turned on an additional light, and the illumination caught the iridescent enamel on the ornament in gentle flickering flashes. Hermione spun the cross, so that the flashes became more insistent. Archaroch felt a pressure within him. The ornament was dangerous. He decided to avert his gaze and say nothing. Call her bluff. Let the anaemic saint do her damndest. And then horror came upon him. He could not look away! His eyes were locked onto the cross by a force which he could neither break nor understand.

Pictures formed within his mind, at first of a physical nature. Great Lyonesse battleships, with guns like the wrath of God. The Saint Thomas Apostolos, salvo after salvo, blowing a whole flotilla of Amentan warships out of the water. The Lyonesse Army, killiad upon killiad, fully armed and as lithe as cats. Then it changed. He saw visions of churches, great and small, filled with kneeling people. Celestial Christians. Catharine's people. He heard Hermione's voice, small and calm and still.

"The Communion of Saints, Archaroch," she said, "links the Church Celestial with the Church Militant, of which the child in my care is a baptised member."

He now saw where it was leading. Hermione had projected the images into his mind, and he was unable to break free. She was focusing power upon him; the cross was like a lens.

"Some of Catharine's people," continued Hermione, "are even now directing their energies towards you. Do not resist them. Your mind could disintegrate into lunacy."

His tension became unbearable. Desperately he tried to break free. But that confounded spinning flashing dancing emblem held his mind as a magnet grips the steel. It was not merely Hermione who now opposed him, she led a company of the heavenly host. Maybe he felt some sense of involuntary relief when he began to speak. Not that he wanted to. Despite himself, his lips uttered a slow monotone recital of events over the past few months, and he barely noticed when Ystelle produced a field notebook and started writing down what he said. Several things became clear, although it was also apparent that Archaroch himself was not fully informed. To the ladies' surprise, they found that the Meneiuses were not the leaders of the earthly faction. The necromancer mistrusted them, and hence had been looking through Simon's eyes to determine their movements. Similarly, he had been informed of the arrival of the celestial forces. He disbelieved the American visitors rumour, but had not grasped the truth until a few minutes ago when confronted by Hermione. As for Merlin's Myster, he knew that it certainly existed, but of its exact nature he was unsure. There then followed an incomprehensible account of the medieval Langarrow, some nonsense about something called a sky tail, of the ancient attempt on the Myster, foiled by the Myrmidons, and of recruiting Arthur Marazion to their evil ends. There was more about a factor from Arthur's Celtic ancestry. This would enable them to reverse a defensive force applied to the Myster by Arthurian priests many centuries before.

Ystelle's thoughts were now in a whirl. Priests or priestesses? A Guinever or a Jennifer? And who was in charge of the evil ones? She surely believed that they were being directed from the Amente, but it might be an alliance rather than a chain of command. But Archaroch's next statement was alarming, at least to Hermione.

"My friends are nearby. They have been summoned, and will shortly be here. You shall be utterly destroyed."

Hermione thought fast. Was he bluffing? Impossible. Psychologically he was at her mercy. But what to do? Thank heavens Ystelle had her automatic; she had been right all along. Moreover, Hermione's fears were soon confirmed. There was a noise outside, followed by a scuffling on the staircase. But Ystelle appeared totally unconcerned, calmly writing in her notebook.

And then the door opened. A smallish elderly man entered, bent almost double and with a cut on the side of his face. He was helpless in the grasp of Georgina Burton-Coggles, Sarissa Major to the Brocelliande Myrmidons.

"As you asked Donna," she said to Canti. "We picketed the house, and when they appeared, seized this one because he seemed to be in charge. The younger fry ran off, and we let them go, not wanting too much commotion. Our Demiarch" (she meant Louise Long-Clark) "is in charge at Miss Trepennick's, and four of the Queen's Girdle are stood too at the rectory, armed with pickaxe handles."

"You are breaking my arm," gasped the creature in her grasp. "Do you have to twist it so much?"

It was none other than Agravain, the Exeter archivist.

"Well done, Sarissa Major," said Ystelle, although it was not clear whether she referred to the military operation or the arm twisting. Georgina assumed the latter, but nevertheless she reduced the pressure sufficiently for Agravain to stand normally.

"Well well well," said Hermione.

CHAPTER VIII
Saint Catherine's Crypt

Both women were thinking fast. Victory was theirs, but how to exploit it? Hermione tried to extract more information from Archaroch, but the intervention had broken her hold, and he could not be overpowered a second time. Meanwhile, Ystelle questioned Agravain.

"Who brought you here?" she asked, although there was but little point to the query – obviously he and at least some of the Menenius gang must have been already present in the village. He stood in sullen silence.

"Shall I twist his arm again Donna?" suggested Georgina, although she knew full well that it was against the Lyonesse Army's rules to ill-treat prisoners. Indeed even threats of violence were frowned on, if not rigidly forbidden.

"Not just yet thank you, Sarissa Major," replied Ystelle, still thinking hard.

What was the relationship between Agravain and the Lords of the Dark World? Or with the Menenius cousins? But Hermione was ahead of her.

Agravain, reasoned Hermione, was an old man, clearly versed in the black arts, and in league with evil lords, of whom Archaroch was a senior servant. Indeed he was a trusted necromancer in the employ of Asfernel, Archduke of the Amente. Therefore, both of their prisoners were likely to be in disfavour with the Archduke, because things could hardly have gone according to his wishes.

"Agravain," she said, "I offer a bargain. We shall take you immediately to Exeter, and there you will open the Diocesan Archives, and give us the Saint Catherine's box of documents. Then you will be allowed to go free. When the box is safely delivered here, Archaroch will also be released. Otherwise we shall hold on to you both until he drops from exhaustion."

There was a long pause. The necromancer knew that in his present situation he was subject to the same needs as an earthly man. To be kept standing within the loop of Hermione's stole until he collapsed was a poor prospect. Also, whenever, or if ever, he got back to the Amente there would be some awkward explaining to do. Given a swift return, things could be glossed over. What was in the box anyway? He did not entirely know. Agravain had been using it as a bargaining point. Quite possibly this was bluff; typical of a devious old man. Things had gone badly so far – failure to conscript Marazion despite that elaborate charade at Langarrow, failure to force entry to the crypt, and now tonight's demeaning business. Best to give way. Confound this ninny of a female priest, and all her goody-good friends.

"I agree," he said, "and Agravain will do likewise."

Agravain protested, but Archaroch pointed out that his earthly demise was only a few years ahead, and if he wanted an honoured place amongst the infernal necromancers, he had better do as suggested. Burton-Coggles applied a supplementary argument, and the old man speedily gave way.

Next day they opened the box. It was about thirty inches long and made of black japanned steel. Arthur thought that it was Victorian, and had been provided when the records should have been moved to Truro. He also noted that a modern padlock and hasp had been fitted since his first visit. They cut through the hasp with a hacksaw, and Arthur opened the original lock as before.

Hermione now advised caution. Some sort of booby trap might have been installed, so Arthur raised the lid with the fire tongs from Laura's library, held at arm's length. All was well however, and soon the company was inspecting the contents. On top, there were some comparatively recent records of little interest to the company, and a curious strip of parchment, beginning 'Crypt candles I believe'. But soon they came to stronger meat, written in an amazing mishmash of languages: English, Dog-Latin, what looked like Welsh but was in fact ancient Cornish, and, surprisingly enough, a little Greek.

Arhur selected the plan of the crypt seen during his first visit to Exeter. (It later transpired that there were three plans. One appeared to be an original working drawing, the second a careful copy, and the third, almost illegible with age, might refer to the ancient church on the hill.)

The second plan showed a structure so large that indeed it seemed to cast doubt upon the veracity of the draughtsman, until Samuel pointed out that both the Choones and Trepennicks owned extensive tin mines and therefore plentiful skilled labour would be available.

In the centre of the crypt was a rotunda, about thirty feet in diameter, with triangular extensions radiating from it, to form a five-pointed star. At first this was thought to form a pentacle of cabalistic significance, until Hermione pointed out that it was not so; the angles were incorrect. Also, there were a number of rooms connecting into the arms of the star. The largest of these extended from an apex beneath the chancel, and formed a rectangular chamber, about thirty feet by eighteen feet, and named 'The Presence Chapel'. Other rooms had equally fascinating names. King's Chamber, Guardroom, Armoury, Priests' Chamber, Morgan's Room, The Chapel of

Guinever, Nuns' Dormer, and, in the central rotunda 'Circle of the Lion and Five Trees'. This last was in Greek; Hermione courteously corrected Arthur's translation – 'Lion' was in the feminine, and therefore 'Lioness'. There were other rooms, apparently stores and domestic offices, and two staircases were indicated, one leading upwards to the sealed door in the tower, the second descending to God knows where.

The crypt had been cunningly contrived. Clearly, the pillars in the nave of the church rested upon the blocks of granite left between the arms of the star, and the Presence Chapel extended beneath the eastern end of the building. At first, the company was too fascinated to consider the implications of the drawing. Then there was some excited speculation, until Jennifer said:

"When I was in Ys, I saw a flag that had a circle of five trees with a lion in the centre. I had forgotten about it until now."

"You're right," said Samuel. "There was such a flag on Lucilla Mantzini's battleship."

Ystelle, Hermione and Louise exchanged glances. It was Louise who spoke.

Saint Catherine's Crypt

"Things are coming clear at last. The national flag of Lyonesse shows a lioness rampant, inside a circle of five cedars, representing the five trees of paradise. There is some sort of link between this crypt and the Brocelliande Myrmidons sacking Langarrow all those years ago. Unfortunately, my Killiad's official history records nothing of it, apart from a single reference to a raid into the earthly aeon, thought to refer to Langarrow. But the Lyonesse Army was more loosely organised in those days. My guess is that the crypt was laid out following contact between my predecessors and Sir Christopher Trepennick, or his father. Possibly it is an enlarged version of whatever was beneath the church on the hill."

"You have to be right," said Hermione. "The Arthurian connection runs right through the whole business. Trepennick's people wanted to be rid of an awkward responsibility, and in some way that we don't understand, Lyonesse assisted them. It would be interesting to know exactly when the crypt was sealed."

There was a pause in the conversation; everyone was trying to assimilate the new ideas. And then Ystelle remarked in response to Hermione:

"Maybe there will be something in the box about it. I nominate Arthur to make a search."

Sure enough, there was a mason's bill, showing that the crypt had been walled up only about two years after the church had been completed. The metal for the leaden strip had come from a local mine. It was all there, although they had problems with the Cornish.

Then Marazion spoke for them all.

"We must get into the crypt," he said, "and give our visitors a chance to follow up their knowledge. There is pretty sure to be information down there, and possibly the spear itself."

"It's not so simple," said Samuel. "To open the doorway I shall need a faculty from the diocese, and the Church Council will be aware of it. Half the village will turn out, and most likely the local press. First class stuff for them, but we want to keep things quiet."

"True," said Ystelle, "and no doubt the Meneniuses would also be hanging about. We could hardly start punt-gunning them in front of the *Truro Times*."

"Perhaps we could find another way into the crypt," said Mary Mordecai. "Dig down into the Presence Chapel and make out it was something to do with a grave."

"You'd have quite a dig," replied Arthur. "The levels show that there are six or eight feet of granite above the crypt. We might get down to the bed rock easily enough, but not much farther, short of dynamite that is."

There was a prolonged pause, and then Caroline Owens joined in.

"Saint Catherine's has a lot of curious features, and one is a large slab just inside the entrance into the chancel. You can't see it because the chancel carpet covers it. I noticed it about ten years ago when we replaced the carpet. Samuel was rector, but I don't think he was about at the time. There is an inscription on the slab. We couldn't read it, it isn't in English letters."

"The slab is made of Delabole slate," said Laura, "but there are numerous people buried in the church. I doubt if it's significant."

"Let's have a look," said Arthur, and so they walked down to the church, and rolled the carpet back. They took the box with them, leaving Louise in charge at Trepennick Chase, and Rosalind at the Rectory. Predictably enough, the slab was engraved in Greek. Samuel struggled to translate, but Hermione had no difficulty.

"It's a right hotch-potch, and no mistake. The first lines are from Saint Thomas' Gospel, and followed by what looks like a mismatch of two verses from the First Epistle of Peter, forced together out of context to give a meaning different from the original. Then there is the last bit, which is the most obscure of all. Probably the inscription is meant to confuse people without previous knowledge, but to give a clue to others – like the Brocelliande Myrmidons on a later visit perhaps."

"But what does it mean?" burst in Jenny. "For goodness sake, can't one of you academic geniuses translate it?"

"Sorry Jenny. 'Lift up the stone and there you shall find me', is a straight quotation from Saint Thomas, and forms the first line. When Our Lord spoke the words he was referring to the transcendental nature of the divine presence. But that isn't what it means here."

"Pardon me," said Samuel. "Are you saying that God is not present in my church?"

"This is no time for futile theology," said Laura. "What does the rest of it mean Hermione?"

"I know what it says. A rough translation would be 'Behold I place in Zion a corner stone as a raging lion,' but what it means is doubtful. The raging lion seems to be a borrowing from the famous devil goeth abroad text. I can't work out its significance. The last part could be a distortion from Jude, something like 'And angels having left their own location he has placed in deepest darkness.' Frankly, your guess is as good as mine."

"It is clear enough to me," was Laura's rejoinder. "The inscription is meaningless to anyone without previous knowledge, and is a message to people like us – like you said. What it means is 'Dig here'. My gardener has a crowbar. Let's get the slab up and see."

In fact it took both the crowbar and the combined strength of Arthur and the younger women to raise the slab, which was about three inches thick and four feet square. Then the company found itself seized by a thought stopping icy dread, as they stared down into the pitch dark void which was revealed beneath. Until Caroline broke a long silent pause.

"Who's going down then?" she said.

There was a second and longer pause.

"I am," said Hermione. "But I'm going down fully vested with my Saint Catherine's Cross round my neck, a hurricane lamp in one hand, and Ystelle's automatic in the other. It's no blasphemy to say God alone knows what we'll find down there."

"You're not suggesting that there is anything alive in the crypt," said Arthur, "surely not?"

"That depends upon what you mean by 'Alive'. We are assuming that the crypt is of Christian origin, but we don't know for certain. It could be diabolical – what price Agravain and his ancestors?"

"Then I am going," said Laura. "It doesn't matter much with someone of my age."

"You might lose more than your life. It's a job for an experienced priest."

"Then I go," said Samuel. "This is my parish."

"Nonsense," said Arthur. "I play prop forward for Cambridge University, and I'm going."

And so they wrangled. Ystelle was the senior officer, therefore it was her privilege. Someone said that Louise was Demiarch to the Brocelliande Myrmidons and hence held the historical authority. Georgina Burton-Coggles respectfully suggested that senior officers should not hazard their own lives in such a way. Caroline thought that apart from Laura she had the longest association with the parish, and being fit and strong she should be chosen.

The only available torch was the small one from Jenny's handbag, and as they argued, they all peered down into the void. The hole took the form of a cylindrical shaft, about forty inches in diameter, and cut down vertically through the granite for several feet. The sides were well finished, chiselled smooth but without any foot or hand holds. It was clear that the shaft opened out into a larger area, possibly paved with stone slabs, but the light from Jenny's torch was feeble at that depth. Little could be seen laterally; visibility was constricted by the cylindrical depth.

"To conclude the argument," said Jenny, speaking in what was for her an unusually serious manner, "I intend to be first into the crypt, because a strong intuition is pressing me to be so. I fancy that it comes from Catharine, but additionally here is some sort of vague historical factor, an instruction that I can't identify."

"Very well. If you are certain sure, so be it," said Hermione.

They obtained a hurricane lamp, a ball of string, and a spare bell rope from the ringing chamber. The lamp was lowered on a length of the string and swung to one side until it rested on the floor away from the area where Jenny would alight. Then she grasped the sally in both her hands, and Arthur and Georgina lowered her cautiously down the shaft, ready to haul back at a moment's notice. Soon Jenny was below the cylindrical shaft.

"I say," she called. "This is quite a place. There are stone tubs with trees in them, and a statue of ..." Then, when she was about a foot from the floor, she released her hold on the rope to drop the last little distance. But to the company's horror, a stone slab hinged down beneath her feet, and she disappeared below into a pit of unseen depth.

There followed a short pause, then a creaking noise, and the slab swung slowly back to its original place. And thus Jennifer was gone, engulfed into a pit containing God knew what. Within the instant, Arthur had knotted the rope round the end of an adjacent pew, and was swarming down, closely followed by Ystelle. Swinging to one side, he retained his hold on the rope until his whole weight was on the floor. Then, kneeling down, he pressed hard on the edge of the pivoting slab that had betrayed poor Jenny. It moved a little; Ystelle joined him, and soon they had the slab pushed hard down, almost to a right angle. The light of the hurricane lamp revealed Jenny, staring up at them, pale faced, but apparently unharmed. The pit was about eight feet deep, and had a heavy wooden door in one side. Arthur wedged the pitfall open by jamming his shoe against the edge of the pivoting slab, and reaching down, he pulled Jenny out easily enough.

"Are you all right darling?"

"I think so," she replied. "My ankle hurts a bit, but I didn't fall all that hard. Odd that I thought that Catharine had wanted me to be first down." She paused for a moment. "I put my hand on something as I landed, and seem to have picked it up."

She opened her hand. To the amazement of all, it contained a Saint Catherine's Cross, a little dulled with age, but still exquisite in its Celtic intricacy and engraving.

Hermione had now climbed down the rope.

"I fancy that you got the right message," she said, "but misinterpreted its source. Clearly the Cross is meant for you."

She examined the ornament as carefully as possible in the indifferent light. It was indeed similar, probably identical, to her own, except that it had an inscription on the reverse, which even Hermione had difficulty in translating.

"This is ancient Celtic," she said after a moderate interval, "and I think it reads: 'Guinever, Mother Superior in the Year of Redemption 541'. I don't doubt that it's genuine. It is known that the widowed and penitent Guinever rose to be head of a religious house, and as such was one of the first women in Britain to be ordained priest. Probably the Cross was preserved in the old Saint Catherine's, but how it came to be on the floor of that pitfall is beyond me."

"Is all well down there?" Caroline Owens' voice came hollow down the shaft.

"Sure it is," replied Jenny, looking upwards courageously enough. (In fact those at the top of the shaft had seen some of what had occurred, and were not now unduly alarmed.)

"Come on down," she continued. "It's an amazing place."

Caroline and Georgina lowered first Laura, and then Mary and Samuel, before climbing down the rope themselves. Laura was in tears.

"It was all my fault," she sobbed. "I said to dig here and get the slab up. But there was a clear warning, 'Angels who have left their own location he has placed in deepest darkness'. I see it all now."

"Oh come along," Jenny replied. "I'm no angel, but I've been decorated for gallantry. Look at my beautiful Cross."

But it seemed at that moment that a shadow passed across the head of the shaft. Several people looked up, although there was nothing to be seen.

"Hermione says that it belonged to Guinever, my namesake of ..."

But Jennifer was interrupted. The bell rope, apparently of its own accord, came tumbling down the shaft to land in an untidy coil at her feet.

"So! You wanted into the crypt, didn't you? And at last you've got what you wanted. Enjoy it, because a few days from now you'll all die of thirst, and go to join your friends among the departed saints. How appropriate, in the crypt of an ancient church. My friend Archaroch will be devastated with mirth – a poetic ending, from his point of view. And I'll have my box back thank you. We have been concealed in the church for three hours past, watching your every move."

The face of Agravain could be seen peering down at them, with an expression of malicious glee. He was flanked by the Meneniuses, oozing oily triumph.

"My dears, what a fitting end to the affair. Langarrow is avenged at last. In due course we shall return and obtain what we desire. I do so hope that the odour of death is not too strong for us. My cousin is a little delicate you know."

And then the slab was slid back into place. The companions were entombed.

CHAPTER IX
Scytales

"They'll be lucky," said Arthur. "I'm not going to be beaten by the likes of them to end my days down here, and that goes for all of us. Let's explore the staircase that leads up to the tower. If we hammer on the masonry blocking the doorway, sooner or later someone will hear. We aren't beaten yet."

"And," said Ystelle, "my Sarissa Major is a woman of considerable resource, as is Louise. We shall be missed, and they will take action. And Margeritos is with them, and Mageritos has an intuitive mind. She will work out where we are. It is not as if a single person had disappeared, as might happen by kidnap. There are eight of us, and the Meneniuses could hardly remove such a number in broad daylight without some sort of commotion."

"True," replied Arthur. "Nevertheless, let us explore the place. Before we lowered Jenny down the shaft, I stuffed the plan of the crypt into my pocket together with the long strip of parchment that I happened to be looking at when Caroline went to borrow the hurricane lamp. Let's have another look at them."

He produced the plan, and they studied it further by the light of the hurricane lamp. Then they explored.

Discoveries were at first disappointing. There was a second pitfall at the foot of the ascending staircase – avoided easily enough – but the stairway was blocked by a wrought iron door in the form of a grill, strongly made and locked shut. Moreover, the stairs went up in a long narrow spiral. Even their combined voices would not be audible above.

By now the company had overcome their initial fright, and were gaining some notion of their surroundings. A main principle with the crypt seemed to be endurance. Almost everything was made either of stone or Delabole slate, held together by iron clamps and rivets. Tables, benches, even chairs, were so fabricated. They found a muniment room, with shelves encased by small panes of glass set into slate, like mullion windows. Inside were leather bound books, surprisingly well preserved and mainly of a religious nature. (Later, Hermione examined them in some detail, and pronounced that despite their historical context, the contents were so dull and complexly worded that perusal was impossible, save by great effort on the part of the reader.)

Stone candlesticks and iron sconces suggested that illumination had been provided for by the architect, but none contained candles or traces of wax, and indeed there were no signs that they had ever been used.

"This place reminds me of an Egyptian tomb," remarked Arthur. "As if artefacts had been brought together for the benefit of dead to be resurrected at some time in the future. Yet it does not feel like a mausoleum. Neither is it a charnel house, despite a clear association with death. As if marble figures were in some way alive and sentient, but locked into the reality of a silent necropolis. Stone tables and chairs. Could these be intended for use by dead people? I fancy not, but it is as close to it as I can get."

Hermione answered him.

"Like I said before," she said, "it depends on what you mean by dead."

"Also," said Ystelle, partly in support of Hermione, "time is not exactly as earthly Christians think. It is more complicated. The psyche is not confined by it, nor in some circumstances are other things. Consider your experience at Langarrow. This was to a degree a re-enactment of what had gone before. Also, how did Hermione predict this, and so place her note on Jennifer's car? The answer derives from Catharine's response to Jennifer's plea during her second visit to Saint Catherine's Wood, which reminded Lyonesse that things needed watching in Cornwall. Georgina won't mind my saying that more is known about Langarrow than in the annals of her Myrmidons. So Donna made an informed guess at the enemies' tactics, and Hermione was advised accordingly. You can work out the rest for yourselves."

Exploration continued. The western area of the crypt included a commissary, and here they found slate chests, some containing sacks of flour – dry and apparently wholesome, with no signs of mould. Others held meat – hams and pieces of salt beef, wrapped in linen and buried under layers of salt. There were even domestic utensils, some cleavers, a flour scoop, and a great broom for sweeping up the flour – a heavy nail studded shaft with a mixed bundle of rushes and birch twigs bound round with iron wire. Most cheering of all to the company were some slate boxes containing a great stock of candles, all of uniform size, and according to Arthur, furnished with self consuming linen wicks, woven to eliminate the need for snuffing – unusual for candles of the time. This discovery caused much relief. They were no longer dependant upon the hurricane lamp and its limited supply of paraffin.

"Let us brighten the gloom," exclaimed Laura.

Soon they were placing candles in the iron sconces around the rotunda, three candles to each, with five sconces, one between each arm of the star. It was as if a fever gripped the company as they hurried to and fro, jamming candles into sockets and lighting them, firstly from the lamp, and then from one to the other. Soon the rotunda was ablaze with light, the beeswax flames burning clear and steady in the still air of the crypt. To a degree the funereal atmosphere of the place was dispelled, and the company began examining the rotunda in greater detail, until Arthur exclaimed:

"The crypt candles. This is the clue to the scytail," and he pulled the parchment strip from his pocket.

"Look," he continued, "where someone has written 'Crypt candles' at the head of the parchment. Perhaps Agravain, it's in a different hand from the rest of it."

"A sky tail?" responded Ystelle, producing her field notebook. "Archaroch babbled something about a sky tail when Hermione had him hypnotised. I assumed that it was an astrological term, and could make nothing of it."

"No indeed. A scytale was a Greek, originally Spartan, method of encoding a message, and was used by the Myrmidons. The word comes from 'skutale', meaning a staff. A strip of parchment was wound round a staff or cylinder in a continuous coil. The message was then written along the length of the cylinder, and the parchment unwound. The words were meaningless until the strip was rewound round a cylinder of equal diameter. It was a bit more subtle than I've said, but that is the gist of it. Pass me a candle."

Someone produced one, and the company watched with both doubt and interest as Arthur wrapped the strip around the wax cylinder. Sure enough, a list of unassociated words assumed an intelligible form:

"I believe in sacred things," read Ystelle to the company,

"In dedicated groves, with cenotaphs,

"In hidden secret holy springs,

"Whose waters raise the souls of those whose epitaphs,

"Are lamps within the pillared halls of time."

"Things are coming even clearer," she continued. "My guess is that we are in the dedicated grove here and now, if five trees can form a grove."

So they examined the miniature trees. They certainly resembled diminutive cedars. The trunks and branches were of wrought iron, and the needles were of copper, artfully corroded to have a green coating of verdigris. But what of a cenotaph?

Georgina inspected the lioness' statue, prancing rampant in the middle of the circle. The great cat was covered in gold leaf, and stood upon a handsome granite plinth. This indeed bore an inscription, in English, and with no mysterious wording:

'This statue is erected to the Glory of God
And in grateful memory of Guinever,
Of Lyonesse and ynys Afalon, Queen.
May her house endure for ever in the hereafter'.

"Amen to that," said Ystelle, "but where are the hidden springs?"

There was no answer to that, so they continued to explore, although Hermione was opposed to entering the Presence Chapel.

"First let us try to find out more," she said.

So they tried the descending staircase. This led into a gallery that communicated with the door into Jennifer's pitfall, and similarly to that at the tower staircase. Otherwise there was nothing of interest, until they came upon a further stairway, descending to an even lower level. This they followed for fifty-one steps, when their way was blocked by a heavy oak door, secured by three massive wrought iron bolts. Curiously, the bolts were provided with a lever mechanism, linked to a chain which disappeared through an aperture in the wall. It seemed to be made of a bronze alloy.

The atmosphere was now dank and oppressive, and unlike the crypt, here the stone work had been left unfinished, chisel marks and the remains of shot holes drilled by Trepennick's miners were easily seen. The stairway was narrow, but there was a wider open space at the foot of the steps, and here the company crowded together as Arthur (in the lead) endeavoured to open the door. A rusty holder for a single candle was pinned to the wall, and unlike the sconces in the crypt, it contained an end an inch or so in length. There was more corrosion on the door furniture, and a wooden lever projected to one side, but served no obvious purpose. It was indeed a forbidding place.

There was a presentiment of evil, and automatic in hand, Ystelle stood close by Arthur, as he struggled to open the door. The bolts were tallowed and withdrew easily enough, and Arthur found no keyhole, merely a sturdy iron latch worked by a rusty ring. And yet the door refused to yield. Moreover, by listening close to the woodwork it was possible to hear a faint but regular swishing sound. What could it be? The breathing of some monstrous beast, some creature of extraordinary form sustained in the depths of a pit by God knows what resources? Or awakened from a centuries old slumber to defend the crypt against such prying intruders as themselves?

"What do you think is on the other side?" Ystelle asked of Arthur.

"Goodness knows, but we ought to find out," he replied. "If there is something sinister around it would be better to be aware of it, than return to the crypt in ignorance."

No one disagreed with this, and Georgina came to Arthur's aid.

"From the state of the latch, and the atmosphere down here, I dare say that the door has stuck with the damp. All that is needed is plenty of push, and I'm your woman. Shove hard with me."

She stepped back a pace, and threw her weight hard against the door. There was a creaking noise, and it moved, perhaps by a sixteenth of an inch.

"Again," she said, and Arthur joined her, throwing their combined weight against the boards. At the third attempt the door flew open.

Ystelle fired immediately. The sound of the shot cracked out loudly in the confined space, and then she fired again, twice in quick succession, while Georgina moved forward to support her senior officer. The light was poor through the doorway, and most of the company could see little of Ystelle's target, not withstanding its nature.

"My God, what is it?" cried Jennifer, as the horror of the spectacle burst upon them.

Ystelle now realised that what she had fired at was a corpse, although in the dim illumination it looked grotesquely life-like. The cadaver had been positioned vertically against an opposite wall by two pegs under the armpits, placed so that the feet were about twelve inches above the floor to give an impression of unnatural height. The thing had been embalmed, but nevertheless a superficial fungoid mould had mottled portions of the skin with a whitish felt, and the eyes had been replaced by vitreous orbs glowing a faint iridescent green from the reflected light. Behind and surrounding the horror was a panoramic scene painted onto the stone, and clearly intended to represent hell. Indeed it could have been taken from Dante's Inferno, and in its way was not without artistic merit.

"It is a very dead man Jenny," Ystelle replied, "and it was stupid of me to shoot at it. Do not be frightened; it can't harm you except by a nervous reaction which you have to be strong enough to resist. A lot of psychic warfare is like that. Later, I fancy that Hermione may try to give him some sort of burial."

The corpse was naked except for a low crowned hat jammed onto its head. Beneath the feet was a small plaque which read:

'Agravain, Rector of Langarrow.
Beware his fate and pass by'.

"His epitaph could hardly be regarded as a lamp within the pillared halls of time," remarked Laura. "And who would want to raise his soul even with the means to do so? What's your opinion Hermione?"

"I think that he was put there as some sort of warning; beware and pass by, to quote the plaque. But it seems to me that it was meant for people entering the crypt from here, not coming down the stairs as we have done. Let's take the message at its face value and find what is causing that peculiar noise."

Such is human nature that their encounter with the mummified rector had displaced their earlier cause for alarm, but they now realised that the intermittent swishing noise sounded much louder than from the other side of the door. Also it was interspersed with a loathsome gurgling. Mysterious, but unlikely to be of biological origin.

With Ystelle in the lead, they moved on along a level passageway. Shortly, this opened out into a sizeable cavern, and here they found themselves standing on a paved shelf beside a small expanse of swirling water. It looked forbidding, although a stone balustrade along part of the shelf reduced the sense of menace. There was a stone altar and slate cross at one end of the open space, and two small passageways led off from one side, although subsequent exploration showed that they ended blindly. Otherwise the place was empty.

"In hidden secret holy springs," quoted Arthur.
"Whose waters raise the souls of those whose epitaphs,
Are lamps within the pillared halls of time."
"Is this the end of the scytail I wonder? I see no pillared halls hereabouts!"
"What price the raise the souls bit?" countered Jennifer.
"We will leave that to Hermione," Arthur replied.

They stood along the balustrade and looked down into the pool. Stone steps led down into the water, suggesting that the place might have been used as a baptistry, but there was no saying what fluid geometry lay beneath, because the waters formed a reversing whirlpool, spinning alternately clockwise and anticlockwise. When in the clockwise mode, the rotation became sufficiently vigorous to draw a column of air down into the centre of the vortex, and this caused the gurgling noise already noticed. Arthur passed a hand through the balustrade, lifted a palm-full of water, and tasted it carefully. It was sweet, fresh, and perfectly clear, typical of a high quality mineral spring.

"So, Mr Agravain junior," he said. "We are not going to die of thirst."

They buried Agravain senior beneath a pile of debris at the end of one of the blind passages. It seemed that further excavation had been intended, because in addition to broken stone there was a rusty chisel lying about, and a tool which Samuel said was called a 'jumper' – a star pointed drill used for driving shot holes. They searched for a sledge hammer to force the iron gate on the tower staircase. Caroline found a broken haft, but no head. After a time they gave up, and returned to the crypt, bolting the door behind them.

Soon they conferred together, and decided that it had become evident that survival was possible in the crypt for several days or even weeks, certainly until rescue occurred or a means of exit could be worked out, but there were diverse opinions on the background to the position. At first sight, it seemed that they had suffered a major defeat. Not with the disastrous consequences so jubilantly assumed by the enemy, but a defeat nevertheless. Until presently, Hermione, supported by Mary and Laura, expressed doubt on this, at least as a simple interpretation of events. They wondered if there were not some deep seated factor working on their behalf. The Menenius faction certainly thought that they had won by destroying the opposition; presumably Archaroch would be so informed. But perhaps things had been 'meant' to turn out as they had. The enemy would be misled into over-confidence, and then dismayed indeed when the company emerged from the crypt unscathed. Hermione developed this idea, and in an historical context.

"There may be a parallelism of events," she said. "I dare say that the original sacking of Langarrow by Lyonesse was made partly to defend the old church against an earlier attempt on Merlin's Myster. Also, the corpse which Samuel has just buried must have been brought here from the old church when the crypt was built, having been displayed there to frighten off Satanists. Rather like country people hanging up dead crows to keep the live ones off the turnips. Doubtless our friend Agravain is a descendant of the Langarrow rector, and is involved in the present attempt as was his ancestor in the previous one. Perhaps he will end in the same way!"

"But how do the Brocellinde Myrmidons fit in to all this?" asked Mary.

"This again is history repeating itself. Consider that extraordinary psychic re-enactment arranged to trap Arthur. No troopers were physically present, but it was Laura's threat of the Myrmidons which caused the rout. Then a few days later, we arrive on the scene for the second time."

"And the Spear of Longinus?"

"That I accept remains a mystery. We still don't know for certain sure that it is the spear behind this business. Catharine the First probably believed so when she authorised the earlier intervention by the Myrmidons, although I doubt if there is much about it in the official history. Georgina will know.

"We are working on a mixture of myth and an informed guess. Let's be practical. If the spear really is in the crypt further search should find it. The most logical place is the armoury."

"Or the Presence Chapel?"

"Maybe, but I'm a soldier. Armoury first."

The armoury certainly lived up to its name, containing a wide range of military equipment apart from firearms. Arthur was appointed expert, although he declared that medieval armour and munitions were a specialised study, and not his forte. Firstly they examined the spears, but Arthur said that none were Roman. They had ornamentation of Celtic character and might be Arthurian, but he thought that at least some were copies made at a later date. The same applied to the swords and body armour. A few genuine Celtic pieces had been used as patterns by subsequent skilful craftsmen. Ystelle and Samuel agreed with him, and it also fitted the theory that the crypt itself was copied from an earlier version. But careful scrutiny did not reveal their objective. So the company returned to the rotunda.

"Show me the plan again," said Hermione, "and let us try to foresee any hazards which may apply to the chapel. There could be a deadfall, quite apart from psychic forces."

The plan indicated what was probably an altar, three rectangular objects that might be tombs, and an entrance through a vestibule with two sets of double doors.

"I enter first," she continued, "but would feel more confident if I had my vestments. Forces guarding this chamber may be of two kinds. Evil, in which case their influence will be restricted by the sacramental power impressed within vestments of the celestial church, or benevolent, when the same power will be recognised as in alliance. Fortunately, I have my Saint Catherine's Cross, which is in some ways similar, but in a more specialised way."

The outer doors of the vestibule were of slate, great polished slabs on wrought iron hinges. Hermione pushed a leaf open and peered inside. The vestibule was entirely empty, and terminated in an identical pair of doors at the farther end. Cautiously she stepped inside. The atmosphere was completely still, but her candle flame guttered for no overt reason. Slowly and carefully the priest walked forward to the second doors, and pressed gently. A leaf opened. Immediately, the company felt a thrust upon them, pressing them back like a storm wind, although no air moved. Nevertheless, Hermione's candle was instantly extinguished. Not that it was blown out; the flame died motionless about the wick. Hermione returned pale faced to the companionship of her friends. "It is not a question of fear," she said, "but one of folly. To enter that place unprotected is to court disaster. Even with a stole it might be feasible, but full vestments are what is needed."

The tension was enormous. The earthly members of the company in particular were both frightened and confused by the recent turn in events; Samuel felt professionally nonplussed. As an experienced priest he accepted the reality of spiritual forces, but had never encountered them in such a direct and indeed physical manner. Perhaps it was not surprising that no one noticed that Jennifer had slipped away, until she returned a few minutes later.

"Donna," she said, addressing Hermione, "you need some vestments, and I have either found some for you, or been given some. Don't ask me how, but I knew where to look. They belonged to Guinever, and were in a chest in the room labelled 'Chapel of Guinever' in Arthur's plan of the crypt. They were wrapped in what looked like white silk. I don't care what anybody thinks; these were hers. Beyond reason, but I know it. Will they serve?"

Hermione examined the garments very reverently, using as much care as possible in the indifferent light. They were not greatly different from her own. There was a linen surplice, once white but now a little yellow with age, an alb, an amice complete with colourful apparel, a maniple and stole, also richly embroidered, and a girdle, of linen but with silk tassels. Additionally there was a pair of unworn doeskin shoes, not strictly part of the vestments, although wrapped in the same way. No remarks were made, but silently Hermione began to put on the garments, Jennifer helping her. She relit her candle, walked through the vestibule, and for the second time opened one leaf of the double doors at the farther end and entered.

The candle flame flickered, and all present felt a brief return of the pressure, but this was little more than momentary; the psychic thrust was now neutralised although they felt a residual tension, probably self-generated. But anxiety for their champion grew among the company, waxing ever greater as the seconds mounted into minutes, and the minutes gathered on in an inexorable pavane of useless inactivity. At last Jennifer broke the silence.

"I am going in after her," she said. "At this moment I am closest to her, and should be at her side facing whatever is in there. I have Guinever's Saint Catherine's Cross."

Ystelle put an arm round her.

"Jenny my dear, Hermione de Lamarac is a gnostic priest of unsurpassed knowledge and ability. With the doubtful exception of Donna Catharine herself, no one in the priesthood of Lyonesse is her equal. She knows precisely what she is about, and were anyone of us to enter the Presence Chapel it would only be an incumberance to her, because she would have to protect a companion as well as herself. None of us can protect her. During the great storm when the enemy attacked the church, in effect Hermione raised the dead. I fancy that what she is doing now is the reverse of that process. You could not help her with it."

"May I at least go into the vestibule? I shall feel closer to her then."

"No harm in that, but no farther, and Georgina and I shall come with you."

The trio moved forward to the inner doors. Nothing could be heard, and after a minute or so Jennifer peered cautiously through a narrow central slit where the leaves did not quite touch.

"I can see an altar," she said, "with two candles burning, and patches of grey mist which form and disappear for no apparent reason. There are some shadows in the candlelight but with nothing to cause them. They are moving about, swirling around and changing form, and there is a great spear lying across the altar. A long black shaft and a curved metal head with some sort of pennant beneath it. And there's a triptych behind the altar, not painted, carved in slate, but I can't make much out. Hermione is nowhere to be seen. I want to go inside and pull her out. She may be lying insensible, overcome by something that we don't understand."

Georgina and Ystelle took her by the shoulders and forcibly drew her back from the doors.

"You must do as we say. We aren't priests but we know more of these things than you do. Please believe it. There is nothing you can do but pray. Come back through the outer doors to the rest of the company."

Reluctantly, Jennifer agreed; indeed she had little option.

Grim faced and silent the company continued to wait, Jenny clutching her Saint Catherine's Cross with the metal digging deep into her hand, while Samuel shifted uneasily from one foot to the other. It was all happening in his parish, and he felt that he should be playing a more positive part. Mary stood close by him, as if trying to give her husband some sort of emotional support. Arthur was hopelessly nonplussed – this was an aspect of history far beyond his frame of reference. Laura alone seemed relaxed. She trusted an intuition that Hermione was past mistress of her profession and would not be overcome by any entities, good bad or indifferent, which dwelt within the Chapel.

And then the doors opened, and a surge of relief flooded through the company as they saw Hermione emerge, unscathed and smiling gently.

"You may all come inside now," she said. "Nothing will harm you. The powers were defensive, but not truly hostile. Once they understood my purpose they became actively on my side."

"But what was in there?" exclaimed Jennifer. "I could see shadows moving and misty images coming and going. It was alive with power. I was frightened myself, and terrified for you."

"My dear, nowadays life as you experience it, is interpreted in terms of phenomena. That is to say of causes and effects. You hold the match to the candle, and the candle lights; so the match is the cause, and the lighting of the candle is the effect. But humanity is also concerned with the noumenal, and here we must think in analogies. Analogous reasoning is similar to the phenomenal in that there are two sides to it. Not firstly cause, and secondly effect, but one side of the analogy and then the other. When Christina Rossetti wrote 'My heart is like a singing bird whose nest is in a watered shoot' she was communicating by analogy. The literal interpretation of the words is ridiculous, and yet one knows what she meant, and what she wrote was clearly true. Much artistic and religious thought is analogous; most parables are analogies. To understand what was going on in the Presence Chapel, you must realise that these two types of reality can become intermixed. Factors of the psyche, noumenal factors, can become so powerful that they bridge into the phenomenal. This means firstly that one may become aware of things by pathways which are not dependant on the physical senses, and secondly that material objects can be influenced by similar means. This is an over-simplification, because one side of the analogy may be outside objectively conscious thought. Consider Salvador Dali's famous painting 'The Persistence of Memory' – you remember it – the picture with the glutinous watches and a landscape with a strongly emphasised perspective. Here, Dali makes a statement through analogy about an aspect of the human condition. The painting is one side of the analogy, and the human condition the other. One can grasp the meaning, but it is impossible to articulate it. Note that the painting itself is essentially phenomenal. It is made of a canvas covered with oil-bound pigments applied in a recognisable form. But the message is noumenal, it communicates with the human psyche in a manner which can not be put into words. Suppose that the reverse process applied? From the noumenal to the phenomenal? From the unseen to physical reality? That is what was happening in the Presence Chapel. Have no fear. The ghosts – for the lack of a better word – were essentially on our side, and are now at rest. You may enter with impunity."

But Laura had had enough of Hermione's exposition, and interrupted her, albeit politely.

"My reverend dear, we all know that you know what you are about, and are content to take your word that things are safe. No need for a deal of advanced theology to justify your advice."

Hermione smiled gently by way of reply, but to the surprise of most of the company, Georgina Burton-Coggles came to the priest's support.

"With respect Miss Trepennick, I know as a Sarissa Major that ignorance is often a big factor in fear, and what Donna de Lamarac was doing was to allay Jennifer's ignorance by explaining the background to what happened. According to our theology the greatest virtue is gnosis – Christian knowledge. Ignorance is the underlying cause of evil as well as a factor in fear. The two go together."

Poor Samuel was becoming increasingly out of his depth. It was all highly heretical by Anglican standards, although he accepted Catharine and the power of their beliefs. And what of those vestments? Once again, Hermione read his mind.

"The initial psychic risk was largely averted by the vestments that Jennifer was instructed to find for me. For the sort of reason which I have tried to explain they acted as a barrier to forces from the other side by denying them access to the thresholds of the personality. Undoubtedly, they belonged to Guinever, but they are not Arthurian. I recognise them as ancient vestments of the Celestial Church, and they could only have come from Lyonesse."

"From Lyonesse?"

"Yes Samuel. Without doubt. They must have been brought here by the Brocelliande Myrmidons. As you know, Guinever was the first queen of the celestial Lyonesse, and she is an ancestor of Catharine. Someone is watching over us. Have no fear."

"Let me go in first Jenny," said Arthur. "We can't leave it all to you ladies you know."

All present moved forward slowly into the chapel, which notwithstanding Hermione's assurance retained an atmosphere of covert power. She had lit two candles (which had already been present in the chapel), and they were still burning. A large crucifix was suspended above and slightly behind the altar, and this supported a Christ who was depicted not as awaiting death in calm composure, but suffering immense and mortal agony. The triptych behind the altar was utterly different, and portrayed three scenes of the triumphant saviour. All were meticulously carved, and despite the inert nature of the slate in which they had been worked, had a commanding vigour which was difficult to describe. Joy, victory, triumph; a surreal factor was involved. But what of the spear? Hermione spoke slowly and carefully.

"That is not the Spear of Longinus," she said. "It is an elaborate histrionic fake put there to confuse people. Perhaps it resembles Malory's brief description in the Morte d'Arthur, but it is a sham, have no doubt of it."

"You are right," said Arthur. "It's no more Roman than I am."

CHAPTER X
Secret Springs

The companions left the Presence Chapel disconsolately enough, but before doing so they examined the three tombs, each complete with a carved effigy. All bore the name of the deceased and with the same Celtic inscription:

'Ni bydd a fydd fel a fu, bwriai'i ffydd heibo i'r ffin.'[2]

Laura expressed interest, but fatigue was now rising as their mood of exploration gave way to exhaustion; stress from their struggle with the Chapel and disappointment over the spear sapped the vitality which had driven them forward. And so they retired to the Nuns' Dormer – the least inhospitable of the domestic offices. Here they chewed wearily upon some hard tack found in one of the slate chests. It resembled ships biscuit, tasteless, but not unpalatable.

"Maybe these were brought back by Sir Christopher from the Spanish Main," remarked Jennifer.

It was not much of a joke, but helped a little in the circumstances.

"My revered ancestor," said Laura, "may not have been a culinary expert, but he built this place and certainly knew a bit about tin mining, and the allied art of tin streaming."

"Tin streaming?"

---

2 Nothing will be as it has been; he sent his faith beyond the veil. H. de Lamarac.

"Yes Jenny. The old method of separating the ore from the debris. The spoil was crushed and carried into a stream of water flowing over slightly sloping surfaces. Tinstone, or cassiterite to give it its proper name, is heavy, and so it was retained and the waste was washed away. Tradition has it that one of our mines had an adit not far from here where the tailings were discharged. Water flowed out of it when I was a girl, but there hasn't been any for years now. 'Merlin's Well' we called it. The water flowed intermittently, but in a regular pattern. There was no obvious reason for the stopping and starting, though why people thought Merlin had anything to do with it is a mystery. He'd been dead for donkey's years before the Trepennicks started digging tin mines!"

"Hidden secret holy springs," quoted Mary. "I wonder."

"I wonder too," said Caroline, "but we could all do with some water. I'll go and get a bucketful, but don't fancy it on my own. Why did they bolt the door on the inside I wonder? Any volunteers?"

Arthur and Georgina accompanied her, the latter arming herself with an axe from the armoury.

"Have no fear," said de Lamarac. "He won't come back to life."

They found a bucket in the commissary, and returned without incident.

"We had a look at that lever beside the bottom door," remarked Georgina. "It goes through to the other side of the wall, and we found that it would move up and down, but the other end is not connected to anything. It ends in a clevis, but the clevis bolt is all rusted away. There's a shaft comes up from the floor, with the remains of a clevis bolt still in a hole in the end of it. But it's creepy down there and we didn't hang about."

Conversation continued for a little while, but it was now late in the day, and soon the company composed itself to sleep.

Meanwhile, both Rosalind du Lac and Louise Long-Clark had recognised that all was not well, so in the late afternoon Rosalind took Samuel's bicycle and hastened to Trepennick Chase. They could think of no immediate action, but sent Trudie home to help care for her brother – Hermione was among the missing party, and he had been left in charge of one of the Myrmidons. Pearl Esyllt accompanied her, and this left the Sarissa Major and the Demiarch to take stock of the situation; Michelle de Ligny was on a visit to Polly Penvithick.

"They went over to the church I know," said Louise, "but didn't come back. Apart from Caroline. She returned twice, at least so far as I can gather. At first to borrow a crowbar. The gardener had one, but then she came back a little later for a hurricane lamp. There was one where Laura had said there was, but we had to find some paraffin. Caroline said nothing on the whys and wherefores, but there were several people about at the time which could explain why. Oh, and I forgot, she also wanted a ball of string."

"I suppose the church has been checked?" said Rosalind. "Not that they would be likely to wait there for as long as this without letting us know."

"True enough, but let's go over again and have a better look round. I didn't pay much attention before – only confirmed that there was no one about."

They found the crowbar in some long grass near to the lychgate, where the Meneniuses had presumably abandoned it. Of the lamp there was no sign, but they found a part-used ball of string under a pew in the nave. And so they had little enough to go on, but later in the evening Laura's chauffeur (who was also a bell ringer) returned from belfry practice:

"There's a new bell rope gone missing. Stolen most like. What are things coming to when people help themselves to church property? Put us out as well; it was for the tenor bell. The present rope is so worn it's getting dangerous. We had meant to do the job tonight."

"So," said Rosalind, "a crowbar, a hurricane lamp, a ball of string, and now a missing bell rope. There must be a connection, but I can't see what it is."

They talked on for a while, but it was now late in the day. Long-Clark had a further word with the Myrmidons on picket duty, but otherwise they could think of no positive action and gave up until morning.

But the morning brought some surprising news. About nine o'clock, a breathless Trudie arrived at the Chase. She was riding her mother's bicycle, with Simon in a seat on the back.

"Miss Esyllt sent me to tell you. I took Simon for his walk this morning, and Merlin's Well is running with water. All down the dry stream bed, and Miss Esyllt thinks it's got something to do with Miss de Lamarac. Miss Esyllt's gone down to the well. Can I leave Simon here until she comes for him? I'm late for the college."

And so she went pedalling off.

"It does seem to be too much for a coincidence," said Louise. "A crowbar, a hurricane lamp, a ball of string, a bell rope, and now a dry spring suddenly coming back to life. I wonder."

"I think," said Rosalind, "that the company has explored its way into some underground place, and either got lost there, or met with an accident. First they want the crowbar, presumably to lever something out of the way, and then the hurricane lamp to light their passage. The ball of string and the rope don't quite fit, but they could have been used for all sorts of things."

"Like lowering a lamp down a mine shaft before climbing down on a rope?" It was Pearl Esyllt who spoke, having arrived at the Chase a few seconds before and entering unannounced. "I've been down to the spring, or Merlin's Well as they call it, and the water is flowing copiously and crystal clear. But something remarkable came down floating along. It may or may not be significant."

She produced a candle, partly burned down, and about four inches long. It was clearly of good quality, over an inch in diameter and with the slight yellow tinge of old beeswax.

"It doesn't look as if it had been in the water for very long," she continued. "No discolouration or erosion of the wick. As if someone had dropped it into the water only a few minutes before I noticed it. Any ideas?"

The time was now around nine o'clock in the morning, and the company in the crypt had been astir for some time. Arthur had brought more water, and on his return, conversation was resumed on the function of the mysterious lever, beside what they had taken to calling 'Agravain's door'.

"The thing that puzzles me," said Arthur, "is that it must have been put there for some good reason, but what reason? There's nothing much down there, only the passageways and the spring. Perhaps there is a concealed door that the lever is meant to open. There are supposed to be some pillared halls hereabouts!"

"Let us all go down and have another look," said Ystelle.

The lever itself could be moved by applying moderate force, but pulling upward on the shaft produced no movement. Either it was stuck fast or had some great weight attached to it.

"Perhaps we could replace the rusted bolt," said Caroline. "Any strong piece of metal would do if it would fit through both the clevis fork and the bush in the end of the shaft."

"There might be something in the armoury," said Georgina, "but nothing suitable comes to mind. We need a round bar, about an inch thick."

"The jumper," cried Mary. "The old drill thing that Samuel remarked on – it is lying about close to where we buried Agravain. Any volunteers to go and get it?"

However, the jumper refused to enter the clevis, because the blunt end had been mushroomed out by repeated blows from a heavy hammer, and the drilling end was expanded into a case hardened rock cutter, shaped like a striated star. Eventually, Arthur managed to break the mushroomed metal away by striking at it tangentially with a piece of granite, and presently they persuaded the shaft of the drill into place.

"So," said Samuel. "Let us proceed empirically. Nothing would surprise me these days, but it seems likely that the shaft was originally raised, and dropped down when the clevis bolt rusted through. I doubt if anything dramatic will happen if we lift it up again."

However, the lift proved far from simple. Georgina, Arthur and Caroline leaned their combined weight upon the lever, while as many of the company as could get a hold pulled upwards on the clevis joint. But to no avail, the mechanism was stuck fast. Then Caroline said:

"Let us try to fix up a second lever. There was a sledgehammer handle lying about somewhere. We could jam it under the clevis with a lump of stone for a fulcrum, push down on the other end of the handle, and try to heave the thing up. I reckon it's worth a try."

The handle was nearly four feet long, having broken off where it had fitted into the hammer head. They wedged it into place as Caroline had suggested, and she and Arthur stood on the end of the handle, Jennifer clasping Arthur's hand to hold them steady; they had a mechanical advantage of perhaps four or five to one. Meanwhile, the rest of the company pressed hard down on the original lever, or heaved upwards on the clevis. Still nothing moved. Then Samuel picked up a piece of granite, and started hammering on the end of the vertical shaft, striking alternately from right and left. Suddenly the shaft released; the mechanism flew upwards and Arthur and Caroline were precipitated to the floor, where they would have gone sprawling save for Jennifer's restraining hand.

"Hooray," she cried, but their attention was soon demanded by the gurgling from the nearby whirlpool. The sound magnified into a vigorous roar, and hurrying to the balustrade, the company were in time to see the water disappearing downwards into a pitch-black void. The noise in the confined space was enormous, and was indeed exacerbated by a deluge pouring in from an opening in the side of the chamber, which had been concealed beneath the rotating surface of the pool. This inflow now formed a cataract crashing down into a seemingly bottomless abyss, with a startling and indeed frightening effect. The staircase could be seen leading downwards, until it became obscured by a combination of darkness and furiously whirling spray.

"Golly," said Ystelle. "Abandon hope all ye that enter here."

She had a partly burned crypt candle in her hand, and extending her arm, she let it fall into the void with the flame still alight. They watched its descent for a surprising distance before the light was extinguished, whether by the water or the velocity of its descent would have been impossible to say.

Soon after this, Merlin's Well was drawing fair local attention. A renewed visit was made by Pearl Esyllt, accompanied by Rosalind and Louise Long-Clark; they found several people already standing about, including Nanskillien, the village constable. Louise spoke to him:

139

"I'm a visitor here, officer," she said. "They tell me that this flow of water is most extraordinary, but no doubt you will be able to explain it to us."

Nanskillien was indeed flattered to be so addressed by this cultured highly elegant woman.

"I'll try ma'am. It's the first time I've seen it running with water, although I've lived round here man and boy for fifty years. My grandad reckoned it had last run about 1906 or 08, couldn't remember for sure, when he was a little lad. But it never ran continuously. It would flow for three hours, then run dry for three hours, and then start up again. Day after day, regular as clockwork. Folk say that Merlin had put a spell on it, but a more likely reason is something to do with tin streaming."

"Tin streaming?"

"Yes ma'am." (Nanskillien was enjoying himself.) "The old way of separating the tin ore from the useless rubbish that came out with it. They put the powdered ore into a long channel with a stream of water through it to wash away the muck and leave the heavy tinstone behind. A bit like the gold miners in the Klondyke, so I'm told."

"But why three hours?"

Nanskillien scratched his head.

"Couldn't say for sure ma'am. Possibly they spent the three hours when it was dry taking out the washed ore, and then refilling the channel ready for the next flush. Or could be there wasn't enough water to keep it running continuously. I dunno, it's all mighty peculiar."

As if to reinforce Nanskillien's wordy explanation, at that moment the head of water in the channel started to diminish, and after a few minutes was no more than a trickle.

Meanwhile, Pearl Esyllt's intuitive mind had been working like a needle. She calculated that their friends were somewhere underground, that they were in danger, and the enemy was involved. And then logic reinforced intuition.

"I say Mr Nanskillien, there must have been some way of getting into the old mine. A shaft, or adit hereabouts?"

"A good question ma'am, but none too easy to answer. There's an awful confusion of disused tin workings round here. You ladies must have seen the old engine houses, and the mines often led one into another. Mind you there were no steam engines in the days when Merlin's Well was built, so most like they went in by an adit."

The three women exchanged glances; it was du Lac who spoke:

"Perhaps the stream comes out from an adit. I can see what looks like a masonry arch, bricked over inside, but the brickwork doesn't match the masonry. It doesn't look so old, and is rougher than the stonework, as if it had been built in a hurry."

"True enough ma'am. I can't explain it, but you see the iron grating across the channel – that's been replaced a time or two to keep boys from crawling in through the hole where the water was coming out. Last time, Miss Trepennick paid for it; let me see, it must be twenty years back now. The parish council was for walling it up altogether, but she wouldn't hear of it. No way. She put the money up herself, but not before they'd given in to her and she'd won the argument. Very determined lady Miss Trepennick. Best not to cross her. There was one lad climbed in there and never came out for fourteen hours. I was a young constable then and we were searching the country for him, not knowing where he'd gone you see. Later on folk said that he was never the same again, but then he came from a daft family to start with." (Nanskillien paused for breath.) "But this is clearly not a constabulary matter ma'am, so I'll wish you good morning. If you want me again, the police station is in Fore Street, three doors past the chapel; always pleased to oblige a lady."

"One last question officer, if I may bother you further," persisted Rosalind. "Are there any other adits or streams or such like coming out of the hillside?"

"Yes to be sure ma'am. There's Saint Catherine's Brook just on the far side of the road – you can see it from the bridge behind you. Come to think of it, there was no water in it when I came down. Most peculiar. Let's have another look."

At least to the intuitive Pearl Esyllt, it was no surprise to see that the brook was now brimming with water.

"Well now, there's curiosity for you," said Nanskillien, and off he went towards the village.

Not so the ladies. They turned in the opposite direction and followed the narrow lane (which at that point runs alongside Saint Catherine's Brook), until presently the stream turned underneath the road to disappear into the hillside, about a hundred yards away. The companions climbed the roadside wall, and scrambled onwards until they reached the source of the water – an archway not greatly different from that at Merlin's Well. There was a difference, in that here the flow was culverted, and instead of a metal grid, access was denied by a row of parallel slate slabs arranged vertically in the water. Also, the brickwork was in poor repair; indeed a rough aperture had been broken through at one side. Stooping low, du Lac entered. She could only just stand upright inside, but found that the adit was smoothly floored with stone slabs, and the water could be heard rushing past beneath. A few odds and ends were lying about – the place appeared to be used by hobos as a refuge. It was almost dark inside, and although they had no torches, they moved cautiously forward until they found their way blocked by a heavy wooden door. It had a ring operated latch, but was locked securely.

142

"No way ahead," said Pearl, "but I feel we should return and get in somehow or other. God knows where the key is though."

"Don't worry about it," said the resourceful Rosalind, "I'll take the charge out of a grenade, and blow it open."

Down in the crypt, conversation had continued.

"Who's going down the steps then?" said Arthur.

"No one," replied Samuel. "Not until we've thought this through, if at all. There is nothing about it in the plan of the crypt, so far as I can remember and to go down there without more information could be suicidal."

Ystelle leaned over the balustrade, almost dangerously far.

"Listen," she said, "there's another noise, above the water. A sort of mechanical sound, like primitive machinery."

Sure enough, despite the roar of the deluge, a regular clanking could be made out, together with an occasional groaning sound.

"Either we have set something in motion," said Caroline, "or the lowered water level is allowing the sounds to reach us. Has anyone any idea what might be causing them?"

No one had any pertinent suggestions, so Hermione proposed that they return to the muniment room, and search for further information.

They found two slate drawers, and Hermione removed a vellum manuscript for later study. Also, there were numerous ancient drawings, many illegible from age, and their significance could not be deciphered from brief inspection.

"These might be Ophite Diagrams," said Hermione, but as no one else knew what Ophite Diagrams were, she received no reply. There were several primitive maps or plans, and a few line drawings, probably of primitive machinery. One, according to Arthur, was a ballista, or siege engine.

"This really is odd," he remarked. "Such things went out with the invention of gunpowder."

But Ystelle and Georgina were unconvinced.

"What is that big wheel for?" asked the latter.

"To wind up the mechanism before they fired the missile – usually a big stone. Somewhere there will be a bucket to put the stone in."

"There are what look like buckets round the edge of the wheel," said Caroline. "Like the Ferris Wheel at Exeter fair."

Laura entered the debate.

"I think it's a water wheel. Something to do with mining before steam engine days. Look, that could be the channel to deliver the water."

Arthur took a deep breath. It seemed a pointless argument in the circumstances. Jennifer put her arm round him.

"Arthur dear, you musn't mind us women disagreeing with you, but I think I see what it is all about. The thing is indeed a water wheel, and my guess is that we've set it working. That's what happened when we were heaving away with the lever. This must have opened a sluice, and let the water into the buckets. The Trepennicks certainly built things in those days."

Poor Arthur, she was right of course, the drawing was undoubtedly a water wheel. Hermione comforted him.

"Cheer up Arthur. It's a question of intuition as well as logic. It was logical for an historian to reason as you did, with the armoury and the Arthurian associations. But we women are often an illogical lot, reacting to strange hunches. So Laura knew what the wheel was for, without thinking over much about it. Who can say how? Perhaps Sir Christopher Trepennick is in touch with his descendant in some mysterious way. Who are we to argue against him?"

"I know that the old miners used water wheels to work pumps," said Mary, "but unless the mines were driven to lower levels, why would the Trepennicks want a pump? It doesn't make sense to me."

Laura re-entered the argument.

"The Trepennicks required power for other things than pumping. Breaking up the tin ore for a start. Usually this was done on the surface; back-breaking labour provided by grossly exploited women. Bal Maidens they were called. But later on, the job was done mechanically using machines which today are called 'Cornish Stamps'. I dare say that my ancestors built such devices. They were good engineers, and often ahead of their time."

"That would tie in with the noises that I heard," said Ystelle. "I want to see what goes on down the whirlpool staircase, from curiosity if nothing else. I vote we explore. We can always climb back again if the stairs don't lead anywhere."

The steps were wet and somewhat irregular in height, but well cut and surprisingly clean. Nevertheless, it was a tense experience. The treads were about three feet wide with no handrail, and so they descended carefully, keeping close to the wall, and shielding their candle flames as best they could, but the flight of steps proved to be shorter than they thought, leading them past a sizeable empty conduit leading away into the rock, before coming to a stone platform beside a masonry chamber. Here the deluge was trapped, crashing into the chamber with much spray and indeed frightening force. On the further side was a second larger conduit, carrying the water away, and with a raised footway to one side. A massive sliding door, or penstock was suspended above the arched opening, and they could see a corresponding gap in the footway at this point. Clearly, a mechanism for raising or lowering the door had been installed by Trepennick's engineers.

The mechanical noises, just perceptible from the balustrade, were now readily audible, and, daringly enough, Arthur ventured forward along the footway and into the archway of the conduit.

"I say," he called. "There is a water wheel! And a big one, with buckets like bath tubs."

But at that moment, a further noise came to the ears of the party waiting on the platform, and slowly, very slowly, they saw the great sliding door begin to descend.

"Come back, darling," cried Jennifer. "Come back at once. It isn't safe here. The door is coming down and you'll be cut off."

At first Arthur failed to understand, until she started to run towards him along the footway, ignoring the danger of falling into the torrent. On seeing her action, Arthur returned; probably more to prevent her hazarding herself than because he appreciated what was happening. In fact he passed under the door easily enough, and the companions watched in fascination while the great penstock came lower and lower. And then Ystelle exclaimed:

"We shall have to run for it. When that thing closes, the water will build up and fill the shaft, drowning the lot of us. Back up the stairs at once. I'll come last and help Laura. Don't stop to think. Do as I say, and don't argue."

They reached the top of the steps with about ten seconds to spare, and gathered behind the balustrade in a small rather frightened group.

"My fault," said Ystelle, "I should have been more circumspect before suggesting an expedition down the steps. Let's go back to the crypt and have another think."

They stood about for a brief time, staring at the swirling water, but lacking any alternative idea, moved off as Ystelle had proposed.

They reached Agravain's door a minute or so later, and then further calamity closed upon them. To their dismay the door was bolted on the inside! There was no doubt of it. Since Georgina had first helped Arthur to force the door open it had not been unduly difficult to manage, and now by pushing and pulling on the latch ring they could feel the bolts juddering to and fro within the hasps. Oh horror horror. Who was responsible? The Menenius faction must be in the crypt. Presumably they had used some method unknown to the Christians to lower the penstock and thus restore the water level within the shaft. What if the Meneniuses could raise it further, flooding the area up to Agravian's door? They would be drowned like rats in a trap. Also, even if no further hostilities ensued, they could not survive long where they were. By comparison, the crypt now seemed like fair accommodation, but down here they had no food, merely plenty of water. Moreover, they had only a limited reserve of candles. Arthur attempted to break open the door using a large stone and the chisel previously found in a side tunnel, but the chisel was blunt, and the door heavily constructed from oak boards. Also, if he succeeded, what would they find on the other side?

There was much confused discussion on this. Previously, they had lit a candle in the single socket on the inside of the door, and this seemed to be still alight – illumination was visible through the chinks, and the lever was as they had left it, partly contradicting the theory that the Meneniuses had raised the water level. Arthur's activity with the chisel had made a considerable noise, but no answering sounds could be heard, although psychology suggested that if Agravain junior were present he would be jeering at them through the boards. A chill feeling began to grow within the company – was some supernatural factor involved? They were intensely aware of Agravain senior, buried only a few yards away under a pile of stones. Who could say what factors might be at work within this psychically active place? Hermione played down these fears, saying that essentially the crypt was of friendly origin, but Samuel at least wondered if there was something which she was keeping from them, to avoid undue alarm.

They returned to the area at the top of the steps, sitting close together beside the stone altar, and extinguishing all save one of the candles to conserve their reserve of light. None of the company smoked, but Caroline had a box of matches (obtained originally to light the hurricane lamp). So they had the means of relighting a candle, but courage failed at the thought of sitting in the dark.

What to do? No one had any useful ideas, beyond making a further assault on the door. Arthur attempted to sharpen the chisel by grinding it against a stone, but the granite did not give a good surface for the purpose. Time passed, slowly indeed, with the whirlpool reversing and gurgling and their solitary candle burning lower and lower. Presently, Mary selected another partly burnt candle, and lit it from the remains of the older one; there was an unspoken question in everyone's mind on how long the candlelight could be maintained. Were they to perish thus, from cold and starvation in this strange and desolate place? Or would the door be opened, and God knows what be released upon them? Even Hermione felt a measure of doubt, and Jennifer alone retained her full confidence; snuggled close to Arthur she maintained a profound belief in Catharine of Lyonesse, and thinking strongly of this lady, that surely they would be saved.

"Listen," she said an hour or so later. "The sound of the whirlpool is changing."

Sure enough, the gurgling assumed a different pattern, and on looking over the balustrade, Jennifer saw the waters descending once more into the depths of the pit.

"There's our way out," she cried. "Down the steps again and across through Arthur's archway. The water must flow out somewhere. Let us follow the stream."

This made some sort of sense, but as yet the company had not fully recovered from their previous excursion in that direction, and subsequent isolation at the top of the steps. They were unconvinced.

"What if we are trapped by the water?" said someone, and a series of ideas were brought forward, with Jennifer continuing to lean over the balustrade. Until suddenly she had them on the alert.

"There is someone coming up the steps," she said.

What new devilry was this? Ystelle drew her automatic, and with the safety catch released, took up a position at the end of the balustrade where she could see down the steps, but without exposing herself unduly to whatever malevolent being was about to come upon them. Georgina stood close by, armed with the sledgehammer handle, and Arthur picked up a large stone.

All Ystelle could see was a bright light coming steadily towards her, but what, if anything, was carrying it could not be made out. Cautiously, she leaned further out over the balustrade, whereon the beam of a powerful torch almost dazzled her.

"Greetings Donna," came a voice, above the noise of the falling waters. "Is all well up there?"

It was Rosalind du Lac.

"We came in through an adit above Saint Catherine's Spring," continued Rosalind, a few minutes later. "Donna

Louise is waiting at the top of a water wheel with Pearl Esyllt and two of the Myrmidons to give me a rear guard. Not that there seems to be anyone physically present in the mine workings, although I am glad we have Pearl with us. It is a spooky place. We found you by working our way along an underground stream, and didn't explore otherwise, but we saw into a great cathedral of a cavern, with pillars supporting the roof. Goodness knows what it was for. I would recommend that we move out right away. The water follows a three-hour cycle, so there is plenty of time, but the sooner we start the sooner we shall be outside."

No one disagreed with this and two hours later the company were in Trepennick Chase, drinking coffee and brandy, and wondering if it all had been true. Then Hermione produced the Celtic parchment which she had taken from the muniment room – to be translated, from Morgan le Fey, she said.

CHAPTER XI
The Last Chronicle
Of Morgan Le Fey

Translated from the Brythonic by Hermione de Lamarac.

This is written as I approach the end of my earthly life, believing that despite numerous misdeeds, I shall continue to serve Guinever, my priest and queen in the world to come.

So God me save, following King Arthur's voyage to our healing care in ynys Avalon, it became clear to the remnant of his chivalry that the old order was indeed at an end. And now I labour hard under the authority of Guinever to preserve what may be against diabolical forces, and the evil men whom they control.

Even yet, articles of great sanctity exist which were once in Arthur's care. The first and greatest of these is the Sangreal, and this I have placed in an iron box, so strongly enchanted that none save an appointed one will be able to open it before the end of time. The second is the Spear of Longinus, used to lacerate the body of Our Gracious Lord, as verily recorded in Holy Writ.

The Sangreal is of great virtue, even as the second article was originally of wicked intent. But good can come of evil, even as good came from the evil conception of Myrddin

Emrys[3], my great mentor and tutor in the mystical arts. Myrddin was conceived of a virgin in a sickening parody of Our Lord, got by an incubus upon his holy mother Aidan, a nun in the order of which Guinever is now mother superior. But the intent was early perceived, and so the nuns baptised Myrddin immediately upon his birth, and the dark power imbued within him was converted into the Christian good, and Myrddin became a veritable Πνευματικοσ[4]. And it is often thus with sinners who come under the healing influence of a mighty priest. Not only is absolution given to the penitent for wrongful deeds, but the evil force within him is redirected to impel his soul into the paths of virtue.

Guinever knew that she could not remove the energy latent within the spear, nor indeed whether it would be proper to do so, and thus she sought to remould the nature of this energy to render it virtuous – available to Christian men to apply the power of the Paraclete for good works and to oppose the powers of darkness. This she did by her sacramental authority. Even as a priest is both a person in herself and an ordained channel for the recalling of Our Saviour to her people, so the nature of the spear is twofold – the iron and wood of its material substance, and a ghostly power associated with this. And therefore it follows that the spear is itself like unto a sacrament, and Guinever applied her own authority to it. This she did at the high feast of Pentecost, using a subtile

---

3 Myrddin Emrys is the correct and original Celtic name for the wizard Merlin. I have left it in the ancient form.

4 This is a gnostic term which has no simple translation from the Greek. It refers to the highest of three spiritual classes of Christian people. Its occurrence here indicates that both Morgan and Guinever had considerable theological expertise.
H. de Lamarac.

combination of baptism and the Eucharist. She consecrated water as for a baptism, and then placed this in a chalice, sacring it as if for the mass. So there was an epiclysis, and Guinever combined the absolution of baptism with the divine recalling[5] of the Holy Office. Therefore the directing of the energy which cleaves to the spear was transferred to an Authority far beyond our own. And because of this, it would be indeed presumptuous for mortal me to predict what the ultimate outcome of this divine redirection will be.

But it is permissible to forewarn earthly Christians who are to follow me of some events which are yet to come[6]. In the nature of man let us put in the first place possibility, in the second will or volition, and in the third the being in the realisation of the act. The first of these faculties is derived in essence from God, who bestows it on the people of his creation. The other two must be referred to the human agent because they flow from the springs of his will, and free will is allowed us by the Father. Thus we have the power of seeing with our eyes; but it is in our power that we make a good or bad use of our eyes.

---

[5] Morgan used the Greek word 'Αναμνησις', inserted untranslated. This means 'Bringing back' in the physical sense, and is therefore a stronger word than 'Recall' or 'Remember'.

[6] The remainder of this paragraph could be an almost literal quotation from the Celtic monk Pelagius, and was probably inserted both to borrow authority from this noted theologian, and to make it clear that Morgan did not believe in an absolute predestination. Clearly, she considered that all people were morally responsible for their own actions, and also rejected Saint Augustine's opinion that Pelagius was at fault by trying to amalgamate Druidic theology with the Christian faith.

I now foresee that much strife will be caused by the Spear of Longinus, not springing from the weapon itself, but from the will and volition of demons and evil men to possess and misuse it. Furthermore, these powers of darkness will disturb the aeons[7], and the earthly soldiers of virtue struggling for the light will be caught up within movements of time and space beyond their comprehension. Shortly, indeed too shortly perhaps, although I oft times wish that it may be soon, Guinever and I shall also cross the aeons into an afterlife, but it is clear to me that we or our successors in the Celestial Church shall continue to be involved in the defence of the holy articles. I now approach my earthly death, and by grace can verily see into the world to come. Our Lyonesse, wherein we now dwell, is doomed to sink beneath the waves, but we have the glorious promise of a new and greater Lyonesse about to arise in low heaven – an aeon not far removed from that containing the earth. Therein we ladies shall dwell in peace and fellowship with God and one another, but without the perfidious male to tempt and plague us, destroying our amity and distracting our minds from the greater good. But the saints from this halcyon world will continue to watch over earthly events. Let the demons be warned that if any power of darkness interferes with the aeons, we shall do likewise, lending our aid to the Church Militant by direct and physical means.

Shortly before the disasters which preceded King Arthur's departure to Avalon, the king placed the Spear in a chapel of

---

7 'Aeons' appears to be used in the gnostic sense, meaning a simultaneous combination of time and space, c.f. the first chapter of the Epistle to the Hebrews. It is interesting to note that this concept was not apparent to earthly minds (other than those of the Gnostics) before the scientific development of cosmological theory during the twentieth century.

great holiness, and arranged for it to be guarded constantly, both by holy people and his trustworthy knights, and thus it was defended at all points, spiritual and temporal.

Alas, these provisions could not be maintained following the end of Arthurian Chivalry. What were we to do? Where ignorance prevails, imagination takes the place of knowledge. Many and various were the proposals made for the further keeping of the Spear, and while Guinever believed that her baptism of the dreadful weapon would do much to direct its potency towards virtue, it remained necessary to find a secure haven to lay it to rest. Therefore, to prevent wild imaginings being applied to this mystical article, we resolved to place it in the keeping of simple people – rustic villagers, with a priest of strong but simple faith, all of whom would follow our informed instruction without the deviations of self will. Also, lest the Spear be lost in the watery cataclysm about to engulf Lyonesse, the site of preservation must be on secure ground, perhaps to the south in the region of Saint Corentin[8], although I favour Saint Juliot's chapel nigh to the great Castle of Tintagel, and Guinever has faith in the church of Lansallas[9],

---

8 A church dedicated to Saint Corentin survives to this day in the village of Cury, close to Helston. Corentin was a widely respected Celtic bishop, and it may well be that the present Saint Catherine's Church was originally so dedicated, and the name altered in Saxon times by a translingual gloss. Moreover, Saint Catherine of Sienna was not born until 1347. Catherine of Alexandria (martyred about 310) was a much earlier saint, probably well known to the Saxon church, and a more likely source of translingual error. Other explanations are possible. Catherine of Alexandria may also have been known to the Celts, or the Spear may have been moved to Saint Catherine's under unknown circumstances.

9 A modern village of this name exists, one league to the west of Polperro.

within the see of her friend Saint Ildierna – one of the great women bishops of our Celtic Church. Wherever, it shall be received within a crypt constructed beneath the church, and there triennial rites shall be enacted to reinforce the majesty of the divine power protecting the Spear.

It has to be warned that as the centuries pass, the enchantment[10] which we have made will fade, and in time even the best of men may lose their volition to maintain our will. Attempts will then be made upon the Spear by the evil ones. And these will take several forms; there is bad blood among those that dwell in Langarrow, and I foresee that they will grow worse in the ages to come. At first, such attempts will I think fail. Guinever will be queen in the new Lyonesse, and indeed is destined there to found a dynasty which shall reign in virtue and latter-day chivalry beyond anything known on earth.

Further in the future, I foresee a great and formidable assault upon the Spear, of which the outcome is shrouded in mist. The time itself is doubtful, but may be towards the end of the second millennium of Our Lord. Our enemies will use necromantic means to muddle both time and space, and strive as I may, my skill will not penetrate the complexities of these forthcoming matters. The muddling makes it impossible to see into this future, because the events when they occur will themselves be a recalling of earlier ages, and indeed of things

---

10 'Enchantment' is an inaccurate translation, but I cannot think of a better one. H. de Lamarac.

10 Here again, Morgan indicates that she follows Pelagian theology,

which have taken place in what by then will be the past.[11] Be it as it may, Lyonesse shall respond to the pleas of earthly Christians; the Communion of Saints will never desert its allies struggling for the light!

Extraordinary force will be brought to bear in response to resistance made at first by local Christians against evil men desiring to enter the sacred crypt. Then there will be great fury in the hearts of demons, following humiliations by an Angel of the Light. Therefore, the enemy will bend the natural movement of time to compel a battle outside the province of the late millennium, so to destroy the earthly ones by transferring the context into a fatal arena unknown to them. I am vaguely aware of ancient things returning to the fray, of an Arthur and a Guinever; yet I pray God that the might of our Lyonesse will also be present to their aid. There will be a fearful conflict, in which the earthly ones cannot stand alone. Impressions of darkness come upon me, of caves and passages far beneath the earth, and also of a great empty moor and a battle fought in biting cold beyond endurance.

Therefore, let whoever read this be ever vigilant in their intercessions, remembering that all things are made possible by the Father, but it is within their own volition to ask aid of the Communion of Saints. We of Lyonesse shall ever be ready, although unable to intervene unless called upon, because even Guinever herself is not permitted to infringe upon freewill.

---

[11] Here again, Morgan indicates that she follows Pelagian theology, and denies absolute predestination. Thus she forewarns, but does not necessarily foretell.

God bless the Church Militant, and all who serve within it.

Written by Morgan le Fey, in the Year of Redemption of Mankind, 545.

CHAPTER XII
Lucilla Mantzini

"What are we to make of it, Hermione?" asked Louise Long-Clark, as Laura refilled the tea cups for the second time.

The companions were discussing recent events, and felt that things had arrived at a sort of uneasy stalemate. Thus they knew how to enter the crypt, and indeed had done so, even defeating a counterattack by the Menenius gang in the process. But the enemy were also aware of the access route, and neither side knew for sure where the Spear of Longinus was located. Indeed it now seemed that it might not be in the crypt at all. Also, it was difficult to forecast what moves the enemy would make. If any. Canti feared that they might back off, and renew their attack in a year or two's time. She had placed guards on the church, and what they now called Rosalind's Adit, but the Lyonesse army could not remain in Cornwall indefinitely. How much did Agravain and Archaroch know? The Meneniuses had moved out of the village again, but nevertheless they were probably aware that the Christians had escaped from the crypt, although there was no explanation for the locking of Agravain's door. So what to do next? Obviously, a more systematic search of the crypt was needed, and this should include the muniment room, whence Hermione had removed the manuscript.

"It is almost certainly genuine," Hermione replied to Louise. "Arthur and I have spent a fair amount of time working on it, and are as sure as we can be, short of carbon dating."

Jenny took a deep breath.

"It is historically interesting," she said, "but does it give us any insight into the present situation?"

"Of course it does," said Laura. "Le Fey's earlier predictions were clearly accurate, although they were made years before the present Saint Catherine's crypt was built. Consider her foreknowledge of the Langarrow business, to say nothing of the humiliation of the enemy by an Angel of Light."

"Who or what was meant by an 'Angel of Light'?" asked Caroline. "Some form of divine agency or intervention?"

"No indeed," said Samuel. "It is clear enough to me. Morgan was referring to Hermione. There can be no doubt of it."

Poor Hermione, she coloured deeply at Samuel's comment, but was unable to contradict him.

"Let us move on," she said and Laura returned to the fray:

"We must assume that le Fey's guidance for later events is also valid. Therefore the enemy will not back off as Ystelle fears. Far from it; they are now more angry than ever, and are gathering for a new and greater assault. So far as possible we must prepare for it, but just how is beyond my wits."

"Beyond mine also," said Samuel, who felt as parish priest that some sort of leadership was expected of him.

"Frankly, I am out of my depth. What is this business about crossing the aeons?" he continued with a perplexed expression. "It all seems speculative to me."

The Lyonelles exchanged thoughts. Louise responded, speaking with great care:

"It is difficult to know precisely what was in the minds of our foremothers such as Morgan and Guinever when that chronicle was written, but their knowledge was accurate so far as it went. Their methods were derived from Christian writings now dismissed by the earthly authorities as extracanonical, but which were vital in the rapid growth of the early church. You yourself have experienced crossing the aeons in your visit to Lyonesse. Morgan accepted the reality of this sort of thing as an act of faith; it is improbable that she really understood what was involved. In the modern Lyonesse these matters are included in what we, for lack of a better term, call physical theology. God himself can not be defined in this way, indeed it would be presumptuous to attempt it, but the mechanisms of transference and spiritual communication can be so interpreted."

Unfortunately, Samuel was now more bemused than ever. He did not doubt the verity of what Louise was saying; the difficulty was that the concept was alien to the way in which he had been conditioned to think. Louise was a skilled telepath, but she lacked the great ability of de Lamarac, although scientifically she excelled her. What Louise said was factual; unfortunately Samuel could not assimilate it. Hermione recognised this.

"Samuel," she said. "Perhaps it will clarify things to consider two factors. Firstly, our three familiar spatial dimensions are enclosed within a fourth dimension which can not be visualised because it lies outside normal human reference. Astrophysics treats of it mathematically. The curvature of space is a bending of three dimensional space through this fourth dimension. I can't explain it better than that, because the mathematics are beyond me. But there are other universes, or aeons, which exist in parallel with the one which you know, separated from it in a way which can not be readily understood because their three dimensional spaces are outside your three dimensional space. In medieval times people believed in a heaven above the sky, and a hell beneath the surface of the earth. These concepts may have been an oversimplified memory handed on from earlier Christian ages. Notions of up and down were in a sense true, but not three dimensionally true. Lyonesse exists in a different aeon, and we have the means of transporting you to and from it. Hell, for what the name is worth, is the abode of Archaroch and suchlike demons, together with lesser persons whom they exploit and control. Our name for this horrible place is the Amente."

Hermione paused. Samuel made no spoken reply, but she recognised that he was now receptive.

"The second factor concerns what is often referred to as the supernatural. I would quarrel with the prefix. The term is misleading because nature is bigger than visualised. The explanation of many so-called miraculous events lies in transference between aeons. This is not supernatural. It may be inexplicable in everyday human terms, but not once you appreciate the form of the greater reality.

"Telepathy, clairvoyance and most of the so-called psi phenomena are related to this. The human psyche is dimensionally unconstrained, although it is conditioned by experience to think within the usual limits. In Guinever's time, people were more open to ghostly beliefs and accepted by faith factors which modern man rejects, because, as he sees it, they are contrary to scientific reason. Telepathy does not take place by electromagnetic radiation, but by a transdimentional linking of minds. It is not supernatural, nor is belief in it unscientific. It is just that earthly science has not explored what is involved."

"Would you like some more tea my dear?" Laura did not want a profound discussion to spoil the party. She was happy to accept what Hermione said, simply because it was Hermione who said it. Samuel was not so credulous.

"What has all this to do with theology?" he asked. "Are there any early authorities involved – New Testament references or such like?"

"Several of them. The Apocrophon of Saint John is the most direct. In describing the dominion of the Paraclete the writer states: 'It is not boundless, nor are limits set to it'. The second half of the sentence refers to the earthly universe, which is unlimited three dimensionally, but not boundless because of the curvature of space. If the fourth dimension is included, we have the first half of the sentence. There are other references, but I am going to have another muffin."

But Hermione had aroused general interest, and the next question was from Jennifer.

"What is an apocrophon?" she asked.

"Originally all that it meant was something that was secret, but time has caused a distortion, and now it signifies outside the pale – unauthorised, or dubious."

"What about that business at Langarrow, just after you left the note on my car?"

"Time and space form a continuum. This is harder to recognise than the concept of parallel universes, but it is so. Events that are past can be reawakened. It is not possible to pass forward through time. There is no absolute predestination. Much of the future is uncertain."

"Surely there is nothing about that in Holy Writ," said Samuel.

"I hate to contradict a gentleman, but there is indeed. To return to the Apocrophon, shortly after the opening of the book, Saint John, while in a dejected condition, recounts the risen Lord returning to assist him. The Saviour is described as being like a small child and an old man, but simultaneously. Saint John was trying to describe something which was beyond normal human experience, and for which he had no direct vocabulary. The phrasing he used was the closest he could get to what occurred. It was like trying to describe the colour blue to a man blind from birth."

Laura was now interested, almost despite herself.

"What is the Apocrophon of Saint John? I've never heard of the book. Has it something to do with Revelations?"

"To answer the second question first – not much. It is a gnostic gospel, only available to earthly Christians in Coptic translation, and the translator took liberties from Saint John's Greek. Like much of Gnostic Christianity, it is concerned with the teachings of the risen Christ. This leads us into a faith which goes beyond that followed on earth. It is exceedingly powerful. It is also a traditionally secret theology, at least on earth, if not in low heaven – the aeon from which I come. There are reasons for this. One is that it may interfere with free will, the second of Morgan le Fey's factors in the nature of man. The second is that it is dangerous. Gnostic writings can convey an awareness into the unconscious mind of matters which differ from the meaning, or apparent lack of meaning, in the direct interpretation of the script. This may apply to knowledge outside usual human experience, and which therefore cannot be easily expressed in words. So people who meddle without guidance are experimenting with things which they are unlikely to understand, and this is hazardous indeed. But enough of this, I am spoiling Laura's tea party!"

Alas for Hermione; she had the company's intense interest, and they ignored her last remark.

"You have my full attention," said Arthur, "but I don't see how this relates to Morgan's Chronicle. Could she foretell the future, or couldn't she? Are there really going to be extraordinary battles in some plane which we can't visualise, let alone understand?"

"Oh dear. We are getting confused, and it's all my fault. Morgan did not believe in an absolute predestination. No more do I. Therefore she cannot foretell absolutely; she merely forewarns. You must distinguish between the will of God and the will of man. One can know God by his footprints, but His will cannot be spied out so that it might be grasped. He makes no preparations like a man does, and this gives His enemies no breathing space. But human will can be foreseen, and this is the basis of Morgan's predictions. I believe that the evil ones will endeavour to do as she predicts because they clearly have the volition to do so. Whether or not they succeed may well depend on us."

"Let's have another look at the manuscript." It was Louise who spoke, mainly because she feared that a further assault was imminent, and that it would be on a larger scale than anything so far encountered. "It is the last three paragraphs that are important, where Morgan writes of a great and formidable assault upon the Spear."

"It looks formidable to me," said Arthur. "Is she predicting something like that business at Langarrow, only more so? She writes: 'The enemy will bend the natural movements of time to compel a battle outside the province of the late millennium'. If she is correct that means now. But what can we do to be ready for it?"

"Good questions," replied Louise. "It may be possible to work something out, mainly by a mixture of logic and intuition. What do you think Hermione?"

"Nothing definite. Morgan certainly believed that something serious would happen, and I agree that we should prepare for it. It might be possible to study the physics and chronology of the position, and so narrow down the probabilities. There are limits to what even the most powerful of necromancers can do in the way of bending time. It is akin to a problem in physical theology, except that there are evil forces involved as well as the Paracletic ones. It is no good asking me. As I have already explained, I can't understand polydimensional mathematics."

There was a long pause while the company digested this. The earthly members felt dependant on the Lyonelles, but the Lyonelles themselves were in a quandary. Ystelle and Louise knew that their troops could repel any physical attack, except by an improbably large hostile force. But what if the contest was staged in an earlier Cornish time frame? A major psychic assault was also on the cards.

Under Hermione's leadership, this was unlikely to succeed, but what if she were physically disabled? Pearl Essylt was a competent gnostic priest, but she lacked Hermione's immense knowledge and ability, as indeed she would be the first to admit.

"What we need is more information," said Louise at last.

"Surely," replied Samuel, "but how to obtain it? We seem to need someone who is even more gifted in the esoteric sciences than are you ladies. But whom? I can't help. There are no earthly authorities."

There was another pause, and then:

"Lucilla Mantzini," said Ystelle and Hermione simultaneously.

"The admiral?" said Samuel. "The lady from the big battleship?"

He felt an excitement at the name, almost a sense of fear, recalling the extraordinary impact which she had made upon him. As an experienced priest he was well aware of the diverse traits of the human character, but Catharine's brief introduction to Admiral Mantzini had led on to an awareness of an ability so intense and incisive that he felt dwarfed by it. Then he felt Ystelle's eyes upon him.

166

"None other, but we must not assume that she can be released. Under Catharine herself, she is the supreme commander of the Lyonesse navy, and this is a vitally responsible post. It will be best if I contact my husband. He sees Catharine regularly every week, and his duties include looking after our expedition here in Cornwall. Once Catharine understands the position, she will follow her usual practice of seeking the opinion of the officer concerned. If Lucilla feels able to come to help us, most likely she will do so."

"She will come," said Samuel. "She said that she was my ally, and with someone like her, what she says, she means."

Four days later, Lucilla Mantzini called her first meeting. To say the least of it, her manner was direct.

"Let us take the offensive. From now on the enemy's side of the struggle be will be increasingly dominated by Amentan influence. How much their earthly minions know of the position is doubtful; let us assume that Agravain is best informed. Much of what he knows he will not himself understand. Give me the opportunity, and I shall forcibly explore his psyche. This information will supplement Morgan le Fey's Chronicle, and the calculations which took all day yesterday. Therefore, firstly we kidnap Agravain. Secondly we bring him to a secure place; I suggest the crypt. Thirdly, we extract all relevant information from him. Fourthly, I wipe our tactics from his memory. Finally, we release him where we found him. Have you a map of Exeter?"

This left the company a trifle breathless. What she said was audacious, illegal, and at least to Samuel, underhand. His misgivings were short lived. Once again, he felt the same unsettling effect as Lucilla smiled upon him.

"I sympathise with your feelings Samuel," she said. "Understand me; I am entirely on your side. This business goes beyond Saint Catherine's Church, and those of us gathered here. The latent power in the Spear exceeds most people's imagination; our opponents are evil in the extreme, and we must fight them on their ground. We have no choice. They will force the issue."

She was right of course. And yet she had not forced her opinion upon him. He was now certain that within her extraordinary personality she was kind, good, and profoundly Christian.

"Are we not going a bit far?" said Arthur. "Surely all that is necessary is to obtain possession of the Spear, and make sure that the Amentans or whoever don't lay their nasty hands on it. Once the other lot know that we have possession, surely they will back off, and that will be the end of it. My opinion is that it is in fact in the crypt, and a more thorough search will find it."

"You raise two points," she replied. "Firstly, the enemy will attack us from malice, and I would teach them a lesson which they will never forget. The Amentans have been a threat to Lyonesse for centuries, quite apart from the evil which they have wrought on earth. Donna Catharine has had enough of it, and so have I. Stephen Zabuloe and I had a long meeting with her. Our remit is now to permit the Amentans to have their battle, and utterly defeat them. Not only shall we recover the Spear. We shall use it against them. Your second point concerns its location. I know where it is, at least approximately. Jennifer knows precisely where it is, although the knowledge is not on the top of her mind. Five seconds from now, it will be."

All eyes turned to Jennifer.

"It is in the crypt, inside the commissary," she said. "It is disguised as a broom for sweeping up the flour. A bunch of twigs is bound round its head, so it is not obvious what it is.

Most of us saw it, but I had no idea that I had assimilated the knowledge at an unconscious level. Lucilla, you are a remarkable woman, but you frighten me!"

CHAPTER XIII
Pearl Esyllt

Four persons were detailed to capture Agravain: Arthur, Caroline, and the Sarissa Majors – Rosalind du Lac and Georgina Burton-Coggles, with Rosalind in charge. A further force was to be held in reserve, conveniently close to the point of action. There was much discussion on approaching Agravain, until Pearl Essyllt came to the fore, partly because he had never seen her.

"From what we have been able to find out," she said, "my guess is that he is a satyr, and a genuine bibliophile, but with esoteric tastes in sex and literature. Probably he is fond of young women; either that or paedophilia. Laura's friends say that he has never been married, fosters the impression that he lives for his work, and is reputed to have a private collection of books which no local people have ever seen. This may correlate with satanic practices, and some sort of deviant sexuality. They often go together."

"But he works for the church," said Jennifer, perhaps a little naively.

"Yes indeed, but diabolically this could be an advantage. It gives him access to sacred things useful for sacrilegious purposes. He would have to be careful, of course. It may help to mention that I was a lawyer during my earthly life, and am not unaware of byways among the human kind."

Laura's enquiries had uncovered other factors in his life style. He had rooms in Exeter, down a side entry off Southernhay North, but he also owned a rambling country property in Clyst Saint Nectan – an isolated hamlet close to the Exmouth road. It was widely believed that he was a wealthy if eccentric man, not so old as he liked to pretend, and that the house was used to store his private library. It was looked after by two equally mysterious middle-aged women, together with a jobbing gardener. Occasional visitors were received, but they came and went without local contact.

Pearl's plan was essentially simple. It was to write to Agravain from a London address, using ambiguous wording about 'literature' and 'artefacts' in which he might be 'interested'. An hotel address would be suitable, because if he telephoned there, he would be told that the guest had moved on. A few days later she would telephone him, adding a little female allurement to increase his interest.

"I was not a barrister for nothing," she said.

The telephone rang seven times.

"Agravain: Diocesan Archives." The voice sounded slightly hollow as it came over the wires.

"Good morning Mr Agravain. Margaret Keinach here. Have you received my letter? I shall be in the West Country shortly, and would like to meet you."

"Who gave you my name?"

Pearl had anticipated the question.

"The gentleman for whom I am acting as agent. He wishes to remain anonymous for reasons which I shall explain when we meet. The legal position is doubtful. I have a copy of the Zohar, probably in Moses of Léon's own handwriting, and also a privately printed version of what is believed to be the Pistis Sophia, but from the original Greek. I can photocopy a page or two for you if you wish." (Coincidentally, Pearl had a copy in her luggage.)

"The Pistis Sophia? In the Greek?" (She had his interest now.)

"You heard."

"That takes some believing. Where did you get it from?"

"One opinion is that it was stolen from an Orthodox Monastery. The original manuscript had existed there in secret for centuries past. May I say that at this stage, we don't care for too many questions. Better to meet. Then you can make a decision, and if you aren't interested, we part amicably with no harm done. What do you say?"

"How do I know you're genuine – I don't know you from Adam."

"From Eve might be a better expression. I have been known to tempt an older man occasionally if I like the look of him. But what if I were to tell you that my principals have the original manuscript?"

There was a lengthy pause. Pearl could sense her quarry thinking.

"Very well. I agree to a meeting. In Exeter?"

"Why not. My principals understand that you have a house in the Southernhay area, but it might be wiser out of town. Also more discreet. You know how people talk. Man of the church seen with a younger woman and all that. Do you enjoy a bottle of wine? I like Chardonnay myself. L'Amoureux is a good one; slightly aphrodisiac. So, shall we say dinner together, one evening next week?"

"You will post me some of the Sophia?"

"To your Sothernhay house? I shall need the address."

Thus it was agreed. Pearl was to meet her target in a car park near the cathedral, and then drive him to the 'Bull and Griffin', a discrete distance from Exeter. Except that she would pull off the road at an agreed point for the kidnap to proceed. And so she posted him a few pages photocopied from her version of the Sophia, and caught the next train back to Truro.

Meanwhile, activity was continuing in Cornwall. Caroline had borrowed a van in which to confine the captured Agravain, and the formidable Admiral Mantzini laid her plans for overwhelming him. She proposed to enrol the support of Hermione's newfound psychic allies in the Presence Chapel, and this re-emphasised the question of the locked door below the crypt – both worrying and enigmatic. There were only two feasible routes of entry, either down the shaft beneath the chancel, or via Rosalind's Adit and the tin mine.

"There is no possibility," said Samuel, "of someone raising the slab in the chancel within the time he would have available; neither could he have come up the stairs from the water wheel without our seeing him. It is entirely baffling. Goodness knows what can have happened."

Arthur joined in.

"Could there be some sort of psychic explanation? A few weeks ago I would have scoffed at the suggestion, telekinesis or whatever it's called, but not now. Particularly where that crypt is concerned. What do you think, Hermione?"

"Probably not. We are now sure that that crypt is of Christian origin, and although it is psychically active, the force is on our side. I assume a more mundane explanation."

Then it was Arthur's turn to receive the Mantzini treatment. He felt a new factor developing in his thoughts, and looking up, he realised that her exquisite face was directed towards him. She smiled, ever so gently, and he also sensed a transient jealousy on Jennifer's part; unreasonably enough, she resented the sudden rapport between himself and this extraordinarily beautiful woman.

"The door was bolted mechanically," he said (or rather found himself saying). "The mechanism controlling the water wheel is linked to the chains and levers attached to the bolts. We all wondered what the arrangement was for, but now I see its purpose. To quote Sir Christopher Trepennick, 'They were intolerant times'. If his brotherhood sought refuge in the crypt and were pursued there, as a last resort they could escape through the mines – it is unlikely that king's men would have had the courage to follow them. Conversely, stannery workers couldn't enter the crypt, even if they weren't scared off by Agravain senior. There may have been more to it than that, but the theory fits the facts. It also explains why there was so much food stored in the crypt."

No one disagreed with this; indeed they all felt somewhat overawed, because what Arthur said now seemed obvious. Only Jennifer sensed the procedure which had unearthed the information from his mind.

"And what do you make of it my dear?" Mantzini asked her. "This crypt is indeed a strange place, and I look forward to seeing it myself, instead of through other people's experience."

Fascinated, Jennifer gazed at Lucilla. As their eyes interlocked, she knew in a moment of both intuition and self-knowledge, that the lady's affections were essentially sapphic. If there were cause for jealousy, Arthur would be the aggrieved one, not herself.

"I agree with Arthur's analysis," she said.

"Mr Agravain?" said Pearl, trying not to sound unduly on edge. "How good to make contact with you by more than reputation. My car is over here, and do please call me Margaret."

He was wary, understandably enough. The transactions purportedly on offer involved biggish money, and were certainly illicit, if not actually illegal. She also had to be wary. A man of his type was probably aware of the nature of noumenal factors in human behaviour; he must not be allowed to sense the sort of ability which she possessed as a gnostic priest. He took his time, but nevertheless, when it came his response was clearly affirmative.

First, he looked her over, noting the smooth taut nylons on good legs, and the short and matchingly tight skirt, bought in London for the occasion. She pushed her bust forward and smiled.

Not that she relished the role that she was playing. By nature she was no Jezebel, and indeed was poles removed from the type of woman who would exploit her sexuality to entrap anyone, even a deeply evil man such as Agravain. Nevertheless, her legal experience had taught her that circumstances altered cases.

"You have an interesting name, Miss Keinach," said Agravain. "I believe it is Welsh for 'Hare'. Maybe you are difficult to catch? But Margaret is less formal. Please call me Hubert." Things might turn out easier than she had thought. If kept sexually aroused he would clearly be off his guard in other directions. Best to keep him simmering. She had purchased a few licentious items from a firm of dealers remembered from her time at the London bar – a priapus and some comparable statuettes of well endowed men and women in immodest detail – risqué, to say the least.

"There are a few minor things in the back of the car," she said. "Fancy a quick peep? I am not naive you know."

He was getting the message – evidence was being offered that this was no confidence trick.

She had positioned two or three of the artefacts on the rear seat of the car, covered by a travelling rug. Opening the rear door, she perched on the seat and leaned across, scissoring her legs to show him her suspenders, together with the white skin above her stocking tops. He was hooked, indeed obviously. The grotesque anatomy of the priapus was barely necessary to complete his arousal. Nevertheless, she smiled coquettishly enough, while exposing the goblin within the semi-privacy of the car.

"It's a trifle public here," she said. "Let's move on to the 'Bull'. I am booked in there, but will run you home later in the evening."

She returned the statuette, bending well forward to offer him her buttocks, before steering him into the front seat. All was well so far. He was too aroused by what he had seen to think about much else. Once out of town, all she had to do was make a quick turn into the agreed side road, and Rosalind's team would take care of the rest. She slid into the driving seat, permitting her short skirt to ride up as she did so, and started the car.

All went well for a mile or two. Then fate intervened. At first the tail-back seemed no more than a mere annoyance as they inched forward in bottom gear, but Pearl found it increasingly hard to maintain her role. It seemed best to keep talking, but on what topic? Salacious wit perhaps? Soon Agravain's hand had found its way onto her knee. Even under the circumstances there were limits on how far she was willing to go, and therefore she felt inclined to remove it. But she was reluctant to diminish his arousal, and so it seemed best to let it remain. Flashing blue lights appeared ahead – nothing much to worry about – obviously there had been an accident. She might be a trifle late at the rendezvous with Rosalind, but the Sarissa would surely wait. And then:

"Police Diversion", read the sign, leaving her no option but to turn off to the right.

Panic at first, but thank goodness; the diversion led into the very road where the van was parked. In fact she could now see it some way ahead, drawn part way onto the grassy verge. Then a new problem came to mind. She was driving in a long slow-moving column; it would hardly do to draw up at the van for people to witness Agravain being forcibly bundled about from one vehicle to another. Better to drive past – Rosalind would surely see her – and follow closely behind until there was an opportunity to turn off at a convenient point for the kidnap to proceed.

Also, the traffic would flow faster once she had passed the van. This was certainly causing an obstruction. The road was a narrow country lane, and normally little used, but now cars were moving in both directions with an unmarshalled contraflow to get past the van. Confound Agravain, he now had his hand half way up her thigh. She had to keep calm, but it made it hard to think clearly. What was that racket coming up from behind? The off-side mirror revealed a motorcyclist – a policeman with his siren wailing. He shot past and stopped at the van. She was now four vehicles behind it, but stationary, while cars came past in the other direction. Perish the constable, he was moving Rosalind on. She could see his mouth moving, obviously in conversation with whoever was driving – probably Arthur. At least Arthur had a British driving licence. Then the van pulled off the verge, and moved forward. Heaven help her, she must overtake it, but there would be no chance along the narrow lane. Moreover, she was not familiar with the local geography, and it was doubtful if Arthur would see her in the mirror. Perhaps it would be best to think ahead to their arrival at the Bull and Griffin; the chances of a successful kidnap as planned seemed increasingly remote.

Agravain's hand was now at the top of her stocking. He was fondling her bare skin, and trying to unfasten her

177

suspender. Why O why had she not put some tights on? It was an insane situation. Here she was, an ordained woman from low heaven, who had led an exemplary earthly life, and yet was now allowing an evil old man liberties far beyond anything which she would have previously tolerated. 'Needs must when the devil drives', seemed appropriate.

"My dear," said Agravain, "why not abandon your booking at the Bull? We are now travelling in the general direction of Clyst Saint Nectan, where my house is. Come home with me. My establishment is efficiently managed, with two housekeepers who will be delighted to provide hospitality. You can telephone the pub from the house, and explain what has happened. It will save some driving, and we shall be able to have any exchange we wish in total privacy." As if to emphasise the suggestion, he moved his hand onto the crotch of her knickers.

"Steady on Hubert," she replied, bringing her legs together and pushing his hand away. "You are taking my attention and may have us up the hedge."

The traffic was flowing faster now with the van out of the way, leaving less time to think. How was she to respond to Hubert's invitation? In the circumstances she could hardly plead modesty, or he would surely smell a rat. The situation was beginning to resemble a Greek tragedy, with herself as the victim. A road junction was now visible a little way ahead. It seemed to be an A road with the traffic turning right. Perhaps she would be able to overtake the van, or at least get close enough for Arthur to see her. Thank heavens Lucilla was available at Saint Catherine's; she had enormous intuition, although a difficulty of communication existed in that Pearl herself had little notion of her present whereabouts. The van was now approaching the junction, where the police motorcyclist was directing traffic. Indeed she could now see the van turning right. All would yet be well.

"Turn left here," said Agravain. "It will take us to Clyst Saint Nectan." Suddenly her mood changed. Clyst Saint Nectan it is, she thought, her sense of confused panic transmuting instantaneously to one of accepted challenge.

CHAPTER XIV
Clyst Saint Nectan

There was a further confusion of traffic at the junction. As Pearl turned left, she noticed an emergency ambulance intermingling with a funeral procession, including a chauffeur-driven Rolls Royce, with a police car escorting the ambulance, blue lights flashing, and all trying to turn right, down the side road. The policeman with the motorbike was doing his best to sort it out, but it was getting dark, and there were vehicles all over the place.

"It must have been quite an accident," said Agravain. "Never mind, soon we shall have you safely home. First we can discuss a few details, and then my lady cook will be ready to give you a supper to remember. I hope you like the house. One of the bedrooms has a four poster, with a big mirror overhead in the tester. The housekeepers are a pair of dyed in the wool lesbians, and very discrete."

Pearl gained little impression of Clyst Saint Nectan, but at first sight the house appeared to consist of a small original structure, which had been added to during Victorian times in a hotch-potch manner. The car belonged to Jennifer, and they parked it in what looked like a converted stable. As a precautionary measure, Pearl had in fact booked a room at the Bull and Griffin, lest a suspicious Agravain telephone the place to check on her, and also, for camouflage, she had located a weekend case on the rear seat. Agravain carried the bag into the house in a somewhat possessive manner, but they left the risqué figurines behind, following a further smirking inspection by the stable lamp. Then he ushered his visitor into a heavily furnished study, before leaving her to her own devices while he gave instructions to his domestics. So Pearl examined his bookshelves. Two of the cabinets were locked, their glazing obscured internally by a fine silk brocade curtaining, but the remainder showed a proliferation of texts, essentially of an occult nature.

Pearl had been careful not to refer to any literature which was beyond her own experience – a wise policy to judge from what was becoming apparent. A grudging respect was unavoidable, at least for the old man's scholarship. Syriac was not one of Pearl's languages, but she recognised a version of the Odes of Solomon, known to her from the Greek translation in the Pistis Sophia. There was much cabbalistic material, but, surprisingly, no copy of the Zohar. But she paid small attention; her mind was working hard. Somehow she had to get a message through to the company. Then Agravain re-entered the room.

"May I use your telephone to call the 'Bull and Griffin'?" she said.

He agreed readily enough, and having apologised for failing to arrive, she left a simple message to be relayed to her 'principals' merely saying that if anyone called, she had gone to Clyst Saint Nectan.

She now had to conduct a negotiation which seemed on the borderline of insanity, by representing a party who did not exist, in selling documents which did not exist, to a man of demonic background, who was versed in the black arts, and desired to further his occult abilities. Moreover, it had become clear that when financial arrangements had been brought to an adequate state of negotiation, he expected sexual freedom of her as part of the bargain. And she was herself much to blame for the position she had got into, having used female allurement to draw the man into an ensnarement. Best to play for time. Given an opportunity to think, Lucilla would work out some suitable tactic.

Delay proved easier than she had thought. At first the conversation went badly. Agravain was indeed interested in the Sophia, but had no wish to purchase the manuscript, merely to have sight of it to confirm that the printed version as offered had been transcribed from a genuine original. As the cost of the copy was comparatively low, he was little concerned about the price. He took a similar attitude over the Zohar – a photocopy would meet his interest. Thus Pearl had no opportunity for a prolonged financial haggle, but it seemed that he wanted to talk. Building from his assumptions on what lay behind their meeting, and her knowledgeability on occult documents, Agravain had come to believe that she was at least a novitiate to the black arts. From this, he appeared to be appraising her as a recruit for his own satanic practices. These included a large erotic element. He desired her not only for his own immediate use, but also as a female acolyte to participate naked in a Luciferan Chapel. Only young woman of high physical desirability and suitable psychological attitude were suitable, he said.

"I lead a small association of adepts," he continued, "and the rewards are considerable if you can be of genuine service to the great ones. Riches and influence will come to you, to say nothing of the heady sense of power which the arts provide. Over events and people. It is good to observe apparent misfortune falling upon those whom you dislike. What say you, my dear? Are you interested? Would you like to know more?"

Playing for time, Pearl replied with a cautiously qualified affirmative, but his response took her unawares.

"Take your clothes off then my dear, and let's have a look at you. Nothing but the best may appear before the Lords Asmodeus and Asfernel, not to forget my friend Archaroch. May I assume that you have no artificial aids, implants or so forth? Do not try to deceive, because they will be detected the first time that Archaroch feels you over."

O dear God, what was she to do? It was a nauseating request, and yet she dared not snub him. Fighting down panic, she slowly unbuttoned her blouse, while he watched her movements with an interested smile. The clock seemed to be ticking never so loudly and slowly as she lowered her skirt, and removed her shoes. Her slip followed, and trying to avoid his growing smirk, she released her suspenders, and removed her belt and stockings. Such was her embarrassment that the hooks of her brassiere seemed reluctant to come undone for her fumbling fingers, but at last the garment fell away.

"Permit me to lower your knickers for you," he said. "You may be a little shy to do so yourself."

And then the study door opened.

The housekeeper showed no sign of surprise at the sight of the now stark naked visitor.

"Supper is ready sir," she said. "If you are otherwise engaged we can keep it hot for a little while —"

"No, no, Phillippa, it's all right thank you. Miss Keinach will dress, and we shall be with you directly. The Tudor Bedroom is made up I take it? Our visitor has not been shown upstairs as yet, but her case is in the hall."

"Will madam require a nightdress sir? I can put something out if I know what is wanted."

183

"You are very considerate Phillippa. No doubt Miss Keinach has one in her case, but perhaps she would like a change. What would you suggest?"

"Perhaps madam would like the green satin. The one slit to the waist with chinchilla fur round the hem. Or there is the rose-pink topless. Madam has exquisite breasts, and it would emphasise her nipples."

"Put both of them out please Phillippa," said Agravain. "Miss Keinach can decide later when she sees them. Now let us proceed to supper."

The repast was indeed of the quality promised by Agravain, indeed amazingly so, considering how little time his domestics had had to prepare it. But poor Pearl was little able to concentrate on the food and wine with which Phillippa plied her. Firstly, she must exploit an opportunity to assess the extent of Agravain's necromantic ability, because he could no doubt be persuaded to show her his Luciferan Chapel and the associated facilities. A little work on his vanity was all that was needed; a modicum of flattery should do the trick. And the information could turn out to be highly valuable. Secondly, she had to think of a procedure to further his kidnap. By now, the company would have deduced where she was, but what would Lucilla expect her to do? Some sort of telepathic communication might be possible, but it was risky. She did not know the extent of Agravain's psychic powers, but no doubt they were considerable, and he might sense something of what was going on. Best to keep him on the boil erotically. His nature was such that he would be able to think of nothing else. But this led her into a further problem. How was she to do this without permitting the final intimacies? Already he had fondled her womanhood while removing her ultimate garment, and Phillippa's expressionless but direct observation during the procedure had exacerbated her humiliation. The thought of full submission was utterly odious. And yet this sacrifice might be something which she would have to accept. She now knew that Agravain was so much aroused by her, that temporarily he was more in her power than she in his. Must she exploit this to the advantage of their cause?

Agravain's thoughts clearly continued to be focused on the licentious, so she led him on with a question on her proposed duties in his diabolical chapel. Dark ritual took diverse forms, as Pearl well knew; quickly she strove to recall lectures from her priestly training, not least a synopsis of the tutorials taken by Hermione in person. Procedures included the so-called Black Mass, in which the Communion Service was said more or less in reverse, often under an inverted or headless crucifix. Strange substances were placed in the chalice, and a naked woman served as an altar, sometimes kneeling on all fours, at right angles to the congregation. The logic of the mass was to win Luciferan favour by performing acts of extreme sacrilege, believed to be pleasing to the dark lords. However, this seemed to Pearl to be a coarse and primitive procedure for the sophisticated likes of Hubert Agravain. Enquiry made it clear that she was indeed correct.

"May I see your chapel?" she said. "I expect that it forms an eminently appropriate setting for the most elegant of liturgies!"

He was flattered, so much so that vanity temporarily overcame erotic desire, and he readily agreed to show her round.

It was a great rambling house, constructed to avoid any arrangement of floors on distinct levels, and thus she was led through a bewildering labyrinth of interlocking rooms and passages that seemed to be devoid of logical lay-out. In addition to several short flights of stairs, there were corridors with slight slopes, oddly angled corners in unexpected places, and long mirrors, at least some of which had been curved to give a false sense of perspective. Twice she thought that a corridor existed where in fact there was none, and one room proved to be of dimensions quite different from the impression gained on first entering it. Thoughts of the Chaos came into her mind – that place of dreadful habitation on the further side of the Amente where rationality ceased to exist. Agravain sensed her confusion, and was clearly satisfied to note it.

"You like my house, my dear? It grows on people with our sort of temperament, and given time I fancy that you would learn to enjoy the sense of escape from the accepted spatial rules. It generates this in sympathetic minds. Wait until you see your bathroom; I look forward to our later evening."

But the architectural peculiarities were as nothing compared to the chapel itself. At first the room seemed square, yet it was not square. None of the angles were at exactly ninety degrees. The ceiling swept up into a dome, but the apex was not central; the thing was slightly lob-sided. Curving lines on the ceiling twisted into interlocking whorls and wreaths, which at first seemed to form a pattern. But as the eye followed the arrangement, the pattern broke up, and either disappeared or reformed into a different system, which in turn dissolved if one attempted to follow it. Sometimes the lines began to coalesce to form a recognisable object, a flower or a small animal, or an image which was vaguely suggestive or even obscene, but in all cases any attempt to concentrate on such met with irritating failure. The same sort of thing was continued elsewhere. There were several caryatids, one of which was enclosed in what looked like writhing snakes, and there were wall paintings showing impossible mechanical effects; thus a river appeared to flow circuitously around the fresco, although logic dictated that part of its course had to be uphill. The floor alone was normal, consisting of an elaborate mosaic depicting people and animals in some sort of macabre dance.

Suddenly, Pearl had the measure of it. The thing was a parody of physical laws. The powers of Celestial Christianity were, as she well knew, not limited by the restrictions on time and space which applied to their earthly contemporaries. Dimensions were involved beyond the three familiar to her earthly friends, and the divine authorities could move and communicate along pathways which appeared inexplicable or even miraculous to the earthly mind, but in fact followed laws of a higher physical reality. Indeed, Louise and Hermione had endeavoured to explain this to the company, albeit with indifferent success; but Agravain's chapel was adorned in a twisted parody of the same. The devil was lies, and the father of lies. This distortion of the reality was designed to act upon the minds of initiates, persuading them to accept false hypotheses, and through these to worship both him, and much of what he stood for. Ignorance was the underlying root of evil, but this technique fortified ignorance by a distorted parody of the truth, worse than mere blind ignorance in itself.

Furthermore, this twisting of initiates within the dark areas of their minds, was intended to condition them for the more blatant satanism to be enacted within the chapel – for their benefit, or enslavement, depending on how you looked at it. The rituals would presumably be based upon a mixture of sadism and sexual obscenity; but Pearl now found that alternative thoughts were stirring in her mind.

"One form of Ceremonial Magic," she said, "controls demons by diverting higher powers of Christian origin to compel the demons' obedience to you as their master. A dangerous game, but highly rewarding to those who have the stomach for it."

It was clear that she had struck home. He looked at her searchingly, but made no reply for several seconds. She realised that the man's pride and deep seated arrogance made him desire that such as Archaroch be subservient to him, and not the other way round. Meanwhile further thoughts flocked into her mind, seemingly uncontrolled, and growing into a ferment racing about at increasing speed. 'Saint Nectan, Saint Nectan's Glen, Saint Nectan's Well' – there seemed no logic; indeed how had she come to be aware that the Glen and Well even existed? Nectan, she knew, was a major Celtic character. He had several dedications, including some in Brittany. Also, he was of Arthurian background, being a son of the legendary King Brychan. He had died a martyr's death; something to do with cattle rustling – obviously a hardy man. Moreover he was a brother of Saint Keyne, which virgin lady had endowed a Holy Well with the curious power of granting dominance to women, apart from converting people to the Christian faith.

"Go to my brother's well," Keyne seemed to be willing her; "Go to the well, to the well, TO THE WELL; and we shall be there."

"Tell me, Hubert," said Pearl, "what do you know of Saint Nectan? I believe that there is a famous well and waterfall dedicated to him hereabouts. Do not underestimate the power of these Celtic saints, nor forget that in their time Christianity was more broadly interpreted than it is today. They were not above using ghostly authority to make a potin or two, or bothering about whose side they were on in the process" – it was as if someone were talking for her, but through her lips – "I believe that his waterfall is fed by a hot spring, some source recently assessed during the Cornish geothermal energy project" – Pearl barely knew what geothermal energy was, but the words came spilling out. "Fancy a moonlight bathe, in the nude of course?"

Agravain continued to hesitate. Pearl grasped that while he was not averse to her suggestion for its own sake, he was trying to work out whether she was implying something further – namely that she knew how to invoke Nectan to their diabolical advantage. Was she making him some sort of offer? (In a sense this was correct, if not in the way that he thought.) So now it was his turn to play for time.

"Why not?" he said. "A moonlight saunter, followed by fornication in the Holy Waters of a Holy Well! We can discuss other matters a little later. I like your style my dear; we are going to get on famously!"

"Come on then," said Pearl. "Let's take my car. I think my case is still in the hall; we can share a towel."

Saint Nectan's Glen proved to be a long narrow defile, with a stream and path under overhanging trees. Intermittent moonlight shone between drifting clouds, while a moderate breeze stirred the trees, although all was dank and still along the floor of the ravine. It was a brooding sort of place. Clearly, the Glen was psychically active, and the atmosphere affected them both, although in different ways. Agravain appeared to be stimulated by this, and developed an anticipatory excitement surprising for an older man. Probably he thought that he was about to combine an extension of his arts with a stimulating act of sexual sacrilege, using a woman who would be a willing and unusual partner. Pearl recognised that there was much latent energy about and believed that this would be applied to her assistance, but despite her gnostic background, and unlike Agravain, she found it somewhat frightening, and indeed had to steel herself to walk onward without showing dismay. Twice, Agravain paused to fondle her. Perhaps this helped, because it prompted her to discourage his hungry fingering by urging him on towards the waterfall and well.

"Wait until you've got me in the pool," she said.

So they moved slowly forward. It was indeed dark under the trees, and they had no torch, but presently the sound of the waterfall became apparent, and they emerged into a small clearing where the cascade came tumbling down into a sizeable pool. There was more light here, with the moon riding high above the trees, but Pearl's fear intensified. Nectan was buried behind the waterfall, and the Communion was with her. Victory she believed would be hers, but to achieve it had she to sacrifice her chastity to this vile man? The moment of truth was fast approaching. She stood almost motionless as his eager fingers removed first her garments and then his own; a quick naked grapple, and they plunged together into the pool.

Even as he fondled her, she looked up towards the summit of the fall, and saw, or thought she saw, two figures standing side by side, a man and a woman, not against the moon, but with the light obliquely upon them. Within the instant, she knew what she must do.

"Hubert Agravain," she said, placing her hands upon the back of his neck, and speaking in the Greek use, "I baptise you in the name of the Holy Trinity, Father, Son and Paraclete, and thus enchain the demonic entities within you. Also, I subjugate you to my will, through the power of my friends and allies, Saint Nectan and Saint Keyne, whose spirits haunt this place." And she pushed him under the water, before he could reply.

He surfaced, spluttering, probably more confused than anything; but there was more to come.

"I mark you with the sign of the Cross," she said, drawing the symbol on his forehead with her wet finger.

And then she knew, in a manner which went beyond knowing, that within the Glen he was powerless. Her ancient friends held him in fetters that surpassed logic, but from which he could in nowise break free – she had the mastery of him.

"What fantasy is this…?" Agravain began, but found that his tongue froze between his teeth. His face was indistinct in the moonlight, although she fancied he had an expression verging on the catatonic.

"Get out of the water, and dress," said Pearl.

He obeyed instantly, but even as she spoke, she realised that a tall man and a woman had appeared nearby: dark figures, looming out from the shadow of the trees. Agravain had also seen them, and stood stock still, shivering naked in the moonlight.

"So, we meet again, Mr Agravain." The voice was that of Georgina Burton-Coggles.

There was no need for Arthur's support, nor indeed for any physical pressure by Georgina. Wretchedly enough, the terrified necromancer dragged his clothes onto his wet body, and suffered himself to be led meekly away down the glen.

CHAPTER XV.
The Wisdom of the Just

"How did you find me?" asked Pearl, as Arthur sent the van rolling back to Trepennick Chase, the kidnapped Agravain safely in custody, and with Jenny driving her own car.

"Not too difficult, Donna," replied Rosalind. "Lucilla seemed to know more or less what was happening by using her own methods, but apart from that, a little deductive reasoning plus your telephone message at the Bull and Griffin sorted it out. Also, we had the rearguard in Laura's Rolls Royce, and they spotted you at the Saint Nectan junction. So we drove on to Saint Nectan, parked at an observational distance from Chateau Agravain, and in due course followed you to the glen. You can guess the rest for yourself."

"Surely, but how did Arthur and Georgina get to the top of the waterfall?"

"They weren't at the top of the fall. Nobody was. You saw them yourself, down by the pool. None of us was anywhere else. What puzzles me, is how you got the better of the old man. I thought that you must have bashed him with a rock, but he shows no marks."

Pearl decided to say no more on the subject; not at least until she had spoken to Hermione. So she changed the topic.

"Does Lucilla still intend to have Agravain into the crypt? How are we to get inside? I don't fancy heaving that slab up again, and lowering him down the hole."

"It would be poetic to throw him down," Rosalind replied. "But Lucilla and Louise were proposing to open the door from the outside by borrowing the chauffeur's portable drill and hole saw. My opinion is that they will have the door open by now – easy enough to put your hand through some holes and ease the bolts back. Pity to hack the old woodwork about, but needs must I suppose."

Lucilla's party assembled in the rotunda. She herself; Ystelle, Hermione, Michelle, the two Sarissa Majors, and of course Agravain himself. Poor Hubert, bewildered by the labyrinthine entrance via Rosalind's Adit, he could not readily appreciate the significance of his surroundings, or indeed even where he was.

Hermione began:

"Mr Agravain, as you know, I am a priest in the service of Catharine of Lyonesse. We wish you no harm by Christian standards, rather that you renounce your satanic practices for a virtuous life. In fact it is within our ability to force this upon you, but force is forbidden. The volition must come from yourself."

She paused. The crypt candles burned steadily in their sconces, the lioness stood as still as ever upon her granite plinth. Agravain said nothing, but they were aware of the atmosphere of the place pressing in upon his dissolute mind. Lucilla read the mixture of alarm and incredulity temporarily within him. And yet the man was no coward. Even in dire circumstances he retained a professional interest in what was taking place.

"Where am I?" he asked.

"In the crypt of Saint Catherine's Church."

"What do you want of me? Christian conversion is out of the question. I worship Lucifer, the great angel of light."

"Maybe, but my Orders are from a higher authority than yours. To answer your question, we require information on the tactics of your Amentan allies. Their strategy is already known to us. Having failed in their initial attempt to seize the Spear of Longinus, they propose to lure us into a trap, by bending the rules of space and time. So they seek a contest to defeat us. Indeed to take possession of us, earthly Christians and Lyonelles alike, in addition to securing the Spear for themselves. You, their major earthly confederate, are aware of this. It is you who knows, and we know that you know. The Meneniuses are of lesser account."

"This is fantasy. No Amentan lord in his senses would go to the expense and trouble of such a harebrained scheme. Be reasonable. If you intend to use me ill, so be it, but do not trifle with my intelligence."

As previously arranged, Lucilla now took over the interrogation. He was lying, desperately so, as she well knew. He still feared the dark lords far more than the Christians, and believed that if he betrayed them to save his skin, retribution would be dreadful beyond words. Therefore, she thought, push him hard at once, before he had time to discipline his thoughts into a series of plausible lies, and then impregnate these into his deeper mind to resist her interrogation.

"Beware Hubert. You have recently experienced the power of Celtic Saints. This is but little compared to the resources within this crypt. Open your mind to me now, and we shall help protect you from the consequences. I am Lucilla Mantzini, High Admiral of Lyonesse, and I give you my word."

He became stubborn, perhaps to gain time.

"How can someone like you protect someone like me from the supernatural might of the Amente? Why should I believe you?"

Lucilla did not argue.

"We shall continue this interview in the Presence Chapel," she said.

Agravain found himself gripped between the two Sarissa Majors, his hands pinioned behind him by a webbing sling from a carbine rifle. Hermione was now fully vested, and standing beside Lucilla, who was breaking naval regulations by wearing her Saint Catherine's Cross, resplendent on the bosom of her admiral's uniform. Ystelle and Michelle waited to the rear, as the Sarissas propelled Agravain into the vestibule of the Chapel, towards Hermione and Lucilla, awaiting them at the inner doors. The candles burned steadily enough, but all of the women were conscious of a force similar to that experienced during the company's first attempt at entering the Chapel. Precisely what Agravain thought could not be discerned. Hermione opened the double doors, entered the Chapel, and lit the altar candles.

The remainder of the company were little affected by her action, but poor Agravain, white in face and trembling in limb, he shrank back within the grasp of the Sarissas who constrained him. Lucilla knew that his inner energy was absorbed in resisting the forces of the Chapel, and gently enough, she slid her own psyche into his mind. At first he barely recognised this, merely becoming aware of a moderating influence which seemed to be regulating the otherwise terrifying impact of the Chapel. He became calmer, and the Sarissas moved him forward towards Hermione and the altar. Lucilla continued to control the pressure upon him, but he now realised that she could withdraw this protection at any moment.

"Hubert," she said. "The entities within this place are not at war with you as such, but rather with the satanic power within you. Your involvement with the Amentans is an

195

expression of the latter. Rid yourself of this, and you also rid yourself of the hostility contained within this Chapel."

Both she and Hermione sensed that he was overwhelmed, not entirely by fear, but also by perceiving that at the deepest level, Lucilla wished him no personal harm. This factor both surprised and startled him; notions of charity were alien to his thoughts. What was he to do? This devastating woman had him in her power, and he dare not, could not trifle with her. Moreover, it was only recently that the Amentans had discovered that the Christians had not perished within the crypt, but were in fact all alive and as he now realised, becoming belligerent. News of their escape had much annoyed Archaroch and his peers. Gold had been expended to no purpose, and more importantly, there had been a loss of face – a major matter in the Amente where pride was a maximum virtue. A furious reaction to the Christians was in hand, indeed he was involved in it. They were to be entrapped, enslaved, and subject to ongoing humiliation. If he betrayed the plans, he would be subject to the utmost ferocity of Amentan wrath. But what if he managed to outwit this extraordinary woman, and the enterprise failed nevertheless? He would be left on the wrong side. Samuel Mordecai and his contemptible group of parishioners was one thing. Catharine of Lyonesse was a different matter. Should he change sides? This seemed to be more or less what Lucilla was suggesting to him. But he was underestimating the lady.

"Hubert," she said. "Do not think of trying any hounding and hareing with me. You are considering changing sides to save your own skin. Don't. We can extract the information from your mind by applying psychic force. Alternatively, you can provide it of your own volition, and seek the protection which we can provide. But this must involve a genuine change of outlook, and no attempts at cheating. Your mind is transparent to me, so abandon all thoughts of duplicity."

Agravain made no reply for several seconds. He was over a barrel. He knew enough theology to recognise that Mantzini would not force his conversion, even though she might have the spiritual resources to do so. It was against rules which she was not allowed to break. And yet if he did not, as she would put it 'repent', he would be forced to give information inimical to his interests with the Amentans, apart from being mentally annihilated by the entities in the Chapel. But any repentance, and change of sides, would have to be sincere. And how could he himself be sure of what he truly believed? Mantzini would know if he were less than honest, she could see into his mind, even into the darkest recesses barely known to himself.

It was from these recesses that his answer came. A further presence became apparent in his mind. This did not pressurise him, as did Lucilla, but encouraged him to explore his own nature, looking back to earlier years before he became a confirmed Satanist. Nothing was said for several seconds. Then he realised that Hermione strove to help him.

"Hubert," she said. "People can be roughly divided into three types. Two small groups, the exceptionally good, and the exceptionally bad, and then a much larger group, the Psychikoi, or men of the middle, who may incline to either good or bad according to circumstance or influence. I believe that you are one of these last, and I would aid you with empathy and compassion."

Suddenly, and to his own surprise, he gave way, overwhelmed by an influence which he could not understand. The Sarissas released their hold, and he knelt before the priest.

"Bless me Mother, for I have sinned," he said.

"Eulogia kusiou kai elios elthoi elphumas te autou Theia chasiti kai philanthropia pantote nun un kai aei eis tous aionoas ton aionon."[12] replied Hermione; he was fluent in Greek, as she well knew. She continued, using the ancient Lyonesse liturgy, not dissimilar to that of Saint John Chrysostom. Agravain was as clay in her hands. Both she and Lucilla knew that their victory was complete.

"Our joint enemy," said Agravain, next day, as they met in Laura's library, "proposes to lure you into underground chambers I know not where, but within the mine, bringing the Spear with you. This will be done by sending the Meneniuses to you as emissaries, offering a negotiation. They will claim that items of great value and interest are interred down the mine, in such a way that they can only be recovered using cosmic powers invested in the Spear. Thus the Amentans will argue that they have the information, but we have the Spear. Therefore, they will say, let bygones be bygones, and let us co-operate to mutual advantage. Plausible enough it seems to me."

"But what," said Arthur, "would happen if we accepted the offer, and went with them into the mine as you suggest? Presumably with the resources which Ystelle and Louise have available, the enemy could hardly expect to overpower us."

"True. At least in the way that they expect you to think. Firstly, they would haggle over how many of you should accompany the Meneniuses; this to put you off your guard. Secondly, they would give way to your demands, so, thirdly, leaving you with a false sense of security. In fact, numbers might give little advantage because of the enemy moving events into a different aeon by necromantic means."

"What form is the proposed shift to take?" asked Louise.

---

[12] The blessing of the Lord be upon you by His divine grace and love for mankind, until the ages of ages. H. de Lamarac.

"That I cannot readily explain. This sort of thing is beyond the resources of earthly Satanists, but not I assure you of the Amentans."

"So, presumably we are intended to walk in like sheep through Rosalind's Adit or wherever, carrying the Spear, to find ourselves at the mercy of a powerful Amentan force in another locality and time frame. Thence we are removed to the Amente, and a hellish fate."

"More or less," agreed Hubert, laconically enough. "They have a plan of the mine. I gave it to them."

"I am aware," said Samuel, scratching his head, "that my Celestial Allies are determined to bring the conflict to a final conclusion, and although a peacemaker by nature, I appreciate their point of view. But surely, it would be stupid to proceed along such lines as the Amentans will ask."

Lucilla joined in: "They haven't asked anything yet. I need to talk to the Meneniuses. We receive them with tact and caution; noting their proposals, but insisting on some little delay to consider the same. Also, Hubert requires time to renew his contacts. He should return to Saint Nectan before he is unduly missed. Therefore we take him home, and await the Menenius' pleasure."

(Eight days later)

The Bell & Anchor Hotel
South Parade
Penzance
Cornwall

17-4-1982

Revd. Samuel Mordecai, M.A., D.D.,
The Rectory,
Church Lane
Saint Catherines
Cornwall

<u>In confidence</u>.

Dear Reverend sir,

Though I speak with the tongues of men and angels, and have not charity, I am become as a sounding brass or a tinkling cymbal. My cousin and I look back with sorrow over the events of the past few weeks, and reflect with the utmost sadness on the extent of the dreadful misunderstanding which has developed between us. Our original approach to your excellent self was made, I assure you, with the most sincere hope that a rational agreement could be reached to further our mutual benefit by exploring the ancient resources undoubtedly associated with the Church of which you have the honour to be the incumbent. Unfortunately, we then failed fully to explain the objectives of our proposed activities in this connection, which resulted in an understandably negative reaction on your part. One thing led to another, and a degree of hostility developed, for which I must freely and readily admit, we are partly responsible. However, I would humbly request you to appreciate that this was largely caused by the malign influence of Hubert Agravain Esquire, who is not party to this present communication. We understand that you also have suffered malign influence from the misguiding interference of persons from beyond the veil, and would respectfully remind you of the Witch of Endor, and the fate which may await those who attempt to further their interests by such means.

It is known to both of us, that an article of great historical significance was long since committed for safe keeping to a crypt beneath your Saint Catherine's Church, and that this article, namely a Roman Spear with biblical associations is presently in your hands. What is known to me, but I fancy not to your good self, is that there are other valuable items interred within nearby tin workings, and that these goods are likely to be of mutual interest. They include Arthurian artefacts wrought in precious metals, altar furniture from the Celtic Church, and vellum manuscripts of unknown but contemporary content. Substantial monetary value is involved, but, and perhaps more importantly to yourself, the religious and historical importance of what is at stake could also be of great concern.

We are aware of the location of this wealth, but there are metaphysical factors involved in its recovery. These I feel unable to describe in detail; suffice it to say that there are obstacles which can only be overcome by the cosmic forces associated with the Spear.

Therefore I would suggest a meeting to discuss the position. At present we see through a glass darkly, but I feel sure that with a modicum of goodwill between us a rational agreement can be reached, much to the benefit of all concerned. My cousin and I shall give ourselves the honour of calling on you at the Rectory, one week hence (24th of the month) at ten o'clock in the morning, when in the lack of any communication to the contrary, we confidently trust that you will be able to receive us.

With every cordial sincerity,
Charles Menenius.

Slowly and carefully, Samuel read the letter to the companions, which now included Hubert. (Both Lucilla and Hermione were unreservedly confident of him, following his experience in the Chapel.)

"Well," observed Laura, "one has to admit that they've got cheek. People say that the devil quotes scripture to his purpose, but for sheer audacity, that letter takes the cake. Cordial sincerity indeed! What do you make of it Hubert?"

"An embarrassing question, considering that I wrote it. Do not let us get into a fury over the perfidiousness of the other side. The question is how to react to them."

"With premeditated duplicity." It was Lucilla who spoke. "They ask for a meeting with Samuel, but can hardly object if he asks his lady secretary to be present. The cousins have never seen me, and I shall wear civilian clothes. Perhaps they'll think I'm the Witch of Endor."

CHAPTER XVI
Through Pillared Halls

"It is good of you to receive us," said Percival Menenius, following some preliminary civilities. "Charles and I would have preferred to talk to you as men talk to men, but we have no objection to the presence of your secretary. Is she a local lady?"

Lucilla assumed her most bewitching smile:

"I wasn't born here, but my heart is firmly established in Cornwall" – true enough, so far as it went. At least the cousins seemed satisfied by her reply.

Samuel began:

"Your letter suggests co-operation in the recovery of valuable articles from a tin mine. What exactly have you in mind?"

"Celtic jewellery, mainly in gold and semi-precious stones, weapons and armour, some of it ceremonial and richly ornamented, possibly including swords mentioned in the Morte d'Arthur. Chalices and altar candlesticks in silver or silver gilt, and such-like church plate. There are also manuscripts which may contain direct information on the historical Arthur. I have to say that we are not fully informed ourselves; there is no reliable inventory." Samuel and Lucilla had to restrain their amusement. Agravain had certainly briefed them thoroughly! Samuel continued:

"So you believe that these things can be recovered using the Spear of Longinus? We are aware of the extraordinary paranormal forces associated with Saint Catherine's Crypt, but your proposal involves a change of location. How certain are you of the facts?"

"I assure you Reverend sir, that we are as confident as it is possible to be under circumstances such as we have here. Moreover, what have you to lose in the event of failure?"

And so it drivelled on. Samuel felt guilty at the subterfuge of his tactics. Not so Lucilla. She was better informed than he on the extreme evil of the Amentans. The Meneniuses were small fry by comparison, but were well capable of doing the bidding of their demonic masters. It was agreed that Samuel, his 'secretary', Arthur, Ystelle and Rosalind would conduct Charles and Percival into the mine, entering by Rosalind's Adit. They would then ascend to the crypt, permit the cousins to witness the removal of the false spear from the Presence Chapel, and (having foisted it onto the Meneniuses) invite them to co-operate in removing it to the lower area of the mine, where, so Agravain reported, a spatial transfer would be forced upon the Christians. The true Spear was to be entrusted to Georgina and the Myrmidons. Unfortunately for the Amentans, the transfer was partly dependant upon the cosmic forces associated with the true Spear. Hermione and Lucilla would not prevent a transfer. Instead, they would insure that it did not work out in the way that the Amentans intended. Also, Hermione, Georgina, and a substantial force of the Brocelliande Myrmidons were to be stationed at a suitable point in the mine.

It was clear, at least to Lucilla, that the Meneniuses felt a degree of trepidation as they entered the mine, even though, according to Agravain, they had some indirect knowledge of the place. Not that they were intimidated by the company. On the contrary, it was something to do with the atmosphere of the old workings. Maybe no more than a reaction to the darkness and claustrophobia of the underground passages and confined rushing waters, but she fancied that ancient Celtic forces, benevolent to her, but not to the cousins, were also involved. The Myrmidons had been concealed fully armed within the 'Great cathedral of a cavern', (as described by Rosalind) and here the Meneniuses hurried onward, even though they merely passed the entrance. Not that they feared an overt assault; rather a vague undefined hostility.

Lucilla thought of the 'Lamps within the pillared halls of time', described in Arthur's skytail. She glanced briefly into the cavern. It appeared to have had doors fitted during some earlier epoch – a few pieces of decayed timber hung onto rusting hinge pins. Within, she had a momentary glimpse of a twin arcade of carved pillars, reaching upwards to an unseen roof. It was obvious that the cavern had precious little to do with tin mining; it had been contrived for an alternative purpose. Presently, they reached the crypt, but Samuel refrained from showing the cousins much of it, leading them directly to the Presence Chapel.

They baulked at entering the chapel, so Rosalind held open the inner doors, while Ystelle walked up to the altar, picked up the false spear, and returning, presented it to Percival. He and Charles inspected it with considerable awe.

"A great pity that Hubert Agravain cannot be here," observed Percival, "but alas he is indisposed. Fortunately a procedure was intimated to us two or three weeks ago."

Then Charles caught his eye, and he said no more.

"Let us ask our new friends to accompany us to the third level," said Charles.

The company agreed readily enough, and thus they returned down the staircases.

The ladies went first, followed by Percival, now permitted to carry the spear, leaving Charles, Arthur and Samuel to bring up the rear; with Percival a trifle inconvenienced by his burden. Slowly and carefully, they descended the whirlpool stairs, the men falling increasingly behind the women, until they reached the transverse walk (where earlier Jennifer had come to the aid of Arthur).

"We are to look out for the Mithraic Altar," said Percival. "Then follow a passageway to the left, onto a downward stairway which descends to the third level, whereafter the vibrancy associated with the Spear will direct us to an alternative exit."

They found the Mithraic Altar followed by the descending steps, and so strode on confidently enough, with Charles now in the lead. Percival followed close behind. At first the duo seemed to be following memorised instructions, but presently it became clear (at least to Lucilla) that they were out of their bearings. This did not much concern her. Clearly, there was the hazard of getting lost in the mine workings, but their route had not been too complex for it to be retraced to the whirlpool stairs. Soon Charles came to a halt, and there was a muted conversation between the cousins; they seemed to be expecting the spear to direct them, somewhat after the fashion of a water diviner's hazel twig. Lucilla permitted them to mutter together for a minute or so, and then offered some persuasive 'help':

"Perhaps we she should go back a little, and try to pick up a lead that was missed previously because of undue enthusiasm."

The cousins reluctantly agreed, and thus she gained further advantage. Her objective was not to block the Amentans' strategy entirely, but to divert their offensive in a manner which would give the Christians a final victorious result. Archaroch was presumably following the activities of the Meneniuses and directing them by some form of psychic link, but the devil alone knew exactly what he was about. So cautiously, she began to infiltrate Percival's mind, edging her persona into his unconscious as gently as a moonbeam into fog. At this level of telepathy, she found no definitive thoughts, merely a murky pool of unformed notions superimposed on ingrained ideas. Archaroch's influence was also present (although unrecognised by Percival), and this factor exacerbated the tension within him. The spear was not performing as expected, and Archaroch was annoyed. But she had to be careful. Easy enough to dupe the Meneniuses, but Archaroch must also suspect nothing, and he was a different kettle of fish. A moment's concentration served to stimulate Percival's arm muscles so that the spear seemed to give a pronounced upward jerk of its own accord. But contrary to what she had expected, he promptly dropped the weapon.

"The damn thing's alive," he said. "I'm scared of it."

Lucilla sensed Archaroch's reaction – relief that the spear was becoming active, and irritation with Percival for a fatuous response.

"Pick it up again," said Charles, 'and don't be an idiot. We're getting somewhere at last. Hang on hard, and see what happens next."

"Proceed"; an apparently spontaneous notion sprang up in Percival's mind, although neither he nor Archaroch suspected that Lucilla had introduced it. The message was what they wanted to receive, and was therefore not closely questioned. But how or when would Archaroch make his move? Not yet awhile, Lucilla thought. He wanted to get his clutches on the rest of the company, Hermione in particular, but nevertheless, Lucilla realised that Percival also anticipated action – he was looking forward to witnessing the humiliation of the Christians, and receiving his promised rewards.

And then it became clear to her that Archaroch himself was becoming confused, and therefore vulnerable. Best to force his hand. She decided to lead the party towards Rosalind's Adit, and thus to an exit from the mine. Percival continued to believe that the seemingly spontaneous gyrations of the spear, with parallel indications arising in his mind, were derived from the evil force associated with the true weapon. Thus Lucilla found it simple to edge him towards the adit.

So they proceeded backward in a series of stops and starts, moving upward from the third level with poor Percival becoming increasingly agitated. The Christians were also aware of a growing tension within their own faction, although this was somewhat relieved by the unexpected appearance of Jennifer Parsloe, coming towards them along the gallery, hurricane lamp in hand.

"Hullo folks," she said. "I have a message for Arthur, but it can wait for a minute. Carry on exploring."

It was clear to the Christians that she did not wish to speak in front of the Meneniuses, who in fact took little notice of her, being fully occupied with the spear.

Jennifer's arrival broke the continuity of the recent events, indeed so much so that for a time the ambience of the party approached that of carnival. It seemed that the whole venture had gone off somewhat at half cock, and that shortly they would all emerge from Rosalind's Adit with the situation no different from when they had entered it. Until they reached the entrance to the pillared cavern. For no pillared hall was visible; where previously the portal had been graced by no more than a few shards of decaying timber on rusting hinge pins, now there were substantial wooden doors, well made from oak planks, and furnished with heavy wrought-iron fittings.

Lucilla thought fast. Clearly, Archaroch had arranged a relocation in time, similar to the recent business at Langarrow.

But what reaction did the necromancer expect of them? There were three possibilities: continue forwards to the adit, retreat, or open the doors of the pillared cavern, and enter. Percival's mind was almost gelatinous with glee, but he seemed to expect retreat – a flight backward into the depths of the old workings. Therefore – press ahead!

"How fascinating," she said. "The spear certainly has some extraordinary powers. No doubt we shall soon be shown the secret treasure. What are its instructions now?"

Percival hesitated. The spear waved around in circles, and then pointed towards the entrance to the adit.

"This way," he replied, and they were off again along the gallery.

Soon they reached the open end of Rosalind's Adit, although both the wooden door and the brickwork closing off the arch had disappeared. And there they stood; looking out from the archway, to find themselves viewing a countryside different from that remembered. The overall form of the landscape was unaltered, but there were more trees, and the neat stone walls and orderly arrangement of Saint Catherine's Lane had disappeared. Now there was merely a rough track leading away from the adit, with the stream flowing along a meandering bed, unlike the straightened channel which they remembered. But there they did not remain for long. A horde of men was proceeding towards them, and it was immediately apparent that the mob was hostile; at least to the Christians. Not so with Charles and Percival. They ran towards the newcomers, spear brandished triumphantly, and exchanged greetings with the leaders of the horde. Arthur and Jennifer recognised several ruffians from their experience at Langarrow, but it seemed unwise to hang about, and the Christians fled back along the adit with all the haste which they could make. Fortunately, by now they were reasonably familiar with the route, and thus made better time than the pursuing mob, Arthur and Rosalind assisting Samuel to a fair turn of speed.

Lucilla recalled that by Hubert's account, the Amentans' plot was to lure the Christians into the depths of the mine, and there force a spatial transfer upon them. However, contrary to what was expected, the Christians had emerged from the mine. Probably Archaroch had the brute force of the Langarrow mob already available, and hence was using it to drive the Christians in the direction that he wanted. So, Lucilla reasoned, she had two tactics available. Either she could lead her party into the pillared cavern, or retreat further to the crypt. The narrow whirlpool stairway could easily be defended; Ystelle had her automatic and six clips of ammunition, and there were plenty of rocks to hurl down the steps. Moreover, the penstock was shortly due to fall; the resulting flood would drown both the Meneniuses and the Langarrow lot. But the pillared cavern seemed the better option. She knew that Hermione and the Myrmidons were immune to Archaroch's actions; they would still be on station as arranged. And Georgina had the true Spear.

And so they fled. Ystelle brought up the rear, pausing occasionally to drag odd pieces of debris into the path. The enemy was provided with lanterns, but the resulting illumination was of indifferent quality, and it was clear that they were making a slow pursuit. Soon, Lucilla was raising the latch on the double doors. The leaf refused to open; the doors appeared to be bolted on the inside.

"Hermione," she called. "Open up please, it's I, Lucilla."

The door opened slightly, revealing Georgina Burton-Coggles, handgun at the ready. They slipped in rapidly, and Georgina rebolted the door, which was secured both by iron bolts into floor sockets, and a massive wooden bar which dropped into slots affixed onto both of the leaves.

"Thank you, Sarissa Major," said Lucilla. "There may be an assault on the door at any moment. Can you get your women into position?"

"Yes Donna. We have anticipated something of the sort, and have plenty of fire power."

She gave a brief command, and Lucilla saw the Myrmidons take up stations one behind each of the nearer pillars, handguns directed towards the doors. Some of their lamps were extinguished, leaving the doorway well illuminated, but little light elsewhere.

Lucilla took stock of the situation. Georgina, she knew, was a highly competent Sarissa Major, with twelve Myrmidons under her charge. Her troops were heavy infantry. Besides firearms, they carried grenades, and short stabbing sabres. Their firearms were truly dreadful weapons. Known as 'Dragon Guns', each had a pair of superimposed barrels. The upper was a small calibre self-loading carbine, dimensionally identical to those carried by Ystelle's light infantry. The lower barrel resembled a cross between a pump action shotgun and a blunderbuss. Each cartridge contained twenty-eight lead bullets about the size of peas, and at short range the effect could be devastating. At twenty yards, Georgina had calculated, the charge would scatter more or less over the area of the doorway. Heaven help the men of Langarrow if they forced their way in!

But there was little time for reflection. Noises in the gallery indicated that the enemy was without. Lucilla stood with her ear against the planks, but the timber was thick, and she could only hear unconnected noises.

"Try this Donna," said Georgina, and gave her a thin metal mug from an army water bottle.

By pressing the base of the mug against the door, and placing her ear in the cavity, Lucilla found that she could hear a surprising amount of what was going on. There was a lot of confused talking, but she able to discern an argument between the cousins, and a man who appeared to be the leader of the Langarrow faction. His name sounded something like Colgrin Sturmey, and the dispute was to do with opening the door to the cavern. Both the mob and the Meneniuses were expecting the supernatural force within the spear to achieve this for them indirectly, by compelling obedience on the part of the Christians. Some notion to this effect was being communicated to Charles by Archaroch, but Charles was unable to interpret exactly what the necromancer was instructing him to do. Thus a demonic procedure was thought necessary to mobilise this aspect of the weapon's resources. Considering the general rumpus going on outside the door, the poor communication was scarcely surprising, although of course even if Charles got the message, the spear would not function thus, because they had the wrong spear.

"Lend me a mug, someone please," said Hermione, and accepting one from a trooper, she joined Lucilla at the door.

"Odd that Archaroch did not brief them beforehand," was Hermione's first comment.

"Not so," Lucilla replied. "The Amentan mind always fears treachery, and the necromancer would not want to be too forthcoming with his earthly allies, in case they rebelled in their own interests, and used the information against him. Also, Agravian is supposedly their lead man, not the cousins."

"Sturmey, can't you get your men to shut up," Charles was heard to shout, "I'm trying to concentrate."

The excitement died down somewhat, and then:

"Why not break the doors in sir," replied Sturmey. "They're strong, but there's plenty of us, and they're not so strong as all that."

Georgina had now joined the eavesdroppers.

"Why don't we open the door," she said, "with them thinking that the spear is responsible. Then I blow them off the face of the earth."

"It's a good idea tactically," Lucilla replied, "but my remit includes destroying Archaroch and his diabolical henchmen. This lot are small fry by comparison. But hold on, I'm trying to get into Charles' mind. Earlier I had a rapport with Percival, but lost it when we fled from the adit."

"I think I've sensed something," said Hermione. "It's jolly vague, but it seems to me that Archaroch is fed up with the Menenius lot, and proposes to take charge in person. He will appear shortly, but outside the adit. It will take him an hour or two to get here, and he may bring some others with him. This gives us time to think."

The Amentans' strategy was clear enough. It depended upon a combination of physical and psychic assault. The latter would be unlikely to succeed against persons of the calibre of Hermione de Lamarac or Lucilla Mantzini, but if such citizens of Lyonesse were subject to simultaneous physical restraint, victory could be obtained. Hence Georgina's proposal continued to make sense, except that the Amentans would back off as soon as her Myrmidons opened fire, leaving a lot of dead underlings behind them, but with they themselves unscathed. Therefore Lucilla wanted to lure the Amentans into a situation from which that they could not escape by an easy retreat from the earthly aeon.

"Hermione," she said. "What do you make of this place? I don't doubt that you and Georgina looked around while awaiting events."

"It is clearly the 'Pillared Halls' referred to in the scytail. And there are some epitaphs about, although I have not had much time to investigate them. Consider the rows of structures between the pillars and the walls. Some, or all of them are tombs. Have a look at the name on the biggish one to your left."

Lucilla, supported by Samuel, quickly inspected it, as well as possible by the light of a hurricane lamp.

$GWYNHYVARBRENHYNES$ read the inscription.

"What does it signify?" Samuel asked.

"It's in Brythonic – ancient Celtic. Gwynhwyvar is their rendering of Guinever, and 'Brenhynes' means 'Queen'. I don't doubt that it's herself. Undisturbed for a millennium and a half."

"What else can you tell us?" was Lucilla's next question.

"The place is something of a catacomb. I suspect that King Arthur himself is buried here, together with many of his followers. There are passages leading off from the end of the hall away from the doors, but we haven't explored them." Hermione paused for a moment, and then continued. "There is an ancient British legend that in a time of absolute need, Arthur and his knights will awaken to their country's aid. Perhaps there could be something in it, but I fancy that their courage and spirit would rise again through the personalities of modern people, not by a physical returning from the dead."

"I believe in sacred things," quoted Samuel.

"In dedicated groves with cenotaphs,

"In hidden, secret, holy springs,

"Whose waters raise the souls of those whose epitaphs

"Are lamps within the pillared halls of time.

"So that is really Guinever's tomb," he continued. "This place is certainly powerful, and the poem is coming true, we are in the pillared halls; but what next? Do we await the arrival of Archaroch? And what is the condition of that extraordinary body of men outside the cavern doors? Are they the same as they were centuries ago when Langarrow was in its hey-day?"

"To answer your last question first," Lucilla replied. "Yes they are, but it may be more accurate to consider ourselves as being pushed back to them, rather than them moved forward into the present day, although it isn't as simple as that. The Langarrow men have the same physical needs that you have – they are not incorporeal creatures. I think that we await the arrival of Archaroch much in accordance with your question, but arrange for his visit to be on our terms. As for what next, I have some ideas, but let us do a little more eavesdropping and try to see a trifle further into the Menenius mind! The longer we can maintain the deception with the spear, the better."

And so they returned to the double doors. The argument over forced entry seemed to have partially abated, awaiting the arrival of Archaroch, but the Meneniuses were still minded to open the door on their own account, but by using the supposed kinetic properties of the spear.

"I tell you that the thing has enormous powers," said Percival. "It should open the doors by direct psychic energy, but it would be a lot more fun to make the Christians open them for us. If you know the procedure, all you have to do is point it towards your enemies, and they will be obliged to obey your every command. So when Archaroch arrives it would be great for us to have got the doors open and have the other lot running round in circles to order."

"Fair enough Boss," said Sturmey. "Is there much in it for us, apart from the gold?"

"Why not?" said Charles. "I'm in favour of making their women strip. Get every stitch off that stuck up tart of a secretary. She's a right looker, but I'd like to see her blush.

And I'll have the dark-haired plump one dance the can-can. With her knickers off of course!"

"Nice men," observed Hermione. "I feel almost disappointed that they don't know I'm here. But let us prepare a reception for the necromancers."

"Hold on a minute," Lucilla replied. "I fancy that there is treachery afoot. Sturmey has a plan."

"Mr Menenius," said Sturmey. "If we can get the hang of the spear, why do we need Archaroch? With a weapon as powerful as that, we can get everything we want without being beholden to the evil lords. I say we have another go at opening the door with it for a start."

They continued to haggle. The cousins were clearly frightened of crossing Archaroch, and stridently explained the possible consequences to the Langarrow gang. The latter seemed to be largely won over. Now reluctantly, the Meneniuses agreed to make one further attempt on the door.

Lucilla approached Georgina.

"Tell me Sarissa Major," she said, "what is the longest fuse setting on an army grenade, and would one blow that wooden bar apart – the one helping to secure the doors?"

"Yes Donna. Any delay from three to twenty seconds, and a grenade probably would shatter the timber like you say. If I follow your thinking, wedging one into one of the slots, but under the bar, would blow it out of the way, probably without breaking it."

"Excellent Sarissa Major. My plan is this. We place a grenade as you suggest, and we all, except for one volunteer, withdraw into a passage at the far end of the cavern. The volunteer sets the fuse for twenty seconds, and follows the rest of us at a rate of knots. The grenade blows the bar aside, and the door opens. This convinces the Meneniuses that the false spear is genuine, and working for them."

"What next?" Ystelle asked. "I fancy that it would be amusing to have the necromancers chasing their own men around the tin mines."

"True," Lucilla replied, "but I doubt if the Meneniuses have the audacity to go forward without them. My guess is that they will wait until Archaroch arrives, and then inform him that having mastered the use of the spear, they have forced the doors with it. 'Please sir – look for yourself. There was a big bang, and the door flew open, but unfortunately the Christians have disappeared.' What Archaroch will make of it is anyone's guess."

There was general concurrence with Lucilla's plan. Ystelle suggested pouring a little paraffin over the bar – this would be ignited by the explosion, and add to the dramatic effect. Arthur insisted on being the person to pull the pin out on the grenade, claiming that he was the company's swiftest runner. Cautiously, he and Jennifer paused for a few moments at the exit from the cavern, to observe results. The noise of the explosion was concentrated by the confined space, and they had a momentary glimpse of excited faces behind a cloud of blazing paraffin. Then they fled to join their companions, a furlong or so along the tunnel.

"Tell me darling," said Arthur. "What is the message that you have for me?"

"Nothing much in words. An instruction from Catharine, directly into my mind. You and I are to stick together to the end of the action. It's meant to be that way."

"I don't want you to get hurt. Thank heavens the Myrmidons are around, guns and all!"

CHAPTER XVII
Sir Christopher Trepennick

Arthur and Jennifer found the remainder of the party awaiting them in a cavern smaller than the pillared hall, but similar in style and finish. It became clear that they were indeed within a catacomb of interconnecting chambers and galleries, which like the pillared hall, had little to do with tin mining. There was a second exit from the cavern, and the party formed a compact group, with several dragon guns covering the entrance, but the Meneniuses seemed in no hurry to mount a pursuit.

"They are waiting for the Amentans," said Lucilla.

The tactic which the Lyonelles were following was initially to defeat the enemy, and then separate the Amentans from their earthly underlings. Thirdly, Archaroch and his peers would be dealt with in isolation. But how this was to be achieved was not clear – at least not to the earthly Christians. Some of the party explored the cavern, more to relieve their tension than for any specific purpose.

"I say," said Arthur, "There is another tomb here; very grand, and the only one there is. It seems to be inscribed in both Brythonic and Greek." He brushed at the dust with the side of his hand, and continued: "Good heavens, it's got my name on it, at least in Greek. I can't translate Brythonic."

ΑΡΘΥΡ ΒΑΣΙΛΕΥΣ ΤΩΝ ΛΩΓΡΕΣ

"Arthur Basileus tôn Lôgres," read Hermione, and then translated: "Arthur, King of Logres. It's himself all right – the Brythonic has the same message. Surprising that they did not bury him beside Guinever, but then she died some time later than he, and is in the company of a few of her nuns. This probably explains it."

She paused for a moment, and then said:

"Hush. Someone is about in the passages, not I fancy from the Meneniuses."

All listened carefully. Sure enough, faint noises could be heard coming from the second exit. What did this imply? Were Archaroch and his accompanying Amentans closing in using some sort of pincer movement, with the Langarrow mob entering from one entrance, while the necromancers attacked from the other? For certain, the Meneniuses, and probably the Amentans, did not know that Samuel's original small party was supported by a dozen heavily armed Myrmidons. Therefore any assault would lead to mayhem, and bloody mayhem at that. Neither Ystelle nor Lucilla were necessarily averse to killing enemies were they forced into it, although like most professional military they disliked taking life if it could be avoided. But it seemed doubtful if they would thus get the better of the Amentans. Some degree of stealth was called for. Moreover, under the circumstances, victory was far from certain. Easy enough to shoot down some men from Langarrow, but could they also deal with a simultaneous psychic assault led by Archaroch?

They peered uncertainly along the passageway. It ran straight for about a hundred yards, and then veered gently to the right. They had powerful torches, but could discern nothing other than smoothly finished granite walls. Soon a slight movement of air became apparent, bearing with it the faintest suggestion of aromatic odours, vaguely reminiscent of a Levantine souk or maybe a Byzantine church. And then an overwhelming sense of the impending came upon the company. Faces pale in the lamplight, the Myrmidons stood awestruck, looking to their Sarissa Major. She in turn glanced towards Ystelle and Lucilla, her senior officers, but they were as overcome as she. The remainder of the company gathered about Hermione, who, crossing herself, continued to gaze into the tunnel, as if trying to see through the very granite in which it lay.

"I shall say the Collect for Purity," she said, "and would ask you to join with me."

But even as she completed the brief prayer, resonant enough in the Greek use, the noises in the tunnel became louder, and then clarified into an irregular sequence of tinkling notes, similar to those of a small bell in erratic motion. Hermione was aware that some factor of enormous power was approaching, and was half tempted to fly before it. At least the Meneniuses and the Langarrow mob formed an enemy which she could understand. Meanwhile, Arthur stood with his arm around Jennifer, his mind almost paralysed, but becoming aware of an ancient intuition now crystallising into intelligent thought.

"Have no fear," he cried, but before he could continue, a light became visible, approaching them round the bend in the tunnel.

Slowly the light grew stronger. So far as could be seen, it was coming from a source close to the floor of the tunnel, and thus they watched as the illumination slowly gathered brightness. Seconds passed, while Hermione held her breath. And then behold a small solitary boy appeared, a lanthorn in his left hand. The lad was clothed entirely in white, and he bore a censer, swinging it rhythmically as he walked. A tiny bell was attached to the censer; thus both the aromatic perfume and the noise were explained. With expressionless face, he came steadily onward, paused at the entrance to the tunnel, and addressed Hermione, clearly, solemnly, and in fair English, but with an intonation reminiscent of things long past.

"Priest and Donna of Lyonesse," he said, "I bring you greeting from the Reverend Sir Marrock Nacien, a priest descended from Saint Joseph of Arimathea, and whose thurifer I am."

"I thank you, young sir," replied Hermione, with equal courtesy, "and would send respect to your master for his kindness towards me. Are you able to relate the nature of his regard?"

"Verily Donna, if you wish it. But my bidding is to lead you to Sir Marrock, who presently awaits you. Pray follow me."

Jennifer felt as if she were dreaming; certainly the boy's vesture and unexpected appearance had the preternatural clarity sometimes associated with dreams. And yet the lad was real enough. She decided to speak to him:

"You have the advantage of us – tell me please, who are you?"

His answer was startling, and given with some degree of pride: "Mistress, it is Richard Trepennick that I am, of the parish of Saint Catherine in the county of Cornwall. My father is Sir Christopher Trepennick, esquire and merchant adventurer. I believe, my lady, that you are none other than the Lady Guinever. So the Reverend Mr Nacien tells me. Therefore I would do you honour."

He bowed to her, gravely, and with exquisite aplomb.

There was an uncertain pause, until Arthur decided to accelerate matters.

"Let us do as the young gentleman asks," he said, looking round the company. "I pray you lead on young sir."

And so they found themselves formed up behind the lad in a kind of procession, walking pair by pair in an apparently spontaneous sequence. First the two priests, Samuel and Hermione, secondly Arthur, with Jennifer on his arm, then Ystelle and Lucilla, with Rosalind, Georgina and the Myrmidons bringing up the rear. There were still no signs of pursuit, and thus the thurifer led them off serenely enough, censer swinging and bell tinkling, taking them along a serpentine path which sloped slowly upwards. Presently he began to sing in a clear confident treble:

"Hear our prayer: and send incorporeal spirits to dwell with us.

"Let them teach us the things that Thou hast promised us: and let them dwell in us that we may embody them.

"And Thou wilt give precepts for our work: and establish it according to thy will.

"And Thou wilt guide us: for we are thine."

Only Hermione recognised the words.

"Good grief," she said softly to Samuel, "it is a gnostic canticle from a second century liturgy. Who is this Reverend Marrock Nacien I wonder?"

"There is a hermit called Nacien mentioned in the Morte d'Arthur," Samuel replied, "as a descendant of Joseph of Arimathea. I know nothing apart from that, but even taking the record as factual, it was centuries before Christopher Trepennick's time."

"True enough, but I vaguely recall something from Arthur's conversation with Sir Christopher, shortly after the Choones shot a minor villain in your very church. Sir Christopher described a liturgy which he did not understand, sung by an ancient priest in a foreign language. My guess is that it was Greek. Most of the educated Romans could speak the language, and it is likely that some of the Romano-British could do so as well. Therefore the Reverend Marrock Nacien was the priest referred to by Christopher, and the liturgy a direct remnant from the early Celtic church, probably as known to King Arthur."

"As used to reinforce the majesty of the Spear?"

"Indeed so Samuel. Even as mentioned by Morgan le Fey in her testament – where she refers to triennial rites. How much Catharine knows of this is beyond me, although I suspect little or nothing. What seems to have happened is that in their twisting of the aeons to suit their purpose, the Amentans have to a degree outwitted themselves. Some of our ancient Christian allies have been caught up in the Amentans' meddling with the aeons, and praise be are now in the same location as ourselves. Essentially they are on our side, and I dare say that we shall be glad of their aid!"

Richard's path was indeed tortuous. At one point the passage narrowed and assumed a series of sharp right-handed bends, alternating with gentler left-hand curves. Arthur claimed that this was to make the route more defensible against an enemy moving in the same direction as themselves, assuming that the defending swordsmen were right handed. Twice they passed wrought iron gates similar to those in the crypt, but left wide open. Samuel wondered about locking them behind the company, but Hermione was opposed to this, even assuming that Richard had the keys. Occasionally, other passages branched off. It was clear that they were in a confused mixture of catacomb and tin mine; moreover, any attempt at retracing their steps without guidance could end in disaster.

"I doubt if the Archaroch faction could follow us along here," remarked Georgina, "even assuming that they dared to try. I wonder how Ystelle and Lucilla intend to proceed. It would be a novel form of victory to destroy one's enemies by losing them down a tin mine."

"Perhaps," said Rosalind, "but I fancy that Archaroch will have some diabolical resources available. He is a nasty piece of goods, with much psychic ability, which might help him to track us. Also, they have some sort of map of the mine. My belief is that our officers will lead him on, and then take the offensive. We can't hang about down here ourselves for long. We don't have enough rations."

But then the path sloped downwards, until they found themselves walking along the side of a long narrow underground lake. The water was perfectly still, looking like an immense black mirror in the light of their torches.

"Creepy, isn't it?" remarked Jenny. "Fancy a dip?"

But before Arthur could reply, the company came to a bridge, a single slender stone arch, very well made, and leading off to the left across the lake. As Richard led them over, Arthur noted that a parapet was on one side only – presumably a further aid to defence. Then amid an aura of increasing tension, the company joined a long flight of shallow stone steps, rising from some moorings on the farther side of the water. The stairway passed through open gates within an extensively carved stone arch, and as Richard slowly led his procession up the steps, it became clear that they were approaching the end of their journey. The walls of the stairway had been plastered, and soon some wall paintings became visible – it was not possible to examine them in detail, but they were surprisingly well preserved, and had a Byzantine feel about them. Stylised saints stood tall and thin in extended vertical perspective, the serenity of their faces complemented by the brilliant celestial blue of the background. It all seemed crazy to both Arthur and Samuel. In essence the mine and catacombs were Celtic if not Romano-British, but this artistry was Greek, like to that of the Orthodox Church. Hermione paused for a moment, and directed her torch onto a picture close to the head of the stairs.

"That is Joseph of Arimathea," she said. "Remember the Glastonbury legend? See the staff bursting into flower, and he holds a chalice, presumably the Sangreal, and a spear, indeed our spear, rests against his shoulder. I wonder what awaits us at the top of these steps."

Her question was soon answered. Even as Richard gained the summit of the stairs, a familiar male figure appeared from the shadows.

"Greetings, Reverend sir and Mother," he said, addressing Samuel and Hermione, with a bow to the latter. "Christopher Trepennick, once more at your service. I would hope that my son and heir has discharged his duty faithfully." Without waiting for a reply, he fell into step beside Samuel, and continued: "Welcome to Saint Catherine's, both you and your people."

They entered an approximately circular chamber, lit by several sconces of candles. A few wooden benches stood in a semicircle, with a table at one end, covered by a white cloth.

"But we have only just left Saint Catherine's," replied Samuel, naively enough.

Trepennick paused for a moment to think; he too was having difficulty in adjusting to the unusual nature of what was going on.

"You are now within the period of my earthly life," he said. "But nevertheless, Catharine of Lyonesse is aware of our meeting."

Lucilla decided to intervene.

"Both of you gentlemen are correct," she said. "We are now in the crypt beneath the ancient Saint Catherine's, having

225

left the sixteenth century church behind us. Don't bother unduly about it, for we must concentrate on the business in hand. I beg you to proceed, Sir Christopher."

"You have the true Spear?" Sir Christopher asked anxiously, "and have not been misled by counterfeits?"

He was quickly reassured. Indeed at his invitation, Georgina placed the weapon on the table at the end of the crypt.

"Shortly you are to meet Sir Marrock Nacien," Christopher continued. "A priest of great renown amongst us. He is descended from Saint Joseph of Arimathea, whose mortal remains were at one time preserved within this very crypt. They now occupy a tomb in the Presence Chapel beneath the second church. Therefore when you are near to that tomb, you are near to the relics of a man who walked and talked with our Saviour. But enough of this. Sir Marrock is above. I shall send Richard to advise him that we await his pleasure. In the meanwhile, please be seated."

And so they occupied the benches, the Myrmidons sitting to the rear, except for four whom Georgina posted to guard the stairway. Hermione, Samuel, and the senior officers sat closer to the table which they now realised was some sort of altar. Christopher stationed himself at the foot of an ascending staircase, presumably awaiting the arrival of the priest.

Thus they waited, it seemed interminably, although in fact the period can only have been a few minutes, until a faint chanting became apparent from the descending stairs.

"I don't recognise the language for certain," Hermione remarked to Samuel as the sounds became louder, "but I think it's Syriac – not a tongue in which I am entirely fluent."

"Indeed?" replied Samuel. "I know that it is still used as a liturgical language around the Levant, and in England it is also called Western Aramaic. How close it is to the Aramaic spoken in Israel in the time of Joseph of Arimathea is doubtful."

The chanting ceased, but some supporting music continued, and a small procession entered, coming down the ascending staircase. First came two musicians with simple reed instruments: shawms according to Jennifer. They were followed by Richard Trepennick, his censer discarded for a large and exceedingly beautiful Celtic altar cross – silver inlaid with gold, and ornamented with semi-precious stones. This he placed on the table, behind the Spear. Next was the Reverend Marrock Nacien himself: tall, thin, and clean shaven but with shoulder length white hair. His vestments were not dissimilar to those in modern use, but included a scapular of some religious order. Lastly came six laymen, two of them acolytes, carrying tapers, and with surplices over purple cassocks. Nacien addressed the company.

"Who is your captain?" he said.

A direct reply was difficult. It had been tacitly assumed that Hermione was the spiritual authority, supported by Samuel, and that Ystelle was in charge of the military force. If anyone was in overall command it was presumably Lucilla, but her authority was mediated by circumstances. Nacien noticed their hesitation, and at least Lucilla sensed that he disapproved of it.

"As you will know," she said, "some of us are from Lyonesse, where we have a different style of leadership."

Nacien was unimpressed. He continued, without waiting for further response.

"I believe that one of you is named 'Arthur', and I shall recognise him as your leader. Will he please come forward?"

Somewhat diffidently, Arthur complied.

"At your service, Reverend sir," he said, but was taken aback by the priest's next question.

"Are you familiar with the Odes of Solomon?"

"Indeed not," he had to reply; in fact he had never heard of the Odes.

"No great matter. I assume that you are an educated man?"

Poor Arthur. He felt a little aggrieved by this last question, but thought it wise not to show it.

"I am a post graduate scholar of the University of Cambridge," he replied.

"Ah yes, the junior University. You are fluent in the Greek and Syriac?"

"Greek moderately, but without fluency. Syriac, not at all."

There was a long pregnant pause, and then:

"A pity; we shall have to make the best of it, and proceed in English. Needs must. All languages are known to God."

"May I ask what we are about?"

"If you feel so. Your courage must not fail you. There is about to be a mighty battle against forces of the most extreme evil. My task is to reawaken the ancient merits of the Spear of Longinus, that it may support us strongly in that which is to come."

He gestured to one of his laymen, who distributed copies of a missal, leather bound but little worn, not surprisingly, as it turned out that this was the liturgy only used once in every three years. Hermione in particular was fascinated by it. The original missals were on vellum, bound in a heavier leather, probably calf skin, and handwritten essentially in Greek, but with a few initial paragraphs bilingual in Greek and Syriac. All copies were exquisitely illuminated, although as Hermione subsequently discovered, no two were exactly the same. (Later, Nacien claimed that they were the work of Celtic nuns, possibly in part by Guinever herself.) Further examination showed that the books had been modified at a later date by the insertion of leaves of inferior parchment between the original vellum pages. These leaves accommodated an English translation – the script which Nacien now proceeded to use. He bade Arthur stand behind the altar, facing forwards, holding the spear vertically in front of him, and with the end of the shaft on the floor. The remainder of the company remained seated, with Nacien's musicians and laymen standing to the rear. Richard, who had retrieved his censer, appeared to be functioning as some sort of altar boy. Nacien stood behind him, at the focus of the semicircle. It was clear that he modified the missal to suit the circumstances.

Thus he began by addressing Arthur as a mortal of high renown, revenant in time of need. It was difficult to follow precisely what Nacien was about, but he appeared to building a link between Celtic saints and the Spear, Arthur serving as a bridge, besides being important in himself. Then he asked the support of his congregation by singing one of the Odes of Solomon:

'He who has led me down from the higher regions which are above,

Has led me up out of the regions which are in the depth below.

Who has there taken those in the midst,

He has taught me concerning them.

Who has scattered my foes and my adversaries,

He has bestowed power on me over the bonds to unloose them.

Who has smitten the serpent with the seven heads with my hands,

He has set me up above its root, that I may extinguish its seed.

Thou hast led thy aeon above decay,

So that all may be loosed and renewed and thy light become a foundation

for them all.'

Samuel felt disturbed by what was going on. The whole liturgy seemed to him to be bordering on ceremonial magic, and he did not know what attitude he should take. Hermione squeezed his hand.

"Don't worry," she said softly. "This may sound like a lot of necromantic mumbo-jumbo, but in fact it isn't. I'm not sure how much of it Marrock understands himself, but he is following an ancient ritual requesting great ones from the other side to give us their aid. The Spear is acting as a material focus for their forces. Like a magnet, a mustering point for those who would aid us. Remember that Christianity is essentially supernatural; in the early days this was recognised more readily than in your time."

Samuel was reassured by Hermione's advice, and sang more easily; the haunting notes of the shawms emphasised the numinous nature of the liturgy, and he became aware of unseen powers, akin to those of the Presence Chapel. Hermione squeezed his hand again.

"That's better Samuel. We must not resist aid from the other side. Such will not be pressed upon us. It must be asked and accepted by the volition of the suppliants."

Meanwhile, Sir Christopher slipped away down the descending staircase, carrying a silver ewer, and returned shortly, having filled the ewer from the underground lake. He presented it to his son, who, a few minutes later, passed it to the priest. Nacien said a prayer of consecration, before sprinkling the water over both Arthur and the Spear. It seemed that the lake's water had some special significance. The shawm music recommenced, and they sang a further Ode of Solomon.

'A stream came forth and became a great wide flood.

Dams and buildings could not hold it,
Nor could the art of them who hold the waters.
It was led over the whole land and laid hold of all.
They who were on dry sand drank;
Their thirst was quieted and quenched,
When the draught from the hand of the Highest was given.
Blessed are the ministers of that draught,
To whom the water of the Lord is entrusted.

For they all have known themselves in the Lord and are saved through the water of Life eternal.'

Some more prayers and a blessing followed, but Nacien had barely completed his task before one of the Myrmidons came hurrying up the stairs.

"Sarissa, we have seen lights on the other side of the lake," she reported to Georgina Burton-Coggles, "but the bearers seem to have withdrawn back into the tunnel. Are we to open fire if they reappear?"

"Now all things shall be to me!" cried Arthur. "Do not fire. Let the enemy advance and we shall use the portcullis. Call back the guards. Let Guinever bear the Spear, and congregate in the chamber concealed behind the altar, but look out through its doorway and follow my actions. All will become clear, but we must act at once."

"Do as he says," said Lucilla and Sir Marrock, as it were with one voice, and all obeyed, the remaining pickets being speedily recalled from their posts. How Arthur knew of the existence of the portcullis was a mystery to all save Nacien.

"Have no fear," he said. "For a while the spirit of the great king lives within him to guide and fortify, and likewise, Jennifer is his queen."

Arthur took up a powerful torch, and stood staring down the staircase towards the end of the bridge, one hand on a peg projecting from the wall. He directed the torchlight down the stairs, but was careful to stand to one side, offering a small target to any party advancing up the steps. Time passed slowly, indeed it seemed an eternity before anything happened. And then Arthur pulled out the peg. There was a slight rumbling noise, followed by a thud, and a horrible scream from the descending stairs. Arthur stepped sideways into the centre of the stairs, and stood there for three or four seconds, before making off across the crypt and up the ascending staircase. Ystelle and Lucilla were watching from the chamber doorway, and they saw not one, but three Amentans come chasing after him. Archaroch was in the lead, brandishing the false spear, and shouting some sort of gibberish – in the Inchthonic language according to Hermione.

Cautiously, the companions looked down the descending staircase. Arthur had dropped the portcullis as the enemy reached it. The Amentans were in the lead, and he had timed the drop to separate them from the Meneniuses and the Langarrow mob. Two unfortunates had been pinned beneath the spikes; one appeared to be dead, but the second was writhing horribly and screaming. Then a musket banged, sending a ball crashing harmlessly into the farther wall of the crypt.

"Let us follow Arthur," said Sir Christopher. "They will be unable to raise the portcullis. It weighs nearly a ton, and also has a latching mechanism which can only be released from this side. Come up into the church."

They looked out from the west door, left wide open, in time to see Arthur disappearing across country, with the Amentans in pursuit, the spear waving furiously.

CHAPTER XVIII
King Arthur

Arthur was following intuitions of uncertain origin, although he knew that they had to be trusted. Thus he had no objective explanation for his knowledge of the portcullis and the mechanism controlling it, but the information was there in his mind as clearly as if he had made a lengthy study of the ancient church. Moreover, he knew that the water consecrated by Nacien came from the 'Holy springs' referred to in the scytail, and without conscious planning, he had separated the Amentan enemies from their underlings. This was exactly what Lucilla and Hermione desired, although until a few minutes ago no one could see how it was to be achieved.

So far so good, but what now occupied his mind concerned the demons chasing after him. Being a prop forward for his university, and an exceptionally fit young man he did not doubt his ability to outrun his pursuers, but where was he running to? Or leading them? The countryside was roughly familiar, if markedly different from twentieth century England. It appeared to be the early afternoon of a winter's day: not freezing, but cold and with clear visibility. He came upon an open expanse of moor, and maintained a steady cross-country pace, glancing back occasionally to keep a moderate distance ahead of his pursuers. Logic suggested that they believed that the false spear was capable of forcing him to do their will, and they were experiencing a merely temporary problem in learning to apply its energy. Long live their illusion!

He realised that he was running in the general direction of the old village of Langarrow, and despite the tension and responsibility upon him, he felt a strong professional desire to see the place. Archaroch's party seemed to be flagging. He could lose them entirely, have a quick look at Langarrow, and then return to the old Saint Catharine's; it would be a fair distance to cover, but not beyond his strength. What did Lucilla want him to do? He had no idea, because he was reacting to strange intuitions. He increased his speed, and was soon approaching Langarrow.

The geography was fairly similar to what he remembered; as a historian he was not surprised, country routes remained unchanged for centuries. There was the occasional person about in the muddy lanes, and he drew some curious glances, but no overt response. Until he glimpsed the tower of Langarrow church half a mile or so ahead, when the unexpected happened.

"Arthur, Arthur, I say Arthur!" came a man's voice from a tumbledown hovel at the side of the track. "For God's sake come over here, and fast."

It was Hubert Agravain.

Arthur obeyed instantly. The old man pulled him thorough an empty doorway into the remains of what might have been a labourer's cottage.

"Do not go near Langarrow," continued Hubert, emphatically enough. "That is what the necromancers want. Archaroch has been in touch – believing that I am still loyal to him. He thinks that you are being driven to Langarrow by forces within the spear, and when they get you there you will be taken prisoner. If the spear fails, they have a gang of ruffians on hand. Circle back to the church. Hermione and

Nacien will have collected their wits by now; they are well able to overcome the necromancers by Christian means."

Arthur realised that curiosity had overcome his inner promptings. He did not doubt that Hubert was correct.

"How come you are here?" he asked, still startled by the shrewd old man's sudden appearance.

"Two and two together," came the reply. "I was aware of Lucilla's stratagem with the false spear, and hence not surprised when things started to go wrong for Archaroch. My instructions were to undergo transfer to Langarrow, make myself au fait with the situation in time for the arrival of Archaroch in person, and await the return of the Meneniuses' gang. The map of the mine suggested that your party would surface through the ancient Saint Catherine's, which happens to be on the top of a hill visible from the tower of Langarrow church. The distance is a lot less as the crow flies than it is across country, and fortunately I had the foresight to bring some binoculars with me. I couldn't make out who emerged from Saint Catherine's, but I saw one figure flee off at pace, pursued by three more. You can guess the rest for yourself."

"Archaroch isn't far behind me," said Arthur, trying to think quickly. "How will he react if I loop back to the church?"

"Difficult to say. Maybe best if you head off along the side of that wood until you strike the track between Saint Catherine's village and Langarrow. Then turn right for Saint Catherine's, and so back to the church. Archaroch's lot will come past here shortly. I shall accost them, and say that I've seen you make off as I've just said. Keep a look out, and check that they are still following you." He paused for a moment, listening.

"My God, they're coming," he continued. "Stay hidden, and try to overhear the conversation."

He hurried outside, just as the necromancers arrived panting along the track.

"Greetings My Lord," cried Agravain, "and congratulations, I see you have the spear!"

"Never mind about that now you fool. What are you doing here? Your orders were to wait at Langarrow."

"True My Lord, but I pray you not to worry about it now; it can be explained later. As I understand things, you are using the spear to drive Marazion into Langarrow, but I saw him make off over there, towards the Saint Catherine's road. Probably he remembers the route as leading to Langarrow, which explains why he is heading for it. But if he gets too far ahead, the spear will cease to control him. Therefore I counsel haste."

Cautiously, Arthur peered out through a fissure in the stud-work wall. He recognised Archaroch from Ystelle's description of him, although the magus was not wearing his necromantic robes. Longish back hair, and a tall man, slightly stooping, and giving the impression of being in indifferent physical condition. The other two were portly, indeed over weight, and also appearing less than fit.

All seemed to be in early middle age, although Arthur was aware that normal human considerations were less than valid.

The necromancers conferred among themselves for a minute or so, at a level which Arthur could not overhear; then followed a brief expostulation with Hubert, and they were off as the latter had suggested, spear horizontal, and the heavy weights puffing along in the rear. Hubert watched them out of sight, and returned to the cottage.

"Try taking the track through the wood," he said. "I don't know where it leads to, but the general direction is right. With a bit of luck you'll get in front of them, and they'll follow you back to Saint Catherine's."

And so Arthur was off again. He reckoned that it was about three o'clock in the afternoon; there was still a fair amount of light left – probably an hour or so until dusk. Certainly enough time to return his adversaries to the mercies of Queen Catharine's priests, if all went well. Thus he ran steadily onward, but continued to reflect on why the evil ones were so concerned with him in person. Their desire to obtain possession of the Spear of Longinus he could understand, but where did Arthur Marazion fit into the equation? His activities were being guided in part by a fey intuition; perhaps this was interlinked with whatever was motivating the Amentans. Logic suggested that if he were to bring the necromancers to conclusions with Hermione and Nacien, he should not have gone haring off as he had done, but this was contrary to what had prompted him in the crypt of the ancient church. Hubert had said that time was needed for the priests to prepare their wits; however, he felt that there was more than that involved. Press on regardless, trust to intuition, and see how things develop seemed to be his best procedure.

The track was narrow, but smooth and well trodden. Presently he came upon a roughly constructed bridge which carried him across a stream (it was in fact Saint Catherine's Brook, as Arthur subsequently discovered), and soon he found himself in a clearing, with some small dwellings, wattle and daub, but with well-slated roofs, and what looked like a chapel at one end. There were a few people about, and Arthur felt it best to maintain his pace through the settlement; the track clearly continued beyond the chapel. But the residents thought otherwise.

Initially, he was accosted by a middle-aged man who fell into step beside him, and Arthur, for no overt reason, felt that his arrival was not entirely unexpected. The man spoke to him, presumably in Cornish which Arthur could not understand, but the intonation suggested a question, so in the lack of any better idea, he replied in English.

"My name is Arthur," he said.

The man laid his hand on Arthur's arm, gently and detaining him, while inclining his head in a courteous gesture.

"Arthur?" he responded, a little uncertainly.

Arthur nodded, and came to a halt. The man smiled broadly, and again inclined his head, this time with great deference.

"Yr Amherawdyr!?"[13] he cried, bringing more people gathering around. There was an animated conversation, presumably in Cornish; and then an older man addressed Arthur:

"You are Arthur, Arthur of Marazion, come back as king, even as Father Nacien said?"

"I am Arthur Marazion —" but before he could continue, a woman called out:

"Cyfarch galow, Arthur yr Amherawdyr, Arthur y Brenin."[14]

Ignoring the growing excitement, Arthur concentrated on the English speaker:

"Thank you for your welcome, but I am in haste. Can you direct me to the road to Langarrow, the one from Saint Catherine's village?"

"To Langarrow? They are all bad men at Langarrow. Would you lead us against them? We are few and they are many, but with Arthur Amheradwyr leading us? Even as Father Nacien said, victory could be ours, with our evil oppressors put to the slaughter."

---

13 The Conqueror.

14 All hail, Arthur the Conqueror, Arthur the King.

Arthur scratched his head, he would have to go carefully. Then he replied:

"Langarrow oppresses you, and you want me to put a stop to it?"

"Indeed. They extort tribute, and take our cattle if we have no money. If they find a comely woman, they carry her off and sell her to the Saracens. Not only us, but all villages around. No one in this part of Kernow[15] is safe from them."

Arthur recalled Louise Long-Clarke's description of her forbears' Brocelliande Myrmidons in action against Langarrow. But what was he to do now? He must not tarry in conversation with the villagers, sympathetic though he might be. Renewed contact with Archaroch was much his first priority.

"I cannot explain now," he said, "but if the Lord spares me, I shall return as soon as I can."

The spokesman (his name was Ephraim Choone) inclined his head once more.

"I shall guide you," he said, and so they were off, making a fair pace along the track beyond the village.

They were only just in time. Their track joined the Langarrow road about half a mile from the village, and they had barely reached the junction before Arthur spied Archaroch's party emerging from a field, perhaps a hundred yards away and towards Langarrow. They saw Arthur at once, and made towards him, the spear still waving furiously.

"I must avoid these men," Arthur exclaimed to Ephraim, and set off in the opposite direction, more or less towards Saint Catherine's village. Somewhat to his embarrassment, Ephraim came with him.

---

15 Cornwall.

239

"Your enemies are my enemies," he said as they started.

The road was heavily rutted and uneven, and with the light starting to fail, the going was less than good. Nevertheless, they were travelling in the right direction, and now indeed Arthur became glad of his companion's presence; Ephraim was well familiar with the locality, and clearly on the Christians' side.

The Saint Catherine's road (if 'road' were a fair description) was narrow, and long years of traffic had worn it down to below the level of the adjacent countryside. This, in combination with the stone walls on both sides, restricted visibility to a narrow vista along the length of the road. And thus disaster struck. As the companions turned a sharp corner, they found themselves confronted by a considerable body of men, led by Charles and Percival Menenius, and bearing a farmyard gate with two badly mangled corpses. Such was the Langarrow mob, disgruntled and angry on its return from the ancient church!

If Arthur had had a moment longer to think, he and Ephraim could probably have escaped by making an about turn, and relying on Arthur's skill as a rugby player, charged Archaroch's party to send them flying, spear and all. But alas, he and Ephraim attempted to scramble over the wall to one side of the road, and were hauled down ignominiously by the gang of exultant ruffians. They were rough indeed, and it is likely that Arthur would have died there and then, had not Archaroch arrived in triumph, and as exultant as the men from Langarrow.

"There, you see," cried the necromancer. "Observe how the spear drove the fugitives straight into the arms of our own people! No, no, Mr Sturmey, you may not kill Marazion now, but perhaps you will have the pleasure a little later on. Any way you please, and no doubt as slowly as possible." He paused for a moment, being still somewhat out of breath.

"Congratulations," he then continued to the Meneniuses. "Things have turned out well despite setbacks in the mine. These chronological transfers are tricky things you know, and we had some slippage. Never mind. Now we have both the Spear of Longinus and Arthur in person. Let's get him back to Langarrow for questioning. I fancy that the power in the spear will force him to reveal his mind. Otherwise my friend Colgrin Sturmey can use other methods. Soon we shall have them all at our mercy. I remember being humiliated by that gnostic cow Hermione de Lamarac. Colgrin will be raping her before she's much older – revenge is sweet."

"I fancy the dark-haired plump one," said Charles Menenius. "Jennifer, I think they call her. What about him?" (He indicated Ephraim.)

"He's called Ephraim Choone, and of no account," growled Sturmey. "Head man of a hamlet in the woods. Always does what we tell him. Send him back home to get some money together for our next visit. Looks frightened out of his life to me."

And so Ephraim was released, but Sturmey had not finished his say.

"Funny do at Saint Catherine's. When he" (pointing to Arthur) "dropped a portcullis onto us, he pinned two of my best mates. I don't think their Excellencies saw it, being too occupied with chasing him up the steps. But that ancient priest Marrock Nacien was there, may the devil take him, and later he let us raise the portcullis just enough to get our mates' bodies out. How come he was there? And what's it to do with him?"

"Marrock Nacien?" Archaroch asked in confirmation, with a concerned note in his voice. "That varlet is in the succession of Celtic priests acting as custodians of the Spear. We must beware. He has Catharist knowledge; probably it is of no matter since we have the Spear, but he and his ilk kept it from the rightful possession of the Luciferan church for many centuries. Just think of all the evil which we could have worked with it had it been available."

"He's also the priest for Choone's village," said Sturmey. "Saint Ildierna's they call it, and he's no friend of ours. Wouldn't do to kill him though – not a holy man like him."

Despite the precarious nature of his position, Arthur felt a professional interest in Sturmey's point of view. The man had scant respect for either humanity or the Christian faith, and yet he was prevented by superstitious fear from harming a priest. Could this be exploited? Also, the name of Ephraim's village and presumably church was surprising. Saint Ildierna was one of the people mentioned in Hermione's translation of Morgan le Fey. To apply the title 'Saint' to a living person was not unusual in the Celtic Church, but it was extraordinary how things from the past kept coming back into the situation. Thus Ildierna was one of their women bishops and a trusted friend of the first Guinever; Jennifer was in some mysterious way associated with Guinever. Was there something here beyond coincidence? Certainly he fancied so. All of this was interesting enough, but he seemed to have made a mess of things, indeed badly so. Having successfully separated the Amentans from their earthly underlings he had now permitted them to join forces again. And quite apart from the risk to himself, Lucilla's desire to bring the Amentans to conclusions could well be jeopardised. Sooner or later, Archaroch would realise that the Meneniuses had been swindled, but what could he and his confederates do about it? Nothing, so far as Arthur could see. Presumably they would return to the Amente, no doubt in chagrin, but without having suffered the defeat visualised by Queen Catharine. Then there was Agravain. How did he fit into things? Odd him turning up like that. Were Lucilla and Hermione mistaken in trusting him? Perhaps his response in the Presence Chapel had been no more than a clever but totally insincere charade. Presumably he had now gone on to Langarrow, but could Arthur rely on him?

Meanwhile, a three cornered debate was in progress amongst Sturmey, the necromancers, and the Meneniuses, vigorous if somewhat lacking in cogency. They seemed to be arguing over the spoils – who was to get what – gold, women, and revenge. Until Percival Menenius terminated the exchange.

"O come on," he said. "It's getting dark. Let's be off back to Langarrow, and work out how to get hold of the rest of them from Saint Catherine's village. Should be easy enough, now we have the spear. I'm for hanging their scrawny old crow by her feet over a smoky fire. 'Brocellinde, where the Myrmidons come from' she said. She'll cough to a different tune next time she visits Langarrow."

"Good idea," said Charles. "But pour half a pint of brandy down her throat before you start. Add to the laughs if she's half seas over!"

CHAPTER IXX
Langarrow Revisited

The 'Langarrow Arms' looked little different from when Arthur had first seen it.

Night was falling as he was marched along the ill-paved village street, beneath the inn sign and on into the same untidy drinking room as experienced before. At first he feared violence, perhaps with fatal consequences, but on further reflection thought this unlikely; the evil ones wanted him for some purpose. The intriguing question was what? The Langarrow men were now silent and sullen, and Arthur sensed that they would have cheerfully put him to some sort of painful death. Hardly surprising, since he had recently sent two of their fellows to a similar fate beneath the portcullis of Saint Catherine's crypt. They seemed to be awaiting instructions from Archaroch, but had to be content with a generous ration of beer which he ordered for them, before having Arthur removed to a smaller room adjacent to the bar. They were accompanied by the two additional necromancers, and the Meneniuses. Agravain was already present, although he gave no sign of recognition.

Archaroch opened the proceedings cordially enough by introducing his two subordinates as the mages Perhedron Typhon and Ariouth of Riblah. To Arthur's surprise, he now realised that the latter was female; her carriage and costume had suggested otherwise during his earlier observation. Some food was served, together with a wine of fair quality from dark glass bottles. It tasted like claret. "Mr Marazion," said Archaroch. "You must be wondering what this is all about, and why we have gone to so much trouble to bring you here against your will. The answer is either simple or complex, depending on how you look at it, but either way the situation is greatly to your advantage. You are a lucky man Mr Marazion. Potentially, a man of destiny."

He paused histrionically, as if give his words emphasis, and then continued:

"Unknown to your good self, you are a direct lineal descendant of the great British monarch who defended Post-Roman Britain against the Saxon invaders. That monarch had the support of persons with supernatural skills beyond the comprehension of the modern mind, and from them he acquired the ability to utilise such powers, even though personally he was barely aware of this. You have inherited this faculty. Therefore we desire an alliance with you, redirecting these powers to rectify the unwholesome influence of Christianity upon mankind, and restoring earthly authority to its rightful sovereign, Lucifer, the great angel of light. Moreover, for many tedious years we have suffered grievously at the hands of that dreadful example of devious self-opinionated femininity who rules in low heaven, and styles herself Catharine the Second, Queen of Lyonesse, ynys Afalon, and the Islands of the Dawn. She claims descent from Guinever, widow of Arthur, but even as the powers and authority of that adulterous slut were inferior to those of Arthur her lord and master, so can the spiritual power of Catharine be brought into line by your excellent self, as the inheritor of this Arthurian majesty. The rewards to yourself from such an alliance are beyond easy comprehension.

Not only will the great Prince Lucifer rule over the earth, but also over those areas of low heaven presently forming the realm of the said Catharine. I can assure you that you will find both the great Prince, and ourselves, his trusted servants, more than generous in return for your services. We now have the Spear of Longinus, which forms an essential part of the plan. We could use the Spear to compel your obedience. Should you prove intractable, we may well do so, but would greatly prefer your enthusiastic co-operation. Indeed once you appreciate the advantages to yourself, I can think of no reason for any sane man withholding it."

Arthur scarcely knew how to respond to this, but was preserved from an immediate response by the two other necromancers bursting eagerly into the conversation. They now seemed wildly excited.

"Mr Marazion," cried Perhedron Typhon. "My demonic speciality is the encouragement of all manner of venereal experience, bringing those in receipt of this attention to levels of pleasure which you may find it difficult to visualise. If you give us your loyalty, innumerable women will become available to you. I understand that the one whom you currently desire, Jennifer Parsloe by name, is an accomplished musician, but the tunes which you will play upon her shall exceed the most aetherial notes ever to leave her violin! Soon she will be kneeling naked at your feet. Other women also, and young boys should you wish it. And you own virility will be enormously enhanced. Think of all the female resources of Lyonesse. Some of these are women whom you have already met. How about the supercilious Hermione de Lamarac? Wouldn't you like to teach her what women are for, and what a man can do? After the conquest of Lyonesse you can have a fresh virgin every night you fancy one. Some untutored by me, and squealing in anguish while you put them to the rape. The possibilities are endless, once our rightful rule is applied both to this earth and Catharine's alien realm. All you have to do, is to give us your support."

Perhedron paused for breath, leaving Arthur boggling. What made the fellow think that he wanted some extraordinary harem and the devil alone knew what in extravagant sexuality? But Ariouth took up the running before Perhedron could continue.

"Arthur, my dear," she said. "If I may address a revenant monarch by his first name, my service among the Dark Lords is the encouragement of human strife. All sorts of conflict, ranging from feckless arguments to devastating warfare. It can be both amusing and constructive to observe Satan's opponents wasting their resources in fighting one another; much of course to our advantage. One of the great weaknesses of the Christians is their sectarianism. Conflict is common amongst them. Not so long ago by our standards, you had Christians burning other Christians alive because of minor differences in their theologies. Most entertaining. One God? Perhaps, but how many churches? This brings me to a factor in our present position which may prove to be the most important of all. Catharine and her tribe are, according to orthodox standards, heretical in their beliefs. They are Gnostics, basing much of their theology upon teachings of the revenant Christ, which go beyond the doctrine generally accepted by the earthly churches. It is powerful. Indeed it must be admitted that we of the Amente are frightened by it. Were it to be widely revived upon earth! But enough, there is small fear of that, praise be."

Arthur was becoming confused.

"What has all this to do with me?" he asked.

She seemed taken aback by the interruption, almost as if the import of her discourse were self evident. Arthur interpreted this as showing that she had dwelt on the subject for so long that she had become obsessed by it; so much so that she assumed automatically that all other persons must be aware of her ideas. He decided to humour her.

"Please excuse my ignorance," he said. "It is all fascinating, and you are much better informed than I. Continue to enlighten me."

"It has a great deal to do with you," she replied, petulantly enough. "What is required of you is to support us in reawakening sectarian hostility among the Christians, not merely among the lesser fry on earth, but as Lord Archaroch has already hinted, into heaven itself – the so-called Church Triumphant.

"Triumphant indeed? With your help we shall soon see about that! Let me remind you of the strange circumstances of their Arthurian Church, in effect your church, which originated in New Testament times." She paused for a moment, eyes sparkling with malicious glee, and then continued:

"Our high master had secured a mighty victory in the ignominious death of that pestilential Nazarene, but to our equally great dismay, the Nazarene returned from the tomb a few days later, all alive and vigorous. This led to the formation of the Christian Church. What you may have forgotten is that this included an Interior Church, set up by the Nazarene in the period between his resurrection and recall to the higher regions. This church consisted of a small number of disciples, together with Joseph of Arimathea. It was gnostic in character. Arimathea lived for many years, until in his old age he took ship to the South of France, landing at the ancient port of Elna, with he and his party bearing with them both the Grail and the Spear of Longinus. From Elna, they journeyed along the base of the Pyrenees, establishing Christianity in the process. Indeed you will recall the Catharist reverence for Mount Montségur, where a mighty fortress was later established.

Arimathea then took ship again, probably from Bordeaux, sailing thence to Britain and the early Glastonbury."

Legends to this effect were already well known to Arthur, as indeed to all Celtic scholars. But now he was beginning to get the drift of Ariouth's homily. So he risked a glance at Agravain. The old man caught his eye, and winked, the ghost of a smile moving his lips. 'Play along with her' was what he meant. Easy enough; she needed small encouragement.

"Mr Marazion," continued the she-devil. "The gnostic influence was powerful within the whole of the Celtic Church, spreading throughout Western Europe and using its dynamic power against us. Soon its effects were felt in Britain. You must have noticed the similarity between gnostic thought and the theology of the British monk Pelagius, even though Pelagius died in 420. This gnosticism had much to do with the rise of chivalry, including its dangerous code of high principled behaviour and the spiritual quest for the highest levels of Christian experience. The Arthurians even believed in a higher mass occurring within the spiritual life, where the Nazarene was himself the celebrant, and the Grail the chalice. Far and wide the gnostic effects were felt. The Knights Templar were inspired by the same thoughts, and developed into a college of Christian belief that was one of our most potent enemies. So all went well for them for a time, until the Catholic Church decided to intervene because the free thought of the Gnostics was undermining Papal authority, and diverting wealth away from Rome, and later, from Avignon," – smirking, she paused again and went on in a loathsome gloat:

"So the great virtue of avarice was triumphant, and we were delighted by a magnificent result, although not until after the time of King Arthur and the Celtic Church. It was in 1184 that Pope Lucius the Third set up the Holy Inquisition, and this was followed in 1209 by a great crusade against the Catharist gnostics during the papacy of Innocent the Third. The elder Simon de Montfort was in charge, and he set the whole of the Languedoc ablaze with the bodies of thousands of his fellow Christians, being burnt alive for the glory of the Christian God whom he doubtless thought to serve. On the instructions of the Vicar of Rome of course. Wonderful! There was also great pillage and many of the Cathars were subject to prolonged tortures of the most entertaining kind. Eventually, the great fortress of Montségur fell, and all resistance was at an end."

Arthur thought that she had finished at last, but a peroration was yet to come:

"But unfortunately the gnostic theology is far from dead! It remains on earth only among a small band of adherents, but flowers and flourishes in low heaven under the tutelage of Catharine of Lyonesse. Ah yes, Lyonesse; that dreadful land of harpies and amazons, with many of the former Cathars among Catharine's subjects. The Esclarmonde family enjoys high authority under her. Esclarmonde de Perelha, who suffered death at the stake for heresy, is now no less than Killiarch of the Brocelliande Myrmidons, and Esclarmonde de Foix is one of Catharine's bishops. Memory of their ancient treatment by the Church of Rome must linger still!"

Smiling broadly, she glanced round those present as if seeking approval, but Archaroch and Perhedron had heard it all before.

"I am sure that Mr Marazion is now better informed," said Archaroch. "But the nub of the matter is simple. Firstly, Mr Marazion, you are of direct descent from King Arthur, and Catharine is of similar lineage but on the female side. Therefore, as a woman she is naturally subservient to you. Secondly, you shall stand amongst us bearing the Spear of Longinus to reinforce your will upon her. Thirdly, with the aid of the Spear, you will be able to reawaken the ancient hostilities. The Gnostics of Lyonesse will be stirred up to fury against the Catholics. Thus the whole of low heaven will be raised up to civil war, which will end with the great Lord Lucifer ruling over all."

Arthur realised that some sort of response was now incumbent upon him, but found difficulty in knowing what to say. The situation was farcical. He accepted that the true Spear of Longinus had enormous psychic properties. Certainly, Nacien, Hermione and Lucilla believed so, and they were far better informed than he. Moreover, he had experienced something of its power during the brief time when he had defied the enemy from the head of the stairs beneath Saint Catherine's crypt. But the demons had the wrong spear! Even with the true spear, he doubted if the victory which they so confidently predicted would be achieved. He himself had never met Catharine, but had been impressed by accounts provided by Jennifer and Samuel. This great and saintly woman would not easily be moved to hostility against other Christians. Neither would such subordinates as Ystelle Zabuloe and Lucilla Mantzini; these ladies were nobody's lap dogs. On the other hand, minor events in human affairs could give rise to major results. The First World War had been started by the assassination of a single member of the European aristocracy – the Archduke Francis Ferdinand – and many thousands of ordinary men and women lost their lives in consequence.

True, the assassination ignited tinder which had been smouldering for years, but memories of ancient and dreadful wrongs also lingered among the Cathars of low heaven – or at least Ariouth said that they did. Could an article of great psychic force such as the Spear really re-awaken violent passions which had slumbered for centuries? Even if brandished by a leader charismatically re-born from contemporary times? Not that King Arthur was contemporary with Lucius the Third. Indeed the king had been dead for several centuries before the pope was born; he could have known nothing of the forthcoming massacre of the Cathars. Obviously, the immediate key factor was the old Arthurian association with the Spear, because Ariouth seemed to believe that this gave him a kind of sacerdotal authority. Like the divine right of kings, or some such nonsense.

And so while the necromancers warbled on with notions of conquests in earth and low heaven, Arthur struggled to rationalise the situation. It became clear that both Agravain and himself were in considerable peril. Sooner or later the enemy would discover that they did not in fact have the true Spear, Lucilla having sold them a pup. How would they react? Presumably with the utmost fury. Moreover, the discovery would not further Catharine's policy of pressing a dire conclusion upon the enemy. What best to do? Clearly, the longer the deception was maintained the better. Action was called for.

"Are your sure that the Spear really has the extraordinary properties which are attributed to it?" he asked. "I see that you have it here. May I be permitted to make a little experiment?"

"Experiment?" said Archaroch. "What sort of an experiment? You aren't doubting the impact of our conversation I trust."

"No of course not," Arthur replied soothingly. "It is just that there are big issues at stake, and therefore one has to be sure. May I be allowed to examine the Spear?"

"Indeed you may not. There is no question of our permitting you to handle it until you have demonstrated an unreserved commitment to our cause. We shall require you to prove your loyalty by performing suitable acts of barbarity upon your former colleagues. I shall enjoy watching you put that old fool Mordecai to death by pouring the contents of a boiling kettle down his throat. Only a cupful at a time of course."

"I take your point," said Arthur. "I accept that the Spear of Longinus has great psychic power, indeed I have experienced it, but can understand your reluctance to trust me. Nevertheless, I would ask a minor demonstration. Point it towards Mr Agravain, and tell him to bark like a dog."

Looking directly at Hubert, he risked a barely perceptible wink. The old man responded magnificently, giving a superbly convincing display of outraged dignity at Arthur's very suggestion; no man of his age, and position as a leading earthly Satanist should be subject to any such demeaning procedure! All to no avail. The necromancers thought the idea grossly amusing. Ariouth, who happened to be holding the spear, waved it vigorously in his direction.

"Bark," she said. "Down on your knees like the dog that you are, you miserable little man. You shall be made to crawl before the great ones."

Hubert's performance was indeed masterly. He went purple in the face (subsequently explaining to Arthur that he merely compressed his neck within a tight collar), and going down on all fours, he barked and growled, and whined and snorted, before howling as volubly as any prairie wolf beneath a winter's moon. And then approaching Ariouth, he fawned upon her, rubbing against her legs, and thrusting his nose into her hand. The audience loved it; meanwhile the wine continued to flow. Poor Hubert, they had him mewing like a cat, grunting like a pig, and running round the room flapping his arms and cawing like a crow. Until Arthur began to feel concerned as the instructions became increasingly outrageous. And then Perhedron Typhon came to the fore.

"I know," he cried, "Sturmey has a good number of women in custody awaiting sale to the Saracens. Let us have one in, and make Agravain copulate with her. Great sport, and if the old idiot isn't up to it, perhaps my skills will assist his ardour."

The proposal was received with acclamation, but Arthur intervened.

"No, no," he said. "I am now whole-heartedly on Agravain's side, and it is wrong for us to go on treating him like this. Let us reserve such fun for others a little later on. All I asked for was confirmation of the Spear's efficacy, not a risqué joke at the expense of one of our number. Thank you for the demonstration. I am fully convinced, as we all must be. So let's have some more wine, and give Mr Agravain a double serving. He more than deserves it."

Perhedron disagreed, but Archaroch sided with Arthur, and Hubert was excused further action.

Nevertheless, it was clear that the old man's performance had reinforced the necromancers' confidence in their possession, misplaced though it was. So now Arthur's objective was to bring them to conclusions with the psychic and military forces which Ystelle's people had available, and before they realised how badly they had been duped. The immediate problem was in making contact with Ystelle, Lucilla and the rest of the company. Archaroch had to be so managed that he would lead his people into a conflict in which he would be overwhelmed, with the necromancers taken into custody, awaiting Catharine's decision on their fate. But how was this to be achieved? He decided to play for time, and fortuitously, Ariouth assisted him in this.

"Well Sir Arthur," she said, "are you now prepared to take an oath of allegiance to our righteous cause, and agree to proofs of loyalty as Lord Archaroch has suggested?"

"Probably, but I want time to think things through," he replied. "Frankly, I want to be sure that I really will be getting a good bargain. Not that I doubt your level of ability in this venture, but it would be good to know more detail. Apart from the somewhat generalised promises made by your excellent selves, nothing has been made clear by way of an agreement. I fancy that this also applies to other people – notably Messrs. Agravain and the Meneniuses. Where do we stand?"

As Arthur had hoped, the Meneniuses seized on this last remark. The point had already occurred to them, but it took someone else speaking out to give them the confidence to voice their concern.

"Quite so," said Charles. "Percival and myself have gone to a great deal of time and trouble over this business, and so far all we have received has been a few thousand pounds worth of bullion. I would support Mr Marazion in —"

But he was interrupted by Archaroch before he could go further.

"What do you mean?" cried the necromancer. (He was tired, a trifle drunk, and resented being questioned, particularly by such people as the Meneniuses, whom he regarded as inferiors.) "You are to receive rewards beyond earthly dreams. I will not countenance ingratitude, and would remind you that Lucifer always keeps his word."

"Ah yes, that is all very well, but pray remember my Lord that we have broken the law on your behalf, including making ourselves accessories to murder. No doubt Lucifer keeps his promises, but people's memories are, dare we say, sometimes elastic. With every humble respect, no firm financial arrangement has been agreed between us."

Archaroch was clearly annoyed, so Arthur fuelled the flames:

"It seems to me that Charles deserves an answer. We are people of the earthly aeon and out of our depth. It is not a question of ingratitude or disloyalty, but of information. What are your plans; what is to happen next? You ask for proofs of loyalty, but as Charles has said, he and Percival have already been involved in criminal activities, as indeed have I, also being present when one of their people was shot to death in Saint Catherine's Church. I could be charged with murder. It is we who have taken these risks, not you."

This intervention seemed to cause Archaroch difficulty in controlling his temper. Growing pink in the face, he gasped for breath and started breathing stertorously. For him, the potential gains from his activities were enormous. Even with generosity, the sums needed to reward the Meneniuses were insignificant, but under the pressure of the moment he was certainly not going to attend to such trivialities. Moreover, the Meneniuses were of little further use to him. He had the Spear! Not that he was ungrateful. They had been loyal to his interests – but he would neither explain plans nor justify himself to the likes of them. His annoyance was compounded by Arthur's apparent siding with them. What the blazes were their problems to do with Marazion? The difficulty was that he was reluctant to take forceful measures with Arthur, and he could hardly snub the Meneniuses without offending both him and Agravain. But that wily old man had recognised Arthur's tactics, and spoke up, apparently for tactful reasons:

"Mr Marazion has asked for time to think, and I suggest that we allow him some. It is getting late. Let's have another bottle of Sturmey's excellent wine and then leave things as they are until tomorrow.

"We have the Spear, and nothing more can be done today. What think you Perhedron?"

"An excellent idea. Time to relax from the cares of the day. Sturmey's got a fair selection of local women in his lockup awaiting sale to the Saracens, and doubtless he would be willing to loan a few for the night. I looked them over a little earlier – nice enough – the man has taste. Arthur shall have first choice as a gesture of goodwill. Better to avoid the seventeen-year-old though; we don't want to upset Sturmey. Lovely girl, plump and big breasted, but she's a virgin, which makes her valuable to the Saracens for selling on into some bigwig's harem. Wouldn't do to pick her cherries, would it?" He looked around with hard eyes and a wide grin, but Ariouth entered the conversation.

"I fancy," she said, "that Sir Arthur is a man of educated taste, who fancies something more sophisticated than an illiterate country girl."

She sidled up to him, with an expression half way between a smile and a leer, and almost in spite of himself, Arthur inspected her. A large heavy woman, nearly as tall as himself, and oozing an animal sexuality. What the devil was he to do? Desperately, he tried to think. He could not afford to snub her – a woman spurned and all that. Meanwhile, the Meneniuses looked on in silent amusement. Then to his surprise, Archaroch came to his rescue.

"No offence to you, Lady Ariouth," he said, "but I like Perhedron's rejected notion of Sturmey's special girl. We shall give her virginity to Mr Marazion, as a foretaste of what is in store for him following our victory. Sturmey's main interest is in the money, and as things stand, what do a few ounces of gold matter to us? I shall have a word with him; my gold is as good as any Saracen's. Ask Lord Typhon to give you a few tips Mr Marazion – he will be pleased to ensure that you squeeze the maximum fun out of the girl. Now let us all have some more wine."

Arthur bowed slightly towards Ariouth, and trying not to feel too hypocritical, smiled and caught her eye.

"Maybe we shall have an opportunity to get to know each other better at some future time," he said.

The girl was called 'Kenwyn'. So said Colgrin Sturmey, who, duly satisfied with Archaroch's gold, had conducted Arthur into the secure quarters reserved for kidnapped women awaiting sale to the Saracen marauders who plagued the coasts of North West Europe. Nothing had been said, but it was clear that Arthur was also to be locked in – as yet Archaroch did not trust him. They were accompanied by Perhedron.

"There will be some little delay," he said, "because the village women have to heat the water for Kenwyn's bath. But time spent in anticipation is pleasurable in itself. She's a lovely girl, and I fancy that you will have a memorable night. They will administer a few ounces of white wine to soften her up, and Sturmey has threatened her with the birch. She knows that he means it, and what will happen if you complain. You may have a language problem – she speaks Cornish – but perhaps you won't want oral communication!" And with a lascivious smirk, he took his leave.

The women's prison was surprisingly large. Arthur observed a dormitory with a dozen or so dejected ladies sitting on their beds by the light of two or three candles. Narrow unglazed windows were covered by exterior shutters, and a washroom led off. Perhaps 'sluice room' would have been a better description; it had an iron pump, basins and a few primitive toilets. But Arthur was provided with superior accommodation in the form of a sizeable room, with animal skins on the floor, the stone walls screened by cloth hangings, and warmed from a fireplace. There were a few benches, a large bed with a feather mattress, a long mirror, and an iron sconce with several candles. A brilliant moon shone in through a window furnished with a wrought iron grille, but Sturmey excluded the night air by closing an internal wooden shutter. Then he lit the candles from the fire, grinned at Arthur, and followed Perhedron out of the prison.

So Arthur sat on the edge of the bed and awaited developments. He would have to be careful over what he said to Kenwyn. It would not do to try to explain the whole of the position, but he wanted to give her some words of cheer; namely that he would respect her chastity, things were not as they seemed, and rescue might be at hand. Difficult indeed; if he said too much, it might lead to his betrayal to the enemy. Also, he lacked experience with women. True, he had had girl friends, and to his delight Jenny had accepted his recent proposal of marriage, but women could be curious creatures, as he well knew. The minutes passed slowly, the fire gathered brightness, and the room became warm. Then there was a gentle tapping, and the door opened to admit two women, one older and one very young. The former silently withdrew, and Arthur was alone with Kenwyn.

There had been no exaggeration; she was truly a lovely girl. A little taller than Jenny, she had similar features, if a trifle finer drawn. Copious dark hair, a skin creamy in the candlelight, and well kept hands held demurely across her waist. She was wearing a large white shawl, apparently woven in a single piece from finely spun wool. Arthur stood up, and they contemplated each other in silence for several seconds. She looked him directly in the face, neither smiling nor frowning. He felt that the first word was his responsibility.

"Kenwyn?" he said.

She made no reply, but bowed slightly before continuing her inspection of his face. What next? Speaking as gently as possible, Arthur began his carefully prepared exposition. She made no reply.

He paused for a moment; the girl must be terrified and needed time for his words to sink in. Then he tried once more, still without response. Oh dear! Perhedron had warned that she spoke Cornish. Arthur racked his brains. He had picked up a little Brythonic from Hermione, but next to no Cornish. Nevertheless the girl seemed to be reassured by the kindly tone in his voice.

"Kernow?" he said, emphasising the question.

It was one of the few words he knew; all that it meant was 'Cornwall'.

Her response was disconcerting. Withdrawing a pin, she caused her shawl to fall away, and blushing slightly, stood naked before him, her hands at her sides.

Arthur had seen naked women before, on bathing beaches, but never a girl like this, nor in such close circumstances. She could have stepped straight from a Rubens' painting. Her breasts were indeed magnificent; large perfect orbs which jutted towards him in the candlelight. Despite himself, he looked down. Perhaps her waist was slightly too thick by modern ideas, and her belly was a trifle protuberant – once again he was reminded of Rubens. She was generously made at the hips, with exquisitely formed thighs, and the women had shaved her – her most intimate anatomy was clearly revealed. And then Arthur was assailed by a rush of desire which rose up like a massive tide within him. Clearly, the girl believed that her defloration was imminent, and she could not, dare not, offer resistance. He could lift her onto the bed, and within minutes Kenwyn would be a virgin no longer. Moreover, she might well prefer to submit to a white man, rather than God knew what in a Levantine harem.

Several seconds passed, while Kenwyn remained motionless, save for a swift glance to the shutter above his head. Was there a noise without? Perhaps Perhedron was prowling vicariously beneath the window. And then the shutter was forced inwards by a sharp blow, and turning his head away from Kenwyn, not without difficulty, Arthur saw that a stout iron hook had been placed upon the bars.

"Pull, Pendragon, pull," – the voice coming through the bars sounded like that of Ephraim Choone, the head man from Ildierna Village.

The hook jerked against the bars, a horse snorted, and with a wrenching noise the iron grating was dragged bodily from the masonry. A moment later, a woman's face appeared at the window.

"Arthur darling," she said. "We've come to rescue you," – and then stopped suddenly in mid-sentence.

The speaker was Jennifer Parsloe, his affianced wife.

CHAPTER XX
Kenwyn and Jennifer

Perhaps fortunately, Arthur had little time to think, because Ephraim's voice came immediately, strong and clear:

"Tell Arthur to get the women out of there before Langarrow wakens up to what is going on – get on with it lass."

Jenny had frozen. The unfortunate Arthur noted that her features expressed both horror and incredulity, but allowing her no time to reflect upon his apparent infidelity, he seized the naked Kenwyn as discretely as possible, and bundled her through the window, so that she was impelled into Jenny's arms. It was now apparent that the latter was seated side-saddle upon an enormous heavy horse, massively built and black as jet. (This was Ephraim's 'Pendragon' – a truly magnificent animal, although in fact it belonged to Nacien, Ephraim having borrowed it.)

But there was no time to lose. Arthur flung open the door leading into the women's dormitory, to find several of the ladies clustered in close proximity, presumably eavesdropping.

"Rescue!" he cried. "Some men from Ildierna are outside, and the window is forced open. Come on quickly and climb out."

They all stared at him. For some reason Arthur was reminded of hens in a farmyard, confronted by a strange situation. Blank uncomprehending faces, and then a murmuring amongst themselves.

Dear God, couldn't they speak English?

"There's no time to lose," he said, striving to convey urgency by his tone of voice.

More infuriating delay. Didn't these women want to be rescued? Then at last a response:

"And who might you be?"

The diction was clear enough, but spoken with a slow West Country burr. Arthur struggled to control his temper.

"A friend of both yours and Ephraim Choone," he replied. "But I can't explain now – there's no time."

"Well, I dunno; what does the likes of you want with us? And what have you done with Kenwyn?"

She glanced uncertainly towards the open window, with the other women standing near, mute, inert and stupid. Impasse; seconds ticking away, with Arthur's tension rising.

And then salvation. An authoritative voice came at them from the window, incomprehensible to Arthur, and presumably in Cornish. The women moved as if electrified, and Arthur turning, saw Kenwyn's face in the window, her fingers locked tight upon the shattered masonry of the sill. But this was a different Kenwyn from the silent submissive creature who minutes ago had stood naked before him. It was clear that she was used to being obeyed, and expected to be so now. Indeed the other women were already scrambling up towards the window, with the aid of a bench pushed against the wall. Arthur was helping the last of them through the window, when Ephraim's voice came once more:

"Extinguish the lights, unbolt the outer door, and open it. We've got it unlocked, and want to confound Sturmey with an open door."

Arthur obeyed immediately, glancing round cautiously from within the archway. Despite the moonlight, he saw nothing of remark, until he noticed two figures, literally at his feet. One lay prone upon the ground, with the other propped up, half lying and half sitting against the corner of the entrance. Presumably they were meant to be on guard, but both were breathing heavily, and apparently fast asleep. Then, startlingly enough, a voice from the shadows:

"Hubert here Arthur. All's well so far – I've set the situation up. These two beauties are drugged – I put some opium in their drink. Get back and out through the window as fast as you can, then shout 'Help, Help, Kidnap' or some such nonsense as you make off with Ephraim. Archaroch will conclude that you are still on his side, and the Christians have abducted you."

"What about you?" asked Arthur, concerned for the old man's safety.

"Don't worry about me. I shall raise the alarm and play a prominent part in arranging the pursuit. I dare say the necromancers will join in, because the spear is their new toy, and they'll want to use it. Ystelle Canti will shoot the lot of them if it comes to a showdown. A complication is that Sturmey is due a visit from the Saracens. But don't let's stand talking; get going and fast."

Arthur felt great admiration for the old man's sagacity. Subsequently it transpired that it was he who had contacted Ephraim. In turn, Ephraim had sent a message on to Saint Catherine's, thus appraising Nacien and the other Christians of events at Langarrow.

So Arthur scrambled through the window; it was at the rear of the building, and away from the populous part of the village. Apart from Kenwyn, the rescued women could be seen disappearing into the darkness, but Kenwyn was mounted behind Jenny, and wrapped in some sort of cloak – it was now bitterly cold, with a few snowflakes falling. Three other horses were present, smaller than the magnificent Pendragon. They might have been large Dartmoor ponies. Ystelle was seated on one, armed with a dragon gun borrowed from one of the myrmidons. Ephraim was on foot. He hoisted Arthur across a second horse, uncomfortably enough, and tied his hands to his feet beneath the animal's abdomen, then mounting the third horse himself.

"You're being kidnapped," he said. "So yell like the devil when I tell you to. Sturmey's men will find the open door, and most likely go searching round the village for the missing women. Tomorrow, I shall put out a story that the raid was coincidental, and Kenwyn hit you over the head with a length of firewood. Then out of spite we dragged you out unconscious and made off with you."

Suddenly, all hell broke loose. Ystelle fired the lower barrel of the dragon gun, three charges into the air – a single shot, and then two in quick succession. The noise was terrific. It sounded like a shotgun, with both barrels fired together. Also the extreme quiet of the winter's night seemed to exacerbate the noise; and the horses were moving now, with Arthur shouting out in false protest at the top of his voice. Then they drew level with the inn, and Ystelle sent two further charges flying through the windows, adding to the pandemonium already developing. Hubert's voice was momentarily audible, screaming in hysterical rage, and a number of locals were about, probably the worse for drink, but no sign of the necromancers. Jenny was in the lead. Two or three men tried to get in her way, but jumped for their lives as the mighty Pendragon bore down upon them. Then a shot rang out, and Jenny felt the wind of a bullet flying past her head. Looking back, she saw Colgrin Sturmey and a second man, armed with heavy pistols. It was Sturmey who had fired, but as his companion took aim, Jenny heard the crash of Ystelle's dragon gun returning fire from only a few feet away, and the man's head seemed to disappear, leaving his body momentarily still upright, macabre in the moonlight. Soon they were clear of the village, and with the ground shaking beneath Pendragon's hooves, they cantered away into the night.

"The Lord be praised," said Nacien, as the riders dismounted inside a barn in Ildierna village. "All safe I trust? A bold move by Ephraim, and right swiftly arranged. Welcome to Ildierna, and a happy return to our daughter Kenwyn. We shall have vengeance soon – Deo volente."

Arthur, thankful to be released from the horse, looked about him. All of Samuel's party from the ancient Saint Catherine's were present, with Lucilla still in charge. The Myrmidons had piled their weapons, and were sitting about on benches eating bread and cold meat, presumably provided by the villagers. But confronted by a furious Jennifer, he had small chance to collect his wits.

She screamed at him, her pent-up rage exacerbated by her tension and the peculiar factors behind his apparent perfidy.

"You evil lecherous shame of a man! I can't give you your ring back because you haven't bought me one and it would be burning my hand if you had and I see why Catharine told me to stick close by you because she saw you for the filthy animal that you are not fit to be out of a woman's sight, going after that fat fleshy whore as soon as you get the chance, and her belonging to God knows what evil man letting her out for the pleasure of whoever he thinks fit when you should have been standing by what you know to be right."

She paused for breath, but was interrupted ere she could continue, and to the surprise of the unfortunate Arthur, by

Kenwyn. She addressed Jennifer quietly, and in immaculate English:

"Madam, you should count yourself a fortunate woman to have such a man as this. And I would rather that you did not call me 'whore', although under the circumstances I can excuse your doing so. Both Father Nacien and Mr Choone will tell you that I was abducted by Sturmey against my will, and following the murder of my brothers. How come that I stood naked before your man? I shall tell you. In that building in Langarrow, half way between a prison and a bawdy house, the doors have crevices and the walls have ears. Your fiancé had already imperilled himself by assuring me of his intentions, doing so, thank God, in a voice too low to be overheard. Had he been overheard, all would have been lost, because some spineless hussy would surely have passed word to the evil ones, hoping to gain favour. And further, Sturmey had forbidden me to speak English – he wanted no communication, save of a physical kind. Had you not arrived when you did, in a few moments I would have extinguished the candles and entered the bed with your beloved. Any eyes peeping through the crevices would have seen me remove my shawl, and no suspicions aroused. Then he and I could have conversed quietly, with all safely explained. I trust the integrity of him who is yours, and truly believe that he would have dealt with me honourably, as indeed he had said. Fie upon you, for having such little faith in him."

And so Jenny had the wind taken from her sails. But before she could form a reply, Lucilla intervened, placing her arm around her shoulders, and speaking to her in a voice so gentle that few persons could overhear.

"I know little of what happened at Langarrow Jenny my dear, but what Kenwyn has said is true. Arthur spoke as she says he did – I am aware of her rectitude by means which seem strange to you. She had no designs upon him, and behaved courageously in a difficult time. We are all on the same side, and I am sure that soon you and she will be friends. Think no more of it."

Oh God, thought Arthur, with memories of Kenwyn's loins dancing around in his mind, If Lucilla turns her confounded psycho faculties onto me what the blazes will she find out? What would really have happened if Kenwyn had taken me into bed with her, as she has just suggested? Can I honestly say that she judges me correctly?

Then he felt Ystelle's hand upon his. She spoke even more softly than Lucilla.

"Arthur my dear, I am a married woman who has a warm relationship with her husband; in fact I am missing him dreadfully. Men's desires are not in themselves sinful, because that is the way He made you. Also, He will never permit you to be tempted beyond your ability to withstand temptation. Therefore be comforted, you are guilty of nothing. Lucilla knows that, as do I." She squeezed his hand slightly, and added, in a stronger voice, "Now tell us what happened after you were separated from Ephraim on the way to Langarrow."

The company was much amused at Arthur's account of Hubert's response to the false spear, but before he could complete his reply, the gathering was called to order by Nacien.

"I know these men from Langarrow," he said. "They will be more than furious at what has happened, and may attack at any moment. We should either make ready, or retreat further off. I am reluctant to retreat, because in their wrath they will sack Ildierna whether we are here or not. The people in this village are innocent of serious offence, and they are also my people. I would not have them harmed."

"An immediate attack from Langarrow might be for the best," said Ystelle, "before the enemy realises the true situation. They still believe that they have the true spear, and are only doubtfully aware of the fire-power of Georgina's Myrmidons. Pity I shot that fellow's head off. It must have made them think, and it's small chance he would have hit anyone with his horse-pistol."

"There will be no attack tonight," said Ephraim, glancing round anxiously, "nor any retreat on our part. Look outside."

Someone opened the barn door a little, showing that snow was falling heavily. Great soft flakes, tumbling down from unseen clouds, and covering the land with a smothering blanket, already two or three inches deep. Obviously, Ephraim was right. No organised assault was practicable in such a blizzard – quite apart from the cold and difficulty in walking, visibility was little more than twenty feet.

A subdued hush fell upon the company. What was to be done next?

Ystelle and Lucilla exchanged glances. Things had suddenly become parlous indeed. Half an hour before it seemed that they held the strong cards. Arthur had been rescued, the enemy remained confused, and a further brief encounter would lead to their defeat. In fact Ystelle's strategy at Langarrow was designed to provoke a furious but ill-considered response, because such would lead to victory. Thus Ephraim reported that the Langarrow mob were not all that numerous; Sturmey could muster about a hundred men at the most, and although this tally outnumbered Georgina's Myrmidons, the fact did not unduly disturb the two officers. The fire-power of the dragon guns would more than compensate. Moreover, the necromancers would be taken by surprise, particularly since Arthur's tactics at Hubert's expense had confirmed their confidence in the false weapon.

But now the situation was different. None of them had winter clothing. True, the Myrmidons were wearing their battledresses, warm bullet-proof garments which would give a degree of protection, and maybe the villagers could lend some clothes, indeed Kenwyn was even then being supplied by Mrs Choone, but otherwise the company were hopelessly ill-equipped. Fortunately, Nacien had some clothes in the church vestry, and produced two priests' hooded cloaks and riding boots as worn in inclement weather. So equipped, Georgina's troopers were set to patrol the village, in pairs and on an hourly rota.

Also, food would soon be needed. They had little with them, and the village was only a small place where the inhabitants had already been sorely taxed by extortions from Langarrow. Somehow, resources would have to be found.

"How long do you think the snow is likely to last?" Samuel asked Ephraim anxiously. "It looks to me like the sort of blizzard that could turn to rain, particularly as the wind is from the south west."

"True enough," Ephraim replied, "but I doubt if it will abate before morning, and even if there's a thaw, the roads will be deep in mud. We'll have to wait and see."

CHAPTER XXI
Pendragon

The company spent what was left of the night in the barn, kept reasonably warm by sleeping amid piles of straw, until the next day dawned, colder than ever. The blizzard had abated, revealing a clear blue sky and a bitter frost. There was snow everywhere, giving the village a picturesque appearance – Jenny remarked that it would have made a good Christmas Card – but much of the snow had blown into drifts; indeed in places the track from Langarrow was piled five feet deep.

The village people were cordial, but clearly worried about the position, and could offer little help. Their worry was legitimate enough; usually Sturmey was sufficiently shrewd to avoid squeezing his victims beyond their resources, but given an urge for furious revenge there was no telling what he might do. And so conversation was desultory and without purposeful suggestions, until Arthur suddenly remarked:

"I must return to the church, the old Saint Catherine's, and as urgently as I can."

He felt the same overwhelming compulsion as when confronting the enemy from the head of the crypt stairs. Rationalisation was clearly useless, the problem was firstly to convince the company, and secondly to find a way of making the journey in spite of the drifts and the icy cold.

At first they were all taken aback. Nacien said nothing but paid him a long interrogatory glance, and even Lucilla seemed nonplussed. Arthur's idea seemed pointless. Then Jenny came to his aid.

"Arthur darling, if you feel compelled to go back to Saint Catherine's, so be it. The problem is how to get you there. The distance is only a few miles, but through these drifts and in this cold, without special clothing you'll never make it. Don't be foolhardy, there's no sense in that."

Samuel looked puzzled.

"What do you propose to do when you get to Saint Catherine's?" he asked.

"I don't know," Arthur replied, "but I shall when I get there. I would borrow Pendragon. His strength will serve my need, blizzards or drifts, it is so."

"You're an idiot," Jenny exclaimed. "You can't even ride a horse. I must come with you. I can ride fairly well, and you shall hang on behind me. Pendragon can carry two people easily enough."

Arthur was increasingly aware of inexplicable notions stirring in his mind. Perhaps they were no more than desperate ideas generated by the pressure of the moment, but they felt more like ancient memories, vaguely recalled as if from far back in his childhood. Somehow. Jenny seemed to be caught up in the same emotional flux, bright-eyed and excited, she was sharing in the exhilaration which now motivated him. Also, unfamiliar words were germinating in his thoughts. It was odd indeed; he knew what the words meant, even though in themselves they were strange to him.

"You are thinking in Brythonic," said Hermione.

There was a long pause, until suddenly, and for reasons beyond logic, all present were at their utmost to give Arthur support.

"You are welcome to borrow Pendragon," said Nacien. "He's surely a powerful saddle horse – I ride him myself. You will need some clothes – Choone can help, and you will also need to take some feed for Pendragon. I fancy that something predestined awaits you, but I'm not so sure about Miss Parsloe's going with you. There will be dangers involved."

"I'm going!" said Jennifer, looking defiantly about her. "And there is no arguing about it."

"Very well," Arthur replied, "but I am riding Pendragon. You shall sit behind me. I am aware of an ability to control the heaviest of horses; Pendragon and I shall get on famously."

"Will he be able to force his way through the drifts?" Samuel asked. "Particularly if he is carrying two people, and do you know which way to go? Think carefully, and don't be rash. There is snow all over the place."

"There is a way." For the first time Kenwyn entered the conversation. "Push forward for a little distance along the track to the south of the village, until you come to a bridge across a small river, Saint Catherine's Brook. There's a good flow of water, so as yet the brook won't have frozen. Follow it until you come to the moor. There the snow shouldn't have drifted too much – the country is open and exposed, and the wind will have blown it more or less clear. Soon you will see the church on top of the hill, and you should be able to get quite close without struggling through drifts. I would come and guide you, if we had a second big horse."

Muffled as warmly as possible, they found the bridge easily enough. Pendragon seemed little affected by the cold, wading through the shallow snow, and forcing his way through the drifts as readily as any snow plough. Arthur was at first confused by his own ability to control the massive animal, if not entirely surprised. He had never ridden a horse before in the whole of his life, but the nuances of the art were all there in his mind, loaned to him, he believed, by ancestors from the other side of the veil.

"Darling, this is wonderful," said Jennifer, snuggling in behind him. "Or would be in happier circumstances. You are my knight in shining armour: every lady's dream.

"He took me in his strong white arms,

"He bore me on his horse away,

"Oe'r crag, morass and hairbreadth pass,

And never asked me yea or nay."

She quoted, squeezing herself even closer to him.

"Don't be an idiot, darling Guinever," he replied. "I haven't any armour, shining or otherwise, and we aren't riding the traditional white horse. Pendragon is as black as night." He barely realised that he had addressed his lady as 'Guinever'. Perhaps more surprisingly, neither did the lady herself.

They had some little difficulty in leaving the track to reach Saint Catherine's Brook; Arthur carefully nudged Pendragon down the snow-covered bank and into the two or three inches of water forming the flow of the stream. The horse did not seem concerned by the icy water, but splashed steadily onward, being careful to avoid overhanging branches, many laden with snow.

They reached the church much as Kenwyn had said they would, arriving in the early afternoon. Previously, Arthur had had small chance to take note of the building, but now he made a brief inspection, and with predictable interest. There were some Celtic features, although most of the building was clearly Saxon. Low round-headed arches, simple cylindrical pillars, and an emphatic division between the nave and the chancel were all typical, this last reminding him of the Greek Orthodox practice. Moreover, the window embrasures had been glazed in the central thickness of the walls, while the tower was circular in plan and at the western end of the nave.

All of this was more or less what he expected, but not so the stained glass. The winter sun was illuminating the southern aspect of the church, and exquisite colours glowed with a force which bordered on the surreal; indeed there was a noumenal factor involved which both of the lovers could recognise, but not explain. There were four windows in the south wall, none depicting a biblical scene. The first echoed the fresco beside the crypt staircase, showing Joseph of Arimathea planting the holy thorn, and the second showed a ship at sea, presumably bearing Joseph's party on their journey to Glastonbury.

Then they inspected the third window, and Jenny exclaimed:

"Darling, it's you – the famous scene from the Morte d'Arthur where the young unrecognised hero proves himself by drawing a sword out of the stone. Look, it's your face, there in the stained glass!"

Certainly, there was a distinct resemblance – apart from Arthur's short modern hairstyle, the likeness could have been photographic.

"I wonder why that key is there," Jenny continued. "On the ground near Arthur's left foot. I don't remember a key in the story, but it's prominent in the window." Sure enough, there was a large wrought iron key, with the end worked into an elaborate trefoil. There had to be some kind of significance attached to it, but what or why?

They moved on to the fourth window. This was subtle indeed. It showed a massive wooden chest, beneath a church window, and with the key in the lock. Looking down the lovers saw the same chest immediately before them, but without the key. Thus the fourth window was to a degree a picture of itself, but they spent small time in contemplating it before Arthur exclaimed:

"This chest is mine! We must open it at once. I don't know what it contains, but it's important, perhaps vitally so."

Alas, the chest was locked fast, and of such heavy construction that any reasonable assault on it seemed doomed to failure. They had to find the key, but where to look? Assuming that it was in the church at all. They both felt that it was a conundrum deliberately set.

"Why show the key in the stained glass?" Jennifer wondered, taking a deep breath. "There is some sort of logic in it, but what?"

"I don't know darling," Arthur replied. "But if there is a riddle in the windows, the solution may also be in the windows. The problem is finding it."

Jenny found that she was clasping her Saint Catherine's Cross, indeed so hard that it was digging into the palm of her hand. She now wore the ornament on a chain about her neck, and an awareness of Catharine's concern came into her mind. Was the great lady trying to tell her something? She unbuttoned her blouse, withdrew the cross, and looked at it closely in the now fading light.

"What does the Greek mean?" she asked Arthur.

He inspected the inscription carefully.

"Lift up the stone and there you shall find me, cleave the wood, and I am there," he translated.

"Look; look there," Jenny responded. "The third window shows a grassy background, but Arthur's foot is resting on a flat stone, like a five-sided paving flag, and it's got a Maltese Cross engraved on it."

"So what?" said Arthur, feeling a little extended. "Is there a connection?" but his voice died away as he followed Jenny's glance. His own foot was resting on a similar pentagonal stone set within the church paving. In fact his toe half obscured a Maltese Cross.

"Lift up the stone and there you shall find me," Jenny repeated. "Let's get the thing up and have a look."

The mortar was soft and crumbling, and they scraped away at it feverishly, using Jenny's nail file and Arthur's pocket knife. Soon the stone became a little loose. Arthur placed all his weight on one end, and it rocked slightly, sufficiently so for Jenny to get a grip on the raised portion. A few seconds later, and they had the slab up. Beneath was a second stone, with a recess chiselled into it, and within the recess was the key. There was a little superficial rust, but the metal appeared to have been coated with some sort of varnish and no great corrosion was apparent. Arthur placed the key in the lock.

"You turn it, darling," he said. "It was you who solved the riddle."

"Perhaps it was Catharine," she replied, but did his bidding nevertheless.

The lid was so heavy that Arthur had to use all his strength to raise it.

The first item to meet their eyes was a magnificent sword, wrapped in linen, and preserved by a coating of what Arthur said was a mixture of beeswax and tallow. The hilt was bejewelled with semi-precious stones, and the weapon clearly resembled that portrayed in the window.

"Take it my Liege Lord, because it is yours," said Jenny.

"Not yet," Arthur replied. "We'll have to spend the night here, and must first see to Pendragon. We more than owe it to him, and I believe he is caught up within what is happening."

There was still fair light outside the building, and Arthur found a barrel, with rainwater piped down from the roof, and a metal dipper nearby. He broke the ice, filled the dipper, and took it to Pendragon. Meanwhile Jenny had unsaddled him, covered him with his horse blanket, and was feeding him from the sack of oats which Ephraim had provided. The enormous animal was so gentle that he would eat from her hand. The church had no pews, but much of the floor was covered with a simple straw matting, so Arthur dragged a length out for Pendragon to lie on; they had tethered him loosely in the porch where he was out of the wind and the snow and the worst of the cold – Jenny said that he would do well enough for a day or so.

By now it was almost dark. They had brought no lantern, although fortunately Jenny had retained some matches from her earlier entry to the tin mine.

"The altar candles," she said. "Let's borrow the candlesticks from the sanctuary. Nacien wouldn't mind." Then she added: "We must light the right hand one first. Don't ask me why, but I know that it is so."

Both of the lovers were aware of an increasing sense of the numinous, indeed of some sort of covert power, but this affected them positively. Something great and good was going to happen to them, although they knew not what. How would the action develop? The doors at the entrance to the crypt staircase, close to King Arthur's Chest (as they had come to call it) had been left open, and they inspected the descending steps. The candles only illuminated a short distance, and they stared down into the darkness.

"Would you like me to explore the place?" Arthur asked. "And make sure there's no one down there."

"No darling," Jenny replied. "The crypt isn't within our part of what's happening. There's nobody there; we let the portcullis down again after Sturmey's lot had gone away. Best to bolt the doors shut and forget about it. Now let's go back to your wonderful King Arthur's Chest."

Their excitement was like to that of children opening presents under a Christmas tree. First, they examined the sword, peering close by the light of the candles. The blade showed a herring bone pattern, caused, so Arthur said, by the smith hammering together numerous steel lamina until he had forged a blade of enormous strength. A strip of high-carbon steel was then fire welded along each edge, and the whole ground sharp and polished; a work of art as well as a formidable weapon. The pommel included a large semi-precious stone, possibly a cairngorm, and the hilt was both jewelled and elaborately inlaid with a second metal. It looked like silver in the indifferent light.

The scabbard was in the same style and equally beautiful, but they were soon digging deeper into the contents of the chest, uncovering articles of great mystery to Jenny.

"But darling, what is a couter?" she asked, as Arthur produced an intricately worked metal plate, which he identified as such.

"It comes between the rerebrace and the vambrace," came the reply, "Protecting the knight's elbow but without restricting his arm. Similarly the spaudler protects his shoulder joint." Soon it became clear that they had a complete set of knight's accoutrements. Not merely the armour as such, but silken surcoats, padded tunics as worn beneath the mail, great woollen war cloaks, and a lambrequin which fell down like a small cape behind the great helm. But more was to come.

"What is this great silken affair, like a little tent?" was Jenny's next question.

"There is at least one complete barding," was Arthur's reply, "And your tent is part of it. It's a caparison, an ornamental cloak to cover the horse, but the whole collection of horse's gear is the barding. Look, here is a leather sheet to protect the war horse's chest, and an iron chanfron for his head. But just look at this saddle! And jewelled bridle! The whole set of accoutrements seems to me to be more medieval than Arthurian, as if the Round Table's knights were ahead of their time."

"Perhaps, my Liege Lord, you are overlooking the fact that all this equipment belonged to a king, and being of exceptional quality, was copied later on by men of lesser rank. I said 'belonged', yet it still belongs, because you are King Arthur. Just how this can be is beyond our logic, although I don't doubt that Lucilla could explain it. Accept it. It is so."

Soon they made a frugal meal from some bread and cheese given them by Ephraim, and sat talking side by side in the misericords, wrapped in the chest's great war cloaks.

"It's all too difficult to understand," said Arthur. "I know precious little mathematics, but some scientific friends at Cambridge say that you can't have the same time in two places, any more than you can be in two places at the same time."

"Darling," replied Jenny, "I think that I am beginning to get the hang of these seemingly weird goings on, but unlike Lucilla, can't put it into words. Don't be afraid; Catharine has things under control."

The reality of it was that Jennifer, like many gifted musicians, had a flair towards numerical skill. This gave her a sense of mathematical form. Similarly, she had a feeling for complex musical structures, where the score is polydimensional – both horizontal and vertical, but also involving a range of tempo, and instruments of different tonal qualities. Arthur, she knew, was reacting to impulses, which to fulfil the wishes of Catharine and her allies he had to take on trust. But what if his trust wavered?

She herself was in a stronger position. The nature and training of her mind made it easier for her to come to terms with the apparently impossible chronology in the events which they were experiencing. Thus while she could not understand these factors scientifically in the way that Lucilla could, neither did her deeper mind reject them at the unconscious level. Therefore she felt it was her duty to strengthen Arthur's confidence in obeying instructions which he might not understand, and indeed to do so promptly without doubting either himself or the sources of his information. These last she believed consisted of Catharine, and further persons on the other side who were in close contact with her.

Arthur put his arm round her.

"Sweetheart, if I am King Arthur, you are my Guinever, and this complicates things. We are told that Guinever was an ancestor of Catharine, but I don't see how you could fill that role."

"It doesn't seem complicated to me. It's like listening to a piece of music for the first time. Part way through, you can remember what you have heard, but can only make a rational guess at what is to come. Catharine is well aware of events from earlier times. Conversely, Guinever could not have known for certain what Catharine knows now. Hermione says that in her chronicle Morgan le Fey forewarned us of the future, but did not foretell it. What she wrote has turned out to be both true and to our advantage, but she didn't know for certain. Also, Hermione says that things are not necessarily predestined, even though Christianity will win out in the end."

Arthur gave in.

"My dearest, your eschatology is beyond me. Let's see to Pendragon, and then go to sleep."

"What is eschatology?" Jenny replied, more puzzled than informed.

"Something that comes after the finale. It seems a bit warmer in the chancel than it does in the nave. I'll fold up some of the straw matting to make a mattress, and with the war cloaks we shouldn't be too cold."

In fact they made their bed in the sanctuary, out of the draughts. Perhaps the night ought to have been a spooky experience, with the moonlight shining in through the stained glass, casting deep shadows in various places, and setting the silver of the altar candlesticks gleaming faintly with the reflected light. Yet Jenny felt a sense of overwhelming peace. She was in her beloved's arms, and could see the cross on the altar, clear enough in the moonlight. Arthur had placed his elaborate sword beside her, more she thought for emotional reasons than any fear of physical assault, and occasionally she could hear Pendragon shuffling in his porch, as good as any watchdog to give warning of a stranger's approach. And then her sense of peace became suffused with inexpressible joyfulness.

Catharine was thinking of her; sending her love to her. She knew that the great lady was aware of her loyalty, and indeed was pleased with her. Irrational? – maybe, but wonderful beyond words. Soon she slept.

They were up at first light. Arthur found some timber lying about in the churchyard, lit a fire in a sheltered corner, and heated water in the dipper. They washed as best they could, fed Pendragon, and ate the last of their food.

"What now my Liege?" asked Jennifer, although she knew full well what his reply would be.

"We take up arms and prepare for action. You will have to help me, because of the difficulty of a knight putting on his armour by himself. First we must equip Pendragon."

They began by fitting an iron chanfron, covering most of the front of the horse's head, and followed by the rest of the barding – a thick leather sheet to protect his chest, a magnificent caparison worked in multicoloured silks, a saddle cloth, and finally the great saddle and bridle which they had examined the evening before.

While they worked, it became clear that an exhilarating change was coming over the horse. Although he remained biddable enough, his demeanour gained spirit. He snorted frequently, shaking his head and pawing the floor of the porch with one mighty hoof, he gave the impression of desiring some sort of action

"Easy, easy, my boy," said Jenny, scratching his nose. "There will be plenty of work for you to do soon. More than enough I fancy."

"Darling, you know that the English shire horses are descended from the great war horses introduced to Britain in Arthurian times?" Arthur asked. "It seems that Arthur and Guinever are not the only ones being strengthened from the other side. It must be the war gear that causes the effect."

Equipping Arthur was a more complicated process, exacerbated by the box containing more than one suit of armour – it was not always obvious which parts belonged together. An encouraging factor was that after a few minutes they realised that they both seemed to possess a fair knowledge of what they were about, including the procedure for equipping a knight. By usual standards there was no accounting for this, particularly so for Jennifer, while Arthur insisted that he had no great expertise in what was a specialised subject, even among historians – the information had to be of supernatural origin. However, a minor difficulty arose from a problem in vocabulary. Thus, Jennifer was upset by what she referred to in a word sounding something like 'Ysbardun', and then recognised that she meant spurs, objecting to Pendragon being subject to such devices. And yet in a moment Arthur knew what she meant, agreeing that he would not wish to use the pair of vicious looking rowels riveted onto the armoured footwear; sabatons in the accepted terminology. Finally, and kneeling before him, Jenny buckled the sword belt around her monarch's waist.

"Excalibur!" she exclaimed.

"No, no sweetheart," came the reply. "This sword is called 'Caliburn'. Excalibur was a different weapon. We'll talk about it sometime."

It came as no surprise to find that the armour fitted Arthur as if it had been made for him, and before long he was fully equipped. Mounting Pendragon with the aid of a bench in the church porch, he did not find the metal unduly heavy or cumbersome, but the horse seemed frisky, quite different from his previous docile self.

"Arthur y Brenin, Arthur y Amherawdyr!" cried Jennifer, as she sprang up behind him, pulling her war cloak about her, and gripping the back of the saddle.

Pendragon snorted, thumped the ground with a forefoot, and with excitement in their hearts, they were off.

CHAPTER XXII
Caliburn

Arthur's immediate intention was to return to Ildierna village, but they had barely covered a furlong before they noticed a rider coming across the moor, mounted on a sturdy cob. The newcomer was muffled in a heavy cloak, and making steady progress through the snow, which at that point was about six inches deep. Who could it be?

"Probably nothing to do with us," said Arthur, without checking Pendragon. "He doesn't seem to be coming from Ildierna way, and we don't want to be delayed."

But the rider waved vigorously.

"I think it's Kenwyn," cried Jenny, returning the wave, "probably with a message. Let's go to meet her."

Arthur reined Pendragon in, but before he could turn him, they saw another person struggling along on foot from the general direction of Saint Catherine's village. The second newcomer was also a woman, ill clad against the cold and clearly in some distress. Indeed she appeared to be exhausted, almost to the point of collapse.

"Darling we must help her," said Jenny, apparently oblivious of the fact that she had just counselled Arthur to ride in a different direction, and thus contributing to her fiancé's dilemma. So with uncharacteristic indecision, he did nothing. Kenwyn was the first to arrive.

"Greetings, and the Lord be with you," she said, throwing back her hood. "I have a message from Ildierna, but who is that coming towards us? She looks familiar."

Neither of the lovers could enlighten her, and after another minute, Kenwyn exclaimed:

"Gracious me, it's Ronwen Hartwaker, one of the women out of Colgrin Sturmey's human cattle shed. I must go to her."

She urged her cob forward. Arthur now recognised the lady; she was in fact the large, apparently slow-witted woman who had annoyed him shortly before their escape through the window at Langarrow. Still feeling a trifle nonplussed, he followed Kenwyn, to find that the two women were having an agitated conversation in Cornish. This neither he nor Jenny could understand, so feeling that action was better than words, he removed his magnificent war cloak, and passed it to Ronwen. The lady was shaking with cold; Kenwyn promptly muffled her into the enormous garment. Arthur's kingly armour was now clearly revealed, together with his shield, hanging from the saddle bow and illuminated with a brightly painted picture of the Virgin Mary.

"What's to do?" he enquired of Kenwyn, but both ladies stood spellbound by his changed appearance.

"Arthur, yr Amherawdyr!" exclaimed Ronwen, her chill forgotten, and making a somewhat ridiculous attempt at a curtsy, despite the enveloping folds of the war cloak.

"Never mind about all that," said Arthur, a little impatiently. "What's to do?"

Kenwyn burst into a complex explanation:

"Ronwen says that Colgrin's people started an immediate chase to round up the escaping women, but she doesn't know how it turned out, because the snow came. To get shelter, she hid in an isolated barn, and stayed there all day yesterday with nothing to eat. She daren't go home, and decided to make her way to the church in the hope that Colgrin will respect its right of sanctuary. Perhaps he would, more out of superstition than faith, but there's another factor in that Colgrin's Saracen friends are due at any time, and they will be furious if there aren't any women for them. You may be sure that they will help Colgrin and won't respect the church. What's best to do I don't know, but in humanity, we can't leave Ronwen here."

"Of course we can't," said Jenny, indignantly enough. "No knight errant would ever consider such a thing. She needs food and warmth, and that right urgently."

Poor Arthur. There were now three dependant women, and what did they expect him to do? He decided to play for a few minutes to think.

"What was your message from Ildierna?" he asked Kenywn.

"They want your leadership there. The local people have had more than enough of Colgrin Sturmey's extortion, and they believe that you have been sent back to earth to put a stop to him. And I think Father Nacien had foresight concerning your trip to Saint Catherine's. Certainly he was aware of the chest in the church, and what it contained. Early this morning he and Ephraim Choone decided that a thaw is coming soon; the wind is round into the southwest, and at this time of year that usually means warm rain. The roads will be like bogs, but not impassable. The people want you to lead them in a revengeful attack on Langarrow. Sturmey hanged by the neck until he is dead, and half his followers likewise. It's our fight, and while we're grateful to Admiral Mantzini and her woman soldiers, we want to settle the score ourselves. The quarrel doesn't seem much of her business."

This made things more complicated than ever. Obviously, Kenwyn and the Ildierna residents knew nothing of Archaroch and the satanic involvement in recent events. Moreover, the business was indeed the concern of Lucilla's people. He himself was supporting them, and not the other way round, as Kenwyn had assumed. But how was he to explain all this? Clearly, he could not. And what was he to do with Ronwen?

The second question soon answered itself.

"Is there a safe haven round here where we could take you?" he asked her.

She replied negatively. All the local people were too terrified of Langarrow to provide shelter, but before she could complete her reply Kenwyn burst into the conversation:

"Look over there – those men are from Langarrow and they're coming this way. We must flee."

Sure enough, four men on sizeable ponies were approaching from the same direction as Ronwen.

Flight never entered Arthur's mind. He was Arthur, the King Conqueror, and these men were his people's foes.

"Jump down Guinever," he said to Jenny, as he placed the great Arthurian helm upon his head.

Pendragon seemed to sense his master's wishes, and with the snow flying from his hooves, needed no urging to charge the enemy. Peering through his visor, Arthur saw the four horsemen rein in their mounts, and watched the expression on their faces assume first that of incredulity, and then blind terror. They were armed with flintlock pistols and opened fire immediately.

Possibly they would have been wiser to have waited until he was upon them, for two balls went wide, and the third glanced of his helmet. The fourth weapon failed to fire. Then he found that he was shouting at the top of his voice, incomprehensible Brythonic words which seemed to echo within the confines of his helmet. Who was he? What was he? He hardly knew himself, but it was superb.

He ignored the shield, and drew Caliburn, swinging the great blade two-handed. Suddenly he was into them. He struck the first man upon his left shoulder, beside his head, and the sword cut down into his chest, smashing through the scapula and clavicle as if they were matchwood. The fellow went down off his pony, spouting blood. Arthur wheeled Pendragon, the great animal reacting as it were by nature, and Arthur swung at a second adversary, catching him sideways across the bottom of his rib cage, and almost cutting the man in half. Then Pendragon bucked on his forelegs, forcing Arthur to lean far back in the saddle as he heard the thump of Pendragon's hooves contacting one of the ponies. He saw the rider sprawling, with the pony on its side, and the fourth antagonist making off, flogging his mount for all he was worth. The pony scrambled to its feet; there was a cut on its flank where one of Pendragon's hooves had made contact, but it did not seem badly hurt. Suddenly, Arthur's fury was spent.

"Get up," he said to the rider.

Terrified, the man obeyed, raising one arm as if to ward off the expected blow.

"I shall harm you no further," said Arthur, "but go back to Langarrow and tell them that nemesis is coming upon them all. Feel lucky that I let you go."

And so the man fled, his pony limping slightly as he urged it along.

There was blood all over the place. The second man was already dead, with the first moaning and mortally injured, while their ponies stood motionless, as if bemused by events. Arthur climbed down from Pendragon and looked around, with the war horse whinnying, tossing his head, and pawing the snow with a forefoot. He seemed to be in his element.

The women were coming towards him, Kenwyn leading her cob with Jenny and Ronwen walking behind. Jenny surveyed the scene, pale-faced and somewhat unnerved. Ronwen kept well back, but Kenwyn was made of sterner stuff. Picking up the dead man's powder flask and pistol she reloaded the weapon with great dexterity, placed the muzzle to the head of the dying man, and pulled the trigger. He died instantly, a cloud of smoke from the black powder adding to the macabre impact of the scene. Kenwyn calmly reloaded, took possession of the man's pistol, powder flask and supply of bullets, and hung the holster under her cloak. She then recovered the same arms from the man she had just killed, and passed the equipment to Jenny.

"Use powder enough to cover the bullet were it in the palm of your hand, and don't forget the wads, one to keep the powder in, and one on top of the bullet. Have a practice later on."

She ignored Ronwen. Meanwhile, Arthur wiped his sword on one of the corpses, and replaced it in the scabbard.

"What's to do then?" he asked for the third time.

To his surprise both the women thought the question funny, and as if a string were released, started to laugh. Ronwen stood impassively, still a little distance away, and then began to sob, silently, but disturbingly enough. Fearing hysteria, Arthur resolved on further action.

"We ought to hide the corpses somewhere," he said.

Kenwyn stopped laughing.

"What for?" she replied. "Leave them for the wolves to find, and let's get away from here." She then continued to Jenny, "Which pony would you like? They look much the same to me."

Jenny selected the animal belonging to the man Arthur had first attacked, and hitching up her cloak and skirts, mounted it astride.

"This one's yours," said Kenwyn to Ronwen.

"But I can't ride a horse," Ronwen wailed in reply.

"Now's your chance to learn," said Jenny. "My Liege Lord will hoist you into the saddle."

Next, her Liege Lord surveyed Pendragon, standing tall beside him.

Arthur was now carrying some weight of armour, and sixteen hands of horse looked bigger than before. Kenwyn said nothing, but standing close, she linked her hands together, palm upwards in front of her waist.

"Can you hold me?" Arthur asked, as he put his foot into her hands.

"I think so," came the reply, "but spring up hard, while I lift."

The second attempt proved successful, and Arthur thus surveyed the women, gathered round on the smaller horses. The original King Arthur, he remembered, had introduced the heavy horse to Britain, and now he could well understand why. Pendragon weighed as much as the other three horses put together, and in the absence of effective firearms was a weapon in himself. Certainly, without Pendragon he could not have overcome four armed men.

But what lay ahead? He felt that it was his duty to lead, although Kenwyn had a far greater knowledge of the terrain than he had. Best to compromise.

"You go ahead please Kenwyn," he said. "Then the other ladies, and I shall give you a rearguard, not that I think we shall be attacked."

And thus they went, leaving the corpses where they had fallen, pitiful enough in the trodden snow, and with Jenny leading Ronwen's pony. Almost immediately, they felt a change in the weather.

The bitter cold had lessened, and the wind was rising, carrying spots of rain with it, digging tiny craters in the snow. Progress was fair at first, but the wet snow proved more treacherous than the earlier crisp material, and soon their pace slowed. The rainfall increased to a deluge, and poor Arthur became wet and cold. His armour included a padded tunic, or gambeson, worn beneath the metal, and this provided some degree of insulation, but the fabric became first damp and then sodden. Also he had removed the great helm because it restricted vision, and the rainwater trickled remorselessly down his neck, soaking his shoulders and thorax.

The women were in better case. Their heavy hooded cloaks were densely woven from sheep's wool, which retained a modicum of its natural greasiness and hence resistance to the rain. Kenwyn led steadily on. Visibility was poor, but she seemed to be following a route somewhat different from that taken by Arthur and Jennifer the previous day, and this brought them to a rough track where the snow had either melted or been washed away. The pace improved, with the horses splashing along through the stones and mud, until they came to Saint Catherine's Brook.

But 'Brook' was no longer the word. The track led to a ford, where they found the channel bank high with rushing ice cold water brought down by the melt draining from the moor.

"Holy Mary!" cried Kenwyn. "I wouldn't fancy crossing that, never mind trekking along the river bed. We'll have to find another route."

They were now not far from Ildierna Village, and had entered an area of shrubby woodland – difficult to penetrate, especially on horseback. The track (which led to Ildierna) continued on the other side of the stream, and there was a footpath of a sort on the near side of the channel, but overhanging branches denied them passage except on foot. Kenwyn hesitated for several seconds.

"We had better dismount," she said, "and follow the stream until we come to another track going off to the left. It's in the wrong direction, but will ring us to a junction where we can loop back to the village. It's not far now, thank God."

Reluctantly, they slid down from their mounts, and started leading them along the path. The rain continued, and they were now in poor shape. Ronwen had eaten nothing since her escape from Langarrow, and Arthur was soaked to the skin. Moreover, he had to carry the weight of the armour along the slippery path, stooping frequently to avoid overhanging branches, and leading Pendragon at the same time with Caliburn unbuckled and hanging awkwardly from the saddle. The two other women had fared better, but all were relieved when Kenwyn located the second track. Arthur in particular felt comforted on realising that they were close to where Hubert had intercepted him a few days before. They had to be approaching Kenwyn's junction, and at least he knew where they were.

They remounted, Arthur scrambling up with the aid of a convenient tree, but before they had covered a couple of furlongs, voices became apparent through some nearby trees. People were moving towards Ildierna, along the track towards which Kenwyn was heading, and now close to hand.

"Stop and listen," said Arthur. "They may be hostile."

The strangers were only about twelve yards distant, and although they seemed to be either arguing or grumbling with raised voices it was impossible to make out what they were saying. Kenwyn slid down from her horse, and looked anxiously towards the unknown men.

"It doesn't sound like English or Cornish," she said. "I'll investigate."

And she slipped away, moving cautiously through the boskage, to return a minute or two later.

"There the Saracens!" she exclaimed. "They must have landed further along the coast, and are straggling along to Langarrow by the Ildierna road. Somehow we must get ahead of them and warn Ephraim. He won't be expecting a hostile force coming from this direction, and God knows what they'll do to the village."

"I'll charge through them on Pendragon," said Arthur, "and reach Ildierna in time for Ystelle to get her troops into position."

"You won't get past," replied Kenwyn. "The track is narrow, there's a lot of them, and they're tougher than the beauties you tackled this morning near Saint Catherine's. It's up to me."

She removed her cloak, hitched her skirts up to her thighs, and without further word went running off, back along the track which they had just traversed.

Arthur turned Pendragon to follow her, but Jenny intervened.

"Let her go," she said. "Kenwyn is a hardy young woman who knows what she is doing, and you'll only hinder her with Pendragon. My guess is that she'll ford the brook somehow or other and get to Ephraim in time. Better still, this way the Saracens won't know that Ildierna has been alarmed against them."

"You're right," Arthur replied. "What we must do is create a diversion, delay the Saracens, and give Kenwyn more time."

Jenny's response startled him, and was a trifle incautious. She gave no reply, but producing her flintlock pistol, fired it through the trees in the general direction of the Saracens. The voices ceased, only to resume a few moments later more loudly than before. By now most of the gang had passed on towards Ildierna, but nevertheless Arthur gained the impression that at least some had halted. As for Ronwen, she fled, despite her declared inability to ride, urging her pony in the opposite direction to Kenwyn with Arthur's cloak flapping behind her.

Jenny was reloading her pistol beneath the shelter of her cloak, as Arthur said:

"Come on, in Ronwen's direction, but let's make as much noise as possible to distract the Saracens. SAINT PIRAN FOR KERNOW!" he added, shouting as loudly as he could.

Jenny joined him as they started their horses along the track. She was shouting as loudly as Arthur; the sudden exhilarating urge for action was upon them once more. It was some time afterwards that they realised that they had both been shouting in Brythonic – words which made sense at the time, although on later recollection meant nothing to them.

The Saracens seemed to take no immediate action, but soon the tracks converged, and the lovers could see their enemy standing about uncertainly, about two hundred yards off in the direction of Ildierna. Jenny was leading the spare horse; Kenwyn had left her pistol in the holster, hanging from the pommel of the saddle. Jenny inspected the weapon, and passed it to Arthur.

"It looks dry to me," she said, "and the rain's abated. Let's give them a shot."

"The range is too great for pistols," Arthur replied. "So we'll close up a bit, and try to annoy them into chasing us. I can see a few more looking back along the track. The more the better I fancy."

"Fair enough, but after you've fired, pass me the pistol, and I'll back off and reload them both."

Shouting dramatic challenges, they trotted forward. At a range of about sixty yards, they noticed that three of the enemy were unslinging what looked like muskets.

"Get in behind me Guinever," said Arthur.

Before Jenny could do so, they saw the flash of flintlocks, but no detonations followed.

"Their primings are wet," cried Jenny, as the range closed.

They fired their pistols in quick succession, but both bullets missed, and Arthur tossed his pistol to Jenny. Then he charged, roaring furiously, helmet on head, and swinging Caliburn two handed. But these antagonists had fought cavalry before, and avoided his charge by jumping into bushes on either side of the track. From here, they attempted to disable Pendragon as he passed by slashing at his legs with what looked like narrow-bladed scimitars. Fortunately, none of the blows landed. Arthur saw that the Saracens' vanguard was running back towards him, so he continued his charge for another fifty yards or so, until arriving at a point where the track widened, he wheeled Pendragon to send him rushing back towards Jenny. And now, it seemed by instinct, he had the measure of their slashing tactics. He caused Pendragon to weave across the track, but keeping more to the right than the left, while he swung Caliburn right-handed. Only one fellow tried to attack, and Arthur sent his scimitar flying. Whether or not the man's hand was injured was impossible to tell.

"Well done my Liege," cried Jenny, as she passed him a reloaded pistol. "You seem to have checked their march to Ildierna. Pray God Kenwyn gets there soon. What next, think you?"

"Let us remain here, and defy them. It can't be much more than a mile to Ildierna, so even a quarter of an hour will count. Somehow I doubt if they will be in a hurry to move off with us around to harass their rear."

This led to a stand-off, with the Saracens some eighty yards away. There were about thirty of them, although as Jenny remarked, some might have gone on towards Ildierna. An English speaker shouted some blood curdling threats, ignored by the lovers. Then the enemy moved off towards Ildierna, but keeping in a compact group.

"Lend me your pistol, darling," said Arthur, and trotted off after them, paused at a distance of about fifty feet, and fired both pistols. The first shot went wide, but the second ball hit one of the Saracens, making glancing contact with his shoulder. The wound was probably superficial, but stimulated a furious response. The whole group turned towards Arthur, and yelling furiously, came splashing back along the muddy track towards him. This got them nowhere. He merely wheeled Pendragon, and cantered away before them, the war horse outdistancing the pursuit with ease. Jenny had started the other horses, and they trotted along together for about a furlong, until on glancing back they saw that the Saracens had broken off the chase.

Jenny seemed to be enjoying the situation.

"This could go on all day darling," she remarked, as she reloaded the pistols, "or until we run out of gunpowder. There's not a lot left."

"Don't forget Kenwyn's message," Arthur replied. "We are wanted back at Ildierna. The problem is how to get there with the Saracens in the way. There must be a way round, because there are plenty of tracks, but without Kenwyn we don't know enough about them."

"Perhaps there is an alternative strategy," was Jenny's response.

But before she could develop her ideas, they noticed a bedraggled figure coming towards them from the opposite direction to the Saracens, making painfully slow progress along the muddy track, and leading a limping horse. It was the man whose life Arthur had spared earlier in the day; presumably still hostile, although it was obvious that he had precious little fight in him. Jenny took a long hard look.

"Fortunate for us I fancy," she remarked. "He must know his way round here. So let us oblige him to take us to Ildierna by some back lane route, and then send him on to Langarrow with a cock and bull story to mislead Sturmey."

"What sort of a story?" Arthur replied, feeling a little put out. The women seemed to be making most of the running today, he reflected.

"Tell him that you can see Sturmey's side of things, but have been overwhelmed by the Christians. That the gnostic priests have possession of your personality, that you are compelled to do their will, and can only be released by the power of the spear. Most likely Sturmey will believe the messenger, if we dress up the message carefully enough."

CHAPTER XXIII
Subterfuge

The man said that he was called Isaac Sealey. (He made no attempt to avoid capture – if that were the word.) The lovers soon realised that Sealey was as much a Sturmey conscript as a volunteer, although Arthur was well aware that extreme poverty could force men into behaviour which they would normally avoid. Nevertheless, Isaac was Sturmey's man, and they had to go carefully. Furthermore, they did not know how much he knew.

Assuming a reassuring smile, Jennifer began:

"Mr Sealey," she said, "Arthur Marazion is my fiancé and is in a position of enormous difficulty, if not danger. You must be aware that Mr Sturmey's allies, at present visiting him at Langarrow, have powers allied to witchcraft, but of far greater force. These visitors can do much to enrich you all at Langarrow. Believe me, if their efforts are successful you will enjoy gold aplenty for the rest of your lives; far more than could be earned by labour in the tin mines, or struggling with the Cornish soil."

She searched Sealey's face. The man stood impassively, but she felt that her words were having some sort of effect. At least he was attending to her. She continued:

"You will also know that my fiancé was removed forcefully from Langarrow at the same time as your women were released from Mr Sturmey's pen. Something which you may not know is that your enemies include people with powers similar to those mentioned, but opposed to the wishes of your Mr Sturmey and his allies. Mr Marazion has fallen under the influence of these people, who I would add, do not really belong in Cornwall. One of them is a female priest, called a gnostic, by name the Reverend Hermione de Lamarac, and she is particularly powerful."

Isaac interrupted her.

"Aye," he said. "Sturmey's right mad about it all. And he's getting blamed by Lord Archaroch for letting things go wrong. Agravain's stirring it up as well. A dark horse that one. I dursn't go back, and don't know what to do. Sturmey's lost all the women, and I was in charge of us lot hunting Ronwen Hartwaker, when up comes your man like the wrath of God, and I've two men dead and one run off to God knows where, and it'll be my fault most like. Haven't even got the woman back, and she's a good one. Big and plump, like the Saracens fancy. They'd sell her on into a stew house – she'd fetch good prices there all right."

Clearly, the man was not happy about his relationship with the Langarrow management! He also appeared reluctant to return there. It was complicated, and Jenny and Arthur exchanged glances. Curiously, he showed little animosity towards Arthur, and it seemed wise to discover why. Jenny felt that it was safest to continue the interrogation herself, because if Arthur spoke it would tend to gainsay the notion that he was subservient to Hermione's psychic domination. Best to develop some sort of rapport with Sealey. Persuade him to guide them to Ildierna, and keep on talking as they rode. Briefly, she explained the presence of the Saracens, and their need to avoid them. Sealey agreed to guide them to a point close to the village, but refused to enter it – understandably enough, thought Jenny.

"Take the spare horse," she said, "and ride beside My Lord, but keep close; there may be a way of getting you back into favour at Langarrow. You help us, and we help you. I shall explain as we ride."

Sealey led them along some open ground to the south of the Ildierna woodland, where for most of the distance they could ride side by side. Jennifer found that the wily Agravain had been spreading rumours of the spear's capabilities around Langarrow, probably to support people's faith in the false article. This proved fortunate; Sealey accepted her arguments more easily than she had expected.

"You see Isaac," she said, "after the magicians' jesting at poor old Agravain's expense, Arthur was considering their offer of a voluntary alliance, so the spear was not used to compel his obedience. But later in the evening, as indeed you know, men from Ildierna raided Langarrow to release the captive women, and Arthur was also taken, tied over the back of a pony. The reason for this was not vengeance, as thought at first. My beloved is a man with great powers of leadership." She paused to add to her words dramatic effect, and continued:

"In fact he is none other than the ancient monarch, Arthur the King Conqueror, returned to earth. The magicians' offer to him was generous indeed, but he is now subject by ghostly influence to the will of your enemies. Archaroch must bring the spear to Ildierna to break this influence. Therefore, I would ask you to ride to Langarrow and explain this influence."

Sealey looked at Arthur with an expression of both curiosity and awe.

"So the old tales are true," he said, his voice rising with excitement. "And the king has come back at last. If he leads us, all things will be set to rights, and all men will enjoy their own. Unless the other lot bewitch him with enchantments. May luck forfend."

301

They were now close to Ildierna, and at that moment, the sound of gunfire came through the trees.

"That must be the Saracens attacking Ildierna," cried Isaac, showing some surprise. "God help the villagers!"

"I fancy that His help may not be needed as much as you think," said Arthur, speaking for the first time. "Most of the shooting sounds like the dragon guns the Myrmidons use."

"Please, Oh please Isaac," pleaded Jennifer, "hurry on to Langarrow – Sturmey needs to attack now while the Saracens are still in action and get the villagers caught in the middle. Make haste while yet there is time."

To her relief, Sealey turned his pony, and made off without further reply.

They entered Ildierna as the brief engagement with the Saracens was coming to an end. An occasional musket shot could be heard, but most of the gunfire was the exceedingly sharp crack from the rifled barrels of the dragon guns, at first a few close knit volleys, and then more randomly as the Myrmidons broke the Saracens' attack.

"You are late, King Arthur," cried Ystelle, with gentle irony. "It's all over bar the shouting, but there are injured men out there. I must arrange help for them."

The battle had lasted barely twenty minutes. Ephraim had pulled a pair of farm carts across the lane where it entered the village, and tipping them onto their sides, formed a barricade. A band of village men then took up positions behind the carts, and the Saracens, anticipating an easy victory had rushed forward, only to find themselves caught in a devastating crossfire from the Myrmidons guns. Thus none of them even reached the carts; soon eight of their vanguard were lying dead with three injured, and the remainder fleeing back the way they had come.

"Than God Kenwyn came in time to give us warning," exclaimed Ephraim. "We had only a quarter of an hour, but it was enough."

Then he noticed Arthur, still seated majestically enough upon the massive Pendragon, and to Arthur's intense embarrassment, sank down on one knee.

"Arthur, Arthur yr Amherawdyr," he cried, relapsing into Cornish, and then calling out again, "Cyfarch galow, Arthur y Brenin, Arthur yr Amherawdyr."

Suddenly, there were villagers all around, talking in an incomprehensible mixture of English and Cornish. Even Pendragon seemed to react to the emotion of the occasion, whinnying, snorting and tossing his head. Then Nacien appeared, accompanied by Kenwyn and Samuel, and spontaneously the entire company started to sing. The lovers were confused by the diction; some of the villagers were singing in Cornish and others in English, until Jenny exclaimed:

"It's the Te Deum Laudamus," even as they caught the notes of Hermione's clear contralto, singing the canticle in Greek.

Arthur was close to tears. These people regarded him as some sort of demigod, an ancestral saviour come to their aid. It was like an euhemerism in reverse. Here he was, physically present, a man in armour on a magnificent horse, and they were identifying him with a myth from their past. But was the ancient King Arthur a myth? Many people believed so, but Arthur now knew for certain that he was far more than that – without doubt the king was an historical person. It was all too complicated, but the Cornishmen's trust in him was overwhelming. He must not, could not, allow himself to fail them.

"Whose waters raise the souls of those whose epitaphs are lamps within the pillared halls of time," quoth Jenny as she slipped down from her saddle. "You'll have to say something. Think yourself into the personality of your ancestor, and speak."

She was right of course, but what was he to say? An initial gesture was called for. He raised his shield onto his left arm; the brightly painted picture of the Virgin Mary became apparent.

"Hail Mary, blessed art thou, Mother of God —" began a woman's voice.

He drew Caliburn, and raised the blade vertically aloft. A great hush fell upon the crowd.

Arthur took a deep breath, and as if by magic, words formed within his mind.

"Lift up your heads, O ye gates," he cried aloud, "and be ye lift up, ye everlasting doors!"

He pointed Caliburn towards Langarrow, and continued, "And the King of Glory shall come in."

Then, after a pause he added, "Who is the King of Glory?"

Arthur was in fact quoting from the twenty-fourth psalm, although it is doubtful if he himself were aware of this. But the villagers recognised the famous text, and bursting into spontaneous cheers, took up Arthur's words.

"It is the Lord strong and mighty," – a voice answered his question.

"Even the Lord mighty in battle," called a second.

"Even the Lord of hosts, he is the King of Glory," called a third.

"Arthur, King Conqueror, come back to lead us," shrilled a woman's voice.

It was difficult not to be overwhelmed by the poignancy of the scene, but Arthur recognised that careful leadership was more important than oratory. He raised his sword again, and once more the crowd fell silent.

"My loyal friends and subjects," he cried. "Now is the time to take up arms, but more than pitchforks and bill hooks are necessary. Our enemy has firearms, and swords and pikes. Get out your longbows and make arrows ready. Muster every gun you can find. And attend to the advice of Mrs Ystelle Zabuloe, for she is a veritable Helen of the Hosts, come to your aid."

This resulted in a further cheer. Thank heavens, thought Arthur, they are familiar with the Celtic stories. In the 'Dream of Maxen', the 'Men of the Island' would assemble for no one save Helen, so there would be little resentment from Ystelle's female leadership. But the winter's day was getting old, and it would not do to attack as darkness was falling. He had to plan for next day.

"There is much to prepare," he continued. "Go now to your homes, make ready your weapons, your warmest clothing, and pack some food. We shall muster here at first light tomorrow, and fall on Langarrow before the evil ones have their eyes open. I shall lead on ahead, and you will fall in as Colonel Zabuloe directs."

He paused for breath, among further cheers. Long years of resentment were coming to a head.

"And now farewell my friends," he concluded. "And God bless you all. We march at dawn."

Then suddenly, he was tired: weary to the point of exhaustion. Stirring Pendragon, he rode slowly towards Ephraim's barn, and a Myrmidon opening a door for him, King Arthur left the scene.

The inside of barn was different from when he had last seen it. The straw had been pressed into rough bales, and a fire was blazing in an iron basket, with the smoke disappearing through vents near the roof. He clambered down from Pendragon, and shaking with cold and fatigue felt relieved to be surrounded by his friends.

"Get him stripped," ordered Ystelle. "This man is wet and dangerously cold. Bring that tub back, heat more water, and get some hot porridge ready with honey in it. No, Georgina, none of Nacien's brandy. He can have some shortly, when he is warmer and has had some food. Mulled ale will be all right, there's plenty of beer about."

So they restored him, until an hour later, King Arthur, reduced to a more usual state of humanity, and wrapped warmly in a blanket while his clothes were dried, joined in the strategic discussion for the forthcoming day. Surprisingly, it was Hermione who took the lead.

"There are two issues," she said. "Since we already have the Spear, the first one is to sort out the situation here in Cornwall, and the second is to deal with Archaroch and his lieutenants. Preferably, we shall convey them to Lyonesse, there to await the pleasure of Her Majesty, Queen Catharine the Second."

"May we take the Archaroch issue first," said Arthur. "I have a plan."

Next day dawned bright and clear, with a touch of frost that helped to harden the rain-sodden ground. Arthur set out for Langarrow as agreed the day before, early, and alone. Considerable danger was involved, but curiously he felt no fear, merely a calculated reserve towards the round of bluff which he was about to play upon the necromancers.

It was a beautiful winter morning, and the freshly groomed Pendragon trotted steadily onward, his caparison washed and ironed from the previous day's rain and mud. Also, Arthur's armour was cleaned and polished to a brilliance befitting its original owner, although now concealed by the war cloak worn previously by Jennifer. There was much at stake. If the bluff failed, not only would there be great bloodshed, but also the necromancers would escape back to the Amente and Catharine's instructions be left unfulfilled. And how much of Sealey's story had Sturmey believed?

Meanwhile, Ystelle was assembling her forces. They had grown somewhat, because Ephraim had sent messengers to some outlying farms, and about a dozen extra men had come in. Ystelle looked them over. They were a hardy lot, better armed than the villagers; all carried some sort of firearm, and one man had a primitive muzzle-loading rifle. How far they could be disciplined was another matter. She decided on two groups: namely a vanguard led by herself, including the newcomers, and a reserve under Georgina, with most of the village men and six of her Myrmidons. The remaining Myrmidons were to remain with Lucilla and Hermione at Ildierna, thus providing a rearguard in case the Saracens returned, and also to await the fulfilment of Arthur's plan.

There were few people about as Arthur rode along Langarrow's principal street, to hammer with his armoured gauntlet on the door of the 'Langarrow Arms'. Soon the innkeeper's face appeared at an upper window, and assumed a startled expression at the site of Arthur's helmet, not far below the window sill.

"Who are you, and what do you want?" enquired the innkeeper.

"What do I want?" Arthur echoed, with visor raised and tone imperative. "I want you down here, and now. Who I am can wait until you arrive."

The man obeyed with alacrity, but instead of opening the door, he merely opened a small Judas hole in the panelling.

"Well what?" he said.

"Open this door," cried Arthur. "I do not talk under these conditions."

"I'll do no such thing," came the reply, but before the innkeeper could continue, Arthur had wheeled Pendragon.

"Gwingo, Pendragon, gwingo," said Arthur, or words something like that.

He was speaking Cornish, barely understood by himself, but the huge horse reacted instantly, lashing out simultaneously with his hind feet. The concussive force of the stallion kicking in this way was truly enormous, and at the second impact the door flew inward, breaking away at its hinges.

Arthur wheeled Pendragon again, and bending low to get through the doorway, rode into the bar parlour. The innkeeper was reaching for a blunderbuss.

"Leave it you fool," Arthur commanded, drawing Caliburn half way from the sheath. "You asked me who I am; and I tell you. I am Arthur yr Amherawdyr, the King Conqueror, come to lead his people to victory." He removed his war cloak, and laid it across the front of the saddle.

Open-mouthed, the man stepped back a pace, staring at the gleaming steel and brightly painted shield.

"So what Isaac said is true," he said. "And Mr Agravain's counsel."

"Never mind about that," Arthur replied. "Go and fetch Sturmey. I want him, now."

As the man fled, Arthur noticed several faces looking in curiously past the shattered door, presumably attracted by the sound of Pendragon kicking it in. He rode back out of the inn.

"Don't stand there like sheep," he bade the onlookers. "Go and spread the message that Arthur yr Amherawdyr has returned, armed at all points and ready for action. Go first to Isaac Sealey and the visiting magicians. Time is vital."

Within minutes, the space outside the inn was full of excited people, milling about and asking questions which Arthur ignored, sitting impassively upon Pendragon but hoping that his inner tension was not obvious. He removed his helmet, and looked about him stern faced until Sturmey appeared.

"So you've returned," said Sturmey. "It seems that Isaac Sealey was speaking the truth after all. He's not clever enough to be much of a liar, but we wondered if he'd got the message right—"

Arthur interrupted him:

"Why should he lie? But mark you Colgrin, this is no time for talking. Do not underestimate the ghostly power of the enemy's gnostic priests. They have me in their clutches, but I have stolen away early to talk to you. For success, it is essential that I return to Ildierna at once and supported by the Spear. The forces within the Spear are great indeed, and if they are available all will be carried before them." Arthur paused, because at that moment Archaroch, Perhedron Typhon, and Ariouth of Riblah appeared upon the scene, followed closely by Isaac Sealey.

"What Ho!" cried Archaroch. "So you have escaped and returned to our aid. We shall triumph yet; you advise an immediate assault upon the enemy, aided by the Spear. Sturmey, muster your men. We shall march in one hour."

"Too late," cried Arthur. "Even now the enemy may be coming upon us – an officer of Queen Catharine's, with men from Ildierna, and Myrmidons with firearms. I must ride at once, accompanied by the necromancers, with one of them bearing the Spear. Thus we shall come to Ildierna, and overcome their priests and their fighting force with a single stroke. Have no fear of their strength against you – the Spear will overcome all."

He drew Caliburn, brandished the blade aloft, and looked about him. The crowd responded with a resounding cheer.

"That's right," shouted Sealey, the centre of attention for once. "Like I told you, and like the Lady Guinever said. Let's move, and now – victory is ours."

"Why this precipitate haste?" cried Archaroch. "We have the Spear! What do numbers matter? They are at our mercy, be it now or tomorrow."

"No, no; not so," came another voice; Arthur saw that it was Agravain who spoke. "If we delay, Catharine's women will flee back to Lyonesse, and we shall not have the pleasure of taking possession of them."

"Indeed yes," called Perhedron. "After his troubles Colgrin deserves first turn with that dreadful priest. And what price that Kenwyn girl? Stealthily striking King Arthur over the head, so that he could be captured by the enemy."

"You're right," contributed Ariouth. "And Agravain is also right. We must ride at once, my Lord Archaroch. Vengeance is sweet."

Arthur smiled at her; perhaps leered would be a better word. She grinned back at him and winked: her message unmistakable.

"Come and ride pillion behind me my dear lady," he said, "and we shall lead the van. Look lively you fellows, assist Lady Ariouth onto the horse."

They needed no second bidding, and soon the gross creature was firmly ensconced side-saddle behind him, wrapped in his discarded cloak, and with her arm firmly about his waist. A further cheer went up from the crowd, but Arthur was grateful for his encircling armour plate.

"Give my lady the Spear," he directed. "We shall go first, and it is fitting that she should bear your glorious Lance! And let Agravain also be given a horse. He has done much, so let him witness the victory at Ildierna."

Slowly the minutes ticked by while horses were saddled, the spear brought, and the company equipped for the journey. Arthur was edgy indeed; he feared that Archaroch had smelled a rat – would he yet overrule the majority's wishes? Meanwhile Ariouth pressed herself ever closer against him, as if gaining some perverse pleasure from the feel of the hard metal enclosing his torso.

"Perhaps you would like to join my household when all this is over?" she asked, but before Arthur had to time reply, the little entourage was ready. And so he led off, amid cheers, but thankfully enough. Ariouth was clutching the spear: its pennon waving triumphantly aloft.

CHAPTER XXIV
Colonel Kenwyn

Ystelle had now assembled her vanguard, and was marching towards Langarrow with a fair semblance of column of route, when she found that Kenwyn had joined the column uninvited. She had not the heart to send her back. Also the girl was quick witted, well familiar with the area, and unlike many of Ystelle's little force, spoke immaculate English. She had recovered her pistol from the previous day, and was also armed with an instrument like a cross between a large knife and a cleaver, borrowed, as Ystelle later discovered, from the local butcher.

The previous day Ephraim had drawn them a plan of Langarrow, and this Ystelle had memorised exactly. Her proposed tactics were to provoke Sturmey by making an initial attack on Langarrow, and then back off. Psychology suggested that Sturmey would follow up her retreat and thus be drawn into a skirmish outside the village, only to find himself overwhelmed by Georgina advancing with the reserve troops. Like most professional soldiers, Ystelle disliked pillage and unnecessary bloodshed, and hoped in this way to avoid undue house-to-house fighting – she knew that there were innocent women and children in Langarrow, and if her column of irregulars got loose on the village, God alone knew what might happen. Unfortunately, there had to be an element of conjecture in her reasoning; it was impossible to tell how far

Arthur would succeed in playing his confidence trick on the necromancers.

Ystelle kept Kenwyn beside her at the head of the column, and the march continued uneventfully, until they came to the junction between the Ildierna track and the road between Langarrow and Saint Catherine's Village, where their conversation was interrupted by the sight of Arthur coming towards them from Langarrow. He was riding Pendragon with a large woman seated behind him, and followed by three other horsemen. This was much what they had hoped for, and accordingly Ystelle halted the column. She was confident she could handle the situation, provided that her Cornishmen obeyed their orders.

"It seems I was right," Arthur said to Ariouth. "Get ready to use the Spear to give us swift passage through this lot. Don't be afraid. They will soon give way when they feel its force."

Ariouth wriggled even closer.

"Why not make them fight among themselves?" she asked. "Great fun to watch, and Christians have always have been good at killing each other."

"No, no. Time is of the essence. Don't underestimate the resources of the gnostic priests. We must descend upon them waving the Spear before they've had time either to marshal their psychic force against us or retreat back to Lyonesse."

Ariouth agreed, a trifle petulantly, and thus they approached the Christians.

Ystelle looked back along the lines of her little army.

"Remember instructions," she called out, loud and clear. "Let these enemies pass unhindered, unless they show fight, and then shoot quickly to kill the two horsemen following Arthur yr Amherawdyr. Spare the man at the rear, and leave me to deal with the woman riding behind him who is our King." Sensing the pressure upon her leader, Kenwyn repeated

Ystelle's orders, vigorously, and in Cornish. She was not a moment too soon, because the necromancers were almost upon them as she completed her words.

"Make way," cried Arthur. "Make way, for your rightful monarch, and the sacred Spear of Longinus, which is borne by the lady who shares my horse. Stand quietly aside, and give us passage."

Now is the moment of truth, thought he. Would Ystelle's Cornishmen give way as agreed, or would there be a brief and bloody shoot out? What Ystelle wanted was the necromancers delivered whole and hearty into the hands of Hermione and Lucilla, and indeed this was the main objective behind his visit to Langarrow. But would discipline hold? The tension rose further, while Ariouth brandished the spear, and screamed out some incomprehensible gibberish; most likely an incantation in the Inchthonic tongue meant to reinforce the majesty of her cause.

Either Ystelle's discipline or Ariouth's incantation did the trick – the Cornishmen stood passively to one side and permitted the riders to pass without event. Until Archaroch drew level with Ystelle.

"Halt!" he cried. "This is the halloran who foully insulted me in the company of that mystical bitch Hermione de Lamarac, while I was interrogating a child. Her name is 'Ystelle Zabuloe' and she is the Killiarch of Queen Catharine's personal guard. On no account will she escape my revenge. Therefore she'll come with us to Ildierna, and there'll be no slipping through our fingers in some deceitful way."

"Let's kill her now," said Ariouth, her voice as cold as any icicle. "I could run her through with the spear, or even better King Arthur can cut her hands and feet off, and we'll leave her here to bleed to death."

Then Perhedron joined in their jubilations, his voice leering with malice:

"No, no. Let's have a joke at her expense. We'll make her run to Ildierna in front of us, but stripped before she starts. Great fun to see the expressions on the faces of her allies when she comes trotting down the street without a stitch across her modesty."

Arthur thought desperately. Little did the necromancers know that they were within an ace of being blown to whatever evil aeon awaited their apologies for souls.

"My Lord Archaroch," he said, taking care to keep his voice level, "if Mrs Zabuloe is put to death here and now, you will be unable to enslave her as you wish. Also this is no time for foolery. There will plenty of time for Perhedron's droll amusements later on."

There was a pregnant pause. Perhedron was about to utter further, when Archaroch said:

"You're quite right Amherawdyr. Let her ride behind Mr Agravain. It will be a fair load for the horse, so Hubert, you'll need to use plenty of whip. No doubt you will enjoy reminding Colonel Zabuloe of how she treated both you and me once upon a time in Saint Catherine's Village, and inform her of the fate that now awaits her Ladyship. Get on with it woman. Up with you behind him. As for the rest of you lot, stay where you are."

Ariouth pointed the spear at Ystelle, and gave voice to more screaming gibberish. Ystelle looked hard at Arthur, and nodded, so slightly that it is doubtful if anyone else noticed it. Then she clambered obediently onto Agravain's horse.

"Hello Hubert," she whispered in his ear. "What a wonderful friend you've turned out to be."

And so the little cavalcade trotted off towards Ildierna, passing Georgina without incident.

Ystelle had assumed that her force would remain where it was until Georgina arrived with the reinforcements. She knew that the Sarissa Major could be relied on to lead an effective assault on Langarrow, and judged that while some additional bloodshed might be caused, the price was worth paying to capture the evil ones. But she had underestimated Kenwyn.

The necromancers were barely out of earshot before the latter addressed the column, speaking in voluble Cornish. The gist of it was that things were much as before the departure of Colonel Zabuloe, who had left voluntarily to go to Ildierna for the strategic good of the cause, and in the company of evil ones who would be dealt with effectively on their arrival there. None of this was greatly the concern of them as Cornishmen, nor indeed of herself; the overall situation remained unaltered. Therefore, she herself would lead them into battle against the odious men of Langarrow, and God help the varlets when they got there.

Perhaps surprisingly, the column agreed to this readily enough. Perhaps not so, for in fact Ystelle's female leadership had already been accepted. The psychology of the moment was that since Kenwyn had apparently been appointed by Ystelle as her lieutenant, it was natural for Kenwyn to take over Ystelle's command, and hence no questions were raised over what she proposed to do.

Kenwyn had enormous drive and personal courage, but having no notion of military tactics, she sent her column barging straight into the village, taking random pot-shots at any man in sight. At first she advanced rapidly. The enthusiastic mob which had applauded Arthur's departure had partly dispersed, and Kenwyn's first rush brought her force as far as the Langarrow Arms before they encountered much opposition. Here her way was blocked by a hotchpotch mass of men who had been hanging about there since earlier in the day, probably hoping for an assumed development in their favour following the necromancers' activities at Ildierna. By now, Ystelle's orderly column had degenerated into an irregular straggle, but Kenwyn had sufficient instinctive leadership not to allow her force to undertake hand-to-hand conflict with a much larger body of hardy men.

"Form rank," she called, or something equivalent in the Cornish tongue, and her troop, about twenty-five in number, formed a rough line across the street. The opposition was probably between sixty and seventy strong, although not all of them were armed.

"Fire!" yelled Kenwyn, and a dozen heavy handguns sent a volley crashing into the enemy.

The first reaction by the Langarrow men was one of incredulity. They suffered several casualties, but failed to understand what was happening; because they had ruled the area for so long that they could not comprehend anyone daring to challenge their strength. Then there was panic – a confused melee of men, together with a few women coming out of their cottages to see what was happening. Sturmey appeared, and endeavoured to bring his people into some sort of order. "Rally to me you fools," he called. "There's not a lot of them, and they seem to be led by a woman; that bitch Kenwyn Tregenza. I want her, and that right early."

"Load," called Kenwyn confidently enough – another volley and they'll break and run she reckoned.

But the second volley was not fired.

"Mistress Tregenza," said one of her followers, drawing her attention. "Look back there. Those men look like Saracens to me."

True enough, the Saracens, recovered from their humiliating defeat of the previous day, had arrived by an alternative route. So Kenwyn's little force was trapped between the men of Langarrow and the incoming Saracens. Moreover, she was hopelessly outnumbered!

"Into the inn," she commanded, whereon a swift charge carried her troopers over the threshold, with the door still off its hinges where Pendragon had kicked it in earlier in the day. As for the innkeeper, he abandoned his family and fled through the back door, leaving Kenwyn to arm herself further with his blunderbuss. (Later, a terrified wife and daughter were found hiding upstairs; they were suffered to leave unmolested.) And then fortune intervened on Kenwyn's behalf, because as the last men of her column disappeared into the inn, they fired two or three shots at the Saracens. It is doubtful whether they hit anyone, but the Saracens became confused, and failing to distinguish between the men of Ildierna and their Langarrow allies, they returned fire into the latter. Thus one fellow was killed and several injured, and the Langarrow men, having recovered from the initial shock engendered by Kenwyn, fired back at the Saracens. From inside the inn, Kenwyn realised that some sort of pandemonium was going on, but otherwise was unaware of what had happened.

So far none of her people had been injured, and they prepared for a vigorous defence by placing the shattered door transversely across the entrance and wedging it into position with some stools. The bar table was propped up behind it to give a further breastwork, and other furniture jammed against the windows. The inn was one of the few two storey buildings in Langarrow, and stood sandwiched between a single storey cottage and the village smithy. Hence Kenwyn only needed to defend the front and rear of the premises. She posted men accordingly, with punt guns ready to blast any attackers thinking to enter by door or window.

She ventured a cautious look from a bedroom window. The scene outside was one of bedlam. The Saracens appeared to have fanned out into some of the side alleys, and kept appearing here and there as if trying to catch the Langarrow people from the flank. There was a deal of noise and confused shouting, but as only a few of the Saracens could speak English and none of them Cornish, little communication was achieved. Meanwhile, Sturmey was running to and fro with blood flowing from a small cut on his face, trying to gain control of the situation. Kenwyn was tempted to shoot him at once with the blunderbuss, but judged it wiser to let the mayhem continue without directing attention towards the inn.

In fact no serious attempt was made to storm the Langarrow Arms. Minutes passed, and Kenwyn checked the building, confirming arrangements for its defence, and noting what supplies were on hand should they have to withstand a siege. There was ample beer and a fair amount of food, and she was interested to find that some of the bedrooms had been occupied by the necromancers, who had left a few possessions lying about. Also she came across a narrow staircase leading up to an attic, not apparent from outside the building.

"Don't go up there Mistress Tregenza," said the man stationed near the window. "It's an evil place. I had a look, in case somebody was hiding there. There wasn't, but it's full of horrible devilish things, not fit for a young lady to see, truly not."

"Come now Zachary," she replied. "I may be a woman, but I'm the last of the Tregenzas, so I must do duty as a man! Therefore I shall examine their evil devices; better to know than not."

"No, Mistress no," cried Zachary, but to no avail. Kenwyn was half way up the stairs even as he was speaking.

Her first discoveries were some distorted images, hardly obscene in the usual sense, but twisted, defying rationality in their interpretation. There was a grouped statuette of children with some vaguely reptilian animals, it being difficult to discern the distinction between them; and a bat held a writhing woman in its talons, apparently copulating with her in mid-air. Also there were instruments of an astronomical nature, inscribed with strange letters and symbols which Kenwyn could not understand. But the mirror was the most disturbing object of all. Slightly concave, it was about ten inches in diameter, and set in a brass bezel engraved with further incomprehensible symbols. The glass had a yellowish tinge, suggestive of great age. She peered into it curiously.

At first, all that she saw was her own face, looking back at her from the glass. It was a little enlarged by the concavity, but there was something else about it which she could not define. It was to do with the eyes; she got the crazy impression that she was being inspected by eyes which were not her own. Then the image began to blur, as if sliding out of focus.

"Come away from it Mistress." It was Zachary who spoke, having followed her upstairs. He seized some sort of ceremonial robe and throwing it over the mirror, broke the spell of her gaze imprisoned upon the image in the glass. But there was small time to wonder at the experience- a few seconds later Kenwyn heard an orderly volley, and hurrying down the stairs to the bedroom below she looked tangentially from the window, to see Georgina Burton-Coggles advancing along the village street. The Sarissa Major knew what she was about, and had divided part of her force into groups of four men, each group in charge of one of the Myrmidons. These were systematically combing through the cottages, expelling the residents, and herding them into a single building. (To Kenwyn's subsequent amusement, this proved to be the prison used by Sturmey to contain his female merchandise.)

The whole business was over in half an hour. Even with Georgina's reinforcements, the Ildierna people were substantially out-numbered, but the Saracens had been demoralised by events, and wishing no further exposure to the fire of dragon guns they made off as best they could. They left several dead, including their leader who was wearing a leather pocket belt containing a goodly sum in gold. To Kenwyn's chagrin, Sturmey was also dead, probably shot by the Saracens, and all resistance was soon at an end. Two buildings were burned down, and there was a fair amount of pillage, but the Myrmidons prevented wholesale looting, and no women were molested. So the battle ended much as Ystelle had hoped.

Georgina expressed surprise at the lengths the Saracens had taken merely to obtain possession of a dozen or so European women.

"No, no," Kenwyn replied. "Women are not the only commodity. Somewhere about you'll find a quantity of tin, obtained either by theft or extortion, and also some kegs of brandy, smuggled in from France. Strong liquor is forbidden in Muslim countries, but there is an illegal market – at a price."

"I see," said Georgina. "Is it all paid for in gold?"

"Usually not. Contraband spices are landed, also opium, and another substance called 'bhang'. I'm not sure what it is, but they say it causes euphoria – a bit like being drunk. There may be a bit somewhere around if you're interested. For myself, I'm more concerned about some muck belonging to the necromancers – in an attic upstairs at the inn. It's nasty disturbing stuff, and I think it should be handed over to Nacien and Hermione, your lady priest."

"I'll commandeer a cart," Georgina replied.

CHAPTER XXV
The Last Battle

Rosalind du Lac watched in silence from her vantage point at the end of Ildierna Village as Arthur's cavalcade came along the Langarrow lane. So, he has pulled it off, she thought, with a wordless paean of thanks welling up in her mind. It seemed to her that the entire sequence of events had been exceedingly strange – from the first to what must surely now be the last, because soon the evil ones would find themselves in Lyonesse, awaiting the wrath or mercy of Catharine the Second. What would her beloved queen do with them? Rosalind had no idea.

Then she noticed that her Killiarch was returning, riding somewhat ignominiously behind the fourth and last horseman. Moreover, there was a large woman riding with Arthur – presumably the dreadful Ariouth, although so far Rosalind had barely set eyes on any of the necromancers. Therefore things could not have gone entirely to plan. Her concern increased as Arthur came up to her, and paused for a moment.

The harridan riding behind him was carrying the false spear, and this she waved furiously in Rosalind's direction. The woman was wildly excited, and uttered a stream of words in a language which Rosalind recognised as Inchthonic, although she was unable to speak the tongue.

"I think that the Lady Ariouth is ordering you to curtsy and stand humbly to one side," said Arthur, while treating

Rosalind to a magnificent wink. "Please do as she says. Things will become clear a little later on."

Rosalind stepped back a pace, obeyed, and saluted with excessive smartness. Ariouth chortled with malicious glee, but Arthur moved Pendragon on before she could attempt further diabolical humour at the Sarissa Major's expense. Shrewdly enough, Agravain held his pony back a little for Ystelle to have a quick word with Rosalind out of earshot of the necromancers.

"Follow along behind us Rosalind," said Ystelle, "but at a discreet distance. This nonsense will soon be over."

Delighted, Ariouth filled Arthur's ears with a detailed account of what was in store for her enemies, until they entered Ildierna Village, where they found Lucilla, Hermione, Nathan and Samuel awaiting them, supported by Ephraim and most of the villagers. For what happened next, Arthur denied all responsibility. He came to a halt a few feet away from Lucilla's party, where Ariouth, brandishing the spear, screamed out some foul Inchthonic invocation, and then continued in English:

"Kneel down the lot of you, and beat your foreheads on the ground. We are your masters, and by the mystical powers in the Spear of Longinus, I command you!"

Unfortunately for her, Pendragon chose that moment to rear up on his hind legs, tipping her backwards over his rump, so that she was deposited hugger-mugger into the mud and icy puddles of the unpaved village street. And to exacerbate her dismay, a nearby chicken flew off, squawking and flapping into Archaroch's horse, sending it shying about and crashing into that ridden by Perhedron.

A great roar of laughter surged up from the onlookers, and went rolling around the village, putting up rooks noisy from the adjacent trees. Soon the roar changed into a lusty cheer, even as Rosalind du Lac appeared on the scene, and showing perhaps more charity than sense, assisted Ariouth to her feet. The latter was now insensate with rage. The false spear had slipped from her hand, but possibly she still believed in the authority of it, because she slapped Rosalind across the face. The action was foolish indeed. Ariouth was a large heavy woman, but she was no match for Ystelle's highly trained Sarissa Major, and within three seconds she found herself flat on her back in the mud and water.

"Come on du Lac," screamed a village woman. "Kick her, kick her, kick her hard."

Further female invective followed, all of which Rosalind ignored, but closely watched the scarlet-faced Ariouth sprawled in the mud at her feet.

"Get up woman." It was Ystelle who spoke, having slipped down from Agravain's pony.

And then confrontation gave way to farce. Perhedron leapt from his horse, and snatching up the false spear addressed his enemies:

"I abjure you in the name of almighty Lucifer, who by this weapon broke the body of that milksop Nazarene whom you so stupidly revere. Stand, and deliver yourselves into our power, we who are the almighty one's rightful officers —"

"Oh, do shut up," said Ystelle. "You're only making a fool of yourself."

In reply, the furious Perhedron lunged at her with the spear. She side-stepped, but despite this, the thrust would not have landed. Flash! Caliburn came down like a lightning bolt, striking the shaft of the spear a few inches away from Perhedron's hands. The blow failed to sever the timber, but the spear was torn from his clasp, and landed spike down in the earth. Arthur pointed the sword at him.

"You are now subject to the will of Catharine of Lyonesse," he said. "I advise you to accept the fact, and throw yourselves on her mercy."

"Never!" It was Archaroch who spoke. "I admit that as yet the spear has failed us, probably by the machinations of your priests. Let them beware. This day will be remembered. We shall now return to Langarrow, and thence to the Amente, taking the spear with us. We ask mercy from no one, and shall fight another day!"

Lucilla joined the fray.

"You are going nowhere," she said, "until we tell you to. Get down off that horse, and come quietly with me. There is a village lockup which will hold the lot of you for the time being."

"You, you; I know you. You are Admiral Mantzini, that vile virago who has sunk our ships and bombarded our coasts. I return to Langarrow. It is useless to prevent me. Soon our ally Colgrin Sturmey will appear and overcome your petty defences. Beware of Amentan wrath!"

"Empty threats, Lord Archaroch, as you will soon come to realise. Get out off that horse before we pull you off. As for you Ariouth, stand still and stop shouting, or I'll set the village women onto you."

"I shall confer with my colleagues," said Archaroch. "You realise that you're in an impossible position. You have been subject to both chronological and spatial transfer at my instigation. There is no way that you can return to your origins without my assistance, and this you will find it difficult to obtain. As for ourselves, we can easily remove back to the Amente, leaving you where you are now. No doubt you will enjoy the experience."

In fact, this was largely bluff, as Lucilla was well aware. Archaroch either did not know or was choosing to ignore the resources of Lyonesse, now reinforced by possession of the true Spear of Longinus. He must have developed doubts about the false spear, but presumably remained unaware of the facts concerning the genuine article. Leaving him in ignorance seemed the best strategy, at least for the time being. She saw that the minds of all the necromancers were in an illogical frenzy – they had not yet adjusted to the reversal in their fortunes. Also, Archaroch was lying when he said that they could easily retreat to the Amente. She was not clear on the exact circumstances, but in this Lucilla believed that she had him in her power.

"You may confer in the lockup," she said.

A little later the hour was enhanced by Kenwyn, who returned to bear tidings from Langarrow, riding at a canter on the best horse she could find. She reported to Lucilla.

"From what Miss Tregenza tells me," said Lucilla to the rest of the company, "Langarrow is taken, and Sturmey is dead. Well done indeed Kenwyn and Georgina. Your success is enhanced by the capture of what sounds like Archaroch's equipment for managing his transportations across the aeons, a procedure which becomes highly complex when time is involved as well as spatial movement. Georgina is sending a cartload across to us, and I fancy that it will include his armillary astrolabe and Doctor Dee's Mirror."

"What is a Doctor Dee's Mirror?" asked Arthur, now divested of his armour.

Agravain answered him:

"John Dee was a court astrologer to Elizabeth the First. He developed a method for using a mirror to obtain information, somewhat after the fashion of gazing into a crystal ball. Working with an Irish clairvoyant he had a fair measure of success. It is said that they received communications in Inchthonic, although at first neither of them could speak the tongue."

"What has that to do with Archaroch?" said Jenny, addressing the question to Lucilla.

"It's to do with what Morgan le Fey described as 'Meddling with the aeons'. Archaroch needs the mirror to see where he is going – an analogy would be to compare it with what you call radar. Otherwise he can't navigate through time. Spatial transfers are simpler. Therefore if Kenwyn has confiscated his mirror, he is stuck where he is, even without our preventing his movements."

"What's to do next then?" asked Samuel.

"First let us consider the situation here. Kenwyn reports that a pile of gold has been recovered, some from the Saracens, and a deal more from Sturmey's hoard. I would propose that Father Nacien distributes it as fairly as possible to those who have suffered most at the hands of the Langarrow clique. Also, it would be good to arrange rescue for the women previously sold to the Saracens. There is a lot of money available; perhaps a privateer could be fitted out."

"And then?" persisted Samuel, speaking with an uncanny feeling of tension, almost of anticlimax.

"Apart from the necromancers, we all go home. We can overcome the time factor by taking them with the rest of us to Lyonesse, and then transferring Jenny, Arthur and yourself back to Cornwall. Ystelle has been in rapport with her husband, and Catharine proposes to hold the evil ones in Catharine the First's Castle of Lonazep, until she decides what to do with them. Louise, Pearl, and the remainder of our people can follow a little later. I suggest we move tomorrow; it would be good to spend another evening with Ephraim's people, before leaving for the old Saint Catherine's."

Alas, things did not turn out quite as Lucilla had hoped, although it was a wonderful party that evening, even if somewhat marred by thoughts of missing womenfolk. Langarrow was amply nourished by contemporary standards, and the Myrmidons arrived back with two cartloads of consumables, in addition to Archaroch's equipment in Georgina's charge.

Next morning was also something of an anticlimax, because Lucilla did not want the local people accompanying the party to Saint Catherine's to say farewell.

"No, no, Amheradwyr," she said to Arthur. "To these people, our coming was a mystery and our going must be a mystery. We want no witnesses; otherwise extravagant tales will arise, ranging from a direct ascension of saints, to diabolical witchcraft. If people first appear, and then disappear to no one knows where, it may be thought strange but not supernatural."

They arrived at the church shortly before midday. Permission had been given for Arthur to retain Caliburn; the remainder of his equipment they replaced in the chest. Meanwhile the necromancers became increasingly strident, vowing retribution upon all concerned, so much so that their noise threatened to attract the attention of passers-by.

Hence to avoid publicity Lucilla advocated a withdrawal to the crypt, and they conducted the necromancers down the staircase. The ancient vault continued to feel charged with unseen forces, and if anything the atmosphere was enhanced by the illumination – meagrely provided by the lamps carried by the Myrmidons for their original entrance from Rosalind's Adit. At first this had a suppressing effect on the necromancers, until Archaroch burst out:

"This place is unwholesome for man and beast. We shall retaliate, cost what it may. You may have overcome the Spear of Longinus by some sort of gnostic manipulation, but there are other powers to come to our aid. I offer a negotiated arrangement without loss of face to either side."

"There will be no deals," replied Lucilla, her voice as cold as ice. "And you never had your hands on the Spear. The weapon in your possession was an elaborate fake. I shall show you the true article. If you please Sarissa Major."

Georgina passed her the Spear, and Lucilla pointed it towards him.

"Walk over to the altar," she said.

Archaroch's countenance was only indifferently illuminated, but it seemed to pass through a series of contortions which in other circumstances would have been wondrous to behold. Desperately he wrestled against the very force which he had so confidently expected to use for his own evil purposes. And then, pale as death, he approached the holy table.

"Untie him please," Lucilla requested of Georgina. (For the journey to the church, the Myrmidons had pinioned the necromancers' arms.)

Archaroch was soon unloosed, and stood shuddering before the altar.

"What do you know of this, Agravain," he demanded of his one-time ally. "You filthy double-dealing turncoat."

Agravain was standing next to Hermione; perhaps he was grateful for her priestly proximity, so great was the malevolent tide which he felt flowing in his direction. In fact Archaroch was not particularly surprised. Duplicity was so common amongst his fellows he had already assumed that Agravain had been coerced by a mixture of threats and bribery.

To his surprise, it was Hermione who replied and her answer amazed him.

"Hubert Agravain is a converted Christian in the service of Catharine of Lyonesse," she said. "I took his sincere confession myself, made voluntarily at as his recent baptism."

Archaroch's terror increased. She was about to force him into obedience to her God, using the power of the Spear! Such was the nature of his mind that so he thought, falling into the common error of assuming that other persons' motivations were similar to his own. Also he assumed that Hermione was lying when she said that Agravain's confession was voluntary. He had known him for many years, and judged it unthinkable that such a man would truly convert to Christianity other than through psychic force. And horror of horrors, such force was about to be applied to himself!

"Kneel," said Lucilla.

Obey he did upon the instant. In fact he had no option, but no sooner had his knees touched the floor, than he collapsed insensate upon the cold stones of the crypt.

Lucilla pointed the Spear at Ariouth. There was a brief pause, but before Lucilla could utter, the she-devil started to scream, a dreadful high-pitched screeching that echoed eerily round the crypt and indicated almost mindless terror. Lucilla was unmoved. She had no intention of forcing a spiritual conversion upon anyone; indeed she was expressly forbidden to do so. But despite her formidable ability she was surprised by the extremity of the necromancers' reactions, and now regretted using the Spear. It was a superficial action, and not in accordance with her usual standards of behaviour. Nevertheless, she was not put off by the creature's uncontrolled yelling. She knew that this was caused by thoughts which had delighted in the sufferings of others, and were now followed by the unjustified assumption that sadistic procedures were about to be applied to itself.

Not so Jenny. She lacked insight into the extreme evil of her opponents.

"For goodness sake Lucilla," she exclaimed. "Can't you stop her making that dreadful row? We all know that you won't injure her, but she's terrified of you. She thinks that you are going to roast her alive, or some such."

Arthur said nothing. He remembered Ariouth's gloating homily on the fate of the Catharist Christians, but nevertheless, he was relieved when she stopped screaming and subsided into a cowed silence. Perhedron alone of the necromancers maintained a semblance of dignity. He seemed to be looking about him, as if anticipating some sort of action.

Meanwhile, Archaroch had made a partial recovery from his emotional seizure. His quivering ceased, and his breathing became more regular; then he opened his eyes, and sat up. Unbidden, one of the Myrmidons offered him water from her bottle. This he accepted, and got to his feet.

"Thank you madam," he said, with great courtesy. "I shall remember your kindness. My hour of victory is coming upon us, and shortly you will all be in my power. Yesterday, I made a generous offer of negotiation to Admiral Mantzini, your arrogant fool of a leader, but this was crudely rejected." His voice took on a note of increasing glee, as he continued: "The period of time transference is ending, now. Look about you."

A quivering became apparent in the structure of the crypt, and soon developed into a considerable shaking, such that at least Arthur thought that they were experiencing an earthquake. Plaster fell, the clean whitewashed walls became dingy as with age, and with a great crash, the walls of both the staircases fell in, together with one end of the vault. There was now no way out.

"You see," crowed Archaroch. "There is no escape for any of you, save by the will of myself and my masters. We have returned to your aeon, twentieth century England. Do not think that your Spear will help you – it cannot influence the movements of time and space, merely command the will of humans. Even were you to use it to destroy all three of us, you would not procure your escape from this place."

Perhedron Typhon took up the victorious paean:

"You have been entirely outwitted. Why did we make a great disturbance in the church? To lure you down here. Why did Lord Archaroch pretend to faint under the psychic strain? To gain a few more vital minutes lest you had us to Lyonesse before reversion of the aeons. Ariouth's ridiculous screaming served the same effect. You thought you had the victory, and poor fools, relaxed your guard. It is you who are at our mercy now. Soon you will all be in the Amente."

Then followed yet another detailed gloating on the fate awaiting the Christians. Ariouth looked forward to the Myrmidons being made to fight each other in gladiatorial games. Perhedron was going to present Lucilla to his master, Lord Asfernel, Archduke of the Amente, as an ornament to his harem, and Hermione would be compelled to perform naked in a temple devoted to satanic worship. But Archaroch's approach was more subtle.

"Mr Marazion," he said. "To you I am inclined to be lenient. I believe that at heart you are on our side, but have been deluded by that mistress of malign witchcraft, Hermione de Lamarac. Recant, now while I give you the opportunity, and all could yet go well for you. You shall have an honourable place in my homeland; Arthur Amheradwyr could prove a worthy servant for our Great Master. You will be allowed to retain your Jennifer, and I shall also give you Ystelle Zabuloe. No doubt you will doubly enjoy taking your pleasure upon her, knowing that she is another man's wife. And she should prove a suitably hardy woman to keep your harem in order."

Lucilla was thinking furiously. To a degree she blamed herself for what had happened, although there was no way in which she could have foreseen Archaroch's restricted time factor. Amentan time manipulations were strange and unpredictable, not infrequently to the Amentans themselves. Yet all was by no means lost. She believed that Archaroch was in part bluffing about an immediate return to the Amente, because he was dependant upon aid from the other side. It was different from his previous brief encounter and defeat at the hands of Hermione and Ystelle. Then his visit was fleeting and much simpler; no time transference was involved. Now Georgina was holding his astrolabe and Dee's mirror. Therefore he could not readily navigate his own return to the Amente, and it was doubtful how much his colleagues on the other side knew of the position. Moreover, he might have enemies who did not want his return.

Hermione was standing perfectly still, with an expression indicating intense concentration. Arthur's immediate thought in response to Archaroch's invitation to change sides was to draw Caliburn and behead him with it, but second thoughts prevailed. Were they all to find themselves in the Amente, Archaroch's offer would at least protect Jennifer and Ystelle. What was the chivalrous decision? Then he rejected the second idea. There could be no compromise with evil such as this. Ystelle also gave the impression of intense concentration, but there was no overt sign of action from any of the companions. This the necromancers interpreted as confirmation of their victory.

Time passed, minutes ticked past slowly, half an hour, three quarters, an hour, yet still the impasse continued. And then there was a further movement of the strata containing the crypt; not this time from either of the collapsed staircases, but directly above their heads, in the very ceiling of the ancient vault. It seemed as if their drama would end, not in victory or defeat, but with all the actors buried beneath a cascade of falling stone.

Meanwhile, in Saint Catherine's village, the absence of Samuel and his party was causing concern; in particular to Mary Mordecai, but also to those members of the company who were not involved in the expedition to the mine. Moreover, the unexpected disappearance of the Reverend Samuel Mordecai was raising comment in the village.

"It's very worrying," said Mary. "No one thought that they would be away for as long as this, and tomorrow is Sunday. Who's to take the services? Perhaps we could ask Pearl to fill in. The villagers would be enthusiastic, but what if the diocese hears about it?"

"Do not fear," replied Laura, confident as ever. "All manner of things will be well. I know it.

"Also I'm the senior churchwarden, and if necessary shall ask Pearl to officiate tomorrow. If the diocese doesn't like it, they can refer the bishop to me, and he'll remember the conversation for a long time."

The meeting was taking place in Laura's library, but before more could be said, there was a knock at the door, and a maidservant entered.

"Excuse me ma'am, but there is a small boy in the hall. He's almost hysterical and is demanding to see Miss Esyllt. Auntie Pearl, he keeps calling her. Could she see him for a minute – I don't know what best to do with him."

"Thank you Helen," replied Laura. "Please bring him here into the library. Miss Esyllt can comfort him with Miss Long-Clarke helping her."

Thankfully, Helen moved the child forward. It was Simon Penvithick, but he wanted no comforting; indeed not, his message was important, and well he knew it.

"Please Auntie Pearl," he began. "The nasty man has got Auntie Hermione and Mr Mordecai and Auntie Ystelle shut up in a cave, and Auntie Hermione's been telling me in my mind to get you all to go and get them out and I know where it is up on top of the hill and hurry up or you'll be too late and you'll need a ladder…"

But Louise was already in action.

"Telephone the rectory Laura if you please and tell the Queen's Girdle troops to come over at once. We shall move off immediately. Simon is referring to Saint Catherine's Wood. Time is vital, I know it. We shall need picks and crowbars and all the force we can muster."

Arthur held Jenny close against him. Noises could be heard above their heads, and there seemed to be a further slight movement in the strata covering the crypt. Soon the roof might come crashing down upon them.

If we are to die, may it be swift, he thought, and at that moment a sizeable stone slab became detached and landed almost at their feet, revealing an aperture in the ceiling. A few smaller stones followed, and then a face appeared in the hole.

"They're down here," cried a voice. "And look all right to me. Get the ladder down, quickly." It was Louise Long-Clarke.

In fact the crypt had an arched roof, with the apex only about three feet beneath the floor of the church. According to Arthur, the Celtic miners had operated by first sinking a shaft, and then excavating laterally to hollow out a vault; the staircases were put in afterwards. Louise had uncovered the original shaft. Soon the reunited company were standing outside in a fine sunny day.

"How did you know where to dig?" Samuel asked.

"Not too difficult," Louise replied. "We found that near the old font there were only a few inches of earth over the flagged floor of the old church. We scratched about in the grass, and Simon found the end a length of metal. Pearl said that it must have been detached from the font. That is where we dug down."

Jenny picked up the metal, a leaden strip about four feet long, and brushed away the soil to reveal a series of letters. 'ΝΙΨΟΝΑΝΟΜΗΜΑΤΑΜΗΜΟΝΑΝΟΨΙΝ', she read, but this time without surprise.

Lucilla put her arm round her and held her close for a moment.

"At last the combat is over," she said. "And you have played a brave part in it. Now we have the victory."

The moment was poignant indeed. Samuel was close to tears. Hermione took his hand in both of hers.

"Farewell old faithful priest," she said. "It is time for us to depart, but remember, I shall be watching over you always, for as long as earthly life may last."

Arthur lifted Simon onto his shoulder and took Jenny's hand. Off they went across the sheep pasture, with Samuel walking a few paces behind. Ystelle watched them as far as the stile.

"Time to go home," she said.

CHAPTER XXVI
Epilogue

Catharine dealt leniently with the necromancers. In all too many ways she found them pathetic.

She herself (to use her own terminology) was Gnostic of the Father, and this liberation from self opened her mind to the nature and needs of others. But these particular 'others' were enclosed within their own mentalities; so much so that they were blinded by self conceit. This meant that they could not recognise any truth beyond what they wanted to believe; also they welcomed falsehoods, provided that these justified theories in line with their alien thoughts.

Catharine had no time for retributive justice. She genuinely desired to heal the evil ones, but found their minds impervious to outside influence, however benign. Indeed, at first they had difficulty in accepting that the great queen had them at her mercy. Surely, they thought, it was impossible for persons of their superior quality to be subject to such indignity.

Force of circumstances inevitably compelled a revision of this attitude, but Catharine's compassionate treatment of her prisoners introduced a further problem. Following acceptance of their captivity, they assumed that they would be flogged, branded, hung up by their thumbs or some such, but found instead that despite their confinement within the majestic Castle of Lonazep, they were well fed, comfortably housed, and allowed to wander at will in the bailey surrounding the enormous keep. But instead of interpreting this as an act of humanity on the part of their captors, they assumed that it was because Catharine did not dare to do them harm. A despot might have disabused them of this point of view by in fact putting them to the whip, but Catharine was no despot. Such action never occurred to her, and would have been abhorrent if it had. Thus the necromancers continued in the common error of believing that other persons' volitions were similar to their own.

Catharine persisted for a month or so. The Lyonesse church included many gnostic priests who could have broken the necromancers psychologically (as indeed could Catharine herself), but this was against the rules, as surely as physical intimidation. And so she gave up, admitted defeat, and returned the evil ones unharmed to the Amente.

Arthur gained his doctorate without difficulty, although he was sagacious enough to say nothing about the business at Saint Catherine's!

A little later, the Saint Catherine's people decided to open the crypt officially, so a faculty was obtained from the diocese, and the tower door unblocked at last. The resulting 'discoveries' caused enormous excitement, and several learned treatises were produced. Needless to relate, Dr Marazion was considered too young and inexperienced to play other than a minor part in such important work.

In due time Mr Appleton recovered his health, and so Jenny relinquished her duties as choirmistress, to give more time to her principal career. Matrimony soon followed. On a fine sunny morning she joined Arthur at Saint Catherine's in a ceremony poignant for reasons far beyond the customary. How much foreknowledge was available to the Reverend Samuel in advance of the event they never could determine. Hand in hand with Arthur, she had visited Saint Catherine's Wood (now restored following archaeological excavation) on the previous day, and 'knew' beyond all normal knowing that her queen and mentor was well aware, and sending profound love to Arthur and herself. She longed to see Catharine again but knew that journeys across the aeons were in general forbidden. Recent infringements of the rule had only been justified to counter similar actions by the Amentans, all made with evil intent.

The wedding began with a short voluntary by Mr Appleton. Following this, a quintet of Jennifer's students played some of her first violin concerto – essentially as performed in the crypt of Saint Mary All Souls – with the notes timed to welcome the bride into the church. This music came as a surprise to her, and indeed raised memories which to a degree compensated for the lack of Catharine's physical presence. But this experience was as nothing to what was to follow.

It seemed to the congregation that the newly-weds' time in the vestry was a trifle prolonged. On entering the now familiar room, Jennifer had realised that unexpected persons were present; foremost, a tall lady, highly elegant, and wearing a loose fitting jacket and skirt in dark coloured silk. Her appearance was exactly as Jennifer had first seen her, save for the addition of a large hat, typical of those worn to weddings by sophisticated women. Much to her own embarrassment, Jenny promptly burst into tears.

"No, no, no, my dear," said Catharine, gathering the newly married woman into her arms. "This is a happy day. There must be no crying. I absolutely forbid it!"

"Well done Arthur," said Stephen Zabuloe. "You've picked a good one there. Catharine asks you to accept a wedding present, arranged through Laura. It's a converted farmhouse, just outside Exeter, handy for your new job at the University, and for Jenny to catch the fast trains to London.

Haven't seen it myself but they say it's a good conversion. The stables have been retained. You could easily adapt one for a music room. There's a paddock as well. We hope you'll both like it; it can always be sold on if you don't."

Ystelle produced face powder from her handbag, and Jennifer's appearance was speedily restored.

"Laura says we are welcome to your reception," said the queen's killiarch, "and are indeed honoured to accept, but we wanted these few minutes in the vestry to talk and hug you, away from the other guests. There is another surprise for you outside – a gift from Ephraim and Sir Marrock Nacien."

And so a little later, out through the porch, amid confetti, rose petals and photographs. But instead of the phaeton as ordered (to lead the procession of wedding cars) they saw a stableman holding an enormous black horse.

"Beauty, isn't he?" he remarked to the best man. "Queer business though. He arrived two days ago, in charge of a tall woman. 'Rosalind' she said her name was, with the horse called 'Pendragon'. Said about a change of plan for the wedding, cancel the phaeton, and bring this laddie instead. Even queerer, she paid in sovereigns: generous too. She went on about him being a wedding present, and could we stable him until after the honeymoon? Odder still, I had a look at his shoes. Always check a horse's shoes, in case he casts one. Now my dad was a farrier, and I know a bit about horse shoes. But I've never seen such like – not on a horse, though I've seen similar in a museum. Wrought iron, not steel, like we use today. He's well enough shod mind you …"

"Darling, darling," said Jenny to Arthur. "It's Pendragon!! Pendragon – all saddled and bridled, and ready to go. Ystelle says he's our present from Ephraim's people. We're to ride him to the reception, and he's ours to keep, though I can't think where we'll put him."

"Don't worry dearest. Catharine has bought us a country house. Near Exeter, with stables and a paddock. But we can't talk now sweetheart, not with the guests waiting."

Dexterously, he sprang into the saddle, while Ystelle and the bridesmaid lifted Jenny up behind him. They made a striking picture; the tall young man in morning dress, together with the beautiful women seated side saddle, her white silk dress spread out against the shiny black coat of the enormous horse.

"Steady how you go sir," cautioned the stableman. "He's as docile as a kitten, but a stallion for all that."

"Yes, yes, I know," replied Arthur.

Cameras clicked and spectators cheered. Clop-clop, clop-clop, went Pendragon's hooves as he trotted away, with the wedding procession behind him.

SELECTED BIBLIOGRAPHY.

1.   Anonymous, *Epistle to the Hebrews.* Douglas, J.D., editor. (The New Greek/English Interlinear New Testament. Tyndale House Publishing Inc., Wheaton, Illinois. ISBN 0-8423-1213-7)

2.   Anonymous, *Pistis Sophia,* Mead, G.R.S., translator. (John M. Watkins, 21 Cecil Court, Charing Cross Road, London.)

3.   Didymos Judas Thomas, *The Gospel According to Thomas*, Guillaumont, A. *et alia*, translators. (Collins, 14, Saint James' Place, London.)

4.   Dixon-Kennedy, Mike, *Arthurian Myth and Legend.* (Blandford Books, Cassell PLC, Wellington House, 125 Strand, London, WC2 0RB. ISBN 0-7137-2561-3)

5.   Ellis, Peter Beresford, *The Cornish Saints.* (Tor Mark Press, Islington Wharf, Penryn, Cornwall, TR10 8AT. ISBN 0-852025-337-3)

6.   Saint John, *Secret Book of John.* In *A Gnostic Miscellany*, Grant, R.M., editor. (Collins Clear Type Press, 14, Saint James' Place, London.)

7.   Gantz, Jeffrey, translator. *The Mabinogion.* The Penguin Classics. (Penguin Books Ltd., Harmondsworth, Middlesex, England.)

8.   Malory, Sir Thomas, *Le Morte D'Arthur.* The Penguin English Library, Two Volumes. (Penguin Books Ltd., Harmondsworth, Middlesex, England.)

9.   Matthews, John, editor, *An Arthurian Reader.* (The Aquarian Press, Thorson's Publishing Group, Wellingborough, Northamptonshire, England, NN8 2QR. ISBN 0-85030-778-3)

10.   Nataf, André, *Dictionary of the Occult*, Davidson, J., translator. (Wordsworth Editions Ltd, Cumberland House, Crib Street, Ware, Hertfordshire, SG 12 9ET. ISBN 1-85326-338-8)

11.   Squire, Charles, *Mythology of the Celtic People.* (Tiger Books International PLC, 26A York Street, Twickenham, Middlesex, England, TW1 3LJ. ISBN 0-09-185043-6)

12.   Valentinus, *The Gospel of Truth,* Grobel, K., translator. (A. and C. Black Ltd., 4, 5 and 6 Soho Square, London.)

GLOSSARY AND
BIBLIOGRAPHICAL NOTES

Amente: A term of Egyptian origin, signifying regions inhabited by the dead, later adopted by some of the early Christians. Roughly comparable to the Greek Hades.

Archaroch: A ruling demon described in the Fourth Book of the Pistis Sophia.

Saint Joseph of **Arimathea:** Legends abound, but the canonical gospels record that he was a disciple of Our Lord, albeit secretly for fear of the Jews, a counsellor, and a good and just man. Other accounts record that he was sent to Britain by St. Phillip, that he was supported by twelve clerics and a son Josephe (or Joseph II), and built a church of wattles at Yniswitrin – Glastonbury. Also he brought the Holy Grail and the Spear of Longinus to Britain.

Ariouth: A demon described in the Fifth Book of the Pistis Sophia.

Barding: The complete set of armour and accoutrements for a medieval war-horse.

Brocelliande: A legendary land which formerly existed off the coast of Brittany and was a domain of Sir Lancelot du Lac. The City of **Ys** was its capital. The name also applies to a forest in Brittany, more recently called the Forest of Paimpont. Broceliande is an alternative spelling.

Brythonic: One of the two Celtic languages spoken primitively in the British Isles. Brythonic, or P Celtic, is the basis for the Welsh, Cornish and Breton languages, and may have been spoken in Arthurian times. (The second group is the Goidelic, or Q Celtic group, the foundation of Irish, Manx, and Scottish Gaelic.)

Caparison: Part of the barding. A large ornamental saddle cloth, extending over most of the body of the horse; usually embroidered and richly coloured.

Chanfron: Part of the barding. A curved armour plate protecting the front of the horse's head.

Clevis: A U-shaped fork, usually terminating a shaft, and drilled to accommodate a pin or clevis bolt to form a fulcrum or pivot.

Coutar: Part of a knight's body armour. A rounded metal plate protecting the outside of the elbow, particularly when the arm is bent.

Colgrin Sturmey: Originally a Saxon leader, defeated by King Arthur at the battle of Douglas.

Delabole: Site of a quarry in North Cornwall (a few miles south of Tintagel) producing slate of high quality with a wide range of colours, and able to take a high polish.

Epiclesis (or epiklesis): A sacramental transformation, particularly the moment in the service of Holy Communion when the elements become imbued with the substance of the risen Christ.

Esclarmonde de Foix: A Catharian priestess, who reputedly rescued the Cathar relics at the fall of the fortress of **Montségur**.

Escarlamonde de Perelha: A Catharian martyr, burnt at the stake for her faith by the Catholic Church.

Eschatology: The study of the final condition of things, particularly in the theological sense.

Euhemerism: The transference of an historical character into folk lore. A mythologisation.

Francis (Franz) Ferdinand: (1863–1914), nephew of the Austrian Emperor Francis Joseph, and heir apparent to the Austrian throne. His assassination in Sarajevo (28th June 1914) caused the rupture between Austria-Hungary and Serbia, leading to the 1914–18 war.

Guinever (or Guinevere): The Queen of King Arthur. According to legend, following the death of Arthur, she became a nun, and rose to be mother superior of her order. Such ladies were occasionally ordained; hence she may have been one of the first British women to be made priest.

Helen (or Elen) of the Hosts: Elen Lwyddag, reputedly a wife of Merlin. Welsh names such as Fford Elen (Elen's Road), and Sarn Elen (Elen's Causeway) are said to commemorate the routes along which her armies marched.

Inchthonic: A language spoken in hell.

Innocent the Third: Pope 1198–1216. Continued a 'holy' war against the Cathars, in which many thousands were put to death, often with great cruelty. Note also an antipope, Innocent III (1179–80).

Saint **Keyne:** A daughter of King Brychan (6th century), and a sister of Saint **Nectan.** She had a considerable sense of humour, endowing a Holy Well (half a mile south-east of St. Keyne's village) with the power of granting dominance within marriage. Her feast day is 8th October.

Kenwyn: Probably a misreading of Keyne, although there is a church dedicated to St. Kenwyn near Truro.

Killiad and **Killiarch:** Greek – a killiad was one thousand soldiers, and a killiarch was a commanding officer.

Knights Templar: Known first as The Poor Soldiers of the Holy City, the Templars later took the name of The Poor Knights of Christ and of the Temple of Solomon. The order was founded in 1189, led by Hugh de Payns, and received its rule from Saint Bernard in 1128. The Knights' original objective was to ensure free passage for pilgrims visiting the Holy Land. The order prospered, and became well known for well-doing and acts of charity. By 1300 the Templars owned 9,000 manors in Europe, Africa and Asia Minor, but their wealth attracted jealousy, and Philippe IV of France (1286–1314) combined with pope Clement V (1305–14) cruelly to suppress the order and confiscate its property. Charges against the Templars included that they told of Heaven rather than Hell, they worshipped the risen Christ and not the crucified Christ, and they asserted that pardon and grace came from God and were not marketable commodities in the monopoly of the Catholic Church.

Lambrequin: An ornamental cloth attached to the back of a knight's helmet and covering the nape of the neck.

De Lamarac: The original de Lamarac (or de Lamorak) was one of King Arthur's Knights – a son of King Pellinore and a brother of Perceval.

Longinus: A Roman soldier who lacerated Our Lord with his spear during the crucifixion. According to legend, the spear was preserved as a Christian relic, having been given to Joseph of Arimathea by Pontius Pilate.

Lucius the Third: Pope 1181–85. Lucius III declared a 'holy' war against the Cathars, leading to the Albigensian Crusade, 1209–1229, led by Simon IV de **Montfort** (c. 1160–1218).

Lyonesse: A rich tract of land said to have extended westward from Land's End to the Scilly Isles, including the City of Lions, and about 140 churches. Legend claims that the land sank in 1099.

William of **Malmesbury:** An English monk and chronicler (c. 1090–c. 1143), who became librarian and precentor to the monastery at Malmesbury. He left an account of the church at Glastonbury.

Thomas **Malory**: (c. 1400–1471) Famous as the author of *Le Morte d'Arthur*, printed by Caxton in 1485, although the work was completed in 1470. The book is largely a compilation from early French sources, but with additional material. It is the best known Arthurian writing in the English language.

Merlin: The celebrated wizard, who provided King Arthur with excellent advice. The original name 'Myrddin' may be associated with Carmarthen; in Welsh 'th' is written as 'dd', with 'caer' meaning 'castle'. Hence Castle of Merlin.

Metempsychosis. The transmigration of souls.

Mithras: An ancient Aryan god, adopted by the Zoroastrians, but whose cult is also believed to have assimilated the Greek mysteries. Mithraism was widely followed among the Roman legions, and became distributed throughout the Roman empire.

Simon IV de **Montfort:** (c1160–1218), also known as Simon de Montfort the elder. The name derives from the Castle of Montfort l'Amaury, near Paris. Simon IV was largely responsible for the massacre of the Cathars on behalf of **Lucius the Third.** He was the father of the better-known Simon de Montfort, Earl of Leicester (1206–65).

Montségur: The last of the Catharian fortresses to fall to the Catholics (in 1244). More than 200 of its defenders were herded into a snowy clearing and burned alive.

Myrmidons: Myrmidons are said to have originated when Aegina had been depopulated by a plague, and Jupiter granted a prayer of King Aechus, that ants running from an oak tree should be turned into men. Later, myrmidons followed Achilles to the siege of Troy, and were noted for their courage, diligence, and devotion to their leader.

Nacien: Also spelt Nascien. A hermit who appears in Le Morte D'Arthur in several guises. He is mentioned extensively in Volume 2, Book XVI, Chapters 3 and 4, where he gives spiritual sustenance to Sir Gawain and Sir Ector, and in Book XVI, Chapter 4, where he is involved with the Sword of King David. He is also reported to be the son of Joseph of Arimathea. It is doubtful if all the Naciens are the same character.

Saint Nectan: A child (probably the eldest son) of the legendary King Brychan, who fathered numerous saints, including **Keyne** and Gwladys. There is a Saint Nectan's chapel near Lostwithiel in the Parish of Saint Winnoc, and his name also occurs in Brittany and Devon. His feast day is 17th June.

Noumenon: An object primarily of intellectual intuition, or the conception of something; the real under the phenomenal.

Odes of Solomon: An ancient extra-canonical scripture in use by some Eastern Churches, but almost unknown in the West. Not to be confused with King Solomon's Song.

Ophites: An early gnostic sect which drew theological diagrams, typically based on seven or ten separate circles circumscribed by a large circle, said to be the world-soul.

Pelagius: A fifth century British monk who travelled to Rome and had a celebrated disagreement with Saint Augustine of Hippo. Pelagius did not believe in an absolute predestination, and had controversial views on the nature of free-will. He was a near contemporary of King Arthur; the latter is said to have departed to Avalon in 529.

Perhedron Typhon: According to the Fifth Book of the Pistis Sophia, Perhedron Typhon rules over thirty two demons, much given to lechery.

Rerebrace: Part of a knight's body armour, protecting the arm from the shoulder to the elbow.

Sacerdotal: Referring to supernatural power given by God to ordained priests.

Surcoat: A short coat or robe worn over the other clothes. Part of a knight's regalia.

Syriac: Western Aramaic. (A language still used liturgically by the Armenian and some other Eastern Churches.)

Valentinus: An important early gnostic leader and theologian, born in northern Egypt around 100–110, and educated at Alexandria. His major surviving work is known as 'The Gospel of Truth', but these are its opening words – the title page has been lost.

Vambrace: Part of a knight's body armour, protecting the arm from the elbow to the wrist.

Ynys Avalon: The Island of Avalon, to which, according to **Malory**, the seriously wounded King Arthur was conveyed following his last battle.

Ys: Originally the capital of **Brocelliande**, the legendary French domain of Sir Lancelot du Lac.

Ysbathaden or **Ysbaddaden:** Originally a character in the Mabinogion, the father of Olwen.

Zabuloe: A parish and district in North Cornwall, which includes Saint Piran's Oratory, reputedly the oldest church in England.